ℹ*Force of Time*

Adrian Cousins

Copyright © 2022 Adrian Cousins

All rights reserved. This book or any portion thereof may not be reproduced or used in any manner whatsoever without the author's express written permission except for the use of brief quotations in a book review.

This book is a work of fiction. Names characters, businesses, schools, places, locales, and incidents are either products of the author's imagination or used in a fictitious manner. Any resemblance to actual persons, living or dead, or actual events is purely coincidental.

www.adriancousins.co.uk

Before you dive in …

Force of Time is the third book in the Jason Apsley trilogy, preceded by *Jason Apsley's Second Chance* and *Ahead of his Time*. Although I'm super delighted that you've chosen to read this book, you would probably want to read books one and two first.

If you have already enjoyed those two books, crack on, and dive in – I hope you enjoy Jason's latest adventure.

Prologue

1987

Whilst lingering by the open front door, I kept half an eye on Detective Inspector French as she spun on her heels and tramped her way back to her car. Of course, she knew there was more to the story. However, I guess after ten years she would let sleeping dogs lie, as they say.

I wondered if those dogs would soon awaken.

Rubbing my thumb over the brass casing of my now returned Zippo lighter, I stewed over that thought. I'd lost this lighter over ten years ago when my time-travelling partner, Martin, ploughed the yellow Cortina into the large oak tree, killing himself and the evil Paul Colney.

I considered that the lighter represented some voodoo-type jinx that, now returned, would somehow spark the revival of those harrowing few months in the late '70s and destroy my near-perfect life.

I flipped the lid and struck my thumb down on the flint wheel, somewhat surprised to see a flame appear. The flame crackled, then dipped to a small bluish light before dying, briefly leaving a tiny wisp of smoke that soon dissipated. Once again, I pondered the extinguished lighter whilst musing over the last eleven years of living in the past since travelling through time from 2019. Perhaps it would be my good luck charm, and the return of this inane object wouldn't trigger a resurgence of those calamitous events of 1976.

Martin and Paul departed this world on 4th February 1977. Since that event, my life continued on a path of contentment. No longer was I the hapless miserable bastard from 2019, detesting my job and trying to rebuild my life after my divorce from Lisa. Now, living thirty-odd years in the past, I shared this wonderful life with Jenny and my two adopted children whilst enjoying teaching – life couldn't be any better.

Yes, there were complications. Time travel isn't straightforward. Firstly, now having Beth as my daughter and not my best friend from my previous life was somewhat tricky to get your head around. Also, I held knowledge of future events that I could only share with my wife Jenny, and George, my grandfather from my previous life.

That knowledge came with great responsibility – I could affect the future. However, as my failed attempt to stop the Yorkshire Ripper in the late '70s had proven, *time* was not willing to bend easily. In fact, it's fair to say, in the vast majority of cases, *time* followed the laid down path that history demanded.

Although, now super content, I had the nagging concern that life would unravel. There was *other* Jason, as I called him – the man whose life I'd taken when time-travelling back –

what had happened to him? Would he just reappear when I'm least expecting it?

His daughter, Jess, firmly believed I was her father, and I was honoured to take on that role. However, her ex-partner, Patrick, was a Colney – the evil mafia-style family that I seemed to be intrinsically entwined with. Even though David and Paul were dead, Patrick and now Andrew were enjoying life at Her Majesty's pleasure, and their mother, Shirley, had skedaddled to Spain, I fully believed our paths would cross once again.

Of course, trying to understand how you can exist in a time before your mother has given birth to you is a head-spinning conundrum. However, here I was, a fifty-two-year-old man living life eleven years after I should have been born. An event that would have taken place after my parents' deaths because, in this life, they died eight years earlier than in my first existence.

Now that DI French had informed me about the arrest of Andrew Colney, it suggested he couldn't rape Sarah Moore. So, Martin could no longer be born next year, eleven years after his death – yes, living in the past is complicated.

Thinking about what could go wrong wasn't healthy – a prophecy of doom. However, with my somewhat annoying predilection to believe in determinism, I decided one more strike of the lighter flint wheel would influence my fate. If a flame returned, I could relax – life would blissfully continue. If my Zippo failed to light – the demons from hell would be released to tear my world apart.

My thumb thumped down on the flint wheel – a spark, no flame.

I pocketed the lighter and strode towards the kitchen.

Whether the lighter ignited or didn't, that outcome couldn't determine my future life – ridiculous thought.

Or was it?

Part 1

1

1941

The Queen Of Hearts

"Janet!"

Only at the tender age of eight, Janet didn't need her mother to holler twice. For the best part of the last five months, her mother calling out in the dead of night was a regular occurrence – Janet knew the drill.

For good measure, her mother boomed out her name again. "Janet. Now!"

Janet hopped out of bed and grabbed hold of her neatly tied bundle of clothes, which, as instructed, she'd bound with string before going to bed – she knew the drill.

Janet had practised her bedtime routine and now had it down to a fine art. That said, Mother continually drummed it into her since she'd returned home from her horrific, albeit temporary, evacuation to the wilds of rural Norfolk.

A few hours ago, once she'd secured her clothes in a tight bundle, and before climbing into bed, Janet had knelt and prayed.

Her prayers were always the same. Firstly, there would be no siren tonight. And secondly, for Father to be kept safe whilst away at sea. Of course, she didn't know about Father. However, by the sound of that siren, it was apparent her first prayer had fallen on deaf ears. Janet had cause to doubt whether there was any point to her bedtime praying routine because it appeared God wasn't interested.

Mother stood in the doorway to her bedroom holding her hand out to Janet, with the other gripping the front of her cardigan she'd slipped over her nightdress.

"Janet, hurry. Come on!" Mother once again instructed.

Janet rammed her feet into her slippers and skipped over to take Mother's hand.

The haunting *'Moaning Minnie'* air raid siren reached its full pitch as the operator wound around the crank handle, allowing the siren to rise to the crest of its soundwave, delivering the hideous, wailing warning scream to its crescendo. As the sound pitch rose and fell alternately, it filled her soundscape that Janet knew captured the pathos of their situation.

Any moment now, she would hear the whistles of the bombs as they reached their terminal velocity and the *'Kooouuueeee'* sound that always resulted in skull-splitting, eardrum-bursting explosions.

In later life, many children who survived the Blitz struggled when hearing that sound when regurgitated on cartoon shows or war films – but not Janet. With the harsh existence that followed this fateful night, Janet grew a shield-like steel persona that no sound or person could penetrate.

Janet gripped Mother's hand – she could already hear the drone of the engines. As she and Mother negotiated the stairs, Janet prayed she'd soon hear the long-drawn-out signal that Mother had taught her was the all-clear, meaning they would be safe – well, safe for one more day.

Uncle Harry, dressed in his undershirt tucked into his trousers, with his braces hanging in loops almost down to his knees, stooped at the entrance to the cramped understairs cupboard as Janet and her mother bounded down the stairs.

"Come on," beckoned Harry, as he ushered the tiny Janet and her mother into the dark cupboard.

Janet would have to, as she always did, curl up in the minuscule space at the far end of the cramped closet which afforded her little headroom. The claustrophobic feeling of the rising stairs that pinned her to the wooden floorboards terrified her more than the booming sounds of destruction that had already begun its assault on her young ears.

Uncle Harry closed the cupboard door, flicking the latch to hold it tight into the door frame. This was the most terrifying part – that latch locking the three of them into the triangular, coffin-shaped cupboard.

A few months ago, before Janet knew the drill, Mother would take a moment to settle her by stroking her hair as she lay with her head on her clothes bundle and a small blanket tucked around her body. However, now Janet knew the drill, she quickly settled into her designated position.

Because of her slender build, Janet would often be mistaken for a child of much younger years. All the children of her age who lived in the surrounding streets were at least eight or nine inches taller than her. Throughout her life, Janet would always be slight in stature. However, as the years passed, she would grow to become a terrifying woman who could not be intimidated by anyone.

Janet, along with her eleven-year-old friend, Stan, returned to Hackney in the autumn of 1940 after escaping their enforced evacuation at the start of the phoney war. Stan now teamed up with other local children to form a group that, after bombing raids, scoured the debris to help trapped neighbours and bravely smother unexploded incendiary bombs with sand.

Street urchins, Mother had called them. However, like the gang her friend Stan ran with, many groups had sprung up all over the East End. Those brave children soon became known as the Dead-End Kids, and the wispy Janet wished to be like Stan and join the adventure. But unfortunately, Janet was simply too tiny to go rooting around bombed-out buildings – not that Mother would have let her even if she could venture on a growth spurt.

Uncle Harry flicked on the rubber torch after he'd secured the door latch. He shone the beam of light into Janet's eyes, checking she was tucked into her usual position before pulling a blanket around Mother as he cuddled her. Then, below where he'd written the previous night with the thick square red pencil, he marked on the wall—

10-05-1941 11:40pm

Every night, Uncle Harry would record the time of the start and end of the air raid. Janet hoped that the attacks would stop before he filled the wall with his scribbles. Although Uncle Harry was kind, she knew he wasn't her uncle. Neither was Uncle Albert, who'd also lived with them over the past year.

Mother had said that Father was away fighting the war, and Uncle Harry stayed with them to help out whilst Father was away. Janet didn't understand why Uncle Harry slept next to Mother, as had Uncle Albert. She believed that is where Father should sleep. Anyway, if Father had to fight the war, Janet couldn't fathom why all these supposed uncles didn't have to as well.

Mother had said something about some men were better at fighting, and some men were better at doing other things, but everyone was doing their bit for the war effort, as Mother put it.

At the time, Janet had innocently enquired if this meant that Uncle Harry and Uncle Albert were better at things in bed than Father. This had earned Janet a slap, an evening without any tea, and two hours locked in the understairs cupboard – even though there was no air raid.

Janet refrained from further enquiries about Uncle Harry's part in the war effort due to fear of experiencing another night of hunger.

However, bombs and Uncle Harry aside, Janet felt much happier back home with Mother than when she'd been evacuated to live at that hideous farm in the country. Although Stan had been with her, she'd cried every night during her eight-month stay in exile.

Whilst Janet huddled in the cramped space listening to the terrifying sounds, she thought about that distressing experience when in enforced exile in Norfolk.

As far as Janet could ascertain, Mrs Broughton, the farmer's wife, did little or nothing to assist the war effort. Janet had named her *The Queen of Hearts*, a reference to the evil queen from her favourite storybook. Janet firmly believed the hideous woman's only function in life was to inflict verbal and physical pain, presumably to satisfy her evil sadistic desires. Janet had never loathed someone so much.

After school and at weekends, Mr Broughton took Stan to help on the farm. Although Stan was only ten years old, he was taller than most lads of his age and the burly farmer put him to work mucking out the pig pens. Unfortunately, whilst Stan was busy on the farm doing his bit for the war effort, The Queen of Hearts forced the petite Janet to scrub floors and peel vegetables – Janet feared Mrs Broughton would order '*Off with her head*' if she failed with her allotted tasks.

The only respite from this living hell was a few hours on Sunday mornings when Mrs Broughton attended Sunday Service at the village church, whilst the indifferent farmer left Janet and Stan to their own devices. Naturally, Janet cherished those few hours devoid of the suffering of that evil woman's constant vicious verbal assaults.

The day she'd arrived at the school hall in that backward pocket-sized place, despite their name tags slung around their necks which stated otherwise, Stan had confidently claimed that they were brother and sister. Stan had said he wouldn't go anywhere without Janet and, fortunately for her, no one probed Stan's lie.

Due to this made-up sibling alliance, Stan and Janet were left until last to be assigned to a household – no one wanted two children to feed. Mrs Broughton had arrived late to the school hall, so, unfortunately for her, she became burdened with the two runtish looking East End kids who needed a good meal and a scrub in the tub, and not necessarily in that order.

While they'd waited for their transport to the ancient farmhouse, Stan and Janet had had to listen to Mrs Broughton as she hollered at some official, stating she was not happy about having to take in two scrawny young ruffians from the slums of London, as she put it.

Janet firmly believed she would never forget that conversation as the two adults discussed her and Stan's fate. Janet vowed that day that no one would ever make her feel so undesirable again.

"You're not suggesting I take these children into my house?" boomed Mrs Broughton in her usual belligerent manner to the rather officious schoolteacher who'd had the dubious task of allotting billets for the children who'd arrived that day.

"Yes, Mrs Broughton. As you know, the government has stated that any household with spare beds has a duty to house the evacuees. According to the order from the Ministry of Civil Defence, you have no choice!"

"Ridiculous!"

"Mrs Broughton, may I remind you; we are at war! Therefore, everyone must play their part!" replied the tired schoolteacher who knew Mrs Broughton would be difficult.

The bustling farmer's wife was a formidable woman who terrified most of the villagers and probably her sizeable husband with equal measure.

"Oh, no. Children and I don't get along. I can't possibly take these!"

"I'm sorry, Mrs Broughton, you have no choice. If you flatly refuse, I will have to inform Constable Ridley of your decision!"

The oafish farmer's wife had turned and sneered at the two children as they stood a few feet behind them in their Sunday-best, both clasping a small brown suitcase. Stan had held Janet's hand as tears welled up in her eyes whilst she'd tried to fathom how anyone couldn't love children.

"Ridiculous! There's no war! What are Mr Broughton and I supposed to do with two runtish-looking disgusting excuses of children like them?" she'd boomed, before once again pointing an accusing podgy finger in their direction.

"Mrs Broughton. Your task is to look after them!"

The memory of that time with The Queen of Hearts temporarily faded away as the cacophony of booms grew ever closer. Janet now understood why the children had previously had to leave London. However, there were no bombs then; now she was back, the bombs fell every night.

Janet never slept whilst hunkered down in the tight space at the end of the cupboard. Sometimes she'd weep, sometimes she would just count the booming sounds of explosions, and occasionally she would shudder with terror when the house shook and her mother gasped. Every morning she would look out of her bedroom window at the streets around her, surveying the new landscape and spotting the destroyed buildings from the previous night's raid whilst thanking God that her house was still standing.

Tonight would be the last time Janet would have to muster up and pretend to be brave in the understairs cupboard. Not that she knew that when, only a few minutes ago, she crawled into her allotted space, and not because the German bomber planes had stopped droning across the skies.

Ten minutes after Uncle Harry had scrawled the time on the wall, a deafening explosion temporarily removed the sound of those droning bombers above. Her ears recorded a high-pitched squeal, although it wasn't the long-drawn-out tone of the all-clear signal she'd prayed for.

The understairs cupboard appeared to have shrunk. The corner near the door where Mother should be hugging Uncle Harry was now occupied by a humongous heap of masonry attached to a chimney pot. Janet could no longer see Uncle Harry and only her mother's right foot, which now lay partially buried under fragments of her parents' demolished modest terraced house.

For the first time during an air raid, Janet fell asleep.

2

1987

Murder, She Wrote

"Morning, Mrs Trosh," I announced, as I bounded into the school office full of enthusiasm. Not that I always found Monday mornings exciting because, quite often, I would trudge into school with a cloak of doom hanging over me as I pondered the knowledge of the first hour consisting of a physics lesson, my least favourite subject. A double physics lesson that just happened to coincide with thirty fifteen-year-olds from F-Band, the lowest band of misfits whose academic abilities and life prospects could only be described as dismal.

It seemed the moons-of-doom had aligned to present me with a Monday morning where I would try to teach natural science to a disinterested bunch of juvenile delinquents, most of whom were more interested in chewing bubble gum, studying dirty mags, sniffing correction fluid, generally causing as much mayhem as humanly possible, or all of the above, as a classic multiple-choice question would always offer.

Not that I was particularly unhappy about teaching the least capable. No, in many ways, those students presented my biggest challenge and, when I managed to drag a few of them through an O-level exam, I found it hugely rewarding.

Anyway, I had a new vigour about me because the new term had kicked off last week. So, we had a whole new bunch of children, mostly wearing blazers two sizes too big, to drag along the education conveyor belt. With copious amounts of hard work, an equal measure of determination, and a hefty sprinkling of good luck, we would chug out some half-decent human beings at the age of sixteen.

Of course, five years was a short space of time to transform some individuals and, sad to say, some entered the system as naive eleven-year-olds only to ping out the other end as marauding delinquent tossers – to be fair, that was the minority.

Three weeks had now elapsed since the return of my Zippo lighter and, so far, nothing had turned to shite. So, double physics aside, all was good.

Mrs Trosh, our dependable school secretary, efficiently sat at her desk looking, as always, efficient, even though she was now past her allotted threescore and ten that apparently was stated in The Bible as the expected life span of a human being.

"Oh, good morning, Mr Apsley, you do sound chirpy today. Have you had a good weekend?" she replied, as she settled down behind her golf-ball typewriter, which the school had invested in some years ago. Although, at first, Mrs Trosh hadn't seemed too enthusiastic about the engineering advances on offer.

Over the last ten years, technological advances had gathered pace. The school had progressed to computer science lessons as part of the curriculum, and the school office now sported a new IBM word processor. However, Mrs Trosh was not going to use unnecessary electronic devices to type her correspondence. She hadn't trained at secretarial college to then go on to use a machine that corrects all your mistakes.

"No, sir! Learning to type was a skill, and these new machines were simply a way of correcting shoddy work!" she'd often quote.

Although an outrageous gossip and the nosiest person I'd ever encountered, Mrs Trosh delivered some particularly devastating news last week, which I know will profoundly affect the smooth running of the school. However, Mr Trosh, the school caretaker, and our dependable school secretary had announced their intention to retire and would be leaving the school at the end of the Autumn term.

Mrs Trosh and I had had an honest conversation about my concern that she was severing her connection to the one place that provided a platform to extract information and, of course, regurgitate to whoever in the form of gossip. Therefore, as I pointed out to her, she would be missing out. Also, in the future, how the hell was I going to hear the information regarding the groundswell and undercurrents I required to effectively manage my day job as the Deputy Head – my protestations fell on deaf ears.

Time refused to bend. In 1988, when I had started as a student at the school in my first life, Mrs Trosh was not the school secretary. So, I guess my challenge to her to stay on a little longer was futile, as I'd learnt over the past ten years that bending time was an extremely difficult task. The laid-out future, in the main, would continue as it always had.

"My weekend was pretty good ... Jenny and I took the kids up to the ABC Cinema on Sunday. They show re-runs at the matinee performances, so we got to see *Back to the Future* again, which Beth missed out on because she was too young to appreciate it in '85," I replied, as I collected my heap of post from the ancient pigeonhole filing box. Although for me, re-run was an understatement, as I'd seen that movie a million times over the last thirty-odd years. And here I was, now the star of the show, so to speak.

"Oh, I don't like silly films like that. I prefer romantic films. Anything with Cary Grant and Doris Day is my cup of tea. I suppose time-travel nonsense appeals to the kids of today. You see, Mr Apsley, a good story with a romantic ending lifts your mood. You feel that one day the magic could really happen," she stated, whilst clasping her hands to her chest, impersonating, I presume, someone like Grace Kelly as she swooned over Cary Grant. "Now, as for this silly time-travel story, well, how ridiculous! Imagine time-travel, ha poppycock!"

"Yes, imagine. How silly!"

"Oh, well, as long as the children enjoyed themselves," she threw over her shoulder before applying her spectacles to assess her next letter to thrash out on her futuristic machine.

"I presume you're counting down the days now, are you? Marking on the wall how many are left? What is it; thirty-odd to go?"

A moment of silence hushed the room, so I peered up from my heap of correspondence to see why Mrs Trosh had failed to respond.

She turned and beckoned with her head, indicating I should move over to her desk – this was it – a tsunami of gossip was imminent. Would it be tittle-tattle or factual information that I could use? I traversed my way over and placed my palms on her desk, raising my eyebrows in anticipation.

As expertly as always, she delivered her furtive sideways glance before whispering. "So, as you know, Mr Elkinson has completed all the interviews for my replacement. Now, when I arrived this morning, a young lady was just stepping into his office. I didn't catch her name, but I'm sure she attended last week for an interview."

"Oh," I whispered, as I glanced around the office – no idea why, but I seemed to be copying her.

"Yes, oh indeed. So, she's either having a second interview or is being offered the job at this very moment. Now look, I've checked through last week's appointments, and I'm certain I saw that particular young lady here on Thursday last," she stated before performing another quick visual check around the room, then opened the desk diary and pointed to the entries marked up on last Thursday. "So, that means she must be either Miss Brahms or Miss Moore. There! So, Mr Apsley, one of those two names is my replacement!"

I struggled to remember who the school secretary was in my day, as I seemed to recall there were quite a few that came and went, only vaguely remembering the one when I started here was a woman in her thirties and called Morse, or Morris, or something like that.

Back then, my elder brother, Stephen, had commented that the new school secretary was one horny bird. It was a comment that my grandmother overheard and, as I recall, wasn't overly impressed with. I guess in 2019, the comment would be MILF, and I'm sure she wouldn't have been impressed with that either. However, whatever the exact term used, my grandmother put him straight regarding the unacceptable label he and the older boys had attached to the young lady in the school office.

I guess the woman Stephen was referring to would be the lady sitting in Tom's office because MILF was not a label that sat comfortably alongside Mrs Trosh. Unless, of course, you were thumbing through a copy of *Mature Housewives* or some similar equally seedy publication.

"Miss Marple's got nothing on you!" I chuckled. "I reckon you could give Jessica Fletcher a run for her money!"

"Oh yes! I could see myself writing detective stories. You know, I might just do that when I retire! I could be the heroine solving all the mysteries in the town of Fairfield!"

Tom Elkinson's office door slowly opened. The hinges produced a drawn-out squeak, just as they would in a horror movie, raising the drama before the Prince of Darkness, as the teaching staff had labelled him, our aloof Headmaster, peered around the corner of the door frame. As slowly as the hinges squeaked, he produced a thin smile that gradually revealed his teeth – Christopher Lee had nothing on the man.

The difference between Roy Clark, our previous headmaster, and Tom Elkinson couldn't be starker. Over the last three years, I still hadn't formed any kind of relationship with the man. In fact, the day he dished out a verbal mauling to Beth and me when in the sixth form in my first life, which oddly would have been in about six years from now, I had a greater insight into the man that day than I have amassed over the three years working with him.

"Good morning, Jason. Do you have a moment?" asked our vampirical leader in his characteristically slow, deliberate manner.

"Of course, Tom. Good morning."

As I entered the office, I half expected to see the young lady lying motionless caused by the blood-sucking Tom had performed, quenching his thirst before crawling back into his coffin to snuggle down with a colony of bats. To be fair, although an odd man, he allowed me to manage the school's day-to-day running – you could call me the vampire's assistant.

As I closed the door to his study, I noticed a woman enter the main office whilst almost dragging in a girl who I presumed to be her daughter. They looked vaguely familiar, but I couldn't quite place them.

"Jason. Let me introduce Miss Moore. I believe you already know each other?" he slowly gestured with his right hand as if offering me to take a closer inspection.

The young lady turned to face me.

"Hello, Mr Apsley," she smiled, tipping her head sideways.

"Sarah! Sarah Moore! What … what—"

"Sarah will be joining us this week and taking over as school secretary when Mrs Trosh retires."

"Oh, right. Okay." I stood bemused and lost for words whilst struggling to grasp why Sarah had applied for the job.

"Right. I do have to slip out for a bathroom break, so I'll leave you two to get reacquainted," stated the Prince of Darkness as he floated out, gently closing the squeaky door. He possessed the grace and poise of a Stealth Bomber as he glided around the school corridors undetected.

"Sarah, I'm a bit flummoxed. Why—"

"Why would I want this job? Is that what you were going to ask?" she interrupted and followed my walk as I stepped around her and sunk into the free chair positioned next to Tom's desk.

"Well, yes!" I frowned and rubbed my chin. Was Sarah the school secretary when I attended school? Well, I recall the name beginning with M, and as a spotty eleven-year-old in 1988, she would have seemed to be a woman in her thirties. I knew Sarah to be in her twenties, but to eleven-year-olds, I guess anyone above the age of twenty seemed past it. Was Sarah Moore my older brother's MILF? Stephen was now fifteen and completing his final year, so would he and his mates repeat history and regard Sarah as their horny bird once again?

"Well, Mr Apsley—"

"It's Jason. Please call me Jason," I interrupted her.

"Yes. I know. But ... it's difficult to call you that ... you know, being my old teacher and all that," stammered Sarah, blushing and fidgeting with her hair, twisting the blonde strands that lay on her shoulder around in her fingers.

"Not anymore! You're going to be my right-hand man now ... err, right-hand woman, ha!" I babbled. Now it was my turn to look embarrassed.

"Well, yes, as I was saying. I decided to leave the job at the Council because it just wasn't for me ..." she seemed to halt mid-sentence because her tone suggested the next word was *and*, but she'd stopped herself from continuing. Sarah sat open-mouthed and expertly continued with her one-fingered hair-plaiting routine.

"Was there something else?" I questioned.

"I ... I had a relationship with a colleague that didn't ... didn't end well," she stammered and blushed, before continuing. "Oh ... please don't say anything to Mr Elkinson. I didn't mean to say that ... you see, I just had to get away from there."

I shook my head and smiled reassuringly. "Hey, don't worry ... mum's the word. You know, in the position of school secretary I'll need your ear to the ground. So, you and me," I waved my hand, gesturing back and forth between us. "Need to keep the perpetual flow of information, and all away from you know who!" I nodded to Tom's empty chair, whilst half expecting him to reappear in a puff of smoke cocooned in a red-satin-lined black cape.

"Ha, yes, of course. I'm thinking about taking teacher training at the Open University. I know it will take quite a while to complete, but I think that's the career I would like."

"Great idea! There are a lot worse jobs out there, I can tell you."

"Yes. Weren't you a mining engineer before taking up teaching?"

"Err ... something like that." Well, *other* Jason was. I'd spent most of my career as a miserable disinterested sales executive at a sheet metal fabrication company. A job I'd detested and recall spending most of my day pissing off my sales team which, over the years, I now realise was a skill I'd perfected.

Not wishing to pry, but in the knowledge that young Sarah was raped in my first life and became the mother of my now dead time-travelling partner Martin, I was a little concerned about the relationship she'd mentioned that had gone south – a delicate subject to approach. However, I thought I'd dip my toe in.

"Err, not wishing to pry, but at the Council Summer Ball you were at a few weeks ago ... was that the young man you've fallen out with?"

"Scott? The bloke I was arguing with when you stepped in."

"Yes. Sorry about that."

"No, Mr Aps ... err, Jason," she blushed again and, although she had stopped a moment ago, her finger shot up to start the hair-plaiting routine. "No, you were right to intervene. Yes, that's him. We split up, and then the office atmosphere became toxic. I think it was the catalyst to make me move on. Anyway, that council job wasn't much ... bit of a dead-end job, really."

"Yes, I'm sure you're right."

"Oh! No, I didn't mean your wife has a dead-end job. I know she's one of the senior managers at the Council."

"Ha, it's alright, Sarah. I know you didn't mean that. Anyway, I think you'll make a fantastic teacher."

"Thank you. I hope so. That night at the party ... did you know the police caught a rapist prowling around near the Broxworth Estate?"

"Yes, I had heard." DI French had alluded to that fact the day she returned my Zippo lighter.

"Well, I was so lucky! Scott and I had a massive row on the way home. I got out of the car and walked the last mile. I was a bit silly because I decided to take a shortcut through the school playing fields leading off Coldhams Lane. It's so dark through there. When I was about halfway down the lane, I heard something behind me ... God, I was spooked! I sprinted like a bat out of hell, I can tell you! When I reached Eaton

Road, a police car stopped and checked I was okay. Apparently, they'd arrested a man lurking in the cut-through lane! He could have been the rapist! You know, they've charged him with multiple attacks … I think I had a lucky escape!"

"Blimey! Anyway, I think you saying you were a bit silly about cutting across the playing fields isn't right. It's not right that a lone female can't walk about town without the worry of what might happen."

"No, I know. But that's just how it is, isn't it?"

"I'm afraid so. Do you know who they arrested?"

"I'm not sure this is related to that night, but the police have arrested Andrew Colney! Would you believe after that incident with his brother David and then Patrick attacking my dad!"

"Hells bells! That is something. Christ, that bloody family!"

"Oh, I know. It makes me shudder thinking about it."

"Well, don't. You're safe now. It sounds like many others are too, now they've caught the scumbag. I'm just pleased you're okay."

So that confirmed what I'd suspected when Frenchie had turned up a few weeks ago telling me they'd arrested Andrew Colney. In my first life, he was Martin's father. In this life, the police had caught him before perpetrating the heinous crime, so Sarah is safe. Therefore, Martin would never be born. I mused for a moment that based on my parents dying eight years earlier this time, in theory, I was never born either – what a headfuck!

The Prince of Darkness, or PoD, which we often used when referring to our leader, re-entered the office. Presumably, he'd completed his call of nature, probably sucking the blood from a few unsuspecting students on the way back to his office for good measure. Hopefully, some of those delinquents I was about to try and teach physics to, and not the well-behaved bunch who'd be attending my afternoon lessons which were a much more measured and pleasant affair.

This morning's lesson featured thermodynamics and the effect on matter. Not that I thought for one moment that lot had any usable matter between their ears to grasp the subject, and although I'm no expert, I suspected snorting correction fluid wouldn't help.

"Are we all nicely reacquainted?" asked the Prince of Darkness, before grinning. I couldn't see any blood dripping from his mouth, so I guessed he hadn't sucked the life out of a few students when swooping through the school corridors.

"Yes, I think so."

"I think Sarah will make a terrific addition to the team."

Sarah beamed whilst sitting with her hands in her lap, appearing delighted by my assessment regarding her suitability for the role. She seemed to have now completed her one-fingered hair twiddling routine. "Thank you, Mr Elkinson. I'm really looking forward to starting."

"Good. Well, let me introduce you to Mrs Trosh. Although you will remember her from your school days, I presume? Spend as much time with her today as you like, and then we'll see you bright and early tomorrow morning," he delivered in that trademark quiet demeanour.

When the police apprehended Andrew Colney, time had bent in my favour, well, certainly in Sarah's. Unfortunately, PoD was about to inform me of another time-bend – this time, it was most certainly not in my favour.

3

The War Of The Roses

"Jason, I would like you to sit in on the next meeting. I have a Mrs Crowther here with her daughter, Lisa. The girl is from the Howlett School. However, there was a nasty incident, so she'll be transferring here. So, I think it's best you join the meeting as we're going to have to keep a close eye on this young lady."

"Crowther. Did you say, Crowther?"

"Yeeessss," slowly replied the Prince of Darkness in his usual languid cadence, whilst raising his eyebrows in an equally phlegmatic manner. "Do you know the family?"

Did I know them! Christ, yes, I bloody well knew them! Lisa Crowther in 2006 became Lisa Apsley! And Mrs Crowther spent the subsequent ten years informing me what a pathetic useless tosser of a son-in-law I was!

I knew when I'd spotted the woman enter the office, I recognised her. But time had shifted. Lisa had attended the Howlett School in my first life and at no point transferred to the Eaton City of Fairfield School. Why had time changed? What did this mean?

"Err ... no. No never heard of them," I managed to babble out whilst my mind whirred around. However, PoD's raised eyebrows suggested he hadn't swallowed my lie.

"Very well." PoD held out his arm to Sarah as if coaxing her to his lair. "Sarah, let me introduce you to Mrs Trosh. Jason, I won't be a moment."

Sarah hopped up and disappeared with PoD into the main office, where I spotted Jayne Stone, a fellow teacher, who appeared to be in deep conversation with our nosey school secretary.

"Jayne," I hissed through the doorway. As she turned, I gestured with my head, indicating I needed a quiet word.

Mrs Trosh loudly tutted, presumably because I'd addressed our part-time teacher incorrectly and should, in her eyes, have addressed Jayne appropriately by the use of her surname. However, unfortunately for Trish Trosh, she had no grounds to complain because, unlike Roy, PoD had no such hang-ups about the use of first names when out of students' earshot.

Jayne and Mrs Trosh's relationship had never quite recovered from an incident that involved Jayne and a then-married man about eight or nine years ago. A group of thirteen-year-olds had burst into classroom seven only to discover Jayne and the man, now her husband, as they snogged whilst spread-eagled across a desk. Mrs Trosh had been aghast by the unsavoury sordid caper but still managed to gossip about it for some years, resulting in her relationship with Jayne taking a deep dent that no experienced panel-beater could straighten out.

"Jayne, I know you're in this morning to start working on the school play, but I need a favour."

"Yeah, sure," she smiled, full of enthusiasm, which I knew would in any moment evaporate.

"I have a meeting with PoD, err ... Tom. Can you take my class this morning?"

"Oh ... err. Yes, go on then. You owe me, mind," she replied, narrowing her eyes whilst placing her hands on her hips. I guess she was trying to think what my first class was, or more concerningly, who she'd be teaching.

"Oh, brill, thanks."

"What class is it?"

"Physics ... F band," I replied, avoiding eye contact.

"You're joking! That bunch of delinquents! Jesus, Jason, you've pulled a stroke there! I'll have to suit up with a stab vest and police riot shield to teach that lot!"

"Sorry!" I replied, my smile morphing into a grimace.

"Bloody hell," she hissed. "You owe me!"

"Thanks, Jayne."

Colin, Jayne, and I were the three teachers who taught most of the science lessons. Jayne had become a close friend of Jenny, and Colin was now technically my son-in-law after marrying my daughter, Jess. Although in reality, she was *other* Jason's daughter, and Colin was *other* Jason's son-in-law. However, apart from the Time Travel Believers' Club members, which consisted of myself as Chairman, Jenny as the Chief Operating Officer and George as Chief Executive, to the rest of the world, Jess was my daughter.

We often discussed and bartered off lessons that involved teaching F Band pupils. However, if one took a class from another, the debt could be huge. Escaping unscathed from any lesson with F Band was a real feat. You had to have your wits about you throughout the whole class, keeping an eye out for flying objects and generally hideous behaviour that came straight out of the Millwall Bushwhackers' football hooligans strategy handbook – if such a thing existed.

I'd taken my son, Christopher, to the FA Cup match at Kenilworth Road ground to see Luton play a couple of years ago. Not that we often attended, but Fairfield Town were so awful, an occasional trip to see Luton play was a treat.

That particular match witnessed one of the worst scenes of football hooliganism ever encountered. After we'd escaped the stadium, miraculously avoiding the flying seats that were unceremoniously ripped up and lobbed by the Millwall faction, I berated myself for not remembering this incident the first time around. I guess I could be excused as I was only eight years old at the time.

Jenny's brother, Alan, a police officer, had been drafted in to help police the game that night. He wasn't injured, as forty-odd were, and the experience gained when policing the miners' strike had given him a good grounding for the horrific events of that evening. Although the miners were nowhere near the level of the Millwall Bushwhacker crowd, and there were uncorroborated reports that the police themselves had acted violently at the Battle of Orgreave in 1984.

Alan had concerningly loved that battle and the incident in Luton. Subsequently, I harboured grave concerns regarding Jenny's brother's suitability to uphold the law. And now, unbelievably, some idiot in the Fairfield Police had deemed it a good idea to transfer Alan to the Traffic Division, thus placing her fight-crazed brother in charge of a high-speed squad car – a terrifying thought.

Anyway, F-Band had adopted the Bushwhackers' tactics with frighteningly good precision, and Jayne would need to be ready with her tin hat on to survive the next hour.

PoD swooped back into the office, following my twelve-year-old ex-wife accompanied by my ex-mother-in-law, who he'd asked to enter his lair. Behind PoD's back, Jayne bared her teeth and held her hands aloft as if impersonating a monster chasing Shaggy and Scoob. I stifled a snigger – she was funny, although, I accept, totally unprofessional.

Although Tom stayed blissfully unaware of his nickname, never had one phrase fitted so well to describe a man. I think it was Jayne who'd coined the phrase after she'd had us all in fits of hysterics when impersonating him in the staff room one lunchtime.

She'd attached a couple of plastic fangs one of her daughters had used during Halloween dress-up last year and donned a black teacher's gown, which we never wore now Roy had departed. She then proceeded to swoop around the staffroom pretending to sink her fangs into the other teachers, only for Tom to enter the room to witness the event – although he appeared utterly oblivious to the joke.

As I've always been a bit of a Halloween scrooge – the time I now lived in afforded many advantages. Back in 2019, the crazy hysteria about a rather stupid festival used to literally do my head in. I detested dress-up, which included the stupid resurgence after the millennium for the desire to wear Christmas jumpers. Both dress-up requirements delivered stomach-wrenching dread in equal measures.

Gary Oxney, the Managing Director at Waddington Steel, when he wasn't swooping down perfecting his seagull management style of shitting on us all before returning to his nest, would always get excited as Christmas approached, placing a company directive demanding that all colleagues were to wear Christmas jumpers to the office commencing from December 1st – no exceptions.

I passionately hated it, and Lisa would always buy me a new ridiculous jumper each year and proceed to take the piss out of me as I left for work in some hideous garment liberally splattered with flashing lights. Martin always dragged out his penis-nose Rudolph jumper. The said jumper had Rudolph on the front with a large red penis-shaped nose that he would proceed to wave about – I seem to remember it lit up as well. The words across the top of the jumper, as I recall, were – *Rudolph has a shiny hooter!*

Anyway, I digress – where were we, ah, yes – Halloween. Gary Oxney was also pumped up about this festival and insisted on a Halloween dress-up day in which all employees were expected to participate. As the sales executive, I had to lead by example. I threw a sicky one year to miss the event and was royally dressed down on my return for my lack of leadership, as he put it.

Martin would always don his Bananaman outfit on the day, although I never quite knew what the correlation was between a banana and ghostly ghouls. I think he just liked costumes that had phallic undertones.

I'm led to believe the festival originated in Scotland or Ireland, so, to be fair, we exported it over the pond, only for the Americans to give it back with bells on. However, I doubt that many twelfth-century Scotsman ran around the moors dressed as a banana. That all said, Guy Fawkes Night was also a bit ridiculous. Why we still celebrated burning a Catholic to death, hell knows.

I recall each 31st October, whilst sitting in darkness after insisting that all lights must be off and blinds to be closed, I would inform Lisa that we would pretend to be out when the bunch of local morons in fancy dress banged on the front door shouting 'trick or treat'.

One year, after the children had sweetly called out trick or treat fully expecting me to open the door with bags of sweets and chocolate, a small lad – who could only have been about ten years of age and clearly distraught with the lack of offer of said treats – lifted the letterbox and bellowed through informing me that I was a miserable motherfucker. To be fair to the lad, in 2018, he was probably right.

Anyway, back here in good old 1987, Halloween thankfully hadn't hit the ridiculous heights it surely would in thirty-odd years.

"Take a seat, Mrs Crowther," offered PoD, as he reclined in his swivel chair. I plucked up a chair from the back of the office and placed it at the side of the desk, then sat and studied my ex-wife and mother-in-law.

"Okay. I have young Lisa's primary school report and the limited document from the Howlett School. Your daughter appears to be quite bright. Therefore, we'll be placing her in the top band. Mr Poole will be her form teacher."

Whilst PoD rambled on, I found myself gawping at my ex-wife. I'd seen old school photos, and the little girl in front of me was definitely her. Lisa wasn't what you might describe as a stunner. Still, she would develop into an attractive woman and, based on my previously discovered information, a few other men found her attractive during our pointless marriage – including Martin.

However, the young girl sitting across from me clearly hadn't started to blossom, and the plain, stern-looking lass with her hair in a ponytail sat quietly looking at the floor. I noticed out of the corner of my eye Mrs Crowther looking at me.

"Is this man alright? He appears to have a gormless look about him! Are you staring at my daughter?" she stated in an accusing tone.

Her question awoke me from my gawping gaze. I closed my mouth and found a smile.

"You're not one of those perverts, are you?" she questioned aggressively.

My ex-mother-in-law appeared to have perfected her evil tongue a good fifteen years before I met her the first time. Then, as I recall with a shudder, her tongue was fully refined at delivering cutting remarks and accusations.

"Oh, my apologies. Let me introduce you. This is Mr Apsley. He's the Deputy Head. He'll be ensuring Lisa settles in here," PoD offered with his trademark vampiric grin.

I lifted my bottom off the chair and held out my hand to Mrs Crowther, who scowled back as she shook my hand.

"Welcome, Lisa," I said to my ex-wife, who didn't respond. No change there, I thought.

"So, just to be clear, young lady. The school will not tolerate any behaviour that seems to have transpired whilst you were at the Howlett School. Are we clear?" demanded PoD, as he leaned across his desk. He held that position awaiting a response from the apparent timid girl opposite.

Lisa nodded.

"My daughter is not solely to blame for that incident! I will accept her actions were disappointing, and she is quite clear that she must behave herself from now on. Mr Crowther and I are committed to ensuring she toes the line. I'm sure you're aware that Mr Crowther is a Freemason and an important member of the community. We'll not have our name dragged through the mud! Can I trust you both to be discreet regarding any misdemeanour that Lisa may have been embroiled in?"

"You can, Mrs Crowther," replied PoD.

I nodded in her direction to affirm. Although, at this stage, I was intrigued to know what this misdemeanour was. One thing I did know, Mr Crowther, my ex-father-in-law, was a miserable bastard who, like his hideous wife, fought tooth and nail to ensure that Lisa never married me.

I recall her parents' delight when we divorced, following a *War of the Roses* style break up. Although I didn't piss on the fish and Lisa didn't turn the dog into pâté, but it was pretty messy. Of course, they didn't know the catalyst for our break up was their daughter's inability to refrain from enjoying Rudolph's red hooter that many a man offered her.

The meeting ended with Mrs Crowther leaving the school and Mrs Trosh whisking Lisa off to Mr Poole's class. I took the opportunity to gather some information.

"Tom, what happened with Lisa Crowther at the Howlett School?"

"Yes, all rather unsavoury, I'm afraid. Apparently, Lisa was caught with her father's polaroid camera taking pictures through the boy's changing room window, then using the mucky snaps to blackmail the poor boys for money. Pay up, or the snaps would be distributed amongst her classmates, was the demand. Within the first week on the new term, she'd started quite a lucrative business until one lad informed his parents. As you can imagine, of course, it all kicked off. Quite rightly, last Friday, the school had no choice but to expel her."

"Oh hell!"

"Yes indeed. We are going to have to watch this little madam. The butter-wouldn't-melt routine she displayed this morning, I think, is a cover for her real personality."

"You're not wrong! Evil twisted cow!"

"Sorry? That's a bit strong, Jason. I thought you said you didn't know the Crowther family?"

"Oh, no. Ignore me."

Well, the Lisa I knew may not have been a peeping-tom, so to speak. However, the last few years of our ill-fated marriage had taught me that she was cunning, conniving, and played games. It seems my ex-wife had started at an early age.

I considered there was a need for an urgent meeting of the Time Travel Believers' Club up at the Three Horseshoes Pub. Time had changed, and this was concerning. I planned to give George a bell at lunchtime and arrange the meet for this evening.

4

1948

The Shawshank Redemption

"You'd better get it today, you stupid bitch. You let me down, and you know what'll happen!" threatened Janet, as she turned her attention from the butter dish to Beryl. She stepped forward, closing the space between them to push home her demands.

Beryl backed away, bumping into the large butler sink, visibly trembling as she watched her evil twisted tormentor advance, unable to find any words to respond.

"And, if you think you can mess with me, *bitch,* you've made a big mistake!" spat Janet, as she leant into the stupid girl's face and pressed the butter knife against the soft skin of her neck.

Janet held her position, slowly forcing the tip of the blunt knife into her throat, causing an indent in the terrified girl's skin. Janet looked up into Beryl's eyes, smiled and removed the blade before calmly returning her attention to the butter dish and continued sparingly spreading the butter on the toast.

Beryl remained frozen to the spot, wide-eyed with fear. She could feel her legs buckling as she watched her tormentor move away and calmly continue to prepare breakfast for the thirty-two girls who resided at St. Peter's Orphanage. Although Beryl had the benefit of height over Janet, she lacked the evil girl's confidence.

Beryl had already endured three months at the orphanage after being placed here when her mother had moved to a sanatorium due to the cocktail of drugs prescribed doing little to abate her tuberculosis. She'd never known her father, and her mother always refused to speak of him. So, because her grandparents were too frail to take her in, this left St. Peter's as the only option for the delicate child she was.

Although, at the age of nearly fourteen, and the second eldest child in residence, Beryl experienced gut-wrenching terror at every waking moment – most of which was caused by the eldest girl – Janet Curtis, and her accomplice, thirteen-year-old Susan Kane.

"Am I going to have to do all the work? Come on, you moron, pull your finger out!" Janet waved the butter knife in Beryl's direction, delivering her now perfected skull-splitting stare whilst watching the pathetic wallflower flinch once again. Janet revelled in the power she exerted over her.

Beryl tentatively plucked up a butter knife and helped butter the toast, wishing she had the strength of character to plunge it in the evil girl's chest. Being hung for murdering Janet Curtis would be a welcome relief from this hideous existence.

"Mrs Alderman said I have to do the laundry today. I ... I will get it for you tomorrow," whispered Beryl, frustrated that she couldn't stop the tremor in her voice and the constant blinking that always took hold when in close proximity to Janet Curtis.

"Speak up! You're pathetic. I can't hear you," spat back Janet.

"I said ... I said I'll get it tomorrow. I have to do the laundry today," Beryl whispered once again, without making eye contact with the ferocious girl opposite. She really couldn't fathom how such a tiny girl could be so terrifying.

"Good morning, girls," sung Mrs Alderman, as she bustled her way into the kitchen.

"Good morning, Mrs Alderman," replied both teenagers in unison. Not that either girl cared less about exchanging pleasantries with the orphanage's housekeeper. However, like a well-drilled sergeant major, Mrs Alderman ruled the children with a metaphorical iron rod. She demanded impeccable behaviour from all the girls. Otherwise they would suffer dire consequences. All the girls quickly learnt to mind their manners, and even Janet complied. At first, Beryl had curtseyed in front of Mrs Alderman, only stopping when the controlling housekeeper had demanded she refrained from such stupidity, advising a nod of the head would suffice.

"Now, Janet, please ensure all the children are seated for breakfast and chase up where little Doris has got to. I haven't seen her this morning and suspect she's crying in the privy. Be firm with her. She needs the help and guidance from you older girls."

"Yes, Mrs Alderman," replied Janet, as she stabbed the knife in the butter and smirked whilst she enjoyed watching Beryl flinch.

"Oh, Beryl! What on earth are you doing? You can't slap butter on like that. There's rationing, for God sake, girl! That half-pound has to last until Friday! You're going to have to wise up, young lady. I really don't know what your mother taught you!"

Beryl burst into tears, which was not unusual. In fact, it was probably a daily occurrence. "I ... I'm, sorry, Mrs Alderman."

"You've even spread some on your neck! Damn you, girl, there will be consequences for your stupidity! Good men gave their lives so you could enjoy the life you have now. Wasting food is a sin ... you hear me ... a *sin!*"

The rotund housekeeper roughly grabbed hold of Beryl's hand, crushing her fingers around the butter knife whilst guiding Beryl's hand to the butter dish, showing her exactly how much butter should be spread on each piece of toast.

Because Janet was now the eldest girl at St. Peter's, she could be classed as head girl, not that such a title existed. However, Janet assumed the role that no one had assigned her. This position allowed her to enforce a pecking order, which put her at the top, with Susan Kane taking up the role of her reliable lieutenant. Susan was always keen to implement Janet's demands, leaving the rest as fair game for the two girls who revelled in their reign of terror and intimidation.

In May of 1941, after a team of firemen, assisted by the Dead-End Kids, had miraculously extracted Janet from the rubble in the understairs cupboard, St. Peter's Orphanage in Fairfield became her permanent home.

Unfortunately, Mother and her lover of the day, Uncle Harry, were crushed when the house collapsed in the aftershock of a five-hundred-pound bomb that obliterated the house next door, along with the elderly couple who resided there.

Arriving at the orphanage, meeting the other girls, and what seemed at the time the terrifying Mrs Alderman, had stolen a march on the understairs cupboard in the harrowing experience stakes. At the age of eight, Janet soon started bedwetting again and, after an initial show of sympathy, Mrs Alderman punished the little Janet by forcing her to sleep in a wet bed.

After a few weeks, Janet plucked up the courage to ask if she could return to the farm and live with The Queen of Hearts – anywhere was better than here, she'd thought. Of course, that request was duly met with a beating for her ungratefulness. The bed-wetting continued.

Every day she prayed that Father would come home from fighting the war and save her from this frightening place, where she suffered relentless bullying from the outset due to her slight stature. However, as usual, her prayers weren't answered, and Father never came for her.

A further year passed before Janet learnt that her father had, in fact, completed his duty and done his bit for the war effort, as Mother would say. Not that this meant her father would soon be home to save her from this living hell, because only a few weeks after Mother died in Uncle Harry's arms, Father also lost his life at the hands of the enemy.

Now, nearly eight years later, Janet had fortified her resolve – she'd learnt the hard way. No longer could she be bullied, no longer would she wet the bed, and many years had passed since she'd wasted her breath on praying.

Mrs Alderman demanded obedience from the girls, and Janet was okay with this. She'd learnt to play her, make all the right noises, and keep the other girls in check.

Janet's compliance resulted in the rotund housekeeper turning a blind eye to Janet's control and bullying she exerted on the other thirty-one girls who obeyed her every instruction. Although many of the younger girls were taller than Janet, none possessed her fearlessness. Mrs Alderman said she had spunk.

Her latest victim for torment was Beryl. This particular project was turning out to be extremely satisfying. After locating Doris in the privy and instructing her to attend breakfast, Janet entered the dormitory for the older girls, not specifically denoted by age, but whether they were inflicted with *the curse,* as Mrs Alderman called it.

Five girls shared the small room, linked to the main dormitory via a doorway with a heavy brown curtain that provided privacy from the younger, innocent girls. Janet folded back the sheets of Beryl's bed, noting the sheets still clung to the warmth from Beryl's body. Lifting her dress, Janet removed her underwear. Then whilst squatting on the bed and grabbing the steel tubular headrest, she urinated across the sheets and pillow. Janet might have stopped bedwetting, but she still enjoyed wetting beds.

A couple of months ago, Janet was awarded the task of dusting Mrs Alderman's private rooms. This chore was deemed preferable when compared to cleaning toilets and laundry duty – also affording her the occasional opportunity to remove small items which she could sell.

After a close call when Mrs Alderman had nearly caught her sticky fingers, Janet quickly deduced this was way too risky. Not wishing to cut off her new income, she now selected other girls to steal for her. This new strategy eliminated any risk to herself because if any chosen girl were to be caught, they would never have the courage to point the finger of blame at Janet. Ray Hilton, a lad she knew from school, had connections, and his father was able to fence these stolen items, thus providing Janet with a steady income.

Beryl's latest task was to remove a couple of brooches from Mrs Alderman's jewellery box. Although of low value, Janet's profit would be enough for a few packets of Passing Cloud cigarettes – she liked the pink colour of the box and the sophisticated look it afforded her.

A couple of years back, Janet had marvelled at the movie poster of Rita Hayworth, promoting her latest movie, Gilda. Spotting the poster of Rita in her gorgeous tight-fitting green dress while seductively holding her cigarette is what had started Janet smoking – she wanted to look like Rita. When Janet wasn't bullying the other girls, she would entertain them as she strode around the dormitory, flicking her hair and pushing clouds of smoke into the air. When Janet allowed others to see the real her, she could be quite captivating.

That idiot Beryl would steal the brooches today, or a urine-stained bed would be the least of her worries, thought Janet, whilst she reapplied her underwear and skipped downstairs to enjoy breakfast.

Years later, Janet would reflect on her time at St. Peter's. Although she'd arrived there under tragic circumstances, time at the oppressive orphanage had proved to provide her with invaluable lessons about control, coerciveness, and the power of threat – vital tools she required and perfected in her adult life.

Susan Kane, her trusted lieutenant, became a lifelong friend. They were sisters to anyone who didn't know them, even calling each other so.

Beryl Backman suffered two more years at the hands of Janet and Susan. The experience would leave Beryl terrified of her own shadow – the torment and bullying defining her adult life.

5

1987

Dirty Harry

"Morning, Guv." DC Kevin Reeves stuck his head around the door frame. The cigarette slotted into the corner of his mouth bounced as he spoke, allowing a tube of ash that had previously hung on for dear life to break off and float to the carpet-tiled floor at the entrance to DI French's office.

The DI watched the ash's descent as it landed on the carpet one inch inside the door. DC Reeves trod the ash in whilst the DI tutted.

"You typed up your reports yet?" she asked, ignoring the new grey mark on the carpet.

"Err ... I'm on it now, Guv."

"Right. Well, Andrew Colney is up for his preliminary hearing at the Magistrates' this afternoon. So, you better crack on because I want the file ready."

"Yeah, no worries, Guv. You want the good or the bad news?" asked Kevin, as he still clung to the door frame.

DI French glanced up, annoyed her DC was still standing there and not doing as instructed. "Reeves, stop the dramatics ... what news?"

"On Friday, Uniform had another stab at that bird, Sarah Moore, who Colney was chasing down the cut-through lane to the school when we collared that scum. It was the same officers who caught up with her when she was running down Eaton Road."

"And?"

"Well, as she said, she ran because she sensed someone was chasing her. Of course, we know there was because we nabbed the bastard."

DI French rocked back in her chair, raising her eyebrows. "We nicked the shit Colney because I employed my detective skills ... you might want to remember that and learn from it if you want a decent career! If it were down to you, we'd have sat in the motor smoking fags all night!"

"Yeah, okay, Guv. It was a good collar, though." He grinned.

"Well, get on with it!"

"Yeah, well, the young lass was so relieved to see a panda car, PC Harrison said she hugged him when they caught up with her ... reckon she was scared shitless. Both Uniform boys said she's one fit bird. Best bit of skirt they'd spotted all night. Harrison said he'd used all his self-control to remove her arms from around his neck!" he chuckled, then continued even though the DI's expression suggested she wasn't too impressed with his tale. "Anyway, after Harrison had stopped talking about how fit she is and waxing lyrical about her cute arse, he said the girl wouldn't be able to identify Colney because it was too dark."

"Yes, I ruddy well know all that! It was in the report last week!" barked the DI.

"Yeah, but as I was saying, Uniform had another chat with her on Friday to see if she could remember anything now she'd had a chance to think about it ... if you know what I mean?"

"Reeves, are you suggesting Uniform may be putting words in her mouth ... coaxing a false statement?"

"No, Guv," lied Reeves. "Anyway, she stuck to her story ... so that's the bad news. Ha, the way Harrison described her, I reckon he wouldn't have minded sticking something else in her mouth!" he nervously chuckled, now remembering this was the Guv he was talking to, not the lads in the locker room.

DI French raised her hand and, with her index finger, beckoned the young DC into her office. Reeves stepped forward, concerned as he held a lit cigarette in his hand because the whole team knew that smoking in the DI's office was punishable by death or something close to it.

"Close the door."

Reeves complied, using the heel of his shoe to nudge it shut, causing the faded-blue Venetian blind to rattle and clang like a set of wind chimes.

Those blinds had long since outlived their purpose. At least three slats were missing, and the remaining bent out of shape, caused by previous DIs snapping back the metal slats to survey their CID office. The faded, broken blind fitted in nicely with the rest of the building, which hadn't fared well since replacing its Victorian predecessor in the late '50s. However, funding was low, and there were minimal budgets for increased manpower, let alone décor improvements.

DI French stood behind her desk whilst Reeves awaited his bollocking. Although considerably shorter than Reeves, the DI had an aura about her. Her tray-of-beer chest, which Reeves thought would require considerable effort to move, afforded the DI the stature of a bulldozer that matched her demeanour when giving her team a dressing-down.

"Reeves! That young lady was nearly raped that night! You and Uniform, thinking it's acceptable to throw around lewd remarks about the girl's apparent cute posterior, and what you despicable low-life shits want to stick in her mouth, is totally unacceptable! It's comments like that which make men like Andrew Colney think it's acceptable to run around this town taking women whenever they feel the desire!"

Reeves bowed his head. DI French glanced through the blinds to see her team all gawping in her direction, alerted by her raised voice as she delivered the tongue-lashing to the young and totally immature DC. Apart from DC Megson, the only other female officer on her team, all averted their eyes and returned to their work when clocking her stare.

Adele Megson afforded herself a wry smile, delighted that Reeves was on the receiving end of the DI's mauling. Finally, she might now get some respite from the rest of the team who seemed to take it in turns to pinch and grab the protruding parts of her body, which they did at every opportunity, even though she regularly returned their attentions with a slap.

"Did you hear me?" boomed the DI.

"Guv," he quietly replied.

"What? I'm your senior officer!"

"Yes Guv, err ... yes Ma'am," Reeves replied firmly, standing to attention, now grasping the knowledge that he'd really pissed the Guv off.

"Get out!" boomed DI French, as she returned her sizeable frame to her chair. "And turn that ruddy jacket collar down. You're not the Fonz!"

"Guv," sheepishly replied Reeves, as he grabbed the door handle, pulling open the door, allowing the wind-chime blinds to rattle.

Kevin Reeves, an inexperienced CID officer, played the jack-the-lad type in the team. His brash, confident swagger as a PC was one of the reasons the previous DI had plucked him from Uniform to make up the numbers in the already depleted CID unit. However, Reeves struggled with the DI, not because she was a woman per se, but because she didn't appreciate his boyish banter.

Unfortunately, Reeves was not savvy enough to know when to shut up. Now, concerned he'd once again pissed off the DI, which was a far too often occurrence, he searched for something else to say to see if he could haul back this situation.

"You still here?" called out DI French, as she returned her attention to a report on her desk.

Reeves knew he should close the door and crack on with that report. However, his verbal diarrhoea kicked in, which was not unusual.

"Guv, there was a funny one this morning, which I spotted on my way to work. I was coming up Coldhams Lane where we nicked that bastard Colney." Reeves waited for the DI to look up; she didn't, so he bashed on, probably digging a deeper hole that she would surely bury him in if he didn't shut up.

"Well, some tosser had wedged his car between one of the bus stops and a large oak tree. You couldn't squeeze a cigarette paper between the bumpers and the bus stop at one end and the tree at the other! The Traffic boys were there scratching their heads, wondering how the hell the driver could have positioned it like that. I mean, you'd need a crane to lift it into that space. There was no damage to the car; they just said the front offside tyre was a bit bald, that's all."

Reeves realised he shouldn't have gone down this route and, before the DI bawled him out again, he decided his funny story wasn't going to calm the waters between them.

"It was an old yellow Mk3 Cortina. My dad had one back in the '70s," he threw in as he closed the door.

"Reeves!" bellowed the DI before the door slotted into the doorframe.

Reeves tentatively opened the door and poked his head in. He winced whilst awaiting the DI's wrath, also wondering why he always seemed to run his mouth off.

"What car?"

"Err ... a yellow Cortina ... Mk3."

"Which bus stop?"

"On Coldhams Lane, where I said."

"Yes, but which one?"

"Guv, you alright? You're as white as a milk-maiden's arse!"

"I asked which one! And if you make reference to any part of a woman's anatomy again, I'll shove your testicles in a Kenwood!"

Reeves thought for a moment as he bowed his head, trying to picture the scene this morning, whilst seriously regretting the arse comment. He valued his testicles and was in no doubt that the DI was capable of performing the culinary suggestion.

"The one nearest the Beehive Pub, you know where the line of oak trees are before you get to the Broxworth Estate. As I said, both front doors were open, but not a scratch on it ... God knows how someone slotted it in there."

"Have Uniform identified who owns it?"

"Oh, I don't know. I just thought it was funny. Mike Greaves from Traffic said it was bizarre. He remembered a similar car crashing through the old bus stop and hitting that tree in the exact same spot about ten years ago. He said he attended the scene that evening, and two blokes were lying dead across the bonnet. Gone through the windscreen ... probably not wearing seat belts."

"Index number?"

"No idea, Guv. Brian Thompson, the bus driver who pulled up, said he also remembered the crash because the bus stop was demolished when he pulled up the next day, and the car was still wrapped around the tree."

"So, you took the bus driver's name but failed to note down the ruddy index number!"

"Err ... yeah, sorry, Guv. I didn't think it was important. I knew the bus driver because he's one of my old man's colleagues from the bus depot."

DI French stretched back in her chair, her mind racing at this ridiculous possibility. In 1977 Paul Colney and a mystery man were killed in that exact spot, in an identical car. Only a couple of weeks ago, she'd visited Jason Apsley to return a

Zippo lighter found in that car. A car she was certain Apsley was in that evening it crashed. The coincidence was ridiculous.

"Get hold of the index number, and I want to see Mike Greaves from Traffic immediately."

"Guv?"

"Now!"

"Guv, what about my report?"

"The ruddy report can wait; I want that index number. Also, get hold of archives; I want the file regarding that crash from February '77 on my desk at the double!"

"Guv?" called out DS Danny Farham, as he stuck his head through the doorway next to Reeves.

"You might be interested in this one because it goes back to your days on the beat. And based on the events with Andrew Colney, I thought you should know."

"What?" barked the DI, praying Danny wasn't going to dribble on about some tittle-tattle that had little or no relevance. Although she knew that was unfair on Danny. However, her mood had darkened due to Reeves once again pushing all the wrong buttons.

"You know Patrick Colney has his third appeal hearing this morning about his conviction for shanking some scrote in that prison riot back in '79?"

"Yes, it's first up in court today." She checked her watch. "It's probably started, but I'm not concerned as it will be rejected as the last two were. He was bang-to-rights on that one, and the new evidence they keep concocting will be thrown out."

Danny shook his head as he frowned. "Sorry, Guv. It's bad news, I'm afraid. The gobby bird at the court office, you know the one? Blonde with bad roots that any self-respecting randy male badger would fancy humping."

"No, but go on." DI French ignored the badger reference. Despite her attempts to drag the male-dominated force into the 20th Century, she knew she'd have to be satisfied that she no longer had her chest fondled by the vast majority of the station's perverted inhabitants.

"Well, badger-bird just called and said Carl Hooper, the low-life git who shares a cell with Patrick, has given evidence that he shanked the other prisoner and not Patrick. Reckon old-man Colney has exerted some pressure to get that confession, probably threats to Hooper's family."

Reeves swivelled his head and, wide-eyed, stared at his DS. "No way! Hooper is as reliable as a tart's knicker elastic! No one will buy that!"

"Shut up, Reeves," spat DI French, without looking at him, instead keeping her attentions on her DS and the disturbing news he was relaying. "Well, that may be, but that won't be corroborated. Hooper is low-life scum who we stuck away a few years ago. And, more delicately put than wannabee Harry Callahan here, he's an unreliable witness," fired back DI French, whilst thumbing her right hand towards Reeves.

Reeves revelled in the reference to the Clint Eastwood character that the Guv had chucked his way. He loved the Dirty Harry films and thought maybe she'd see her way clear to recommend him for firearms training.

"Sorry, Guv. But the Appeal Court has overturned Patrick's conviction. They said as he has now served ten of the original twelve years for the attempted murder of Robert Moore, he will be released," stated DS Farham.

"Oh, bollocks!"

"Guv?" questioned Danny. He'd worked with DI French for many years. He'd been a DC when the Guv was a DS, and he struggled to think of any time when DI French had sworn. Well, in Court, when affirming her allegiance under oath that she would tell the truth and nothing but the truth – but never a profanity.

DC Stuart Taylor squeezed his head next to Reeves and grinned. "The appeal judge was Simpkins ... he's as bent as a poof's pipe!" he announced.

Heather French had momentarily mused that she had Abbot and Costello with their head stuck in the door, now with Taylor, she had the Three Stooges peering at her.

DS Danny Farham left the trio, and now she was faced with Reeves and Taylor both grinning at her. Both DCs were as competent as Laurel and Hardy, although they tried to model themselves on Bodie and Doyle and were first to volunteer for firearms training, which of course, she'd always vetoed. There was nothing professional about her two errant DCs, and no way could she let these two loose with police-issue firearms on the unsuspecting general public of Fairfield – it would turn into a scene from Butch Cassidy and the Sundance Kid.

"What?" she bellowed at the two pathetic excuses of an officer, who'd still had their heads poked into her office sporting stupid grins. Both jumped back and scuttled away.

DI French had risen up the ranks due to her hard work, attention to detail, and ability to suffer the constant lewd remarks, even from senior officers, about what they wanted to do to her sizeable chest. If they weren't gawping, they were grabbing. Many female officers she'd known back on her beat days hadn't had the steel to handle the attention, but she had. However, the main reason she now held the position of DI and had a whole unit of officers to command was her detective skills, conviction rates, and ability to follow her hunches.

The hunch now that rolled around her brain was too ridiculous to contemplate. Paul Colney was dead, killed when he catapulted through the windscreen of a yellow Mk3 Cortina, which the unknown driver had launched at high speed through a bus stop embedding the bonnet in a tree. How could an identical car be parked in almost the exact same position ten years later?

The Colneys. Jesus, that family! A few weeks ago, she had the euphoria of nicking the shit Andrew Colney. Patrick was already banged up and she didn't expect him to be released any time soon after that riot in '79. Now Patrick was going to be let loose on Fairfield again. Maybe it was time to issue guns to Laurel and Hardy – by the bounds of probability, with their scatter-gun approach, surely, they would hit Patrick at some point. Even if that also involved killing half the residents of Fairfield in the process – it would be a credible plan.

DI French knew full well that, in her line of work, rarely did coincidences occur; there was always another, more sinister reason. Patrick Colney was convicted in 1977 for the attempted murder of Robert Moore. The latter just happens to be the father of the young lass with the cute arse, as Reeves put it. The very same woman that Andrew Colney fully intended to rape on that Saturday night in August, ten years on from Patrick's misdemeanour. And Robert Moore was stabbed by Patrick in an altercation when Robert Moore had confronted David Colney, Patrick's younger brother, following an accusation that David had sexually assaulted his fifteen-year-old daughter, Sarah, back in 1976.

DI French, or *Bristols* as everyone called her, but never in her earshot, had a hunch she was about to start a rematch with the Colneys.

6

Personal Services

PCs Mike Greaves and Alan Lawrence entered the CID office, still decked out with their yellow hi-vis police vests stretched tightly over their uniforms. Although unaware of the urgency, the duty sergeant had summoned them back to the station stating DI French wanted a word. Also, they were advised to 'blue-light' it back because DI French wasn't known for her patience.

Although not particularly liked in the corridors of Fairfield Police Station, DI French commanded the respect of her colleagues. She'd climbed the greasy pole of success, which in the male-dominated environment of the police force was considered by many as some achievement. Heather worked twice as hard and delivered significantly better results than any of her male counterparts. That said, she had to fight for her promotion which involved battling her way through the misogynistic attitude of senior officers. Many of whom believed her only asset to be her famously large chest that, even now as an Inspector, often formed the mainstay of lewd jokes on the station's lower levels occupied by Uniform.

DS Danny Farham acknowledged the traffic officers' presence with the raising of his head as he gassed away on the phone. Pinning the receiver between his neck and shoulder, he waded through a heap of reports as he frantically tried to locate a particular document from the chaotic piles of disorganised manila folders which lay strewn across his desk.

The remaining occupants of the CID office ignored the two traffic officers as they one-fingered tip-tapped away on their typewriters, occasionally swearing and peering at a mistake they'd thrashed out on their report. A bottle of correction fluid was an essential stationery item in CID.

One officer seemed to be trying to negotiate the information on the one computer. Mike glanced across, trying to read the screen, but the green text fuzzed from the angle at which he'd craned his neck.

Danny dropped the receiver in the cradle. "Right, you two, the Guv's been waiting, so I suggest you get in there on the double!" Danny snatched up the receiver again, answering the call that had come through. "DS Farham, CID. Hang on," he bellowed down the line before covering the mouthpiece. "Reg! You're like a fart in a trance! Stop pissing about and get in there!" exclaimed Danny whilst pointing to the DI's office.

Mike and Alan stepped up to the DI's door. Mike's station nickname was Reg, not a name he particularly disliked and, over his years of service, he'd had worse. However, as the station's Police Federation Representative, and who, by his own admission, could be a bit of an old woman with a propensity to moan and drone on and on, he'd acquired the name Reg in reference to the character Reg Hollis from *The Bill*, a show that had started on ITV a few years back which most officers watched along with many millions of the general public.

"Come in!" bellowed DI French.

"Ma'am," stated both officers, as they entered the DI's office and stood to attention.

DI French sat poring over the file that one of her officers had secured from archives, now familiarising herself with the crash details when Paul Colney and a mystery man lost their lives in 1977.

She glanced up at Mike. They'd joined the force at the same time back in the '70s and had pounded the beat together on numerous occasions. Although the DI knew his nickname, she never used it.

"PC Greaves, I want a blow-by-blow account of that abandoned car you attended to this morning up on Coldhams Lane."

"Ma'am," stated Mike, as he momentarily glanced at his old beat-buddy. Then quickly looked up as the DI glared up at him. Mike was old-school and always showed the required respect when speaking to senior officers. For Mike, this meant standing straight, shoulders back, and complying with their request without question. Also, never look them in the eye unless spoken to.

"We were on our patrol this morning. Alan and I are on a six-two shift today, Ma'am." Mike nodded to his silent partner. "PC Lawrence and I planned to complete a couple of tours of the new bypass, then return to the town centre, before the usual first tour of the Broxworth Estate. After two complete tours around the bypass, which we completed without incident, we negotiated the new roundabout at the Hartford section of the bypass—"

"Mike! I don't want to know the blow-by-blow account of Fairfield bypass and every inch of tarmac laid down to circumnavigate the town! Get to the point, Constable!" bellowed DI French.

"Ma'am." Mike shuffled his feet, lifting his right leg a couple of times, an awkward involuntary action he always performed in a senior officer's company.

"At precisely 9:15 a.m., we turned onto Coldhams Lane after taking the third exit from that new roundabout. Three-quarters of a mile along Coldhams Lane, although I'm not totally sure of the exact measurement ... err, although I could check for you, Ma'am?"

Mike made brief eye contact with the DI, checking whether she would affirm she required the exact distance travelled from the Hartford roundabout to the abandoned car's position. Concerned that the DI appeared ready to explode, Mike suspected he was still providing way too much detail. Although the DI had said blow-by-blow account, so wondered why senior officers were vague with their requests.

To avoid a verbal mauling, Mike decided to crack on with his account. So, once again, avoiding eye contact by raising his eyes, he stared straight ahead and carried on, unperturbed that he could sense the younger officer next to him was about to piss himself laughing.

"PC Lawrence! Is something amusing you?" barked DI French. Although she suspected PC Lawrence's stifled laughter was directly linked to Mike's account of this morning's events. To be fair, back in the day and standing in his shoes, she would have probably had the same reaction.

"No, Ma'am," replied Alan-Rambo-Lawrence, delivered in a high-pitched voice whilst also avoiding eye contact. Alan had earned the nickname Rambo due to his love of being in the thick of the action. When there was a riot or a pub brawl,

Rambo would be the first to attend and always the one to draw first blood.

"Ma'am?" questioned Mike.

DI French nodded, affirming that he should continue with his account of the morning's events. She feared any more interruptions to Mike's flow, and she would be reaping the benefits of the police benevolent fund before he finished.

"Whilst heading in a northerly direction, we passed the Broxworth Estate and noticed a vehicle parked on the grass verge. The position of the vehicle was approximately two hundred yards south of the Beehive Public House. The car was a Mk3 Yellow Cortina XL, which I believe is the model one up from the L and included a walnut dash and a leather gear knob as standard."

"Christ," muttered the DI but refrained from any other comment in fear that Mike would take even longer to deliver his account.

She recalled a case last year regarding some armed blaggers who held up a Post Office whilst wielding a couple of shooters before escaping in a Ford Transit van, which wasn't the most ingenious getaway vehicle of choice and were subsequently easily chased down by PC Mike Greaves in his 3.5 litre Rover SDI. After arresting the bumbling blaggers and probably boring the poor bastards to death, Mike had to relay his account in court. The Judge had actually adjourned after repeatedly advising Mike that he needed to be concise. During the adjournment, the judge threatened him with contempt of court if he didn't comply, ranting that he and the jury had no interest in the history of the Ford Transit van and, specifically, the various models produced with what particular extras each model offered.

DI French now feared she was to learn about the Cortina, and that could very well take months because many variations had been produced since 1962, a car that her father had purchased that very same year in a rather drab pale-blue colour. She wondered for a brief moment why so many cars of that era seemed to be the colour of the inside of a public toilet.

Fortunately, Mike only hesitated at the DI's one-word comment before continuing. "The vehicle appeared to be wedged between the bus shelter and a large oak tree. Upon completing a full inspection, I can confirm the car had suffered no damage. However, the offside front tyre was below the 1.6mm required legal depth, which I measured at 1.1mm. Therefore, as per procedure, I issued a ticket for the offence."

"And?"

"Ma'am?"

"Where's the ruddy car now? And who owns it?"

"Oh, I see, Ma'am. I radioed through to request a vehicle licence check at 9:28 a.m. Upon arriving back at the station at 10:47 a.m., following the request from the sergeant that I believe originated from you, Ma'am, I was provided with the information. Can I check my notebook, Ma'am?"

DI French huffed as she rocked back in her seat. "Yes, Mike. But do please get on with it. You're starting to bore me to death, and I'm in real danger of developing deep vein thrombosis if I sit here any longer, let alone the fact my ears are bleeding!"

Unfortunately, that was too much for PC Lawrence, who, despite trying to control himself, unintendedly blew a raspberry in an attempt to avert bursting into laughter.

"Get out!" boomed the DI at the young PC, who immediately turned and complied with the senior officer's demand.

"Ma'am?" asked Mike, slightly bemused by the reaction of his partner.

Now alone with PC Greaves, the DI dropped the formalities. "Mike, Mike, Mike. You're a good officer. But for the love of God, please get on with it!"

"Yes, Ma'am." He thumbed through his notebook, then straightened up to continue his account. "The vehicle was previously owned by a Mr Jason Apsley, who then sold it in 1977 to Coreys Mill Motors, the second-hand car dealership that's over near the Bowthorpe Estate. It appears the vehicle has remained in their possession for the last ten years."

The hunch she had, although completely impossible, seemed to be panning out in front of her. "Index number?"

Mike glanced at his notebook. "Kilo, Delta, Papa, Four Seven Two, November. The tax disc expired in June '77 but did comply with the index number."

"Mike, sit."

"Ma'am?" questioned the traffic officer, somewhat bemused that a senior officer would continue using his Christian name and now offered him a seat.

"Mike, for Christ's sake, take a load off and push your backside in that chair!"

"Ma'am," replied Mike, as he complied with the request. Although an unusual request, he always followed orders.

"Mike, as I said, you're a good officer. For the moment, let's forget I'm the DI and let's just have a chat, as mates, like we did when on the beat."

"Ma'am." nodded Mike, ready to comply. Although extremely uncomfortable with the request, which caused him involuntarily to lift his right leg – that annoying nervous twitch.

DI French turned around the file she'd been reviewing before Mike had entered her office and subsequently made her ears bleed. She tapped the section detailing the information of the crashed car which had destroyed a bus shelter, collided with a tree, and had Paul Colney and the other man sprawled across the bonnet after traversing their way through the windscreen.

"Index number … Kilo, Delta, Papa, Four Seven Two, November. The same car … at least the same plates!"

"I know, Ma'am, I was just coming to that point. I'm good with remembering numbers and, as soon as I spotted the plates, I remembered attending the scene of that crash in '77. I imagine that someone has placed false plates onto the car. Just lucky that the original plates were for the same make and model. It can't be the same car because it was crushed some years ago when the compound cleared out vehicles that were no longer required for evidence purposes."

"What about the tax disc?"

"Ma'am?"

DI French thumped her rather podgy index finger on the report. "Mike, the tax disc on that car suggests the plates aren't false."

"Oh. Yes, Ma'am, you're right. I hadn't considered that. That's probably why you became a DI, and I'm still a constable."

"I would suggest there are a few other reasons why we hold a different rank," stated the DI, whilst raising her eyebrows.

Mike nodded his total agreement. Not that if asked he would be able to list the reasons, but he was aware there would probably be quite a few.

"You attended that scene back in '77. Why does the report state that Coreys Mill Motors owned the car, but nothing about Mr Apsley?"

"Err ... I don't know, Ma'am."

"The investigating officer at the time was DI Shaw." An apt name for the DI, whose nickname was Sandy, who was nothing short of a puppet to the divisional Superintendent who pulled all the strings back in the late '70s. "There's no mention of investigations into Coreys Mill Motors regarding the car in this report. Were you involved?"

"No, Ma'am. I attended the scene as I'd just been assigned to Traffic and was the partner to PC Hackman at the time. We just dealt with the traffic incident, and I think CID only got involved when Paul Colney was identified as the dead passenger. Ma'am, could you perhaps look up the old DI? He might be able to help shed some light on this."

"Malcolm Sandy Shaw is dead ... not going to get much from him, I'm afraid."

"No, Ma'am."

"So, the car. Where is it now? We'll need to get the forensic boys on it, throw their powder about, and see if we can pick up any dabs."

"Ma'am?"

"The car. Has it been towed in?"

"No, Ma'am. It will need a tractor to drag it out sideways; it's wedged in tight."

"Oh. Has it been secured?"

"Err... no, Ma'am. The keys weren't in the vehicle. So, we just closed the doors and slapped a Police Aware sign on the screen. Although I suspect like a shoal of piranhas, the rats from the Broxworth Estate will have stripped it clean by now."

"Christ," muttered the DI, as she leant back in her chair. There was something ridiculous about this situation, and worryingly it involved a Colney and Mr Apsley, who seem intrinsically entwined.

"Guv," called out DS Danny Farham, as he clattered open her door, causing the Venetian blind to clang.

DI French looked up, but neither she nor the slightly bemused traffic officer replied.

"You remember Harris? DS from a few years back."

The DI frowned, indicating she couldn't remember.

"Guv, Harris was the DS on the Lily Poulter case and was found shacked up with her at the boozer down Prince of Wales Road. When we raided it for operating as a brothel, the DS was caught having a Barclays-bank over Lily's brace-and-bits whilst a few of the tarts fingered his khyber."

DI French remembered the case. It had resurfaced as station chatter when the film Personal Services was released earlier this year. They'd arrested Lily Poulter for running a house of ill repute, offering all sorts of sordid entertainment for the perverted gentry of Fairfield.

During the raid above the rather seedy pub, they'd discovered a prominent crown court judge wearing a nappy whilst a scantily clad middle-aged lady with an ample bosom sponged him down. He'd protested his innocence although struggled to explain the nappy, why he was sucking his thumb and why the said lady seemed to be devoid of any upper body clothing when the officers burst in.

DI French rolled her eyes at her DS's description of the then DS Harris's compromising position. "I take it that you were saying when DS Harris was apprehended and caught masturbating over the naked chest of Lily Poulter whilst a couple of prostitutes were providing him with rectal stimulation?"

"Err, yes, Guv. Nicely put," he chuckled. Before continuing, he took a moment, reflecting that his description of DS Harris's unfortunate incident could have been better described when talking to a senior officer. "Well, when Harris got pensioned-off early, he joined the Border Force up at Luton Airport. Some of the lads kept in touch, and he's just rung through and informed DC Dawson that he's just dealt with some short skinny tart with a tight khyber, big gob, possessing more front than Brighton, who just came in on the morning flight from Málaga."

"And?" questioned the DI, well used to her team's vocabulary when describing female members of the general public. But, in the interest of time, she decided not to correct her sergeant's vocabulary.

"Guv, Shirley Colney has just re-entered the country ... he thought we might be interested."

DI French silently forgave the DS for his derogatory description of the female. Shirley Colney was pure scum – dangerous scum.

Coincidence? No. DI French was too experienced to believe in it. So, the day Andrew Colney faces court, is the same day that Patrick Colney miraculously wins his appeal. Also, it just happens to be the same day the car Paul Colney died in, magically appears in the same spot without a scratch. And if that wasn't enough, it's the same day that ruddy woman, Shirley Colney, graces her patch with her presence. Somehow Jason Apsley was involved – he was the key to what was happening.

"Guv?" questioned Danny, who'd now stepped into her office, concerned his boss appeared to be away with the fairies.

DI French looked up. "Pull the team together in the briefing room. Get them to call their wives, mistresses, cats, or ruddy goldfish for all I care ... all leave is cancelled. You're all on overtime."

7

Morticia

The pubescent-appearing, spotty border-guard thumbed through her passport, back and forth through the pages, as if playing for time. He glanced up every few seconds at her face and then back to her picture in her passport.

"Full name?" he coldly requested.

"It's there on the passport … you're looking at it!" exclaimed Shirley in frustration. If this was going to be what it was like back in England, she had half a mind to turn on her heels and scoot back to Marbella.

The guard huffed and again looked up at Shirley. "Madam, I asked you for your name."

"Shirley Colney. And I ain't no madam. Watch yourself, boy. You wanna be careful who you're calling *madam*. Might be alright for the slag who gave birth to you, but not me! Got it?" she aggressively spat back whilst contemplating slapping the jumped-up little scrote.

The young guard appeared to *get it* because his Adam's apple bounced as he swallowed. He raised his hand in the direction of another guard milling about behind the bank of desks. Shirley presumed he was asking to be excused because he'd now shit himself.

Shirley glanced across to see Ralph, her travelling partner, who stood at the next booth, apparently also receiving a grilling from an equally overzealous guard. Presumably, the British Border Control guards at Luton Airport had decided to be super officious on this drab, wet, cold September morning.

She'd left the wall-to-wall sunshine that, with repeated certainty, radiated down on her luxurious villa, scrumptious gardens and pool, to travel back home. Although, as she now lived in Spain, calling Fairfield home was a bit of a stretch.

Now, back in the UK for the first time in ten years, Shirley shivered because sixty-odd degrees really didn't cut it when she was used to basking in temperatures above ninety.

The tosser in the blue uniform pushed his cap back and bravely held Shirley with a cold stare. "Full name."

"Janet Shirley Colney."

The guard thumbed back to the page with her photo, turned it sideways, and held it up, his eyes flicking from the image to Shirley's face, back and forth. Then, still grasping her passport, he glared at Shirley. "Why did you call yourself Shirley if your Christian name is Janet?" he asked whilst still thumbing the pages of her passport, back and forth, but not once glancing down as he held her stare.

Shirley glanced up to see Ralph had made it through the barrier. He was an Australian National who the UK border guards had let through, whilst she received the grilling from the little spotty git who wasn't much older than her youngest, Andy. If he didn't relent soon, she would make a note of his name, and he might just receive a visit in the night from a few acquaintances who expertly wielded cricket bats, although had never donned a set of pads and stood at the crease.

Shirley leant forward and sneered at the guard who she suspected was still in puberty and doubted his balls had dropped, now delighted she could intimidate him as she did most people who dared to cross her. "I don't use my first name, haven't for years. And it's got fuck all to do with you!"

The border guard made an involuntary jerk backwards with his head as this evil cow, who resembled Cruella de Vil, nudged her head in his direction.

After leaving the orphanage in the early '50s, Janet had preferred to make her way in life using her middle name. She saw herself as a Shirley Eaton type, modelling her style on the young British actress.

Since the extradition treaty had expired between the UK and Spain in 1978, the Costa Del Sol, or Costa Del Crime as some of the British press called it, became an exciting playground for those who needed to distance themselves from the British authorities. The long arm of the law didn't extend all the way to Spain. After a difficult start, Shirley soon carved out an exciting life after leaving Fairfield in 1977.

She'd opened a bar, and her regular patrons soon sieved down to that community who liked to distance themselves from the reach of Scotland Yard. A couple of the regulars liked to brag, to whoever would listen, that they'd taken part in the robbery of a train in Buckinghamshire in '63. However, Shirley knew that was just the beer talking, and suspected their misdemeanours were of a somewhat lesser notoriety.

Shirley had come from relatively low standing in the criminal underworld. Her jailed husband possessed a criminal record to rival most of those in stir, and she was mother to the four Colney boys who, with the Gower family, had run the crime operations in the small Hertfordshire town of Fairfield. Nevertheless, her connections made whilst living in Costa del Crime had elevated her to a respected position. No one pissed her about unless they wanted to suffer the consequences.

∼

Ralph stood waiting on the other side of the border-check booths. He raised his hands in a questioning gesture at Shirley, confused with what was happening.

The treaty between Spain and the UK, signed in 1985, had changed the situation for many of their friends. Although extradition was still difficult, it now meant if you had a UK warrant for your arrest hanging over you, you could no longer leave Spain. Even a day's excursion from the safety in the sun would trigger the extradition order, which the Spanish authorities were now compelled to comply with. Fortunately, Ralph and Shirley didn't have arrest warrants pending, so the apparent interrogation his lover was receiving was somewhat odd.

Although Ralph was Australian, he was born in Fairfield, England. Ralph, along with his parents, had emigrated in the '50s. Before leaving the UK, and during his youth, he'd fallen into the Teddy-boy culture and started to run with the gang, *The Jungle Boys,* as they called themselves.

The gang's entertainment centred around causing as much mayhem as possible in the neighbouring towns, disrupting Saturday night dances, and forcing the girls to kiss them. During weekends in the summer, the gang would often head for the amusement arcades on Great Yarmouth seafront, where their sole target was to start a mass brawl with the local boys.

As a young man, there was nothing Ralph liked better than a good fistfight.

Concerned about the company that young Ralph was keeping, his parents uprooted and left for Australia before their son acquired a criminal record. Fortunately, the police caution he'd received at the age of sixteen hadn't affected their application to emigrate. However, the day he received that caution was when he lost his right eye and subsequently the catalyst for his parents to seek a new life for them all, where they hoped Ralph could prosper from the opportunities on offer on the other side of the world.

The eight-thousand-mile distance his parents put between Ralph's old and new life had little to no effect in improving their only child's fortunes. Ralph struggled to settle into the Darwin life, initially having many run-ins with local youths and then becoming embroiled in local gang culture.

Darwin seemed backwards to Ralph, offering little more to add to the tedious plumber apprenticeship his father had secured for him. This inevitably led to Ralph sliding off the rails and becoming uncontrollable for his elderly parents.

One thing led to another, resulting in Ralph elevating from street brawls to becoming embroiled in serious crime. Not wishing to see the inside of an Australian prison, Ralph fled his adopted country during the mid '70s and skedaddled to Spain, no longer feeling the heat from the Australian authorities or the relentless sun of the Northern Territory, exchanging it for the beaches, beer and birds of southern Spain.

He met Shirley there, initially only as a punter in her bar, which later grew into a friendship when they discovered they'd both emigrated from the small Hertfordshire town of Fairfield.

As their unexpected relationship blossomed, Ralph discovered that Shirley's life in the UK had monumentally turned to shit in the mid '70s. To start with, in the space of six months, two of her four sons, Paul and David, were killed, and at the same time, Paul's identical twin, Patrick, received a twelve-year sentence for attempted murder. Now, the *Filth,* as Shirley put it, were trying to pin a rape conviction on her youngest, Andy. From what Shirley had said from the calls she'd made to a few acquaintances back in the UK, it appeared highly likely that Andy would be convicted and end up serving time with his brother Patrick and her now long-time estranged husband, who'd been banged-up for years.

In an attempt to add some pressure, in the form of threats and intimidation to the legal team representing her son, Shirley and Ralph booked flights to the UK.

This visit would be the first time Ralph had returned to his birthplace since he left in early '55 – just a year after that incident which changed his life forever. Ralph had unfinished business in England. However, time heals, as they say, and as the years drifted by, his burning quest for revenge had abated. He'd got his girl, and life was pretty good. He was learning that dealing with old wounds would not bring satisfaction, only pain.

Notwithstanding the decision to forget his past, this trip back provided an opportunity that was too good to miss. As luck would have it, only a few calls to the right people had provided the information required. The man who'd changed his life when Ralph was just sixteen was apparently still living in Fairfield – what a stroke of luck.

Revenge is a dish best served cold – that's what they say. This particular dish was thirty-two years old, and it was time to serve it up. An eye for an eye as the good-book said – apparently.

Shirley proved to be a difficult woman to woo. She stayed loyal to her husband, who'd been banged up for years. However, his sheer size made Ralph a handy man to have around the bar and, eventually, Ralph had worn her down – now sharing her bed.

Ralph and Shirley were an accepted couple and well respected in their community, which consisted of fugitives from the British legal system, plus many young ladies drawn to the glamour and luxuries the ex-pat gangsters had to offer.

Ralph watched as his lover intimidated the young border guard. Although now in her mid-50s, at five-foot two-inches short with her twiggy-like slender frame, she still cut a vibrant, attractive woman, and Ralph Eastley adored his British bird.

Shirl, as Ralph called her, hadn't wafted in from paradise or Luton Airport as Lorraine Chase had suggested, but the feisty woman kept the rough Aussie in check. At a few months short of his fiftieth birthday, Ralph was Shirley's *Rockabilly,* and he took great care over his quiffed hair to maintain his appearance, ensuring his comb was always at the ready to whip out and keep his quiff in place.

∼

Shirley glanced up and spotted Ralph as he stood waiting on the other side of the border-check booths. He raised his hands in a questioning gesture at her, presumably, like her, confused with what was going on.

"Struth, Shirl, what's the hold-up?" Ralph called out, as he stepped towards the back of the passport control desk.

"God knows! Sherlock Holmes 'ere, got some problem. Bloody Luton dippy git. They're all the same from this shit-hole of a town."

"Step back, sir," stated a thinning-grey-haired, pot-bellied guard as he passed Ralph. He leant across the desk, beckoning with his index finger to the young guard, demanding Shirley's passport.

"Step to the side, madam," the older guard stated as he cupped his hand around her back to guide her away from the desk.

Shirley complied with his request, even though she was close to kneeing the git in the balls because no one touched her uninvited. "Don't touch me! Only the one-eyed Elvis over there has that privilege … and only when I fancy a bit. So, I'd step back if you care about your balls," she spat, whilst pointing to Ralph, before returning her glare at the fat, ageing guard, who seemed unperturbed by her veiled threats.

The new senior-looking guard thumbed through the passport, just as the younger one had. The passport only consisted of twelve pages, with just the one smudged Spanish Ports Authority entry stamp messing up the last visa page. Shirley thrust her hands on her hips as she stared up at the impassive guard. She was sure that if he thumbed through those pages again, she would snatch it off him then unceremoniously insert it up his arse.

"Excuse me, madam," politely asked a young air stewardess who'd swished her way to the desk and now tried to pass the border control as the young spotty guard waved her through.

"Wait your turn, bitch," spat Shirley at the young stewardess dressed in her blue and yellow uniform with her yellow, Monarch-monogrammed, pillbox-style hat perched on top of her immaculate blonde hair. The girl could have only been in her early twenties, and Shirley presumed with her long shapely legs, perfect face-paint, and bright blue eyes, she'd be fighting off the attentions of the randy pilots.

"Sorry?" questioned the blonde bimbo, appearing shocked at Shirley's outburst.

"Mind your language. Step aside, or I'll be forced to detain you." stated the guard to Shirley, as he smiled longingly at the young stewardess who squeezed through the gap between Shirley and the desk before swishing her way past in her four-inch matching yellow stilettoes.

"You've got no chance, shit-for-brains. Tight-arses like that don't look at fat old gits like you! Come on, gimme my passport and get out the fucking way!"

The guard closed her passport and held it out, offering it to Shirley. "Welcome home, Mrs Colney," he impassively offered.

Shirley suspected they were trained on how to deliver a dead-pan face. She snatched her passport from his hand, then barrelled past him, only stopping to lean towards the spotty guard who'd restarted his routine of page thumbing the passport of the next passenger. "Boo!" she shouted to the young guard who had glanced in her direction as he sensed the evil-looking woman's head once again nudging his way. He flinched again.

"Careful powder-puff, you'll shit your kecks!" she cackled at the spotty guard, who paled slightly as she nipped through the gate.

"Struth, Shirl, what was all that about?" questioned Ralph, as Shirley slotted her arm through his.

"Dunno. Let's get the cases and get out of this shit hole. The sooner we organise the right brief for Andy, the sooner we can get back. Anyway, it's too pissing cold in this fuck-hole of a dump."

Although packed with alighted passengers who jostled for position to grab their cases and bags, the throng of returning tourists in the baggage carousel area afforded a wide berth to the odd couple who were clearly to be avoided.

With her black and white streaked hair, Shirley had an aura about her. The man whose arm she held, and towered above her, completed his menacing look with fists of gold rings on tattooed fingers that resembled the size of festering, bloated sausages.

To any onlooker, it appeared The Addams Family and the Munsters had swapped partners at some car-keys-in-the-pot swingers party. Now Herman Munster and Morticia linked arms at baggage reclaim, presumably leaving Gomez Addams and Lily Munster still holed up in their love nest somewhere else.

The other passengers avoided eye contact and were more than happy to watch their cases glide past to avoid stepping too close to the frightening couple.

Shirley's old man, Paul Colney Senior, was unaware of his wife's adultery. Within minutes of arriving back in Fairfield, Shirley knew word would get out, and he would know that his girl had strayed. However, she'd stayed loyal to a man who would probably never be released, and now she had powerful friends whose reach could extend all the way from Spain and keep her husband and his associates in check.

A five-hundred-pound bomb had destroyed Shirley's childhood – the events of ten years ago had destroyed her family. She was forced to flee the town she called home for thirty-six years by the Gower family, who controlled the town's drug and protection rackets. They'd lost faith in her, and once her boys were dead or incarcerated, she'd known escape was her only option. Ten years on, all had changed. Shirley, with her connections, would no longer fear her husband or the Gowers.

Also, whilst she was here, a certain pesky schoolteacher needed dealing with, and her granddaughters needed the guiding hand of their grandmother – it was time for revenge.

Morticia pondered that thought as she watched Herman unceremoniously shove a couple of backpackers out of the way to grab their luggage.

Sic Gorgiamus Allos Subjectatos Nunc – We gladly feast on those who would subdue us. Of course, Shirley had no idea of the meaning of the Latin credo, carved on the tombstone of Mother and Father Addams. However, the doctrine couldn't be more apt – those that had crossed her were about to pay a heavy price.

Janet Curtis was back.

8

Lucky Lucan

"Dad?"

"Evening Jess. Phoning your old dad twice in two days, I'm honoured!" I chuckled.

"Dad, you'd better come. Don's not good, and he won't let me call an ambulance. He says he must see you."

"Oh hell, has he fallen again?"

"No. He's in bed, but I think this is it, Dad."

I detected the words catch in her throat.

"Dad, we're losing him." blurted Jess before holding the receiver away from her mouth and sobbing.

For the last ten years of this crazy second life, my world had settled down to a blissful existence. Since that day when Martin crashed that Cortina, my new life had slotted together perfectly. Yes, okay, sometimes life bashed in the odd curveball, but nothing happened that could faze me compared to time-travelling back forty-odd years.

However, Monday 7th September 1987 just had a feel about it that was starting to concern me. A few weeks ago, I'd had that odd conversation with DI French and the return of my

Zippo lighter I'd lost in the Cortina the day Martin and the evil Paul Colney died. I'd also deduced from that conversation, and the one with Sarah earlier today, that Andy Colney was now secured in custody facing multiple charges of rape.

However, this time, that particular dreadful event of Sarah Moore suffering rape seems to have been averted. Does that mean that Martin was never born? If he was never born, then surely, he never died? But he did, as I was in the car that day. I'd witnessed him as he lay splayed out across the bonnet after he'd catapulted through the windscreen when the front of the car had that altercation with a large oak tree.

After living for ten years in the past, you'd think I would have managed to get my head around this time-travel malarky – but no, it was still a mystery.

Concerningly, I believed after that visit to return my lost lighter, Frenchie knew something.

Although she couldn't possibly know I'd time travelled from 2019 to 1976. She couldn't know I'd helped to end the life of David Colney, who had turned out to be the father of my adopted daughter, Beth. And hell, there was no way she could know that Beth was my best mate back in 2019 when David Colney would be a fifty-nine-year-old serial killer terrorising the south of England.

However, she *did* know something.

Frenchie had pushed me in that conversation to tell her who Martin was, and I could just tell that she knew I was hiding information. I had a feeling that she wasn't going to let this go and would keep on pushing to get to the truth. The trouble was, as Jack Nicholson will say in a few years when *A Few Good Men* is released – *You can't handle the truth* – well, Frenchie couldn't.

Confessing to Frenchie that Martin and I were time-travellers, who died in a car crash in 2019 and travelled back to the 1970s, would be, I presume, hilarious. Although I think the rotund detective had a soft spot for me, I'm sure this tale would push her to have me committed to Broadmoor. In her view, I would be a danger to the general public. I'd probably end up sharing a cell with Peter Sutcliffe, who, despite my attempts back in the late '70s, I'd failed to stop his sick killing spree.

Now, to add to concerning happenings, today, my twelve-year-old ex-wife started at my school. Time-bends, as I called them, were rare occurrences. Not that I could know the laid down path of history in intricate detail, but what happened the first time pretty much happened this time, albeit with the addition of older me and the absence of younger me, if you get my meaning. So, this particular time-bend of my ex-wife, now a pupil at school, was not only unusual but extremely unwelcome.

Although I needed to pull together the Time Travel Believers' Club for an urgent meet, George had other plans, so we'd postponed until Tuesday evening.

Now, this call from Jess had given me a deep sense of foreboding. Don's health had been fading over the last few weeks. He wasn't suffering from anything particular, as in a named disease, but there was a steady decline in his general health. He'd started to develop symptoms, which in my old life I'd have googled to discover all of them were potentially life-threatening – of course, they never were. However, at the ripe old age of ninety-one, I feared they were for my closest friend, Don.

'It's all going to turn to shit!'

"Shut up," I answered my mind talk. The trouble was, I had a dark feeling my mind talk was right.

We left Christopher in charge, babysitting his sister Beth, then Jenny and I scooted off to see Don.

"Jason, slow down! We're not going to be any good to Don if we wind up dead before we get there!" ordered Jenny, whilst gripping the side of the seat as she snatched at the grab-handle like a well-trained navigator in a rally car.

She was right. But Don had become my closest friend, and the thought of losing him terrified me. I would never forgive myself if I arrived late, only to discover he'd already left this world without me at his side. He was my honorary father, and I knew his time left in this world was limited.

After hastily abandoning the motor on the driveway and a frustrating fight with the Yale lock, which Jenny had to take control of as I was in danger of busting the key, we let ourselves into Don's house. We trapezed up the stairs and into his bedroom, where we found Jess perched on the bed holding Don's hand. Don looked to be at peace with his head propped up on the pillow and his mouth slightly sagging.

'Should have stuck your foot down, dickhead! You're too late – he's gone!'

"Shit," I muttered. Not to anyone in particular, and certainly not to my mind talk, which had started to royally piss me off.

Jess spun her head around as we burst into the bedroom. "Shush! He's sleeping," she whispered, as she wiped a tear with the heel of her right hand, still holding Don's with her other.

Jenny squeezed my hand and kissed my cheek. "Darling, go sit with him."

Although I could see the gentle rise and fall of his chest, he looked ashen. I feared his time had come. I knew that Don would never forgive me if I called that ambulance and he ended up dying a few weeks later in a stark sanitised ward up at Fairfield General. Don would want to slip away at home. Anyway, he'd had ninety-one years, so what's a few weeks between friends.

Jenny released my hand and lay her arm on Jess's shoulder. "Jess, come on. Let your father have a few moments alone with him."

Jess nodded and left the room with Jenny. I replaced Jess, took hold of Don's hand, and did my level best to maintain the good-old British stiff upper lip.

"Alright, son?"

My head shot up as Don uttered those words. I'm not sure how long I'd sat there for, maybe only a few minutes, but just enough time for one errant tear to trickle out of the corner of my eye.

"You going all soppy, son? Come on, I'm not dead yet!" he chuckled, then coughed.

"Don?"

"Son, chin up! I've had a full life ... I'm ready now. It's time to meet my maker."

A fresh tear escaped my eye. I caught its salty taste as it detoured into the corner of my mouth after it had slowly trickled down my cheek. "Don, let me call the doctor?"

"No, son. I don't want no doctor, you hear. No bloody doctor."

"Alright, alright."

"Anyway, it would be one of those ones I can't understand, so no point," he croaked out before allowing his head to flop back to his pillow.

Don was no racist; he was a man of great tolerance and integrity, and I knew his comment was just generational. I won't deny it irked me, but this wasn't the time to raise it. Anyway, at school, I dealt with comments like that on a daily basis, not only from pupils but also from my colleagues. Unfortunately, I alone couldn't educate the world and highlight the errors of their ways – I needed the support of time.

"Now, son. Tell me, you still worried about that interfering, bustling policewoman?"

"DI French?"

"Yes, that's her."

"Don, as you said last week, I just have to forget it. Although it's not easy … I'm convinced she's digging for information."

"Listen, son. I need you to stop thinking about it. I know for a fact that it'll come to nothing. I promise you, my boy. It's over ten years since it happened. Nothing will come of it, you'll see."

"I know you're just trying to keep me positive, but there's no way you can know that. I'm bloody convinced it's only a matter of time before she pieces it all together."

"No, son. Take it from me … she'll never know. Just forget it."

"Alright," I replied, mainly to ensure Don didn't get himself worked up about something I needed to deal with. I know he meant well, but he couldn't possibly know that nothing would happen.

'It's just a matter of weeks, maybe only days – then DI French will have you on toast.'

I feared my mind talk was right ... that Sword of Damocles now hung from a threadbare singular strand of twine.

"Now, son. I do want to talk to you about something else. Look, close the door so we have some privacy."

"There's only Jenny and Jess here, and they're downstairs."

"Close the door, son. This conversation is for your ears only."

I released my hold of his frail hand, his thin, tissue-paper skin still held the indents where I'd held it, before nipping over and gently closing the door. Then, retaking hold of his hand, I rubbed the back with my thumb.

"Son, as we were just discussing. You remember the day back in '76 when we dropped that evil shit, Colney, off the roof of the flats?"

I nodded.

How could I ever forget! Although David was pure evil and would progress from child abuser to serial killer, I had essentially murdered Beth's natural father. Over the years, I'd pretty much stopped shitting myself about my collar being felt and thus arrested for his murder. Now, Frenchie turning up a few weeks ago had resurfaced those fears.

"Of course, Don. But you just told me to stop worrying about it. Stop thinking about it, is what you said." I now feared his mind was fading along with his body.

"I did, son. And I mean it. But anyway, I knew there was something different about you that day. Over the years, I've concluded that you know certain things that no one else knows."

"What d'you mean?" This was an odd conversation. Don couldn't possibly know the truth. For many years Jenny and I had wanted to confide in Don. However, George had always warned against treading that path – it would lead to disaster – he would always say, and I knew he was right.

"You moved into that flat up at the Broxworth in the spring of '76."

I nodded. Although that was not strictly true because *other* Jason had moved in then, I just took his place in August of that year.

"Well, as you know, son, I'm a nosey old git. I don't miss a trick!" He chuckled, then coughed again.

I plucked up the glass of water from the bedside cabinet and held it to his lips.

"Son, I don't want that! What good is water to me now? Bottom drawer, there's a bottle of scotch. Let's have a dram together ... for one last time. One for the road, as they say, wherever I'm going," he chuckled, before the regulation coughing fit kicked in, which seemed to now form the epilogue of his conversations.

I really didn't think whisky was the right thing for Don at this precise moment. However, he was right. His time was close, and who was I to deny him his favourite tipple. I slopped out two small measures, then doubled them when I noticed Don's disapproving raised eyebrow regarding the Scrooge-like offering.

"There you go. You need me to hold your glass?"

"Son, I might be dying, but I'm not an invalid! I'm quite capable of holding a small glass of whisky!"

I nodded and passed him the glass.

Don pointed to the dresser by the wall opposite. "Son, bottom drawer, there's a brown envelope. Grab it for me, please."

I ferreted around in the drawer, shoving out the way the neatly folded jumpers, and retrieved the tatty envelope before passing it over to him, holding out my hand to take his glass.

"You open it, son."

Dragging out the content, which was only an old newspaper, I noticed it had characteristically yellowed over the years. Whilst unfolding the paper, I glanced at the date stamp – 8th August 1976. For some odd reason, Don had kept a copy of the Sunday Express from eleven years ago. As far as I was aware, the 8th of August wasn't a remarkable day in history – why had he kept this?

I recalled my mother used to keep newspapers of momentous events. After my parents died in that train crash in 1984, my brother, Stephen, and I had thumbed through the stack some years later. She'd bought every paper depicting the royal wedding of Prince Charles and Lady Diana Spencer, along with many others like the moon landings and Kennedy's death. Of course, my second life cruelly moved my parent's death to 1976, depriving my mother the opportunity to watch and weep at the extensive royal wedding TV coverage and the ability to buy up every newspaper in the local newsagents the next day.

As I perused the unfolded broadsheet, it appeared as I'd thought that this unremarkable day in 1976 had no such momentous headlines. Splashed across the front page was the headline about the Viking spaceship entering Martian orbit – okay, pretty awesome stuff, but not enough to warrant keeping the paper. I flipped over to the back page, held the paper out, and froze. The back page headline was momentous for me and a certain Austrian racing driver.

Lauda claims miracle to survive German Grand Prix

The day I time-travelled from 2019, this paper was laid on the kitchen table in that rank flat that *other* Jason lived in on the Broxworth Estate. That very day I'd sat and read about Lauda's crash, and I'd realised I'd time travelled. This was one hell of a coincidence that Don had kept the very same paper – but why?

"Don, why have you kept this old newspaper?" I asked, glancing up from the back page.

"Flick through to page eighteen."

I raised an eyebrow but complied with his request. The news item on page nineteen was a rehashed article about the missing Lord Lucan. I didn't read it, as I hadn't when I'd opened this page eleven years ago. A full-page advert filled the whole of page eighteen – a public service type advert warning of the dangers of drink-driving.

A few drinks, and you're a real lady killer.

The picture, depicting a man leaning across to look at the dead woman in the passenger seat, was not what caught my eye. Instead, down the side margin of the advert was a list penned in my handwriting. Don hadn't kept a copy of the paper from that day – he had kept the exact copy I had read and the next day made a to-do list in the margin. I gawped at my handwriting and the list I'd written – specifically the first few lines.

Have I time-travelled?

Who am I now?

Why am I not dead?

What's happened to me back in 2019?

Does Beth think I'm dead?

The list carried on down the page to more practical questions, like are my parents alive again, and other equally odd comments that only a deranged nutter or time-traveller would write.

"Son?"

I swallowed hard, then looked up at him. "Don, where did you get this paper? Why … why would you keep this?"

Don sipped his whisky, which was very un-Don like. Usually, he would throw it down in one swift action. But hey, my closest friend appeared frail with laboured breathing and, I guess for once, he'd decided to savour the taste.

"Son, as I said, I'm leaving this world soon. I've always wondered who you really are but made the decision some years ago to forget it. But now I know my time is limited … I just feel I need answers. I got to know you when we were neighbours up at the Broxworth." He took another tentative sip as the glass shook in his hand, causing a small drop of the amber liquid to dribble onto his chin.

"I know, Don. That's where we met. But this paper—"

Don held his hand up. I allowed my old friend to interrupt.

"Son, I got to know you from the day you moved into that flat in the spring of '76." Don pointed with his index finger, the glass still in his hand. "But *you* didn't arrive until August, did you?"

I leant back in the chair, the yellowed newspaper with my list still laying across my lap. "Don, what are you on about? If I moved there in the spring, as you say I did, I can't have moved in there in August, if you get my drift."

The trouble is, he was correct. *Other* Jason, whoever the bollocks he is, moved in when returning from South Africa in the spring of '76. I time-travelled in the August and seemed to have taken his place. Of course, that is not sane talk and wouldn't be the conversation I would want to have with Don. I cherished our friendship and, as he lay on his deathbed, I really couldn't face the thought of him thinking I was a total fruit-loop.

However, Don had this paper with my odd list. And Don knew something.

"Son, I'll admit this is somewhat of an odd conversation. For that reason, I'd decided never to have it. But now, well, I guess it doesn't matter. What I would like to know is the truth. Who are you? You're not the bloke who moved into that flat, that much I do know."

I shook my head. I couldn't go there.

"You know me, son. I'm a nosey git!" he chuckled, followed by the regulation coughing fit, which this time caused his eyes to water. After taking a moment to compose himself, he continued. "So, I went through your rubbish bags a few times, as I knew there was something odd. The day you knocked down that ruffian, Fin Booth, outside Carol's flat, I knew then you weren't the same bloke ... although you look identical. So, I found that newspaper in the rubbish and the list you had written on page eighteen."

Slowly closing my eyes, I continued to gently shake my head. All these years, and he'd never said anything – why? I should have known that I could never have kept the truth from Don. And apart from George urging me not to, why hadn't I confided in him?

'Because, dickhead, telling Don that you're a time-traveller would have ended your friendship!'

"Or so I thought," I replied to the voice in my head.

"Son?"

I opened my eyes. Don's appeared a little watery, not from coughing, and not a look I'd seen for many a year.

"Son, I'd like to know the story of Jason Apsley. I know there's a mystery that's more complicated than that Lucky Lucan." He pointed to page nineteen and the headline about Lord Lucan, who apparently had been spotted in Australia.

Of course, I knew that was probably total bollocks. The chances that Lord Lucan was alive and well living in Australia was as probable as the claim that the guy who works down the chip shop swears he's Elvis – and Kirsty MacColl knew that was a lie too.

9

Operation Pied Piper

"Don, I'm not really sure where to start … what I'm about to tell you is so ridiculous that I fear it will affect our friendship."

Don leant on his elbow as he tried to raise himself up the bed. I jumped up to assist, allowing the newspaper to slide to the floor.

"Don't fuss, boy. Don't fuss!"

I froze with my arms out, positioned like a goalkeeper about to catch the ball. I watched as Don struggled, then unfroze from my position and moved forward to realign his pillow for him.

"Thanks, son."

"You want some water?"

"No, son, but I'll have a top-up."

Don held out his whisky glass, and I topped up as instructed. Not that I thought it was a good idea for him to be slugging down alcohol, but I guess he was right – what did it matter?

"Son, nothing you say could do that. You have been the best part of my life. Whatever you say will be okay with me. I think Jenny and George already know the truth?" He raised his finger at me, pointing the glass in my direction. He held that pose and raised his eyebrow whilst waiting for me to blurt out the truth.

Don is what you would call a down-to-earth type of chap, with buckets of common sense. When all around are losing their heads, Don is the unflappable type who'd restore order to a situation. I can only imagine he had a calming effect on his young comrades in those trenches in Flanders as the German guns peppered their positions with gut-ripping shells.

"Alright. Look, you're right. I'm not the man you met in the spring of '76. You're right, Don. I didn't enter that flat until 12th August 1976, six months after you met me … well, not me … but a man I call *other* Jason. And yes, you're right, George and Jenny both know the truth."

Don slugged the whisky, his more usual way of dealing with a glass of his favourite tipple. "Another."

"Don, you shouldn't—"

"Son, stop fussing! When I've heard your story, I'm ready to go. I just had a word with him up there and told him to hang on before he takes me. I want to hear your story and enjoy a few more drams of whisky … one for the road, as they say." He ended his rant with the now perfected coughing fit.

"Alright, but you're starting to look healthier than me! Maybe whisky is what you need," I chuckled.

I poured another measure out and added a slop into my glass. I was going to need this. When I'd tried to convince George and Jenny that I was a time-traveller, pinged back into another Jason Apsley's life, it had taken weeks to convince them. Now I had a limited time to convince my closest friend before him up there took him away, as Don described it.

"Come on then. Let's hear it. So, you're not the same man who moved into that flat … and I guess that means you're not Shirley Colney's half-brother, either?"

The glass pinned between my thumb and forefinger slipped through the gap, pinged off my knee and bounced onto the floor, the content slopping over the newspaper. The amber-coloured liquid morphed the picture of Lord Lucan to a twisted dark image as the whisky soaked into the paper – a fitting alteration to the perhaps seemingly irrecoverable fugitive.

As I gawped at the image of Lucky Lucan, I heard the thumping of footsteps on the stairs before Jenny burst into Don's bedroom.

"Are you alright? I heard a bang," blurted Jenny, as she stood in the doorway, with Jess poking her head over her shoulder.

"Old butter-fingers here dropped his glass."

"Don, I don't think drinking whisky is what you need!" stated Jenny, as she thrust her hands on her hips. "Jason, why on earth are you giving Don whisky! He's a dying—"

"Lass, I'm not dead yet! And if I die with a whisky in my hand, all the better!"

"Jen, it's fine … just a silly accident. It's not made a mess. An old newspaper has soaked it up."

"I'll get a cloth," called out Jess, as she turned to go.

"Jess, leave it. It's alright, honestly," I called out, as I heard Jess bound down the stairs. "Jen, sweetheart, it's fine. Let me have a few more minutes with Don."

Jenny nodded, then pointed at Don. "No more, Donald Nears!"

Don raised his glass to Jenny as she closed the door. "Sorry, son. I guess that was a bit of a shock?"

"What the hell d'you mean ... Shirley Colney's half-brother?"

Now, this was a serious head-fuck after time-travelling, finding out that my best mate from 2019 is the daughter of a serial rapist, who I just happened to kill forty-odd years before he became a murderous bastard. And my best mate is now my adopted daughter, who is only ten years old, but in my old world is forty-two. Add in that my other daughter Jess, who actually is *other* Jason's daughter, has a child whose father is Patrick Colney, Beth's natural father's brother. And Shirley Colney, who is Beth's grandmother, is the mother of Andrew Colney, who is the father of my twice-dead ex-colleague Martin, who also time travelled. Now, Don tells me that *other* Jason's half-sister is Shirley Colney! Jeeesus! What the hell is going on?

"Your lass, Jess ... although she ain't yours, is she?"

"No, she's *other* Jason's."

"Right. And she don't know that, I take it?"

"No." I shook my head.

"Okay, well Jess has, as you know, over the last few years been dropping me up at the library once a week when she nips up to town to do a spot of shopping."

"Yes, she said you've been researching the history of Fairfield Town Football Club. Although I've got to say, there can't be much history worth reading as the team are shite!"

"Quite," he chuckled and coughed, of course. "Anyway, unbeknown to anyone else, I conducted some research into school records and such because I wanted to dig a little deeper into the list you wrote on that paper." Don nodded to the whisky-soaked broadsheet that lay sprawled out on the floor nursing my upturned glass.

"Also, it tied in nicely with some history I wanted to dig into about my own family. Anyway, I'll come to that in a minute."

"Go on," I interjected, dreading what Don might reveal regarding how my new life could possibly be further entwined with the evil Colneys.

"Well, once I started digging in that microfiche system, I couldn't stop. You know, the number of archives they've got stored on those tiny pieces of plastic is amazing. So, not knowing where to start in my quest to find out who you are and your history, I started with the name Apsley, but that didn't get me far. Just at the point of giving up, I researched the name Colney, and that led me down a rather intriguing path."

I raised an eyebrow but said nothing as I waited to see where this conversation was shooting off to. Why the hell was my whole life centred around the world of the evil Colney family? I guess I was about to find out.

Don finished his whisky, held his glass, but didn't ask for a refill. He had a glint in his eye, and I guess the opportunity to finally relay the results of his years of research had perked him up; either that or the whisky had given him a shot in the arm.

"Shirley Colney married Paul Colney senior in the summer of '54. Delving back into her life, I discovered some interesting information. Shirley, whose actual name is Janet, was born in 1933 in Hackney. Her maiden name is Curtis. Full name is Janet Shirley Curtis. Her mother lost her life in an air raid in January 1941. The father died when his ship, HMS Repulse, a Battlecruiser, sunk after being bombed by the Japs in the Indian Ocean in '41. Janet, who was part of Operation Pied Piper, returned to London during the phoney war before the Blitz took hold later that year."

"Pied Piper?" I asked.

"Pied Piper was the operation name for the evacuation of children from London and other cities, which swung into action in 1940. Peggy took our two girls to live here in Fairfield with her sister, Doris, and her family. I stayed in London. By then, I was a pen-pusher for the Air Ministry."

"So, what happened to Janet, or Shirley as we know her?"

"Right, this is where it gets interesting. Shirley's parents weren't her real parents. At birth, Mr and Mrs Curtis took on Shirley because the real mother was too young to keep the child."

"Go on,"

"The mother was Mrs Curtis's younger sister."

"Who's the sister?"

"Right, son. Here's the thing. Evelyn Harris married William Curtis in 1931 when she was twenty. By the time Hitler had become chancellor of Nazi Germany, Evelyn and William realised they had a problem conceiving. As luck would have it, Evelyn's younger sister, Mary, gave birth under dubious circumstances … wrong side of the blanket, so to speak. The father was unknown, and the lass who was only eighteen needed an escape route from her situation."

"Evelyn took Shirley as her own?"

"Precisely! There were no adoption papers or anything like that. Just the birth certificate stating Mary was the mother. Evelyn just took the baby as if it was her own."

"But, Don. How does this fit in with me ... or, well, *other* me?

"Well, it seems that the younger sister, Mary, who gave up Shirley, didn't heed the lesson, getting herself in the family way almost immediately with her new fella. A dashing looking chap called Arthur Apsley ... they only had one child together, Jason, born 30th March 1934."

"My God. *Other* Jason!"

"Same birthday as you ... ain't that so, my boy? Jason Apsley has a half-sister called Janet Shirley Colney."

"What happened to Shirley?"

"After she was removed from the bombed-out house in Hackney, she was placed in St. Peter's Orphanage, where she stayed until she was sixteen in '49."

"Right, where's that? In London somewhere?"

"No. Children were evacuated. St. Peter's Orphanage is here in Fairfield."

I shook my head. "Never heard of it."

"No, well, they closed it sometime in the late '50s. The building lay derelict for some years until Fairfield Council took hold of the building in the mid '60s and turned it into a children's home. We know that place as Lexton House, over on Coldhams Lane."

"My god!"

"So, you see, my son. You, or whoever you are, have a half-sister. And unfortunately, she's the mother of the four evil Colney sons. Rather amazing that you killed David, who was technically your nephew. And you were instrumental in the episode where Patrick got arrested for attempted murder, and you were in that car that day Paul died with Martin. According to Jess, your other nephew, Andrew, is about to face his court trial for rape. You ain't got the greatest family, have you!"

"Jesus Christ!" I exclaimed. I thought the day Paul Colney died and Shirley disappeared to Spain, I'd finally rid myself of that evil family. However, now I discover that Shirley Colney is *other* Jason's half-sister. That makes Patrick and Jess related … they're cousins! Shirley Colney is not only Beth's grandmother, but she's also Jess's aunt and Jess's daughter, Faith, is Shirley's granddaughter. I needed to draw a family tree, as this was becoming seriously complicated.

"So, son. Where do you fit into all this?"

"What?"

"Well, if you're not the Jason Apsley who moved into that flat on the Broxworth Estate in the spring of '76, who are you?"

"Don, I am Jason Apsley. I have been all my life. My parents were Joan and Neil Apsley."

"Not Mary and Arthur, then? And although you were born on 30th March, it wasn't in 1934, was it?"

"No, Don. Although I'm fifty-two, I was born in 1977 … ten years ago."

10

Cape Canaveral

For over ten years, I'd kept the story of my ridiculous time leap under wraps. Only George, my grandfather in my first life, and my wife Jenny knew the truth about me. So, the decision to keep my real identity quiet was a relatively easy one to make. Obviously, blurting out I was a time-traveller from the 21st Century would pose its difficulties, and the pain I went through convincing George and Jenny was quite harrowing – not a challenge I relished repeating.

Yes, I'd made many time-travel cock-ups along the way with the occasional blurting out of information that only the future could know. Still, I'd always managed to wriggle my way out of the situation when it happened. As the years rolled by, the frequency of my mouth disengaging with my brain became a less frequent occurrence. Now, ten years on, I had started even to doubt that my first life existed.

Of course, I knew it had, as history just rattled on repeating itself. Those world events continued and, like my futile attempts to stop the Yorkshire Ripper of a decade ago, I knew that time was not easily bent – history just barrelled on with its laid down plan.

Jenny had grown to understand that although I knew future events to a reasonable accuracy, it was fairly futile to attempt to change it. The two big world disasters of 1986 repeated themselves. When the Challenger Space shuttle exploded, and the Chernobyl disaster occurred later that year, Jenny didn't challenge why I hadn't tried to prevent it. We both knew a schoolteacher from an unremarkable town in Hertfordshire in the central suburban belt of the UK could not influence NASA and the Soviet Fuel and Energy industries.

If I had tried, I imagined how that conversation would have panned out—

'Oh, hi. Please could you connect my call to the head administrator of NASA at Cape Canaveral and the Director of the Kurchatov Institute of Atomic Energy in Moscow?'

I would wait to be connected to the two men on a party line.

'Oh, hello, good of you to spare some time for a chat. Look, just a quickie. There are a couple of points I would like to raise. Administrator, you need to stop the Challenger Space Shuttle launch because it will blow up just after take-off. And for you, Director, you need to shut down your most successful nuclear power plant because the fourth reactor will explode due to a botched safety test operation.'

'Who am I, you ask? Yes, of course. I'm a grammar school teacher from England. I teach maths and science to eleven to sixteen-year-olds.'

No – that kind of conversation wouldn't work.

World events would rattle on regardless. Of course, I couldn't remember them all, and many of the, well, shall we say smaller events, I'd completely forgotten, only to find my memory banks to be awoken when a particular news item hit the evening headlines.

The sinking, earlier this year, of the roll-on-roll-off ferry, the Herald of Free Enterprise, when many had nipped over to Zeebrugge on a booze cruise, was one such event. It's fair to say Jenny wasn't best pleased with my memory performance prior to the sinking. However, as I pointed out, even if I had remembered said event before the disaster took place, there was nothing to suggest we could have influenced the assistant boatswain to close the bow door because our success rate at altering history thus far could only be described as woeful.

The founder members of the Time Travel Believers' Club, namely me, George, and Jenny, often discussed events coming and what plans we could put in place to stop them. We had made lists when secretly meeting to review the future – something akin to the Secret Seven holed up in a garden shed whilst hatching a plan to catch smugglers. However, our club only consisted of three members, not seven. The fourth member, Martin, had died in that Cortina ten years ago. Also, catching smugglers wasn't high on our list of concerns.

At this point, we had a few disasters on the boil, so to speak, but, as usual, no concrete plans on how to affect their planned outcome. We'd organised those disasters into three categories – Manmade – Natural – Individual. Of course, for the Natural ones, our reviewing process was just about how we could warn the world of the impending doom, as communicating with God and seeing if he could see his way clear to stopping said events would be a stretch way too far.

Our two latest natural disasters up for review were the 2004 Indian Ocean tsunami, or tidal wave, as George called it after initially asking what tsunami meant, and the hurricane to hit the UK sometime in October this year.

The precise date of the tsunami was an easy one to remember, being Boxing Day 2004. Not only was it memorable because of Christmas, but specifically where I was at that precise time. Lisa and I had started going steady that year. My first meeting with her parents hadn't panned out particularly well, which was understandable as I'd proceeded to get pissed and then tell her mother what a great set of tits her daughter had. Anyway, great tits aside, we had lunch at her parents' house on that particular Boxing Day. Fortunately, I'd learnt from the fateful dinner party and restrained from getting tanked and referring to Lisa's chest – what a relief! However, all was not good.

This particular toe-curling event, and I mean toe-curling, literally as well as metaphorically, cemented her parents' concern that I was a total loser who possessed a perverted mind, and Lisa needed to rid herself of me at lightning speed.

The four of us had settled down to lunch at the small bijou, and I guess you could say cosy, dining-room table. All was good; dinner was delightful – the food, that is, not the company – also, surprisingly, I managed to stay sober despite the urge to sink a couple of bottles of red wine to numb the pain of spending the day at Lisa's parents' house.

Lisa and I were still at the stage in our relationship where sex was high on the daily to-do list. So, when Lisa's mother rolled out the cheese board, to break up the boredom, I seductively sucked grapes indicating what I planned to do to Lisa's nipples when we eventually left the torment of her parents' company, and I got my girlfriend home. Unfortunately, and unbeknown to me, Lisa had tucked her legs behind her. So, when seductively grape-sucking and searching between her legs with my big toe to raise the excitement, it all turned to shit. Her mother squealed in shock, jumping back to distance herself from my toes that were now expertly rubbing the gusset of her knickers.

Her parents always held a dim view of me, and to be fair, I guess this particular incident didn't help. Although I apologised profusely, we left soon after and we didn't tick off all our tasks on that day's to-do list. As you can imagine, remembering the precise date of the 2004 tsunami was never difficult.

As for the impending hurricane, that was slightly trickier because I had no idea of the date, only recalling it was in October. However, like any well-planned pre-hurricane preparation that would take place in most counties in Florida, we had a clear plan. Although not hugely scientific, the plan included not parking our cars near trees, keeping the kids off school, and securing potential flying objects from the garden. My explicit instruction was we all had to watch the evening BBC weather forecasts every night until Michael Fish, the weatherman, states that there will not be a hurricane – that would be the cue to launch the plan because with less than six hours from that statement I knew the country would be hit by the worst storm in two hundred years.

Anyway, I digress: back to our categories of future events. Manmade consisted of those disasters directly caused by organisations. The World Trade Centre twin towers being the obvious one. And lastly, and more easily avoidable, were individual acts, like Dr Death, Harold Shipman, who I suspected was already on full steam ahead with his killing spree.

For over ten years, we regularly met and discussed plans to change the future. However, we had achieved near-zero success thus far.

Now, here I was, once again, about to convince a rational human being I was a time-traveller. My initial statement that although I was clearly a man heading for middle age, and my girth over the last few years had complied with the spread request that middle-age demands, I had just informed Don that I was born ten years ago.

"Don, did you hear what I said?" I asked my closest friend as his head lay on the white pillow, looking like our maker was creeping ever closer to taking him upstairs. Not that I was a believer in him upstairs, as Don put it, and this was also one of the reasons I never asked if he could refrain from allowing some natural disasters that would kill many. I figured it could be difficult to pray or ask some mythical god not to send life-threatening weather systems.

Don wheezed out a pathetic cough and, akin to the great Titanic's last few movements in the ice, Don's empty whisky glass he held slowly started listing, sinking into the scrunched-up quilt and away from the safety of his hand.

"Don?"

"Yes, son. I'm all ears. Go on."

"Well, okay. But what I just said, hasn't that blown your brain?"

"Son, I've lived a long life and seen many strange things along the way. But, over the years, I've come to understand that you have a back story that is somewhat out of the ordinary. Now, my boy, I'm ready to hear it. But, if you don't get on with it, I might miss the punch line."

I took his hand in mine and gently squeezed it. His frail fingers had taken on a blue hue; it appeared his body heat had left them, presumably leaving the extremities and protecting the organs in an attempt to stop the inevitable. As King Cnut had failed to hold back the tide, I feared Don's body now failed to hold back the encroaching grim reaper who appeared to be approaching.

So, not to waste time, I cracked on and started from the beginning – 11th August 2019, a warm sunny day when I slammed my Beemer into a white van in Cockfosters High Street – the day I died.

Initially, Don offered the odd nod and occasionally blinked but, as I cruised into the full flow of the events of 1976, I hadn't noticed he'd become quiet. I rattled on with my daft account of the time-travel leap from the 21st Century to the time of flared jeans, the rise of disco, the economic meltdown, and the start of the technological revolution that would irrevocably change the world and the way we live – many say not for the better, which after experiencing the pre and post mobile phone eras, I agreed with.

"So, I guess when Martin and Paul Colney died in that crash, that was when life started to settle down."

I gently nudged his hand.

"Don?"

Don didn't reply. With his eyes closed, he seemed to be sleeping. I wasn't aware my story of time travel had been that boring. Squeezing his fingers to gently awake him, they felt cold to the touch and had now taken on a stiffness, almost a wooden feel. After shaking his hand, I leant up and placed two fingers on his cold neck – he'd gone. As Don feared, I think he missed the punchline.

Today had been bright. The sun rose early and stayed high in the sky, similar, I guess, to 11th August 2019, although I only witnessed the first few hours of that day, so I can only assume it stayed bright all day. If I reach the age of eighty-five and relive that day, I guess I'll find out.

The sun continued to stream in through the windows, causing the moted dust-light to dance in the air as I held Don's hand. I bowed my head and silently wept.

When I felt a hand on my shoulder, it appeared the moted dust-light had moved on or was sitting out this particular dance as it didn't like the tune and was unfamiliar with the required moves. The sun had scooted around the side of Don's house, leaving his bedroom bathed in a grey hue – a fitting colour for this sad moment.

Jenny folded her arms around my neck as she leant down, nestling her face next to mine. I felt her warm tears as they careered down the join of our cuddled cheeks. We stayed in that position for a few minutes, silently mourning the loss of our dearest and closest friend – my honorary father – Donald Nears.

11

The Cooler King

Monday finally gave way to Tuesday, and, at that point, we were still over at Don's house, although technically it was mine as I'd rented it to him for the nominal sum of two quid a week. Jess had stepped up to the plate and called the authorities, and a doctor duly attended and pronounced that Don had passed. The doctor stated the time of death as 2100 hours, although I knew he'd left us an hour earlier.

By the time I'd locked up the house and Jenny and I had decamped to Jess's next door, midnight had passed. It's fair to say that when I awoke later that Tuesday morning after a pitiful two hours' sleep, I was convinced that life was about to take a sharp detour in the wrong direction – I'd lost Don, and the Colneys, a family of psychotic despots, seemed to be coming back into my life.

Colin rallied around with Jayne and picked up my morning lessons. Although this was super kind of them, it was just going to leave me to brood over the loss of my closest friend. PoD and Mrs Trosh made all the right noises by offering sympathy and advising me to take whatever time I needed when I'd relayed the news of Don's death.

I busied myself making some necessary calls to undertakers and, after consulting Don's address book that I'd removed from his house the previous evening, I contacted his daughters who were very matter-of-fact about the passing of their father. I'd never quite grasped what had caused the relationship with Don and his girls to go so wrong, and I guess I would now never discover. Nevertheless, it did bother me, and I felt I would need to probe this a little deeper one day. The Donald Nears I'd been so privileged to have known didn't appear to be the man his daughters knew.

Last evening, Don had mentioned he was also researching his own family, as well as mine, when digging into that microfiche system up at the library. Unfortunately, we didn't get around to discussing what he'd discovered, and I wondered if there was something in his past responsible for the rift between him and his daughters – a skeleton in the cupboard, perhaps.

PoD was completing a sweep of the corridors. He'd taken Sarah on a school tour and then planned to catch up with her to discuss how he would like his secretary to operate.

Back in my days at Waddington Steel, it was called *'Ways of Working'* that aligned to some poncy Mission Statement and Company Values that none of the staff could remember or give two shits about.

Back in my time as a sales executive, Gary, the CEO, arranged a two-day event for the executive team to discuss those very points – ways of working and a new mission statement. However, unfortunately for me and the rest of the executive team, I think he'd swallowed a plethora of those leadership self-help books and wanted to impose those ideas upon us.

Being the miserable bastard that I was, it was one of those sort of events that I dreaded. On day one we were instructed to attend in fancy dress as our favourite movie character. All the executive team threw themselves into the fun, turning up in various guises from Princess Leia to Batman.

After suffering a mental scarring at the age of thirteen when playing Tarzan in a school play that involved a wardrobe malfunction with my loincloth in front of a packed audience, I'd shied away from dressing up – now hating it. So, for this event, I just grabbed my brown leather jacket and a baseball I'd picked up when holidaying in Florida, stating I was Captain Hilts from The Great Escape. It was a poor start on my part and, as my boss seemed obsessed with dressing up, he waxed lyrical about everyone's brilliant efforts but pointed out that I didn't have a motorbike and my jacket was the wrong colour.

I think Steve McQueen and The Great Escape came to mind because I had an affinity with Captain Hilts, as in the urgent need to escape because every day at Waddington Steel was akin to living in the Stalag Luft prison camp. I think Gary actually expected me to arrive on a Triumph TR6 and proceed to leap a few rolls of barbed-wire fencing. I thought at the time I needed to start tunnelling my way out – perhaps I would conjure up a plan, give Charles Bronson, the Tunnel King, a call to assist and start building Tom, Dick and Harry.

On the last day of the two-day event the situation regressed to new lows, which surprised me that could happen based on day one's disasters. Supplied with a white t-shirt and a marker pen, we were duly instructed to pen what we were passionate about across our chest. Misreading the purpose of the exercise, which was quite normal for me, I wrote Formula One Motor Racing across mine and proudly donned the t-shirt awaiting all to finish as we sat in a circle. However, as I soon discovered, the exercise had a different purpose, namely understanding our management styles, not our general personal interests. So, when Gary pulled his t-shirt on with the words *'Remove Poor Performance With Compassion,'* I feared I would be the first target of his passion.

Anyway, the event finished with a raucous honking from all the team as we held hands, now fully gelled together with a new set of corporate values to impose on our teams – what a load of bollocks.

So, whilst PoD was sharing his insights with Sarah, I used his study to make my calls – the last was to George. Unfortunately, I wasn't successful in tracking him down, so I would try at lunchtime or just give him the news later when the Time Travel Believers' Club met up at the Three Horseshoes Pub.

Leaving PoD's office, I planned to catch up with Colin and assess how my twelve-year-old ex-wife was faring on her second day. Presumably, she'd settled down and hadn't intended to continue the lucrative pornographic photographic start-up business as she had at the Howlett School.

In my first life, I could only presume that Lisa had not traversed the path of blackmailing male students with mucky pictures. If she had, would I have suffered revenge porn when we split?

Lisa and I weren't into creating mucky home movies. However, I guess as most couples did, we had employed the use of a camera to spice up a few raunchy evenings. I recall we had invested in a new digital camera before our honeymoon and had on several occasions strayed to the sordid event of snapping away capturing our bedroom antics. I'm not sure what happened to the camera when we split, so maybe those digital images were still in her possession in 2019. As I can assume I'm dead in that first life, that presumably means she's not released said pictures for public scrutiny – well, maybe.

Mrs Trosh smiled sympathetically as I stepped into the school office. I reciprocated, but within an instant, both our faces morphed into shock.

The glass panelled door to the school office swung open and continued its back-and-forth motion a few times before coming to a rest as a somewhat dishevelled gent stood in the reception area of the school office. He raised his hands in the air and shrugged his shoulders.

"How the fuck did this happen?" he exclaimed, keeping his hands aloft whilst awaiting a reply.

Rooted to the floor with a gaping mouth, which grew wider by the second, I could only assume that the lack of sleep, coupled with the trauma of my ex-wife attending school, and losing Don, had caused me to start to hallucinate. Colin had said I should take the day off because he didn't think I was in a fit state to teach and, based on the fact that I was now imagining dead people walking about the school, I guess he was right. I needed sleep at the very least and, based on what stood before me, maybe some professional help or counselling.

"You look like you've seen a ghost!" he exclaimed with his hands still held aloft.

"I have," I whispered, slowly blinking, now hoping that the vision would change when my eyes reopened.

"Oh, Mr Bretton! My goodness, you're back!" stated Mrs Trosh, ignoring Martin's outburst and use of foul language.

She patted her meticulously coiffured hair bun, that involuntary movement she always performed when she'd swoon over Martin.

"I must say you don't look a day older! South Africa must have been a tonic for you! You look as fit as a fiddle!"

"Miss Colman," he replied, but with his hands still in the air, he turned to me and once again exclaimed. "Well? How in God's name has this happened?"

"Oh, it's Mrs Trosh now. Mr Trosh and I married just after you left ... so that's ten years ago. I must say I'm rather astonished ... but you ... you don't look any different!"

Presumably as I continued to gawp and offer no response, Martin decided to hold a conversation with Mrs Trosh.

"Oh, well, congratulations, Miss Colman. Err ... sorry, what was that you said about South Africa?"

"You left us in '77 to take a job in South Africa ... I presume you've been there the last ten years?"

"What?" queried Martin, as he peered at our dependable secretary.

The South Africa story was what I'd concocted to explain Martin's disappearance, and I could now see this going pear-shaped if I didn't pull myself out of this trance.

Before Martin blurted out a story that would surely have him committed to a secure unit, I leapt into action. "Martin, follow me," I ordered, as I grabbed his arm and bundled him out of the office.

Dragging my old dead friend across the car park, I shoved him into the passenger seat of my red Audi Quattro.

"Who d'you think you are, Gene Hunt? You've been Quattroed!" he sniggered. "Where we off to then? Off to run down and nick some low-life scum!"

"Martin, you're dead!" I exclaimed, ignoring the reference to the popular TV show that wasn't due out for at least another decade or so. Although I won't deny it, when I purchased my new car, Gene Hunt cruising about in his Quattro as he hunted down armed blaggers had crossed my mind.

"Well, I guess I worked that one out!"

"What the bollocks is going on? I saw you sprawled across the bonnet of the Cortina, and you were dead … finito … brown bread … dead!"

"Well, I guessed something was up! I remember crashing through the bus shelter, but that was it! Then I came to and found myself sitting there parked up in that bloody car! And do you know what?"

"What?"

"Somehow, the bloody bus shelter behind me was still standing!"

"Well, how the hell are you here now? And how come I seem to be having a conversation with you ten years after you're dead?"

"Look, I don't know! Like I said, I came to in that car. At first, I wondered where you had all buggered off to. I thought it was the same evening until I noticed the sun was rising. So, not unsurprisingly, I thought I'd knocked myself out and woken up in the early hours. As you and Jess were nowhere to be seen, I decided to grab a cab and get home. There was no way I could move that car. It was somehow wedged between the bus stop and a tree!"

"What d'you mean wedged? The front of the car was crushed!"

"No … you're not listening to me! I said it was parked up as if a crane had lowered it into the gap!"

"I saw it! The wheelbase was crushed down that small it would have fitted a Ford Fiesta! Anyway, where have you been for ten years?"

"Fuck sake! I'm just telling you. Before I got a cab, I nipped in the newsagents and bought some cigarettes … bloody hell, good job I had a fiver on me as they've gone up! One pound fifty for a pack of twenty … daylight robbery! Although, back in 2019, I recall a packet costing over a tenner! Anyway, as the bloke behind the counter was grabbing the cigarettes, I had a cheeky gawp at page three of The Sun … fit bird called Maria Whitaker, nice jugs. That's when I noticed the date … 7th September 1987!"

"Hang on. Are you telling me that you have been dead for ten years, and you woke up yesterday morning in the same car that somehow isn't crushed?"

"Yes!"

"This can't be happening," I mumbled, whilst I continued to try and compute his ridiculous story.

"Ha, got to say you've chucked on a bit of timber over the years, and I can see the old grey hairs coming through."

I involuntarily sucked in my stomach in an attempt to give the appearance of a more athletic man. As the years passed, I'd added a few pounds and could be labelled a MAMIL when donning my cycling gear. However, it wasn't the tight-fitting lycra on offer in the sports shops of 2019, more of a dodgy shell-suit get-up.

"Jeeesus Christ! This is frigging nuts. How can you be alive? I saw you there ... dead!"

"I don't know ... I don't know." He defensively raised his hand again. "But for some reason, I've come back ten years in the future." Martin frowned and shook his head, a disbelieving gesture accompanying his ridiculous statement. He shifted in his seat to look at me. "Look, mate, this is how you and me time-travelled in the first place. We both died as a result of the crash in the Beemer when we woke up in the '70s. And now it's happened again in that Cortina."

I sighed heavily before shifting in my seat to face him. "Yeah, I get that, but ..." I whispered, although cut short as I had no idea what else to say. "You haven't aged ... Mrs Trosh noticed it but probably thought you'd just aged well whilst living in the sunshine over in South Africa. What the hell is everyone going to think? Hey, also, you're buried up at the cemetery ... it's an unmarked grave because they never found out who you were."

"You think I'm immortal? Maybe we both are and can never die! D'you think we're going to run around the Earth forever? Christ, you know what, we could be like that Christopher Lambert bloke in Highlander."

"Jenny and I saw that film when it was released last year. I had the DVD back in my old life. Jenny said it was total crap, and so did some film critics when it was released."

"No way! That's a classic!"

"Well, yes, it was in our day ... I guess it must have grown in popularity over the years. Anyway, we can't sit here talking about bloody films! And the thought of being immortal is hideous!"

"Well, you're definitely growing older, mate. What you now? Over fifty?"

"Fifty-two."

"Christ, you're old enough to be my father! Jenny will soon be looking to trade you in for a newer model!" he chuckled.

The mention of his father sent a cold shiver down my spine – presumably, Andrew Colney would appear in court soon, faced with multiple counts of rape.

Sarah Moore trotted down the stone steps heading for the car. I doubted she would remember Martin from when he completed that short spell as the stand-in caretaker back in '77. Although, as I recall, the sixteen-year-old Sarah held a crush for him at the time even though he was her grown-up unborn child. Presumably, and worryingly, Martin would recognise his mother.

"That's Mum!"

"Martin, don't say anything!" I ordered, whilst lowering the side window and sticking my head out as Sarah approached.

"Morning Mr ... err, Jason. Mr Elkinson just wondered if you have a moment? Oh, blimey! Hello Martin. Oh, sorry, you won't remember me," she stated as she stuck her arm through the open window, across my face, offering a handshake to her twice-born, twice-dead son. "Sarah Moore. I was here at school when you were the caretaker about ten years ago," she stated and blushed, presumably now remembering the crush she'd held for him.

Martin shook her hand, holding on to it for a little bit longer than was acceptable. "Yes, I remember you ... of course I do!"

"Oh, really. I must say you've not aged one jot!"

"Well, good skincare routine … it's important, you know."

"Really? Never known a man to worry about face cream!"

"Well, just look at the results!" he smirked, still holding her hand as they stretched across me.

"Yes, very impressive! You must tell me what you use!"

"Oh, you don't need it! You're beautiful! Stunning!"

"Oh, thank you!" she replied, causing the previous fading blush to burst back into life.

As they continued their conversation, I felt pinned to my seat. My eyes were now watching the verbal tennis match as they exchanged this rather odd conversation between mother and son.

The son should know better, and the mother had no idea who he really was. As they continued to exchange pleasantries and started to flirt, I realised my time-travelling loose cannon had returned – now becoming increasingly concerned about what chaos he would inflict on my life this time.

12

Randall And Hopkirk Deceased

"God, she's fit!" stated Martin, as he gawped at Sarah, who gracefully glided back to the school to relay to the Prince of Darkness my message that I would be there in a couple of minutes.

I swivelled my head to shoot him a disapproving look.

"What?" shrugged Martin.

"What d'you mean, *What*? That woman is your mother!"

"Not now, she's not. Remember, Paul Colney was killed! He never raped her, and I was never born!"

"Paul Colney wasn't your father!" I boomed at him.

"What? You're joking, right?"

I shuffled my bum in the seat and turned to face him. "Andrew Colney was arrested a few weeks ago for a spate of rapes over the last couple of months. In our first life, I'm fairly certain he was your biological father."

"He raped Mum … it happened again?" questioned Martin, his eyes bulging at the news of his real father's identity landing in his brain. His head jolted sideways as the metaphorical clapper clanged the side of his skull.

"Well, the good news is, I don't think so. Andrew Colney was apprehended as he stalked Sarah on a night back in August. The police were on to him and caught him before he could act. I'm certain this time that it didn't happen."

"Oh, thank God for that!"

"Yes, for Sarah's sake, and yours."

"Mine?"

"Yes! You and new baby Martin can't very well exist in the same world! It's called a paradox or something like that. Anyway, that's what it's called in the time-travel novels I read. Come May next year ... you should be born." I announced, as I jabbed a finger in his direction. "Now, as you seemed to have reappeared, that could be a bit tricky!" I aggressively bellowed, as I continued to point at him with my finger hovering near his face.

Martin's eyes slowly dropped to focus on the tip of my finger. "Phew. Blimey!"

A moment of silence descended as we both stared out of the windscreen. Like me, Martin was probably thinking about the rather head-screwing fact that he was never born but somehow existed in the past. A thought that often popped into my brain over the past eleven years about my own strange existence.

"She's a free agent then." He grinned as he continued to gawp at the school entrance where Sarah had disappeared through.

"What?"

"Sarah ... she's a free agent ... fit ... wouldn't mind, I can tell you."

"You sick bastard!"

"No, I'm bloody not! She's not my mother in this life. I'm not some mother fu—"

"Yes, you are!" I interrupted. "That's exactly what you're suggesting!"

"No," he responded, although with less conviction.

"Look, I need to get back in. Jenny and I are meeting up with George at the pub after work. Let's reconvene then. Can you amuse yourself for the afternoon then meet me back here at five?"

"Yes, I guess so. Although, I need a shower. I slept on a park bench last night. That taxi took me back home yesterday, but my key wouldn't fit in the lock. I knocked on Don's but got no reply, so I guess he must have been out. Where you living now? When I knocked on your door, some bloke answered who I've never seen before."

"We moved in '77 up where Beth lived in our old life. Jess now lives in your old house, and Don …" My word flow abruptly halted.

"What about Don?"

"Don's passed on now," I added, although I couldn't be bothered to elaborate further.

"Oh, that's sad. We all liked Don, didn't we?"

"Yeah, we did. Look, Don's house is unoccupied. Nip over there and grab a shower and get your head down for a bit." I turned and faced him again. "Martin … Don died last night … so use the spare room."

"Last night?"

"Yeah," I nodded.

"Oh, Christ. I don't know what to say. Jesus, Jason, I'm so sorry."

"Whatever. Okay, take the car. Don's front door key is in the glove box. But don't arrive for another hour because I'm going to have to warn Jess. This is going to blow her mind!"

"Yeah, sure. Okay. Gotta say, I quite fancy burning a bit of rubber in this thing. What's it got ... couple of hundred horsepower under the hood?"

"Martin!"

"Um-huh," he responded, as he retrieved Don's house key from the glove box.

"Getting nicked for doing a ton up the bypass really ain't going to help our situation. Some police officer might recognise you as the bloke sprawled dead across the bonnet of that Cortina! I reckon that could somewhat complicate things!"

"Oh, I don't think so. That was ten years ago! No one will recognise me from back then."

"Maybe not, but we can't risk facing difficult questions at the moment."

"Alright, alright, keep your knickers on!"

"Martin, please don't cause a bloody scene. You were like a bloody loose cannon when you arrived in '77! It took all my energy to keep you under wraps at the time!"

"Oh, so I guess you were well-pleased when I pegged it, then!"

"No, don't be silly. But Christ, when you arrived, you were a bloody nightmare. There was all that business with those women up at Lipton's supermarket, not to mention flirting with your sixteen-year-old mother!"

"I didn't flirt with her!"

"Yes, you did! And now you sick bastard are thinking about knobbing her!"

"That's ridiculous! Apsley, you really get on my tits at times!"

"Ditto!"

Martin held up the palm of his hand. "Okay, mate. Look, I'll behave. I promise."

"Please do!"

"Who else now knows you're a time-traveller?"

"Oh, good point. Just George and Jenny. Jess still thinks I'm her father."

"Okay. Surprised you never told Don."

"Oh, well, I did."

"Oh, what did he say? I can't imagine he was very easy to convince ... Don was a super-switched-on kind of bloke."

"He didn't say anything."

"Really? That surprises me. "

"Well, he ... he was dead."

"Oh. You told him you were a time-traveller when he was dead! What was the point of that?"

"He wasn't dead when I started to tell him ... he died before I could get to the punchline, so to speak."

"Jesus! You reckon that's what killed him?"

"No, no. He was dying at the time." That made me think. Had my story caused his heart to stop?

'You killed your best mate. Apsley you're such a tosser!'

"No, I didn't!"

"No, you didn't what?"

"Oh, nothing. I was replying to my mind talk."

"Christ, Apsley, not only have you fallen foul of middle-aged spread, but you're losing it as well!"

"Look, I better get back in. As I said, wait on the road for an hour. That will give me enough time to warn Jess. Then get back here for five, okay?"

"Yeah, no problem."

"Oh, shit! You're dead!"

"Yes, I know! We've done that ... eaten the pie, got the t-shirt!"

"No, I mean, as far as Jess is concerned, you're dead! She stood and gawped at you when we got out of the car when you and Paul Colney were lying dead across the bonnet!"

"Oh fuck."

"Bollocks!"

"What the hell are we going to do? I need some kip, and I don't fancy the park bench again!"

"Look, I'll tell Jess you're Martin's brother, and you've come over from South Africa."

"She's not going to buy that! Saying I have an identical twin who's ten years younger is a bit of an unbelievable story! I know some women have long gaps in labour when giving birth to twins, but ten years is somewhat stretching it, don't you think!"

"No, not a twin, just a younger brother. She only saw you that evening in the car. She won't remember you. Although I have to say, it's clear to see your bloodline ... you do look like a Colney."

"Yeah, thanks. Looking like one of those psycho brothers is not the preferred look."

"Right, what you going to call yourself?"

Martin pursed his lips as he thought up a name.

"Come on. Any name will do."

"Leonardo. Leonardo Bretton."

"Leonardo! What like DiCaprio? Although that film *Catch me If You Can* was a classic! Loved that film. Can't wait for it to come out again."

"Oh, yeah, that was alright, I suppose. Although I preferred the *Wolf of Wall Street.*"

"No way! You saying that the *Wolf of Wall Street* was better than *Catch Me If You Can*?"

"Yeah, way better!"

"Bollocks was it!"

"Well, if Caroline were here, she'd be arguing that *Titanic* was his best."

"Oh, per-lease!"

"Yeah, I know ... girly film."

"Jesus, what's the matter with us! You're dead, and we're discussing which feature film is the best! Bloody hell, this is like some episode of *Randall and Hopkirk Deceased*!"

"What?"

"Oh, never mind."

"Anyway, I wasn't thinking of Leonardo DiCaprio. I was more on the lines of Leonardo as in the leader of the Teenage Mutant Ninja Turtles ... I had all their comics and loved the cartoons. Mum bought me their games when I got my first Game Boy."

"You're joking, right?"

"No, she did. You can go and ask her if you like!" He pointed to the school entrance where Sarah had disappeared into a few moments ago, appearing almost hurt that I didn't believe he had a Game Boy.

"Oh, for fuck sake! I wasn't suggesting your mother didn't buy you a Game Boy! I was suggesting that naming yourself after some animated pizza-gobbling, sewer-dwelling, crime-busting turtle was a bit stupid! And ... and, just for clarity, I can't very well trot back into school and ask your mother if she bought you a Game Boy in the bloody '90s because that's in the future. And ... and she doesn't know she's your mother, and will never know, because, if it hasn't escaped your attention, you were never born!" I took a breath from my rant before continuing. "And ... and you're dead!" I added for good measure.

"Fair enough."

"Look, Martin, sorry to rant, but you coming back from the dead has been a bit of a shock. To be honest, I think Leonardo is a bit too cosmopolitan. Can we go with something a bit more classic?"

"Yeah, probably. Any ideas?"

"How about Keith?"

"Keith! Really?"

"What's wrong with Keith? You've got Keith Richards, Keith Moon …"

"And?"

"What? You want more? You want me to like name some more?"

"Yeah. Come on, apart from a couple of ageing rock stars, who the hell is called Keith?"

"Oh, I dunno, there must be loads!"

"Keith! Christ," he muttered, as he shook his head in disgust at his new name.

I clicked my fingers, excited to have thought of another one, "Penelope Keith! There you go!"

"Who's that?"

"Margo. You know Margo and Jerry … the Good Life."

"Tom and Jerry?"

"Oh, Christ. No. Forget it. Your name is Keith, and that's that. Now try not to cause utter chaos in the next few hours?"

"Don't worry. I won't get into any scrapes. At least this time, I won't have that psycho Paul Colney following me!"

Once again, a moment of silence descended as we both stared out of the windscreen. I was just about to trot back into school and let this wannabee rally driver cause chaos around the streets of Fairfield when my very own clapper hit the inside of my skull.

"Martin."

"What?"

"Oh … my … God!"

"What?"

"When you woke up in that car yesterday morning, you were on your own, yes?"

"Yes! That's what I said. You and Jess seemed to have buggered off."

"Martin, there were four of us in that car that evening."

Martin had died twice in his life, so by that very fact he should have stopped breathing on a couple of occasions and now be a lifeless dead corpse. But, instead, he stared at me with a sagging mouth, his skin taking on a dead pasty creamy colour as the penny dropped.

"Martin?"

His Adam's apple bounced a couple of times. "The passenger door was wide open when I came to."

"Oh, Christ! I think we have to accept we have that evil psychopathic nutter, Paul Colney, running around town again."

13

Cavallino Rapante – The Prancing Stallion

Martin squealed the Quattro back into the school car park at fifteen minutes past five, destroying the relative tranquillity of the school after the fourteen-hundred marauding pupils had departed for the day.

Fortunately, no pupils were meandering out of school after the various after-school clubs had finished. Otherwise, Martin would have scored a strike as they skittled in the air whilst performing a handbrake turn near the school entrance. Furthermore, Philip Glenister's driving stunt double would have been impressed with his skilful dexterity of the Quattro's controls as he backed into a parking space and revved the engine before killing it.

Whatever promises Martin had bestowed on me earlier, judging by this driving performance, my loose cannonball from 1977 had returned.

Significantly more concerning was that my adversary, Paul-Psycho-Colney, was now probably wandering around the town. Apart from being a dangerous psychotic megalomaniac, from my previous dealings with the one-half of the Colney monster twins, I didn't believe he possessed the nous or brainpower to work out that coming back from the dead ten years later was a bit strange.

I dreaded to think who Paul had encountered over the last thirty-six hours, and the mayhem he'd already inflicted upon Fairfield and its unsuspecting residents.

When I spoke to Jess earlier, she was somewhat surprised that Martin had a younger brother who I'd never mentioned before. Fortunately, she didn't probe any further into his non-existent back story. God knows what her reaction had been when she saw him; I just prayed her memory for faces was poor.

At this point in my first life, Martin would only be a tiny embryo, and I would be in short pants in my last year of primary school – probably enjoying the conker season. I recall my grandmother's despair that I'd filled her oven with my collection as I'd learnt that baking your conkers could significantly improve their chances of survival at the upcoming conker championships in the playground.

Anyway, I digress. In 1977 when Martin time travelled, he was thirty-one, and if he hadn't ended up on the bonnet of the Cortina, he would now be the ripe old age of forty-one. However, he was back ten years later, still thirty-one years old, just about eight and a half months before he was due to be born. I just hoped Jess bought the brother story. Also, I prayed Martin managed not to say something stupid like *"Nice to see you again,"* and remembered his new name was Keith.

After losing Don yesterday, I couldn't risk giving George a heart attack when I presented a dead Martin at the pub. So, the plan was to leave Martin in the Quattro until I had a chance to gently inform George of the news. George was in for two shocks tonight – Don dying and Martin undying.

Naturally, Jenny had been somewhat blown away with the news about our new arrival when I called her at lunchtime. Jenny had struggled to warm to Martin in those few months back in 1977, and understandably she had a deep sense of foreboding about his return. I didn't dive into the detail about Paul Colney, and Jenny didn't ask. That discussion could come later, as I felt she needed to get her head around Martin's reincarnation before I landed the very real threat that psycho Colney was back.

"Come on, Apsley, put your foot down! You drive like a nun who's two hours early on her way for evening vespers! This car has some serious beef under the hood ... what's the matter with you? Give it some welly!"

Martin offered his opinion on my driving technique barely a hundred yards down Eaton Road, probably as a result of informing him that his driving days in my Quattro were over after witnessing his Nigel-Mansell-styled doughnut performance in the school car park.

"Martin, the last time I sat in a car with you driving, you nearly killed a bunch of kids on bikes, took out and destroyed a bus shelter, then embedded the car engine deep into the trunk of a large oak! Not to mention I ended up with a bloodied nose and a severe case of whiplash. So, I think you're in no place to comment on my driving technique!"

"Alright, Sister Apsley! Keep your habit on! Just saying that it'll be last orders by the time we get there."

"We'll be there in about five minutes. Anyway, I don't fancy killing myself in a car accident again, then being pinged off to another era in yesteryear. It would be just my luck I end up in Jacobean England dressed in a doublet, hose, and a codpiece, about to be hanged, drawn and quartered after being caught up in the Gun Powder Plot!"

"Ooo, get you, with your historical knowledge! Jacobean sounds like an obscure malt whisky you'd get in Waitrose."

"I'm a bloody schoolteacher. And although I would've liked nothing more than to be whizzing around the hairpin bends of the Circuit de Monaco in my Rosso Corsa, Prancing Stallion, Ferrari, I have accepted that it's not going to happen! I've resigned myself to teaching kids, most of whom have significantly more maturity than you, dickhead!" I spat back before taking a breather after my rant. It was enough to silence my old dead friend for the rest of the short journey to the pub.

"Right, sit here and touch nothing! Don't fiddle with the controls, and try not to cause any calamities whilst I gently inform George of your reincarnation."

"Aye aye, Cap'n," replied Martin, in a poor attempt at a Cornish accent as he saluted.

Leaving the cannonball in the Quattro, I bundled into the pub to seek out George. He and Ivy, now both retired, often visited relatives over in Aylesbury during weekdays or, if not over there, they'd be preparing their allotment for harvest before the onset of autumn.

Now my older brother Stephen was nearly sixteen, he was more than capable of looking after himself, but my grandmother always liked to be home to prepare his evening meal. This always provided an opportunity for the Time Travel Believers' Club to meet at this time. Unfortunately, Ivy could never join the club – she was far too level-headed to get herself mixed up in such silliness – if only she knew.

"Alright, lad? Usual?"

"George. Yeah, thanks."

"Not seen Jenny yet. Shall I order a Martini and soda anyway?"

"Yeah, she'll be here any moment."

"You alright, lad? You look like you've lost a shilling and found a penny."

"More like lost a gold sovereign and found a farthing."

"Oh! What's up, lad?"

I nodded to our favoured window seat. George clocked that this needed to be a private conversation, and out of the earshot of Brian, the landlord, and Dawn and Dennis, the local soaks, who were all ensconced in their usual places – some things never changed.

After exchanging pleasantries with Dawn and Dennis, the double diamond couple, we settled down in our seats, and I dived straight into blurting out the news of the lost gold sovereign. The grief had stifled me all day, and I think it was a release to just talk about it. Jenny joined us before I'd finished the story, holding my hand comforting me as I relayed the so sad events of the previous evening.

"Oh, lad. That's so sad. I knew he was becoming frail, but nevertheless, it's still a horrible shock."

I bowed my head, holding back the onslaught of another round of tears.

"Come on, lad … Don had a good innings. He wouldn't want you all mopey, would he?"

"George you're right … he wouldn't. What I need to do now is give the man a bloody good send-off, which involves lots of drinking."

"Agreed, lad. He'd approve and be disappointed to miss out."

"Ha, yes, you're right. Right, George, whilst we're talking shocking news, I have another bombshell to land."

"Oh, Christ! Who else has died?"

"Not died … you could say un-died … if such a word exists."

"What?"

"Let's say reincarnation."

"Oh, hell. You're not telling me there's another time-traveller arrived … and after all this time."

"Sort of, George. Not so much *another* time-traveller, but a previous one."

"What? D'you …. oh, hang on. Are you telling me Martin has reappeared?"

I nodded.

"My God. I'm seventy-five this year, and after all that time, I thought I'd pretty much worked out how the world works. I thought nothing could surprise me anymore. When you told me we'd go to war in the South Atlantic, and we'd have a female Prime Minister, I thought you were raving mad. Then as all these things started to happen, I thought I had come to accept what a strange world we live in. But this! A man back from the dead, and twice … this really does take the biscuit!"

"I know … but it gets worse."

"Darling?" questioned Jenny, presumably wondering what could be worse than Martin reappearing.

"Where is he?" interjected George, ignoring my 'it gets worse' statement.

"I left him in the car outside to give me a moment to tell you the news ... I didn't want to walk in with him and give you a heart attack! I've lost Don. I can't lose you too!"

"Ha, yes. I think my ticker might have missed a beat!"

"Okay, well before he causes any mayhem, I'd better go and get him."

"I'll get the dead lad a pint of lager ... this is exciting!" proclaimed George, as he leapt to his feet.

Jenny placed her hand on mine before I had a chance to stand. "Darling, you said, it gets worse. What did you mean?"

"Jen, I don't know this, but if Martin has returned—"

"Paul Colney!" she interrupted.

I nodded, raising my eyebrows. "We have to accept it's possible."

I patted her hand as I stood, leaving her motionless as she stared at her drink, deep in thought. I just had to pray I was wrong. I hoped Paul Colney hadn't journeyed forward and was still rotting six feet under up at the cemetery.

I wheeled Martin in and shepherded him to the seat next to George, where his pint had been duly deposited. For some strange reason, I held his upper arm as if guiding a blind man to a vacant chair. But hey, this wasn't a normal situation.

"Alright, lad? Got you a pint of the amber nectar," stated George in a quite appalling Australian accent whilst nodding towards the fizzing golden liquid. But then it was hard to miss the constant Paul Hogan adverts for Foster's Lager that seem to show at every commercial break. George plucked up his mug of mild and clinked Martin's glass as if this was an everyday event. "Cheers! Good health. Good to have you back, lad," he said, as if he hadn't seen him for a couple of days, not ten years after Martin had died.

"Cheers, George. Gotta say it's good to be alive! Not that I knew I was dead … if you get my meaning," chuckled Martin, lifting his pint to his lips. Then, before taking a sip of the cool liquid, he peered over the top of the glass at Jenny, who gawped at him – similar to my reaction earlier today when Martin had barrelled into the school office. "Jenny," he announced before slugging the pint down in three gulps.

The three of us sat and watched as Martin slowly guided the pint glass back, tipping the liquid down his throat in a well-practised motion.

The Three Horseshoes had a stable clientele, most of whom had been using the place for decades. Now the pub was filling up with pre-evening-meal drinkers, I suspected a few of the regulars would recognise Martin from the times we visited back in '77. Until we could work on a more believable back story, I guess the rejuvenating face cream idea was our best shot at explaining his youthful appearance. The trouble was, the younger-brother story wasn't going to hold water in some quarters – he'd already had a conversation as Martin with Sarah and Mrs Trosh.

"Jenny, I must say, you've fared better than your old man! You're still a well-fit bird with a classy chassis!"

"Martin!" I fired back at him whilst Jenny dismissed the inappropriate compliment with a scowl.

"Sorry," he held his hand up as an apology. "George, you won't get offended if I say you've fared well over the years, will you? Although I see you still like to use a good handful of Brylcreem."

"No, lad. Now look here ... I'm glad you're alive again, but you can't cause all the mayhem you did last time. You're older now. You need to act more mature."

"I'm only a day or so older than the last time I saw you. It might be ten years for you, but it's about two days for me!"

"As painful as it is, he's right, George," I frowned whilst pointing my thumb at the loose cannon, who I feared was packing in the wadding ready to fire off his next ball of destruction.

"Well, Martin, that might be so. But I warn you ... cause anything that will disrupt my life, Jason's, or put the kids in danger, I'll personally kill you. Then I'll cut you up into small pieces so you can't return again!" stated my wife, as she glared at him, causing the loose cannon to shrink back into his seat.

"Another?" I offered, breaking the silence of the now newly re-formed Time Travel Believers' Club, with its original four members back together – just like the Beatles, perhaps. However, unlike Lennon, Martin came back from the dead, and unlike the Beatles, who never re-formed. So, I guess nothing like the Fab-Four, whatsoever.

"I'll get it. Anyone else?" asked Martin, as he prepared to stand.

"Sit down! I put you there because Dawn and Dennis can't see you from their position at the bar. For the moment, we need to keep you hidden." I stated, whilst now realising bringing him to the pub was probably a stupid idea.

"Oh, okay," he grinned, probably pleased he wasn't dipping into his own pocket.

"Darling, I'll go. Dawn will be itching for a quick catch-up. I'll keep them talking."

"Good idea, thanks, sweetheart." I thumbed out a tenner and handed it to her.

"Refill, George?" asked Jenny, as she stepped away from the gang's table, probably relishing the opportunity to escape Martin's company.

"Yes, please, lass."

"Right. So, as I was saying earlier. We have another situation we need to consider—"

"Hi, Martin. You're back then? Mum was only talking about you the other day," interrupted a young man with perfectly coiffured, highlighted hair and a gold cross earring swinging from his left ear. He appeared to be the love child of George Michael and Pat Cash – if that were possible.

"Sorry?" offered Martin, frowning as he looked up at the young man now standing behind Jenny's vacant chair.

This new addition to the conversation was concerning. I thought the only real danger was Dawn and Dennis. Martin hadn't existed in 1977 long enough to make acquaintances. Although, that said, he'd probably managed to impregnate half the female population of Fairfield in those few months, carrying on from knobbing most women in the south of England in 2019, including my ex-wife.

"Oh, hi, Mr Apsley, sorry I didn't recognise the back of your head," chuckled the swinging-earring man. "Craig. I'm Craig," he stated, as he laid his hand on his chest, presumably indicating that his name was Craig and not about to pledge his allegiance to the flag of the United States and bang out a verse of the Star-Spangled Banner.

"Craig Blake. You remember my mum, Nicole? You were the caretaker at school, and you and Mum … well, you know!"

he sniggered and grinned, probably remembering Martin when he was performing his Fairfield shagathon back in the late '70s.

"Oh, yes. Err ... say hello to your mum."

"Yeah, sure. Will do."

Fortunately, Craig swivelled away and joined his mates at a nearby table, after stopping to chat with a woman near the bar.

"Jeeesus! Keeping you under wraps ain't going to be easy. At least he didn't ask how you had stayed so youthful-looking."

"I think, lad, although it's a bit raw, for the moment, you're going to have to get the lad 'ere tightly secured in Don's house."

"Yeah, you're right. Martin, I think you are going to have to lie low for a couple of days until we work out what our next steps are. Certainly, looking up your old conquests will have to be put on ice for the moment."

"Christ, it's just like last time! I didn't exist then, and I don't exist now! Don't tell me I'm going to have to become a bloody caretaker up at the school again."

"Ah, there's a thought—"

"No!"

"You're right. You up there with your mother, Christ no."

"What you on about? That Moore lass is all grown up now, she's not a schoolgirl anymore," questioned George, looking confused.

"Ah, well George, there's another development—"

"So, you're back! Well, you owe me ten years of backpay for your kid's maintenance! I tried to track you down a few times, but someone reckoned you'd pissed off abroad," a voice interrupted me, as had George Michael lookalike a few moments ago when trying to relay my concerns about psycho Colney.

Something suggested this encounter would be a fair few places higher on the Richter Scale of potential Martin-induced disasters than the swinging-earring boy.

14

Danse Macabre

Replacing Craig stood a woman, I guess in her late twenties. I rather rudely outwardly groaned dreading who this was, and what the reference was regarding maintenance payments.

With her hand slapped on the hip of her leather trousers tucked into her slouch boots, loudly chewing gum, her leather jacket barely hiding the lace corset that woefully failed to restrain her ample chest, she was either about to audition for a position as a groupie for Bon Jovi, or the crimped teased hair suggested she intended to apply for the role as Bonnie Tyler's stunt double.

"Well, you back now then?" she questioned, whilst skilfully rolling around the chewing gum in her mouth, dragging on a cigarette, and staring at Martin, who unusually appeared lost for words.

I glanced over to see Jenny still holding court at the bar, entertaining Dawn and Dennis with the latest news on Christopher and Beth. All I needed now was them to join in and the George Michael lookalike lad to stumble back, and we might have to start handing out application forms to join our rather exclusive club.

"I'm Mandy. Remember me?" stated the gum-swilling groupie. Fortunately, unlike Craig, she didn't feel the need to grope her chest when performing introductions. Although it was quite apparent there was a lot to grope, and I shouldn't be surprised that she knew Martin well, based on his shagathon performance of ten years ago.

Martin didn't respond. George looked somewhat surprised at the obvious as Mandy pushed out her chest, which caused the lace bodice to fight tooth and nail to prevent her chest from exploding free – you could say the thin bodice was clinging on by its fingernails.

"Well, you didn't mind these a few years back!" announced Mandy, as she grabbed her chest. "You had a good gawp at them as well if I remember," smirked Mandy, as she stretched her bodice apart after tapping me on the shoulder and nodding downwards, indicating I should have another gawp, as she put it.

Now, I'm not sure that I could instantly remember a set of boobs. But I guess this young lady assumed that if I struggled to recognise her face, the clincher would be a topless exposé to seal the deal. Not sure whether it was her face or her outstretched chest that managed to tweak my memory back to life, but I did recall who this was, and the last time I'd seen her when she'd stood naked in Martin's kitchen.

As the young lady raised her eyebrows whilst exposing the majority of her upper modesty, all I could think of was *"That will do nicely, Sir,"* as Pamela Stephenson had said on that sketch on *Not the Nine O'clock News* – a reference to a piss-take of the American Express Card advert, if I recall correctly.

"Randy Mandy!" blurted Martin with a grin. "How could I forget! You look pretty good, girl!"

"Yeah, that's me. You don't look any different."

"Ah, well, lots of sunshine, and good living has kept my youthful looks in good shape."

"Martin!" I hissed, indicating he should close down this conversation.

Martin glanced at me then back to Randy Mandy. "Err ... look, I can't really talk now. Give us your mobile number, and I'll give you a bell."

"Oh, Christ!" I groaned again.

"What number?" questioned Mandy.

"Err ... your home number."

"Well, I ain't got an office number 'ave I! Anyway, I can't risk you doing a runner again, so you better give me your number. I want your address as well. I'll be going through the courts if you try and shirk your responsibility this time!"

"What?"

"You're a daddy. And you owe me a shit-load of cash. Bringing up a little lad ain't cheap, you know!"

The reference to maintenance pay was now clear. I guess Mandy might struggle to prove Martin was the father of her child. However, whether he was or not, this just added to the mess Martin had created the first time, and I feared the second time was heading to be significantly more calamitous.

"Mandy, Martin has just returned from a works trip—"

"Bloody long one!" she stated, still holding the same pose, hand on hip and chest thrust out.

Martin had taken on a vacant look whilst George continued to do his level best to look anywhere but in her direction.

"Yes, quite." I retrieved a pen from the inside of my tweed, leather-elbow-patched regulation schoolteacher jacket, peeled a beer mat in half, and wrote down my home number, the school number, and Don's address.

"That's my home and work numbers. This is the address Martin will be staying at. I suggest we meet here tomorrow night at six, and we can discuss this situation."

"What you, his dad? It's Martin who owes me, not you."

I held the beer mat up to her. "Mandy, take this, and we'll see you tomorrow."

Mandy reached out to take the beermat, but I pulled it away before she could grab it. "You can have this if you leave us alone tonight … you understand?"

She nodded, still chewing her gum, a feat I seemed to recall that Lyndon B Johnson believed Gerald Ford was incapable of.

Mandy snatched the beermat. "You better be 'ere," she aggressively spat at Martin, whilst multi-tasking – pointing her finger – still chewing her gum – smoking her cigarette – clearly competent and perhaps should consider a career in politics with her sharp mind.

"He will be," I replied on Martin's behalf, who appeared still shell-shocked that the news he was now alive again, or that he was a father, or perhaps a combination of both.

Keeping her finger pointed at Martin, the very act appeared to pin him to his seat. "Well, you don't show, there's a few lads with handy fists live on the same landing as me up at the Broxworth … they'll be paying you a visit." Then, with her threat eloquently delivered, Mandy spun around and sashayed out of the pub.

"Oh, bollocks!" I exclaimed. Why did everything centre around that bloody estate?

"Lad, this *is* a mess. You think she's telling the truth?"

"George, here's yours," stated Jenny, as she gently placed his beer down, carefully positioning the handle so George could pick the mug up with his right hand. Then, quite unceremoniously, she thumped Martin's glass down in front of him, causing the top inch of beer to slop over the side of the glass and slosh onto his lap. "Who's telling the truth? And what's up with him?" asked Jenny, as she returned to her chair.

Martin didn't notice his wet crotch and did not reply to George. Instead, he just repeated the previous action of slugging his pint down in three large gulps.

"Right, before we get interrupted by any other members of the Martin Bretton fan club, I need to bring you up to speed with what's just happened," I turned to Jenny, then looked at George and Martin. "However, more importantly, I need to talk through the other real scary concern, which is significantly more worrying than the possibility that Martin has reproduced."

I brought Jenny quickly up to speed with the two interruptions she'd missed whilst entertaining Dawn and Dennis at the bar. Unsurprisingly, by the looks she shot in Martin's direction, this new information didn't help to soften her view of him. With that information relayed, I moved on to the significantly more concerning situation that there was a very real threat we had a reincarnated dead psychopath wandering around town.

"Lad, I think we might be alright. The local council buried Martin after the police released his body. But I recall Shirley Colney had Paul cremated. I heard on the grapevine that she wouldn't have his body in the ground near her beloved son, David," whispered George, as Jenny and I leant across the table.

The three original members of the Time Travel Believers' Club were now talking in hushed tones, which is something we'd practised over the years. The fourth member, who'd rejoined us, sat chain-smoking, presumably contemplating his newly discovered family.

George continued. "It was rumoured that Colney senior was furious, and although the prison authorities allowed him and Patrick to attend Paul's funeral, the old man refused to go. There was a big splash in the paper at the time, don't you remember?"

"Yeah, now you mention it ... but so what?"

"Darling, what George is saying, is if they cremated Paul, perhaps he couldn't be reborn, so to speak."

"She's got it, lad."

"Well, I don't think it works like that. I'm pretty sure if we nipped up the cemetery, Martin's grave wouldn't be disturbed as if a body had crawled out like a scene from Kill Bill whilst the London Philharmonic Orchestra bangs out their version of Saint-Saëns' Danse Macabre!"

"Kill who?"

"Oh, yeah, sorry ... it's a film in the next century. But look, what I'm saying; I don't think it matters if Paul was buried or burnt."

"Oh, well, if he was burnt, how could he come back to life?" quizzed George. A reasonable question, I mused.

"George, if they buried the bastard, how can he come back to life?"

"Good point, lad," nodded George, pursing his lips as he considered that thought.

"Darling, would you have been buried or cremated in 2019?"

I looked at my wife as she held onto my arm, asking, what was for us, a very straightforward question. However, for a brief moment it seemed a little strange that she should be asking if I knew how my body might have been disposed of in thirty-odd years from now.

"I don't know. I didn't have a will, so I'm not sure what Beth or perhaps Lisa would have sorted out."

"I had a will," stated Martin, whilst he continued to stare vacantly across the lounge bar, smoke drifting from his mouth as he removed his cigarette and stubbed it out in the already heaving ashtray.

The three of us sat back, shifted in our seats, and looked at him whilst awaiting his next sentence. Presumably, he wasn't just informing us that he'd made provision for the division of his wealth on passing and intended to elaborate on his statement.

"I've always had a fear of enclosed spaces. So, after I'd stupidly been potholing with a mate up in the Peak District, I told Caroline that we must make a will. I was explicit in my instructions. When I died, I must be cremated. The fear of waking up in a coffin terrified me." Martin turned to face us. "I made her promise."

"Martin, are you saying that you were definitely cremated when you died the first time?" asked Jenny.

Martin nodded as he lit another cigarette. "Without doubt," he replied whilst blowing a plume of smoke to the already yellowed ceiling.

"Shit! We have to assume Paul Colney is alive again!"

For a few moments, we sat in silence. Jenny's grip on my upper arm tightened, George sipped his beer, and Martin continued to watch the smoke drift from his mouth to the ceiling.

The cloak of doom that engulfed the window-seat table clearly suggested that Paul Colney and Martin Bretton returning from the dead could only spell disaster for all of us.

Part 2

15

Porridge

Junior Prison Officer, Barry Stockhill, marked three crosses on the release form that he'd secured on the clipboard. Then, yawning loudly, as he always did when on the morning shift at Havervalley Prison where he'd worked for eight years, he plucked up his mug of coffee whilst he waited for the first scum-bag who was due for release to appear.

For Barry, discharging prisoners was a part of the job he didn't enjoy. However, it did give him one more opportunity to bully them before they left. If Barry were in charge of the courts, he would issue life sentences to all the low-life scum that entered the penal system irrespective of the crime committed, even if that required taxes to rise to pay for it.

I guess you could say Barry was not a patron or supporter of the Howard League for Penal Reform. But fortunately, for the whole of society, Barry didn't control the courts.

Today's first release was particularly disappointing. Barry knew he could never bully this one because of the powerful family and connections this particular prisoner enjoyed in, and outside, the prison. Although Barry had no particular interest in rehabilitation, and got his kicks from seeing the misery on the incarcerated men's faces, he wasn't stupid enough to make enemies of the wrong sort. So, he knew he'd have to be careful with this one.

Whilst facing the first prisoner presented for release, Barry sported his best sneering face and slid the clipboard and pen across the desk. "Sign where the crosses are," he nonchalantly stated to the prisoner in front of him, flanked by Reg, the senior officer.

"What am I signing for?"

"Your belongings. Presumably, you want them back. If you're illiterate like most of you in here, just mark the form with a cross. You can copy my crosses if that helps," stated Barry, as he did his best to goad the prisoner.

Patrick squiggled illegibly in the three places stated before slinging the clipboard back across the desk.

Barry plucked up the clipboard and studied Patrick's scrawl. "You haven't dated it," he stated, as he turned the board around and tapped his cigarette-stained fingernail to the blank box where Patrick had wiggled the pen over.

Patrick picked up the pen, half tempted to stab it in Barry's eye. However, he thought better of it as he was about to be released after being banged up for ten years. "What's today?"

Barry leant across the desk after plucking that stained fingernail from his nose where he'd presumably been trying to dig at something buried deep in his hooter. "Today, sunshine, is your lucky day … and a very unlucky day for the rest of society. Releasing a Colney back into the community is a dark, dark day."

Patrick gripped the pen and raised it in Barry's direction.

"Go on then … that will keep you banged up in here," goaded Barry, willing Colney to lose his shit.

"Just date it, Colney. Today is Wednesday 9th," stated the senior officer, defusing the stand-off between his junior officer and the prisoner.

Patrick looked at Reg, then complied. Reg was probably the only officer that had respect from the inmates. Although Reg was a filthy screw, he was fair and would deal with the younger, sometimes overzealous, officers when he witnessed them overstepping the mark. On the other hand, Barry was one of the officers who all the inmates would love to shank with a sharpened toothbrush, just as he had with that toe-rag nonce he'd murdered in '79.

Anyway, it didn't matter now. Patrick's old man had persuaded that scum Hooper to confess to the murder during that prison riot in return for a promise of no harm coming to Hooper's teenage son. A threat that Hooper was fully aware old man Colney was more than capable of organising even from inside prison.

Patrick lobbed the board back and smirked at Barry. "That's the last time I'll have to see your ugly mug. Let's hope one of the lifers gets you cornered in the showers—"

"Colney!" boomed Reg, indicating it was a good time to shut his mouth. Patrick grinned at Barry, revelling in the fury of the young guard's face.

The good thing about lifers, the ones that would never be eligible for parole, was they had nothing to lose – so they had power. The screws knew this and took great care when near them. For a lifer, getting caught stabbing a prison officer didn't matter because nothing worse could happen to them even if caught, which was pretty much a certainty. To that group of despots, an additional life term for another murder was no deterrent based on the fact they would never see the outside world again. So, killing a screw would elevate their status – a win-win situation.

"You'll be back, Colney ... you'll be back. Scum like you are born to live in places like this," stated Barry, determined to have the last word.

Patrick held his stare, only moving away as the senior officer tugged his arm. Reg handed Patrick over to Godfrey Stanton, another one of the junior guards, who would escort the prisoner through the various gates to the outside world.

Godfrey was the epitome of the opposite to Barry. He believed all prisoners deserved a chance, clinging to his unwavering faith in the process of rehabilitation.

"Alright, Patrick. All set then, lad?" asked Godfrey, as he helped Patrick through the series of gates and performed the unlocking and relocking procedure.

Patrick nodded but didn't reply whilst he stood as instructed each time they traversed through the sets of gates, waiting for Godfrey to relock each gate they passed through.

Over the years, Patrick had lost count of the conversations he'd had with Godfrey regarding the prison officer's softly-softly approach, advising him that his openly empathetic progressive-minded attitude, although welcome, would not work with the violent nutters in A-Wing.

Godfrey, or *Barrowclough* as he was known, in reference to his similarities to the Prison Officer in the situation comedy, *Porridge*, was simply too soft for the job. Patrick despised the way some of the nutters in A-Wing treated *Barrowclough,* so he'd tried to help the nervous guard toughen up on many occasions. Although his efforts were in vain, it had brought home to Patrick how he himself had changed. Just by the act of wanting to help another human being, especially as Godfrey was a filthy screw, proved Patrick had changed for the better.

"Right, Patrick. This is it, the outside world, my lad."

Patrick turned to look back into the prison and then at Godfrey. "Remember, *Barrowclough* ... don't let the bastards grind you down. That goes for those nutters in A-Wing, and tossers like Barry Stockhill."

"Don't you worry about me, lad. Just make sure you don't come back here."

Patrick sucked in his breath like any self-respecting rogue builder who was just about to deliver an outrageously inflated quote for block-paving your drive. "Back here? Never! I'm never coming back here. Or anywhere like it."

The hefty wooden door slammed behind him, and the lock engaged with the rattle of a heavy bunch of keys. The difference this time, to every time he'd previously heard those keys turn, he was being locked out – not in.

Patrick dropped his bag to the wet pavement before lighting a cigarette whilst contemplating his plan. Depressingly, no one was here to meet him. No wife or girlfriend to rush up and hug him because Jess hadn't stayed faithful. He'd heard she married some schoolteacher. Also, his mother had pissed off to Spain years ago. So, the plan for the moment was to catch the bus back to Fairfield and, before reporting into his appointed hostel, check-in with a few of his old man's contacts who would get him set up and back on his feet.

Plucking up his bag that contained his few meagre possessions, Patrick strode off to the bus station, following the map that had duly been provided upon release. He stepped into the alley that ran down the left side of the prison, which the map indicated would lead to the main road into the local town and ultimately the bus terminal.

Some years ago, Patrick had made decisions about his life. Of course, at that point, he didn't know his release would come much earlier than anticipated. However, now in his mid-thirties, he knew he would have to divert from the life he'd previously led and been brought up to follow.

His old man would probably never be released; Paul, his identical twin, and David, his younger brother, were dead. The last remaining brother, Andrew, would very soon be taking his place in that prison, and Patrick suspected his little brother would end up in *Stir* serving a significantly longer stretch than he had. So, with no family left, Patrick had some radical plans to change his life, and he felt good about it.

The ten years inside had taught Patrick that there had to be something better than this, and he would give the straight and narrow a chance. So, when he'd won his appeal case on Monday, the decision he'd made was a simple one – get back on his feet, shore up his finances, then leave Fairfield behind.

Although he now had a nine-year-old daughter who he'd never met, Patrick had decided to leave that particular scab unpicked. Jess had married and moved on, and although he loved her, he wouldn't try and wriggle his way back in – no, it was time to start taking the right path – forgetting Jess and his daughter was the first step on his way to redemption.

If his plans panned out right, before Christmas, he'd be knocking on Mum's front door in Spain. His loosely contrived plans included opening a nightclub, enjoying the sunshine, and start living life. He expected to be on track by the beginning of next year.

The single-track alley, which cut down the side of the prison walls, appeared under attack from the brambles that assaulted and engulfed the chain-linked fence which separated the lane from a derelict, corrugated roofed warehouse. Patrick assumed the only people who used the alley were released prisoners like himself. The high oppressive wall to his left, and the triffid-like fencing to the right, afforded the lane an uninviting aura that would understandably result in the lane being underused by anyone other than ex-cons.

Enjoying the fresh air and a cigarette, although difficult to put those two thoughts in the same sentence, Patrick almost skipped down the alley, marvelling at his freedom whilst ducking and weaving his way along, brushing the brambles away from his face with his bag.

As he ducked a large thorny bramble, he caught sight of movement out of the corner of his right eye. Halting his jaunt and swivelling around, Patrick dropped his bag, his cigarette sagging in his lips as he gawped at what had caused the sudden movement. Rooted to the broken weed-infested tarmac, Patrick could only watch as his assailant swung the nail-encrusted piece of wood towards him. The force of the blow, which thumped into the side of his head, caused his boots to momentarily leave the ground as his body collided with the high concrete prison wall.

Patrick slumped, his right eye sightless as the socket filled with blood and flapping skin. The noise of his skull cracking filled his head as a heavy object thumped down. Patrick could feel his skull pushing on his brain as another and another repeated whack crushed his head.

He thought of Jess and Faith, his ex-girlfriend and the daughter he'd never met, and the bright sunlight that Spain always offered. He imagined the nightclub, packed with paying revellers, that he now guessed he would never own.

Before his brain surrendered to the fragments of his skull as they embedded their way in, he thought of his dead brothers, David and Paul.

16

Weapons Of Mass Destruction

"Right, you useless mob of delinquent, good-for-nothing wasters," announced DS Danny Farham, as he marched to the front of the CID office.

The team ignored him.

"Listen up!" he bellowed, as the chatter hadn't abated after delivering his earlier engaging opening line. Danny had learnt his motivational team-engaging skills from copying his previous DI, who always believed derogatory put-downs would get the best from his team.

"What, Dawson?" asked Danny, as he noticed the detective constable had raised his hand like a four-year-old in primary school desperate to get the schoolteacher's attention.

"Sarge, are we still on forced overtime through the weekend? Just that I'd promised to take the missus up to Margate for the day. She's a bit put out, to say the least."

"Shut it, *Fawlty*," called out DS Taylor. Dawson was known in the office as *Fawlty* due to his ever-controlling wife, Sybil, who would often arrive at the station demanding that her husband was to come home because his dinner was ready and on the table.

"After this morning's discovery, what do you think?" replied Danny. "Right, eyes forward," he commanded, whilst Dawson presumably shat himself about informing his tyrannical missus that the seaside trip was off.

"Four-minute warning. Confirm. Four-minute warning. Over," buzzed through a police issue radio lying on one of the desks.

DC Reeves, closest to the radio, which everyone was staring at, plucked it from the desk before returning the call sign. "Received. Over."

"Confirm. Bristols is on her way up. Over," came the reply.

The reference to the four-minute warning wasn't aligned to the public alert system conceived by the British Government during the Cold War, but rather the time it took for DI French to traverse her way from the car park to the CID offices.

All ten DCs slid their backsides off the tables and removed their feet from the chairs due to it being a particular bugbear with DI French. The foul mood she'd been in for days suggested it was not the time to piss her off.

DI French's station nickname had morphed over time. Now affectionately known as *Bristols*. Many had assumed it was cockney slang referring to the DI's hefty frontage, but it was so much more complicated.

Bristols bustled her way into the briefing room. If a violent clap of thunder could walk, this was it.

The DI never wasted time with pleasantries, introductions or checking in how everyone was feeling. After she retired in the early 2000s, she did wonder how the hell the *snowflake* generation got anything done and would despair at the constant counselling and pandering that everyone needed. As far as she was concerned, everyone had lost their balls. DI Heather French was a no-nonsense kind of woman who loathed shoddy police work and wouldn't tolerate self-pity.

The DI boomed out, before reaching the front of the now hushed room, "As we all know, Susan Kane is the victim discovered by Uniform this morning up at the Broxworth Estate. Susan Kane, a fifty-one-year-old woman, should be well known to all of us. That said, just because some low-life piece of shite has decided to rid the world of the perennial pain in the backside that we all know her to be, it doesn't mean we don't give it the attention that any murder victim deserves." The DI spun around as she reached the front of the room, slapping her hands on her hips and surveying her troops. "Danny, take us through what we know so far."

DS Danny Farham, or *Bergerac* as he was known by, the name acquired due to his childhood spent on the island of Jersey, nodded then faced the room. "Right. So, Uniform discovered Susan's body just after eight this morning. The rent collector, called," Danny consulted his notebook before looking up and continuing. "Err …Tony Powell, peered through the window when he couldn't get an answer after knocking. He said it was quite common for Susan to avoid answering the door to him, so he'd started turning up on different days to catch her out."

Danny hesitated as the DI narrowed her eyes at him, a non-verbal instruction to stop waffling.

"Anyway, when he peered through the window, he noticed Susan lying on the kitchen floor. His initial thought was she was just hiding and trying to avoid paying that week's rent. Uniform forced entry at eight-twenty and discovered her body. It appears the cause of death was the result of trauma to the head, namely multiple blows from a blunt instrument. We've recovered a heavily bloodstained rolling pin which the boys from Scene Investigations are checking for dabs as we speak."

"No loss there! No one's going to miss that old slag," called out DC Reeves, who instantly regretted the comment as the DI delivered him one of her famous cold stares.

The DI didn't need to speak to register her displeasure with the team. Reeves knew this better than most and wished at times he could train his brain to keep his overactive mouth shut.

DS Farham shot the DI a look and, when satisfied with the nod received, he continued. "Although we'll have to wait for the postmortem results, the force used by her assailant was significant. Due to her head resembling an Italian flatbread dish similar to that which gets served up at Pizzaland that any Mutant Turtle would mistake as lunch, it's safe to assume she was struck multiple times." Danny nodded to the DI, indicating he'd finished, whilst a few sniggers reverberated around the room at the sergeant's description of the crime scene.

"Well?" boomed the DI, frustrated that her team just seemed to gawp at her.

"Guv. I've got Uniform on door to door. Not that I expect any results from that because, as we all know, no one on the Broxworth talks to us," stated Danny.

Reeves jumped in next. "I've put the word out for a couple of snouts I know. I'm meeting them up at the Beehive Pub later."

"Good. Apply some pressure. I want swift answers," stated the DI whilst pointing at the young DC.

"You got it, Guv," replied Reeves, chuffed that he seemed to have received a positive comment from the difficult to please DI.

"Guv, Andrew Colney lived with Susan when Shirley pissed off to Spain in the late '70s. There's got to be a connection there. The fact we've nicked him, and he was up in court on Monday is too much of a coincidence," added Taylor.

"Good work, Taylor. And you know what I think about coincidences," replied the DI, now starting to relax, pleased her team seemed to have started their jobs and not sitting around on their backsides waiting for instructions. "Who was Susan's latest fella?"

"Ma'am," called out DC Adele Megson. "Carl Bowen seems to be in the frame at the moment. We've done him a few times for possession, and he's got a conviction for ABH when he gave his last girlfriend a pasting."

"Bowen! Christ, that low-life. I nicked him in the '70s," replied the DI, as she settled her backside on the table. The very act caused a few officers to exchange glances.

"He's had more skirt than Richard Burton. He must be scraping the bottom of the barrel if all he can get is Susan!" threw in Taylor.

"Ma'am," I'll take *Fawlty* with me and pick him up," replied Megson.

"Yes, let's have him in. He's got to be our prime suspect," instructed the DI whilst ignoring the use of Dawson's nickname.

As much as she hated the unprofessional use of these idiotic names, she knew she couldn't change the silly banter all officers seemed to enjoy. Pushing water uphill would be a significantly more manageable task. And, right at this point in time, she had far too many unpalatable events happening on her patch to concern herself about putting a few officers straight regarding the use of silly station banter.

"Right. Reeves and Taylor, pick up with Uniform. I want to know who's seen or heard what up at that ruddy estate. If you need to put the squeeze on Susan's neighbours, do so." Although as soon as she'd said it, she knew she'd just given Laurel and Hardy licence to kill – a shudder zipped down her spine at the thought.

"Paddon and Suggett, we need to know the whereabouts of Shirley Colney. The results from the postmortem on Susan won't be ready until tomorrow. However, the pathologist is suggesting Susan died over thirty-six hours ago. Shirley Colney arrived back on Monday, so she could have been back in the country when some nutter smashed Susan's body to a pulp."

"On it, Guv," called out both officers. They looked pleased with the task assigned. Within the Fairfield Police Station community, chasing down a Colney was regarded as a pleasurable blood sport. Huge kudos was assigned to any officer who could slap handcuffs on any member of that family.

"Ma'am. Weren't those two best friends? I heard they called each other sisters. Shirley wouldn't kill Susan if they were close," said Megson, as she held out her notebook – the only officer taking notes during the whole briefing.

"Cain and Abel," offered DC Brown. Or *Paddington* as he was known in reference to the small, orphaned bear's adopted family's surname.

"They were brothers you, spazzo!" called out Taylor.

"Alright then, King Lear," replied Brown, knowing full well the uncultured dross he had to work with, day in and day out, would have no idea of what he was talking about. DC Steven Brown, who was now close to retirement, really couldn't wait to leave. He enjoyed the arts, culture and reading books, and throughout his career wondered how he'd ended up as a police officer – a job so far removed from any of his interests.

"He's a bloke as well! We're talking skirt on skirt!" bawled Taylor.

"Yes, King Lear … Goneril and Regan … there you go, you thick arse!" retorted Brown, showing his frustration at the lack of culture his colleagues displayed.

"Oooo. Get the thespian officer over here. I can see you prancing about the stage in a pair of tights!" replied Reeves, causing a ripple of laughter throughout the room.

"That's enough!" bellowed the DI. "Megson, you're too young to remember the terror the Colney family reigned on this town. Shirley Colney may well have regarded Susan Kane as a sister. However, all of you be clear … Shirley Colney is capable of anything. So, do *not* underestimate this woman."

"Guv," replied Megson, or *Gladys* as she was known to the team. The nickname applied due to being Welsh and referring to the tannoy-squawking character in the TV sitcom Hi-de-Hi. Although she felt chastised, *Gladys* didn't know that the DI deemed her the only capable DC on the team.

"Guv?" called out Reeves. "What about Patrick Colney? They released him on Monday … should we pick him up as well?"

Danny shook his head. "Patrick was released this morning from Havervalley Prison. He couldn't have done it."

"Let's pick him up anyway. There are too many coincidences for my liking. Benson and Machin, pick him up and have a word. I don't like Colneys on the loose on my patch, so I want to know the evil git's plans. Also, he must have known Susan Kane pretty well, so dig a bit into what that relationship was like and see what you can get out of him. Turn him upside down and give him a damn good shake!"

"Pleasure Guv, nothing I like better than an opportunity to rattle his cage," called out DC Mell Machin from the back of the room.

The DI stood and thumped her hands on her hips. "Right. Let's get on with it. Remember no time off until we've nailed the git. I want quick results before the Super starts breathing down my neck!" For a brief moment, no one moved. "Oi, stop prancing around your handbags and go nick someone!"

"Guv," came a chorus from the DCs before the sound of scraping chairs and a melee of chatter filled the office as they piled through the door.

DI French shook her head as Taylor and Reeves bumped into each other as they simultaneously attempted to squeeze through the gap. "Christ!" she muttered, whilst watching her two dippy DCs, as they tried to fathom how to walk through a doorway. If it wasn't for DS Farham and DC Megson, the DI feared her team wouldn't achieve anything.

Without her two competent officers, the rest of her team would be incapable of controlling crime, leaving Fairfield to resemble Chicago in the 1930s.

"Danny, my office," she boomed, as she spun on her heels, unable to watch Laurel and Hardy as they fell through the gap, now finally working out how to leave the office.

"Guv?" nodded the DS before following the DI into her office, closing the door and steadying the clanging Venetian blinds.

DI French slumped into her seat and nodded to Danny to sit.

"Guv, you alright?"

The DI huffed whilst shaking her head. "Danny, how long have we known each other?"

"Guv?"

DI French just raised her eyebrows.

"Oh, ten years … ish, I guess."

"And in those ten years, would you say that I've always acted like a normal human being?" The DI spotted Danny smirk, so rephrased. "Alright, I'm not a nutter?"

"Course not, Guv. Look, you alright?"

DI French leant forward, resting her arms on her orderly desk. The only desk in the whole of CID that didn't look as if the whole place resembled a crime scene following a recent burglary. "Danny, something is going on and, to be honest with you, I'm not sure I can get my head around it." She opened up a manila file, took hold of the top sheet and passed it over to Danny, laying it on her desk so he could read it. She nodded at the page.

Danny leant forward and read the report.

"See my point?" she stated before he looked up.

Danny glanced up and shook his head. "I don't understand, Guv."

"Neither do I. But I want to know how a motor discovered on Monday morning wedged between a bus shelter and an oak tree up near the Broxworth can be the very same motor Paul Colney died in. That piece of scum, fortunately for the rest of humanity, died ten years ago!"

"What's this got to do with Susan Kane?"

"Everything and nothing. Danny, I don't know. But I just have a hunch that whoever was driving that car discovered on Monday morning is connected to the murder of Susan Kane."

17

Nessun Dorma

Jenny seemed a bit snippy with me on Wednesday morning after I'd informed her that my twelve-year-old ex-wife had started at the school after being expelled from the Howlett School following her mucky-photo scam. I guess Jenny's reaction was understandable. Although the circumstances were somewhat odd, bearing in mind that Lisa was my ex-wife, and our marriage was in the future – a future that would no longer happen.

Martin's reaction concerned me. Based on the fact that thirty years from now, he and Lisa were to have a *thing*. However, in this life, she was a twelve-year-old schoolgirl with a propensity to resort to the use of blackmail to fund her purchases at the school tuck shop. So, Martin thinking it was hilarious was not the reaction I was looking for.

Although he'd completed that stint ten years ago as the stand-in caretaker at the school, it hadn't turned to total shit as I'd thought it might at the time. So, with Martin once again back from the dead, I thought I'd get him to take over from Mr Trosh when he retired, irrespective that his mother was now the school secretary and Martin had said she was gorgeous.

George had warned me to keep my distance from Lisa at school. He felt it would be better if I avoided teaching her, and under no circumstances was I to engage in conversation with the young lass.

I considered that George's instruction could be somewhat difficult to obey because the Prince of Darkness had asked me to keep a close eye on the little madam, plus I would be teaching her maths. I imagined she was already quite capable at that subject, based on her calculating nature and business head she developed at such a young age when she'd concocted her mucky-photo extortion racket at the Howlett School.

This week had not started well. Not only had we lost Don, but I'd gained a half-sister in the shape of the evil Shirley, re-met my ex-wife, had Martin back to contend with – who also appears now to have a ten-year-old child – and to top it all off, there was the real possibility that Paul Colney, rapist-cum-murderer and generally nasty piece of work, had risen from the dead. I was living my own version of a particularly terrifying horror movie – *A Nightmare in Fairfield* – starring Paul Colney wearing the leather-bladed glove and fedora hat.

The Time Travel Believers' Club newly formed quartet had failed to reach a consensus as to whether it was believed Paul Colney had returned. In our favour was the fact that over forty-eight hours had elapsed since Martin had re-materialised, so if that was the same for Paul, then it was slightly amazing he hadn't caused utter mayhem in that period of time that would surely have slapped him on the headlines of the local evening television news. However, as George had said, we'd better have our wits about us.

On Wednesday afternoon my worst nightmare started to unfold, and it had nothing to do with Freddie Kruger or his stunt double.

"Mr Apsley … yoo-hoo, Mr Apsley," called out Mrs Trosh, as she stuck her head out of the school office door whilst clinging to the door frame.

I'd just whizzed past as I hot-footed my way to my afternoon classes, following a difficult lunch break that involved pondering how Martin and I were going to deal with Randy Mandy when we caught up with her later this evening to discuss Martin's newly discovered offspring.

It had occurred to me that there was a real possibility that Martin had many children across several generations. Now he was here in 1987, I expect he will restart his re-insemination of the unsuspecting female population of Fairfield like some randy version of Dr Who.

"Hang on, Mrs Trosh," I replied, as I barrelled back through the swing doors from the Assembly Hall.

"Price!" I bellowed at a fifth-former who'd just snuck past me as I'd turned.

"Price. Stop!" this time I boomed, so that my voice would carry through the headphones of his Sony Walkman.

Price complied with the given directive, turned and grimaced as I held out the palm of my hand, clicking my fingers as I waited for him to comply.

"Sir?" stated Price, almost pleading.

"You know the drill. Hand it over."

Price and every other pupil knew the drill and the penalties for being caught in the school corridors wearing a Walkman. The first two offences resulted in the cassette tape being confiscated for one week; after that, a permanent impounding sanction would be applied.

"Oh, please, sir?" begged Price, in a whining voice.

I beckoned my hand, showing no emotion as the poor lad ejected the tape from his Walkman before handing over his C90 Maxwell tape – it was the third time – the cassette was doomed.

Based on the fact that Price wore his hair styled on Morten Harket or Patrick Swayze, I suspected this tape had a fifty per cent chance of not being to my liking. Fortunately, Dirty Dancing had not sullied our shores yet, and I was relieved to see *'Take On Me'* scrawled across the label of the cassette tape now thrust into my hand.

"Oh, those infernal machines!" stated Mrs Trosh, as she witnessed the confiscation of said tape. "I really don't know what's the matter with today's youth with their headphones stuck on their heads. It can't be good for their ears, and what about talking to each other. Those damn machines will ruin the art of conversation, you'll see!"

"You wait until they've all got mobile phones! Then the art of conversation really will be over!" I chuckled whilst tapping the confiscated cassette on my knuckles.

"What?" she questioned.

"Oh, don't worry." I dismissed her question, not wanting to explain the future of smartphone technology. "Sorry, what was it you wanted?"

"Oh, yes, Mr Elkinson would like a word," she called out as the doors swung back.

I'd known and worked with Mrs Trosh for ten years, and I knew when she was bursting at the seams, ready to engulf me with gossip. I'd learnt that it was always a good policy to listen and dig deep, as her intelligence gathering skills would put most of the GCHQ operatives to shame. I half expected she was the brains behind U.N.C.L.E, providing all the necessary information to Mr Waverly so that Napoleon Solo and Illya Kuryakin could keep the world safe.

Although I had to cut through the crap, so to speak, there were always snippets of intelligence that were vital to keep me ahead of the game. So, I shot back through the doors, raising my eyebrows, awaiting Mrs Trosh to prepare for her gossip pour.

She didn't fail me.

Mrs Trosh completed her signature furtive sideways glance, then beckoned me closer. "Two police officers are in Mr Elkinson's study! Prior to Mr Elkinson returning from lunch, I tried to ascertain what they are here for." She performed another quick sideways glance before continuing. "Unfortunately, they were very tight-lipped," she whispered, then had a quick glance at PoD's office door. "Although they did let slip that they require a few minutes of *your* time!" she stated, whilst jabbing a finger accusingly at my chest. "I was just about to come and find you when Mr Elkinson returned and ushered them into his study. You're not in any kind of bother, are you?"

"Two police officers?"

"Yes!"

"And they want to talk to *me*?"

"Yes!"

"Oh, Christ!" I muttered.

"Mr Apsley, are you quite alright?" she asked, still in a hushed tone. "I must say, you're now looking a little peaky."

"Err ... yes, yes. No, I'm fine. Look, I'd better see what they want," I muttered before tentatively stepping towards PoD's door, now half expecting that Lisa's money-making scheme had come to the attention of the police after one of the poor unfortunate boys' parents' had made an official complaint. Now I would probably have to have another meeting with my ex-mother-in-law and, God forbid, Lisa's father.

Not wishing to miss out, Mrs Trosh jumped in front of me – she was quite athletic for a lady in her seventies. Then, grabbing the door handle, she stepped into PoD's office, announcing my arrival like a herald at a state function.

"Mr Apsley," she stated, waving her hand forward, indicating I should enter. As expected, she hovered, trying to grab any snippets of information.

As I stepped past our inquisitive secretary there was no trumpeter's fanfare announcing my arrival. However, my heart sank as I surveyed the room.

Based on the fact that both officers were plain-clothed I surmised they were from CID. Either that, or the Hertfordshire Constabulary officers were now enjoying dress-down Wednesdays. I guess the latter was unlikely, so I assumed they were the former. Now, I'm no expert on the level of officer required to investigate specific crimes. However, I suspected that a DI would not be investigating mucky-picture taking, along with playground bullying – which might suggest their visit had nothing to do with a twelve-year-old girl who'd recently engaged in the art of blackmailing and racketeering.

"Ah, Jason," stated the Prince of Darkness as he rose from his chair, his mouth slowly climbing into a wolfish grin. "These two officers require a quick word. I'll leave you to it," he stated before gliding across the room, closing the door after he'd swished out Mrs Trosh.

"Mr Apsley. We have a habit of meeting, don't we," stated DI French, as she gestured with her hand, indicating I should sit in the now vacant vampire's chair.

As I gingerly traversed around the desk, I could only assume that events of the past two days had escalated, and somehow Paul Colney had re-emerged. However, if that were to be the case, this conversation was about to zip off on a bizarre tangent because Frenchie and I would be discussing the crimes and misdemeanours of a ghost.

Grinning like a pillock, I raised my eyebrows in a questioning style whilst trying to impersonate someone whose mouth wouldn't melt butter. I knew I had to play it cool and say as little as possible. Otherwise, that mental institution that has undoubtedly had a padded cell with my name on it reserved for the last ten years would, at last, have its designated occupier.

"Mr Apsley. This is DS Farham," stated Frenchie, as she nodded his way whilst shuffling forward in her chair, presumably to apply her most intimidating posture. I could have saved her the trouble because in all encounters over the years, Frenchie had always afforded the upper hand.

"The conversation we had on your doorstep a few weeks ago. You remember that?"

I nodded, keeping my hands clasped and slapping on my best poker face I could muster up. Although fully aware that wasn't particularly good based on the fact that my ten-year-old daughter, Beth, regularly thrashed me at Snap, and it was rare that I could even achieve better than last place when playing the Happy Families card game.

"Okay. Look, I'm not sure where to start, and this might sound a little odd."

"I doubt it!" I chuckled, but only for a moment. Frenchie's expression suggested that chuckling wouldn't be considered good-form in this situation.

I quickly reapplied my lacklustre poker-face when Frenchie raised her eyebrows whilst shifting her sizeable frontage, which seemed to have held firm over the years and I suspected was her most valuable weapon when pinning armed blaggers to the floor.

"The information regarding the passengers in that car has always been a mystery to me. We both know that you know the answer to that puzzle. To be honest, Mr Apsley, I've been quite content for that mystery to stay that way ... a mystery. However, circumstances have now changed."

"Oh?"

As was quite often in tight situations, my Adam's apple let me down as I gulped loudly whilst the pesky thyroid cartilage shot up and down, highlighting I was nervous. As many of the pupils regularly performed, I considered raising my hand and asking to be excused to use the little boys' room, as I now felt the urgent need to pee.

"Oh indeed, Mr Apsley. You will tell me who was in that car, and you'll tell me now. Otherwise, I will arrest you for perverting the course of justice ... am I clear?"

'Bollocks ... this time, matey, you're royally fucked.'

I was inclined to agree with my mind talk. Whilst my Adam's apple performed its bouncing routine and trying to gather up some saliva in my desert-dry mouth, I desperately tried to conjure up an escape route from this situation. If I provided the Detective Inspector with the facts, I would have to get Frenchie and her muted sergeant to sign up to the Time Travel Believers' Club, and I thought that might be somewhat tricky.

"Well!"

"Um ..." I stated, then winced, as I still hadn't thought of a believable answer.

"Mr Apsley, you have precisely two seconds to start talking. I'm conducting a murder investigation, and my patience is running thin!"

"Murder?"

"Yes, murder. And God knows how, but the events of that February evening back in 1977 when that yellow Cortina ploughed through that bus stop killing Paul Colney has something to do with it. So, start talking!"

'You're going to have to wing it, sunshine. Otherwise, the handcuffs are coming out, and I don't think they'll be the pink fluffy ones Jenny keeps in the bedside cabinet drawer!'

"Oh, bollocks," I huffed, although I intended that to be a silent response to my mind talk.

Frenchie raised her eyebrows. I guess my two seconds were up.

I decided to wing it – where that would lead to, hell knows, either a cell for the night, or a straitjacket, or perhaps both.

"Martin Bretton was driving the car."

The muted sergeant flipped open his pocketbook. "Can you repeat that, sir?"

"Martin Bretton."

"Two t's?" he questioned, as he scribbled the name down.

"Yes."

There I'd said it. My loose-cannon ex-employee from 2019 was now officially here in the past.

That loose cannon, ex-employee's name, would later today enter the Police National Data Base, and I suspected my world would now be the worse for it.

"Go on," stated Frenchie.

I took a huge breath, slowly releasing it through my nose, akin to an opera tenor preparing to bang out the final act in Puccini's Turandot. Somewhat fitting, perhaps, as Calef bangs out his aria, knowing beheading was the price of failure. Although I thought it unlikely Frenchie would behead me for failing to answer her question, but a night in the cells was definitely on the cards.

"Mr Apsley?"

"It's a long story ... kind of complicated," I nervously replied, adding a stupid grin to my face.

She raised her eyebrows at me, then nodded at her sergeant, indicating he needed to be ready to write.

"I planned to pick up my daughter, Jess Redmond, who at the time lived on the Broxworth Estate." I felt this wasn't the time to introduce *other* Jason to the conversation, as that really would be too much for Frenchie to take in.

"Jess Redmond?" repeated the sergeant as he scribbled her name.

"Yes. Although she's married now, so, her name is Poole."

"As in swimming?"

"No, as in Dorset, just along the coast from Christchurch and Bournemouth."

"Australia?"

"What? No, Christchurch is in New Zealand?"

"Poole! P-O-O-L-E!" spat Frenchie at her sergeant, who, now suitably chastised, bowed his head and continued to scribble in his book.

I ploughed on with the basic facts, praying it would be enough for Frenchie and her limited-vocabulary geography-challenged sidekick to bugger off.

"Martin, a friend at the time, drove my car up to the estate and waited whilst I nipped up to her flat, then the plan was to go back to my house to have dinner."

"And how does Paul Colney fit into this? Were you inviting him back for your candle-lit supper as well?" fired back Frenchie with a hint of sarcasm.

"Err ... no."

Frenchie stared at me, waiting for me to continue. For some reason, this policewoman always made me nervous.

"He, Paul Colney that is, jumped into the car as we were about to drive off. He held a sawn-off shotgun to Martin's privates—"

Sergeant Farham sucked in his breath, winced and squirmed in his seat, tightly crossing his legs. Both Frenchie and I glanced at him before I continued.

"Martin drove down Coldhams Lane as instructed, but he had to swerve to avoid some kids on bikes, causing him to crash … I think you know the rest."

"Yes, I do. But why was Paul Colney pointing a gun and instructing Martin to drive? And where to?"

"I don't know?" I lied.

"So, let me get this straight. This Martin chap hits the tree, killing him and Paul Colney. Then you and your daughter decide to get out and casually toddle off home after failing to report the accident that killed two, destroyed a piece of council-owned street furniture, and left *your* car with its bonnet wrapped around a tree? Is that correct?" Frenchie had shifted further forward in her seat, her demeanour appearing to become quite aggressive.

"Well … kind of … ish. Yes, I guess that's about the size of it."

"Why? Why would you leave the scene of the accident? Presumably, you might have needed medical attention."

"I wanted to distance myself from Paul Colney. Also, that car was originally mine, but Martin had purchased it from the second-hand car dealership I'd sold it to."

"Okay. I understand not wanting to be associated with Paul Colney. However, that yellow Cortina, index number—" she halted and glanced at her sergeant.

"Guv?"

"Index number?"

"Oh yeah, sorry, Guv." After thumbing back a couple of pages in his notebook, he read out the licence plate of *other* Jason's old car. The vehicle that I now presumed was a time machine. Should I tell Frenchie that? Hmmm ... no, probably not.

"So, the Ford Cortina, licence plate KDP472N, was owned by Coreys Mill Motors. Martin Bretton was never the registered keeper. And, if Mr Bretton was a friend of yours, why did you never identify him? Why was he buried after no one on this planet knew who he was?"

I nervously grinned whilst Frenchie's questions hung in the air.

Frenchie nodded at the sergeant, who pulled out an envelope from his faux-leather folder that appeared more suited to be tucked under the arm of an estate agent. DS Farham placed two pictures on the desk in front of me before rezipping his folder and plucking up his pen.

"So, Mr Apsley. I have you and your daughter at the scene of a fatal accident. I have you as the last private owner of that vehicle. I have that very same car found parked up on Coldhams Lane on Monday morning, ten years after it was written-off. I have a mysterious man called Martin Bretton as the driver of that car in 1977, who owned some very odd tattoos!" She pointed at the two photographs her sergeant had just placed in front of me.

"What d'you mean, that car found on Monday?" I had to act surprised, as I knew that was the purpose of her statement. Frenchie believed I knew the car was back, but to preserve some semblance of sanity in the room, I had to look surprised.

Frenchie ignored my question, instead, nodding at the pictures of Martin's tattoos that showed one of his forearms – *'Caroline 27 May 2012'* inked in black, and one on his calf, *'20 league titles-Champions 2013'* inked below the badge of Manchester United Football Club.

"Mr Apsley, I want to know everything about your friend, Martin Bretton."

18

Blue Peter Appeal

"Can't you read the sign, dickhead?" questioned Adam, as he stepped back into the reception area, whilst adjusting his trouser fly with one hand and digging in his nose with his other. His index finger fished around up his nasal passage with such intensity the shape of his nostril distorted, affording the impression it would burst from his upper nasal passage, à la John Hurt *Alien* style.

"There!" pointed Adam, the house trustee. "The fucking sign says ring once! Not keep your fucking finger on it!"

Adam eyed up the bell-abuser. It was always good to assess who was staying and what threat they might be. However, as Adam was tall enough to earn a place in the Harlem Globe Trotters team, and his girth making Geoff Capes seem anorexic in comparison, none of the ex-cons that passed through this particularly squalid shit-hole hostel bothered him.

This particular reprobate who'd landed resembled the vast majority of the hopeless wasters who rolled up on their first day at the halfway house. Most of them appeared shell shocked after experiencing a few hours of freedom, and he'd known many 'lifers' who'd wished to return to the sanctuary of their three-metre-square cell because the outside world was too difficult to cope with.

The newest edition, who stood in front of him after abusing the bell, worryingly seemed to ooze confidence. Adam thought he would have to keep a watchful eye on this one. It was difficult to judge his age – prison does that to a man – also, the wild style-lacking beard camouflaged his face. However, Adam reckoned he was between his mid-twenties and mid-thirties, and he looked capable of handling himself.

Adam addressed his guest after removing his finger from his nasal cavity, scratching his arse and sniffing loudly. "Name?"

"Patrick Colney," stated his guest, as he picked up the autumn edition of *'For Him Magazine',* which lay on the heavily ring-stained, chipped, red Formica reception counter, along with some other well-thumbed publications which he was more familiar with. His eyes hovered on the front cover of *Knave,* specifically the nude woman who reminded him of Jessica Redmond.

Adam scrutinised his guest, who continued to eyeball the naked girl on the magazine's cover. "Colney?"

"Yup."

"Patrick Colney?" questioned Adam, dreading that he had heard correctly.

Dropping the magazine, his new guest looked up at Adam. "You deaf, as well as being a big ginger twat?"

Adam instantly realised he would have to ensure the rest of this brief encounter was slightly more engaging and now thoroughly regretted the earlier dickhead comment. If Patrick Colney wanted to keep his finger on the bell, that was fine by him. Thumbing through the sheets of paper on his desk, Adam located the one he required.

"Patrick Colney. Here we go," he chuckled. "Ten years, that's a hefty stretch. But I'm here to help you readjust, okay?" nervously stammered Adam, delivered with a slightly more engaging tone.

The new guest didn't utter a word as he continued to stare down Adam-The-Man-Mountain-Henderson. Or was that stare up?

The fact that Colney had to stare upwards was irrelevant. Colney had the upper hand, and Adam knew it. Whilst performing his well-practised, boxer-style pre-fight stare down, Colney smirked. Adam thought he might shit himself, even though he'd just had a turnout.

Adam rarely experienced intimidation and now wished he'd had more than a perfunctory glance at today's admissions list. If he'd have known a Colney was on his way, he would have worked at getting him relocated to the accommodation over in Luton. Adam managed a tight smile, which was enough to break the eye-hold his new guest seemed to have placed upon him.

"Room eight. Top of the stairs, first on the left. Part of your parole conditions states a curfew required between ten and six. Not that I'm here to monitor that, but be aware parole officers do check, okay?"

Colney nodded as he swiped the key Henderson had placed on the counter before grabbing the strings of his blue duffel bag and bolting up the bare, heavily-worn wooden staircase to the first floor.

"Bollocks," muttered Adam. He'd known Patrick was being released and knew he should've checked which hostel the authorities planned to assign him to. Now, due to his sloppiness, he had a Colney under his roof, which was not a pleasant thought. The only positive he could conjure up was, out of the four brothers, it was widely believed Patrick was the only sane one. Andrew was on remand and the other two, Paul and David, were dead.

Adam stuck his finger back up his nose and momentarily felt relief as his index finger, at last, achieved said task allowing him to wipe his finger down his jeans and refrain from having to snort every ten seconds.

~

Room eight was as expected – housing a tubular-steel single bed, a once-white melamine wardrobe that now sported a yellow film of grime, and a small honey-pine bedside table with a cracked front – a shit-hole.

But hell, it didn't matter. It had a bed, and that was where he was going for the next few hours. He'd not slept properly for two nights, and what few moments of slumber he'd managed had been terrorised with confusing thoughts.

He needed a good kip. Then maybe his bloody brain, which seemed to have gone into meltdown along with Chernobyl's fourth reactor, might make some bloody sense.

After the ridiculous discoveries on Monday morning, he'd laid low on Tuesday as he worked out his next move. Last night he'd watched a documentary, *The Bell Tolls for Chernobyl,* which detailed the events of a nuclear disaster that Paul knew nothing about. He'd then watched some American cop show called *Cagney and Lacey,* which was nowhere near as good as *Starsky and Hutch* or *Kojak.* Whatever had happened over his missing ten years, his brain seemed to have melted like a failed Russian nuclear reactor.

Without kicking off his boots, he flopped onto the thin mattress, causing the springs of the tubular bed frame to annoyingly squeak. It didn't matter – tiredness tugged at his brain, pulling it down into a subconscious state. The moment before he regressed into a deep sleep, Paul thought about his twin brother's broken head when he'd crushed it to a pulp only an hour ago.

A deep-sleep state didn't last long. The events of the last two days were now on replay like that tape machine he'd discovered plugged into Susan Kane's TV. Like that VHS machine that could rewind video pictures, his brain replayed the events of the last two days.

~

Although there was no way he could be speeding down Coldhams Lane, riding shotgun, with his sawn-off pointed at the driver's crown-jewels, and ten seconds later be sitting in the same car ten years in the future, every encounter since Monday morning suggested that, in fact, is precisely what had happened.

Monday morning, he'd awoken in that Cortina. He couldn't understand how he'd somehow fallen asleep and, concerningly, his sawn-off was missing. However, at that point, it was reasonable to assume it was only a few hours later that Friday evening in 1977 when he vaguely remembered sitting in the passenger seat as the dickhead driving careered through a bus shelter.

Paul had headed home after leaving the car and that Martin bloke, who sat motionlessly whilst slumped at the wheel. The driver, who he'd had an altercation with a week ago, didn't have a pulse, so it was safe to assume he was dead. What had happened to that Jason bloke and Patrick's skinny bird, Jess, Paul had no idea. However, with his police record, being in a car with a dead bloke was not a good place to be. So, he'd shot off before the filth turned up and started asking awkward questions.

However, it all started to turn odd when he'd opened the front door to his flat to find some Asian family living there. He'd been greeted with screams from an Asian woman dressed in a bright-red salwar who stood in his hallway. She'd raised her hands in the air, shrieked, and shook with terror when faced with Paul as he stood pulling out the key from the Yale lock. In an instant, two Asian men appeared, running at him with baseball bats.

No one pissed about with the Colneys, and especially not Paul Colney. Notwithstanding his status in the underworld of Fairfield, Paul was savvy enough to know two bare-chested, turbaned, baseball-bat-wielding Asians running full pelt at him meant retreat.

Stumbling out of his flat and struggling to understand why Ma had invited in an Asian family, including two bare-chested nutters, had started to send his mind in a disturbing direction. Paul backed away from the attackers, who stopped chasing when he'd managed to back away ten yards along the landing of Dublin House – one of the three concrete blocks of squalid flats that formed the notorious Broxworth Estate.

"Fucking back up. Come back in here, and I'll crush your fucking head in," shouted the larger of the two bare-chested men whilst pointing and probing his bat in Paul's direction.

"You know who you're threatening? You're a dead man walking," threw back Paul, amazed that these two lads had the stupidity to threaten him of all people. Of course, the only assumption was they were new to the town and somehow had got into the wrong flat.

Whilst pondering this ridiculous thought and wondering where the hell Ma had disappeared to, the front door of the flat next door opened, causing Paul to spin around ready to use his fists on whatever emerged.

A scraggy middle-aged woman dressed in a thin, blue-striped dressing gown bent down to retrieve two milk bottles and a red-top newspaper from the doorstep. When she lifted her head and caught sight of Paul, her grip loosened on the bottles causing her to raise her thigh, thus stopping one from falling.

"What the fuck!" stated Susan Kane, her cigarette in the corner of her mouth, bouncing as she spoke, then sagging downwards as she gawped at Paul.

"Where's Ma?"

"What d'you fucking mean, where's Shirley? Fucking Spain, ain't she! Living it up in the fucking sun, whilst I had to bring up that little rapist twat of hers. Anyway, what the fuck are you doing out? You escaped? You on the run?"

"What?" Paul spat back. He noticed the two bat-wielding turbaned nutters disappear back into his flat. "What d'you mean Ma's in fucking Spain?"

"Patrick, you better get in 'ere. If you're on the run, we can't afford anyone seeing you."

Bemused, Paul stepped into Susan's flat. It wasn't unusual for many to get the twins mixed up. However, Susan was Ma's sister, and she knew the twins well. She wasn't actually her sister – bonded by blood. However, they were bonded from childhood when his mother had taken Susan under her wing at the children's home where they were raised after the war.

Paul wasn't the most house proud. However, he was surprised by the state of the place. Dirty crockery festooned the work surfaces, cascading out of the sink at every angle. It was as if a dirty-crockery-alien-monster had landed and was slowly taking over the world as it oozed from the sink. Even Paul could detect the stale-water smell that powered above the stench of cigarette smoke.

Susan's appearance wasn't much better, and it appeared she'd aged overnight, instantly loading on a couple of stone in weight, now with her flabby frame busting from the open dressing gown and tea-stained nightie. Paul had never been particularly fussy where he stuck his manhood and had often been tempted to take Susan, even though she was Ma's age. However, it appeared overnight she'd morphed from a fuckable mature bird to become a bloated old boiler.

Susan placed the milk bottles on the kitchen table on the rare few inches that weren't covered in a week's worth of unwashed plates and cups. The red-top newspaper unfolded where she'd lobbed it as she dropped her cigarette butt in a mould-skimmed half-drunk cup of coffee.

Paul glanced at the headline—

1985 Heysel Stadium disaster – Liverpool fans extradited

Confused, Paul picked up the paper and studied the date stamp, drawing the paper closer to his eyes that widened in disbelief.

Monday 7th September 1987

"Go on then, you escaped?" asked Susan, as she grabbed another cigarette from a packet from the windowsill, lighting it then flicking the match in the sink, which disappeared into the labyrinth of cups that languished in the grease-slicked dishwater.

"What's today?" he asked without taking his eye from the paper's date stamp.

"I don't fucking know. Who gives a shit? You're the one holding the paper, you twit! Bloody hell, Patrick, have the years banged up in that cell fried your brain? Thought you were the clever one!" Susan took another long drag on her cigarette. "No one misses that bastard, Paul. Sorry I know he was your brother, but the man was a monster. Good riddance, I say." Susan removed her cigarette, flicked the ash in the sink and continued. "Shirley said the same thing at his funeral. Good riddance to bad rubbish!"

Paul dropped the paper on the table before stepping towards Susan. He closed the gap between them, sensing his presence made her uncomfortable. "Whose funeral?"

"Paul's, your brother! Jesus, Patrick, what the fuck's the matter with you? Anyway, have they let you out? I thought your appeal hearing was this week?"

"What year is it?"

"You're not right in the head ... all four of you boys are nutters!" replied Susan, as she poked her finger at her temple, tapping away at it whilst pulling a gurning face. "You get it from your father. No wonder Shirley wants nothing more to do with you lot!"

"Answer me, bitch!"

Susan stepped forward, jabbing her finger in Paul's direction. "Don't you dare talk to me like that! You're not too big to put across my knee! What's the matter with you? You're sounding like your psycho brother!"

Paul swiftly swatted away Susan's arm, then jabbed forward his hand, wrapping his fingers around Susan's jaw, squeezing, causing her mouth to pucker. The force of his action pushed Susan against two dirty orange geometrically patterned plates, which slid off the draining board and smashed as they clattered onto the lino floor.

"Year?" Paul bellowed, still gripping her jaw.

"19 ... 1987."

Paul held her jaw and pushed her head back over the sink. He'd last seen Susan a couple of days ago. Now in less than forty-eight hours, she'd aged at least ten years, stuffed on at least three stone, and looked as rough as the old working girls who touted for business down near the bookies at the edge of the estate.

In his eye line, he spotted a rolling pin that appeared to have doubled up as an ice smasher, based on the fact the small ice cube mould lay broken next to it. Paul shoved Susan away, who stepped back and rubbed her jaw. He could see the terror in her eyes – it was the feeling of power he'd exerted which could be intoxicating.

Grabbing the wooden rolling pin, he turned it around in his hand. A hefty lump, he thought, as he rhythmically gently slapped it in his palm like a policeman with a truncheon.

"What you doing? Patrick?" Susan squeaked out as she shifted away from him, sliding her bum along the edge of the sink. "Patrick? What's the matter?" The cord of her dressing gown caught on the frying pan handle that protruded from the murky water in the sink.

Paul repeatedly slapped the pin in his hand whilst deciding whether it was time to finish Susan Kane off. Should he fuck her first? Or just kill her?

With its handle snagged on Susan's dressing gown, the dirty pan joined the two broken plates on the lino, taking with it on its flight greasy dishwater that splattered up Paul's jeans – question answered.

∼

Paul lobbed the rolling pin on the floor, stood up and stretched his back from where he'd been bent over for several minutes. Then, grabbing hold of Susan's cigarettes from the windowsill, he lit up and pinged the spent match at Susan's head before retreating to the kitchen table.

With his thumb, he depressed the foil cover on one of the milk bottles, discarded the foil on the floor, and glugged down the cool white liquid. Then, placing the half-empty dumpy-shaped bottle down on the table, he took a long drag of his cigarette, wondering why he hadn't previously noticed the milk bottles had changed shape.

The silver foil cap he'd dropped to the floor caught his eye. He remembered his younger brother, David, collecting the tops from all of the estate to send to the Blue Peter Appeal to buy meals-on-wheels vans. David had sent that many tops into the show's collection, he reckoned he was responsible for the totalizer reaching the required target, and in turn, he'd earned himself a Blue Peter Badge for his gallant efforts. Ma had been so proud of David, like she was all of the boys, well, except him, of course. And now it appears that Ma had said '*Good riddance to bad rubbish*' if that Susan slag was to be believed. David died last year – however, as Paul eyed the date stamp on the top of the paper, somehow it now appeared that eleven years had elapsed since his brother fell from the roof of Belfast House.

He tipped the magazines and stack of mail from the roughly painted Windsor chair and flopped down to inspect his handiwork. Then, feeling exhausted from his exertions, he leant back after dropping the cigarette butt in the opened milk bottle. Flipping off the foil of the second pint, he swigged down half the content, then held the bottle aloft as if proposing a toast to Susan, who lay on the lino amongst the dirty frying pan and broken crockery.

"Cheers!"

Paul had lost count of how many times he'd whacked her head with the rolling pin. However, based on the fact that his t-shirt and hands appeared to be liberally splattered with her blood, and Susan's head had pretty much disintegrated, he guessed he must have hit her quite a few times. Apart from the neck down, it was fairly impossible to see that the body had previously held any human form – he suspected the police report would call it a frenzied attack.

Paul grabbed the paper and flipped it over to the back page. The date stamp still stated it was 1987. He perused the headlines.

Sacked Manchester United Manager – Big Ron re-joins West Brom.

"Never heard of him," he muttered. Last time he checked, Tommy Docherty was the Manchester United manager. One page in from the back page, an advert for a car phone caught his eye. NEC were offering a phone for your car, with a free leather carry case. The advert actually stated you could unplug the phone and walk into a field and it would still work. At £899 each, the advert was offering a monthly payment plan. Paul lobbed the paper on the floor with the stash he'd earlier tipped off the chair. Friday's edition of the Fairfield Chronicle now lay facing him.

Colneys' day in Court!

Fairfield Rapist – Colney's court appearance set for Monday 7th September

Sinking to his knees, he grabbed the paper and read the article that stated Andrew Colney, twenty-one, from the Broxworth Estate, was due to appear at Fairfield Magistrates Court on Monday charged with four counts of rape. In a strange turn of events, that same day, his eldest brother Patrick, thirty-three, would be attending his appeal hearing against his murder conviction of a fellow inmate in 1979.

"What the fuck?"

Now at eye level with Susan, whose body lay slumped against the under-sink cupboard, Paul again reappraised his handiwork whilst contemplating the situation he found himself in.

Yesterday, Patrick was twenty-three, and Andy was eleven. He, Andy and Ma lived in the flat next door, and he was the head of the Colney family, making his way up the Mafia ladder of Fairfield – also Susan Kane was fuckable. Now, one day later, his brothers had aged ten years, Ma had disappeared, and

Susan Kane was no longer fuckable, irrespective of whether she possessed a recognisable head.

~

Paul opened his eyes. Sleep was not coming, and his whirring brain now caused the agitation to creep around his body, which usually happened just before he dished out violence to anyone who just happened to be nearby – Paul wasn't fussy.

Only six people in this world could confidently tell the difference between Patrick and Paul. Susan and David were dead. His old man and Andy were inside. As for Ma, well, no concern there – she was in Spain. And lastly, Jess – well, he'd just have to deal with her.

Although he was supposedly thirty-three, and he would have to comply with the parole officer's demands, Paul would, from this moment, become Patrick. All he had to do was avoid Ma. Then this identity switch was going to be simple.

Yanking up his pillow, Paul sat up and surveyed his new temporary shit-hole abode. He lit up a cigarette, blew a plume to the ceiling and pondered his next move.

Three days ago, back in 1977, he'd planned to kill Jason Apsley and Martin Bretton, as they were clearly involved in David's death. Killing them would, he'd thought at the time, bring him back into favour with Ma.

Three days later, in 1987, his focus had changed. No longer did he need to get back in with Ma. He was now dead, and Patrick had always been her favourite of the twins. So, avenging David's death didn't seem to have the same urgency as it had last Friday. However, that Martin Bretton bloke seemed to be dead in that car, so he might as well finish off

Jason Apsley as he needed to deal with Jess – two birds with one stone, was the saying.

After that, well, the world was his oyster, as they say. Patrick had always had the respect of the Gower family, so now Paul had the real opportunity to take control of the Fairfield drugs and protection business.

Paul was super impressed by that new-fangled gizmo machine that could record TV shows and play pre-recorded films; tapes that only cost £6.99 from Woolworths – if the stack of cassettes under Susan's TV was anything to go by. However, what was far more impressive was the fact that Paul Colney no longer officially existed. He would grab this golden opportunity to steal his brother's identity, which would surely instantly elevate his standing in the criminal underworld.

19

Columbo

Whilst Frenchie and her sergeant waited for the information regarding my twice-dead, double-reincarnated, general pain in the arse ex-employee, Mrs Trosh afforded me a few extra minutes to collect my thoughts – bless her. I was going to miss her.

During the handover to Sarah, I just hoped she included an extensive section on how to be super nosey as part of the job description of the school secretary.

"Can I offer you some refreshments, officers?" she stated, as she held onto the door handle whilst leaning into the room, scanning the scene like a nervous lizard about to ping off a rock.

Frenchie frowned, clearly disappointed with the interruption.

The dippy DS swung around to look at our nosey secretary. "Wouldn't mind a cold drink if you've got one, please."

"Oh, yes, I think we have some Robinson's lemon barley water if you like. I bought a bottle when the tennis was on in the summer. Mr Trosh wasn't that keen, so I brought it into school. Of course, I mean the squash, not the tennis," she quantified, adding a silly laugh. "Both Mr Trosh and I love watching Wimbledon. This year was brilliant! Did you see the men's final? That Pat Cash chap is so dashing!"

"Mr Apsley ... do something before I arrest the whole school," calmly stated Frenchie, who I feared would carry out her threat unless I could get Mrs Trosh out of the room who'd now skilfully slithered her way in and stood gawping at the photos of the inked body parts belonging to Martin.

"Err ... Mrs Trosh, we're all fine, thank you. No drinks required."

"Oh ... are you sure?"

"Quite sure! And my sergeant will survive without his barley water!"

"Right-o. Sorry to have offered," stated a suitably chastised Mrs Trosh as she backed out of the room. "You know you must ensure you drink enough; it's good for your skin," she added before closing the door, I guess determined to have the last word.

Quite a perceptive observation from our seventy-something secretary, I mused, as I thought of Jenny, who couldn't fathom my obsession with bottled water. *"It's free out of the tap!"* she would often say.

There were many trends and fads which Jenny and George struggled to believe would come to fruition in the future. Bottled water was one such fad.

George had said that tap water was now safe to drink, as it had been since the late Victorian times, so why would anyone buy it in bottles. He had a good point, which I struggled to answer, but I did suggest spring water bottling companies were a good stock investment option.

Anyway, Jenny complied with my request for the drink and regularly purchased glass bottles of Perthshire Water from Sainsbury's.

Of course, I knew of the plastic bottle issue of my time back in good old 2019. Then, that Jason, the miserable opinionated bastard, couldn't give two shits about the scourge of plastic. Now, new enlightened Jason was recycling nuts, a true eco-warrior, tree-hugging, save the planet gladiator. I guess you could call me the forerunner to Greta Thunberg. However, I didn't actually go around hugging trees or feel the need to camp outside waving protest banners and chaining myself to fences, much like the protesters at Greenham Common a few years back, although that was about the deployment of nuclear weapons rather than climate change.

The irony wasn't lost on me that the protests of the day centred around the perceived need to reduce nuclear weapons to stop the human race from obliterating the world, whilst behind the scenes, almost stealth-like, we blindly carried on destroying the planet through ignorance.

No one thought plastic and fossil fuels were the danger, including George, who really struggled to believe that melting glaciers were a more significant threat to our existence than nuclear warheads.

Climate change was a difficult one to explain in this era. Jenny thought the idea of global warming sounded great because she much preferred wearing her summer dresses than her thick woolly jumpers – I guess I didn't explain that one too well.

Anyway, tree-hugging aside, I would drive across town to the one glass recycling bank in Fairfield to ensure I did my bit to prevent the impending doom of climate destruction in the next century by ensuring my empty glass bottles were recycled.

George thought I was nuts and stated that you'd get a penny back on bottles at the corner shop in his day. If in the future you had to drive to a bottle bank and give it away, then the world in the future was as mad as a box-of-frogs, and he was glad he would be dead by that time.

On many occasions, I did struggle to explain the future. Cultural changes happened slowly over decades, so trying to explain the way of life in 2019 was always fraught with challenges.

"Mr Apsley. It might have come to your attention that my patience is running thin. Can you get on with it, please? Otherwise, we will have to continue this at the station," stated a red-faced Frenchie who rammed her hands in her suit jacket pockets, which exerted extra pressure on the already fully-strained-to-the-limit buttons.

I continued to wing it. "Martin and I worked together at a mining company in South Africa in the mid '70s. After I returned to the UK, I heard he started to mix with the wrong sort ... lost his job ..."

I carried on with my made-up story. Frenchie sat attentively whilst her dippy, presumably now thirsty, sergeant scribbled away in his notebook. Fortunately, he didn't question any more spellings, or geographical locations, which was a stroke of luck as I was making it up as I went along.

Like a well-polished presenter of Jackanory, I concluded my tale. However, my performance was more akin to Gene Hunt in *Ashes to Ashes* than an engaging rendition from Bernard Cribbins.

I figured making out Martin had lived and worked in South Africa, had a girlfriend who was a clairvoyant gipsy tattoo artist, and praying that the mining company *other* Jason had worked at were sketchy with their employees' records, might just be enough to avoid telling Frenchie I was a time-traveller like the nameless traveller in the HG Wells book, with a yellow Mk3 Cortina doubling up as my time machine.

The story went slightly awry when I mentioned that Paul Colney thought the driver of the Cortina was responsible for his brother's death. Which was close to the truth – I had killed David when I dropped him off the roof of Belfast House on the Broxworth Estate back in '76.

"Why did Paul Colney believe the driver killed David?" asked Frenchie, as she started to dig into my ridiculous story.

As she confidently held my stare, with her mop of blonde hair and intense eyes, my vision morphed Frenchie into a Morlock, however-many millions of years before HG Wells suggested. On a positive note, this vision of a Morlock wasn't bare-chested, so not all bad, I guess.

"I have no idea," I innocently threw back, although acutely aware my lying skills were pants.

"That day back in '76, when I was a beat officer, I knocked on Mr Nears's door when conducting door-to-door enquiries."

I nodded, dreading where this conversation was heading.

"You were there with Mr Nears. Coincidently at the time David Colney died." Frenchie raised her eyebrows. The silence descended, the thick cloak of doom crushing down upon me. The thirsty sergeant looked up from his scribbles. Presumably, he'd caught up and was awaiting my answer.

"I was. But as I said at the time, I had nothing to do with David Colney's death." I lied. I could feel the hot flush rising. An unstoppable force as it rose up my neck that might as well have broadcasted that I was not telling the truth about that day. Who needed a lie-detecting machine when my skin already had a built-in colour-coded indicator that significantly outperformed Pinocchio's nose.

"Okay. I think that will have to suffice for now," stated Frenchie. She glanced at her dehydrated sergeant, then nodded at the photos of Martin's body art, presumably indicating he should retrieve them.

My red flush receded.

"I will need to speak with your daughter, Jessica Poole. Perhaps you can both drop into the station tomorrow afternoon. Shall we say five-thirty? Will that be convenient?"

I nodded.

"Good," she stood and offered her hand. "Mr Apsley, you and your family are too entwined with the Colneys. I can assure you that is an unhealthy alliance."

Standing and shaking her hand, I felt the red flush starting to return. My life was so entwined with the Colneys that it would blow her mind if she knew the truth.

"You mentioned a murder enquiry?"

Yes. You may have heard on the local news stations regarding an incident involving a resident from the Broxworth Estate who was brutally murdered on Monday. Susan Kane ... do you know her?"

I shook my head.

"She was the legal guardian of Andrew Colney. Shirley Colney left him with Susan in '77 when she moved to Spain.

The very same Andrew Colney who attended court on Monday charged with multiple counts of rape."

"Oh. How does my old car have anything to do with that?"

"That is what they call the sixty-four-thousand-dollar question. The attack on Susan Kane was brutal. If I didn't know he was already dead, I would have bet my bottom-dollar on Paul Colney as the perpetrator. However, he's dead, along with your friend, isn't he?"

"Yes." Christ, I hoped so.

"Were you aware that Shirley Colney returned to the UK on Monday?"

"What?"

"You're not then?"

"No!"

"Does that concern you, Mr Apsley?"

"Err… no," I lied again.

"Good. Although I can tell you it concerns me. Oh, I may have to talk to Mr Nears again. Give him my regards, won't you?"

"He's dead."

"Oh, that is sad. Please pass on my condolences to his family."

Mrs Trosh opened the door and stood to attention. "Shall I show you out?" she questioned.

"Oh, yes, please," smirked Frenchie. "I must say that was very perceptive of you to know our meeting had concluded. Do you have X-ray vision, Mrs Trosh? Some of my officers could do with those talents."

Our dependable secretary had shown her hand too early. Clearly, she'd had the glass against the wall whilst furiously taking notes, thus detecting when the meeting concluded. If the thirsty sergeant had missed anything, I thought he could compare notes with Mrs Trosh.

DS Farham, clutching his faux-leather folder, brushed past an embarrassed Mrs Trosh. Frenchie stepped to the door.

"I'll ask DS Farham to call you if he missed anything … I'm sure you can fill in the gaps for him!"

Frenchie held Mrs Trosh's stare and smirked whilst Mrs Trosh impersonated Beth's goldfish. A new acquisition to the family that Beth had won at the funfair three weeks ago when she'd successfully hooked the right rubber duck at the fairground stall when attending Fairfield's annual travelling fair. An event to which her disgruntled older half-brother was forced to chaperone her, along with two of Beth's friends.

Frenchie turned around and glanced at me, raising her finger. Then after a pregnant pause, and in true Columbo style, stated – "Just one more thing."

I nodded, wincing inside, dreading there could be worse news than the evil Shirley Colney returning.

"Do you know a Ralph Eastley?"

"No," I confidently replied whilst shaking my head, pleased that I couldn't feel the hot-flush lie indicator returning. This was no lie, as I'd never heard of him.

"Oh, really? How strange. Are you sure?"

Oh shit. Clearly, *other* Jason had known a Ralph Eastley. "Yes, sure. Never heard of him." The flush returned.

"Really? That's very odd. Okay, we'll see you tomorrow, Mr Apsley. Perhaps your memory will have improved by then," Frenchie threw over her shoulder as she crossed the school office, leaving Mrs Trosh and me impersonating Bananarama. I refer to Beth's goldfish, who she'd named after her favourite band, and not directly the three ladies who were already on their way to becoming record-breaking chart-toppers.

20

If You See Sid, Tell Him.

"Jesus, George! It's more than a bit of a problem! It's a ruddy shit storm! Christ, what the hell are we going to do?"

"Darling, calm down. You'll give yourself a heart attack. Now come on, let's think about this logically."

"Logically! What d'you mean logically? This isn't the time to apply First-Officer Spock's logic; this is the time for full-on panic, Corporal Jones style! Jesus Christ! Shirley bloody Colney is back! And it might have escaped your attention, but ten bloody years ago, she was threatening to take our daughter from us! Plus, by the sounds of that hideous murder up at that shit-hole of an estate, I reckon that psycho Paul Colney is alive again and roaming the streets of Fairfield like some bearded grim reaper! Christ, to quote Private Frazer, we're doomed!"

With my rant over, which hung in the air above us as we occupied our favoured window seat, I made a grab for my pint.

"Lad, I've got some more bad news."

I placed my pint down on the beer mat whilst gawping at my once grandfather, now close friend. Since Brian, the landlord, placed my pint down after pouring, I had attempted on five occasions to sup the amber liquid. Each time my hand made that journey towards my mouth, I'd stopped to continue my rant regarding the revelations that had transpired from the meeting with Frenchie and her geographically challenged sergeant.

Now, as George suggested there would be more bad news on the way to assault my eardrums, I let go of my glass and fumbled for my cigarettes. Jenny, who rarely smoked, snatched up my packet and joined me in polluting the air around the window-seat table of the Three Horseshoes Pub.

We waited whilst George awkwardly shifted in his seat, presumably preparing to deliver further devastating news that I feared would have the potential to trump what I'd already heard earlier today.

"You remember Harold I worked with up at the Chronicle?"

"No," replied Jenny and I in unison. We both continued gawping at George as we puffed away on our cigarettes, awaiting what was coming next.

"Hmmm ... okay. Well, I'm sure you do. Harold, Harold Bates. He was at my retirement do. You remember that unfortunate incident with him and a young lass from accounts in the ladies toilets? And the kerfuffle when his wife turned up ... thin fella with a pencil moustache. Looks like the spiv character out of Dad's Army—"

"Walker," I threw in, trying to speed George along and get to the punchline. Whoever his mate Harold Bates was, I really didn't give a shit. I assumed he wasn't the slightly shifty but amiable cockney black-market spiv character who, as a member of Walmington-on-Sea Home Guard, had the ability to purloin petrol coupons and tinned sardines at the drop of a hat. Also, if he was somehow involved with the girl from accounts, well, that was his business.

"That's him, lad," chuckled George, before clocking mine and Jenny's now impatient expressions. "Yes, well, I met up with Harold at lunchtime down at the Three Feathers on Upper Goat Lane, you know the place, the pub with the shove-ha'penny boards on the bar?"

"Yes!" we replied in unison. The frustration in our voices now palpable.

"Well, when Harold and I meet up, he always likes to bring me up to speed on breaking news and such. He was quite surprised I hadn't heard about Patrick Colney and the fact he's been released from prison."

"You're joking!"

"No ... no ... no ... no," slowly repeated Jenny in disbelief, as she shook her head in perfect rhythm as if following a metronome set to a slow beat.

"They released him this very morning!"

"Oh, bollocks!"

Jenny and I slugged down our drinks whilst George, spotting the urgent need for alcohol, hopped up to the bar to grab refills.

"Darling, what are we going to do? Do you think Beth's in danger again?"

"Oh Christ, I don't know," I replied whilst scrubbing my hands across my face.

"Oh my God. What if they are at the house now? They might be kidnapping her as we sit here!" she shrieked.

"Jen. Jen, calm down." Grabbing hold of her hands, I could feel her shaking. "Nothing's going to happen tonight. Christopher is with her, and he's a sensible boy. He won't let anyone in the house … you know that."

Her bewitching green eyes searched mine, I guess desperately hoping that what I had said had some sincerity. I did believe Beth would be safe at home and not already whisked away by the returning Cruella de Vil, like Pongo and Perdita's puppies. One thing was for certain, Paul and Patrick Colney were a fair-few-rungs above Horace and Jasper Badun on the evil-bastard charts leaderboard – if there was such a thing.

"Dad!"

I swivelled around to see Jess flying through the bar with her husband Colin close behind.

"Dad. Dad!" Breathless from her sprint Jess grabbed the back of my chair. Her long jet-black hair draped down, now covering her eyes. Then, parting her curtain hair with both hands, Jess blurted like a machine gun, "He's out! He's out. Dad, he's out. What am I going to do? He's out!"

My daughter, well, *his* daughter, locked eyes with mine. They appeared to be pleading that I would have some magic answer which would make everything alright. She'd unwittingly perfected the frightened rabbit-look, whilst the tremor in her body radiated through the back of my chair as if the 6:22 from St Pancras had just rumbled through the lounge bar.

Jess's hair was in its monthly chameleon cycle of ever-changing colour. Like a mood ring and fitting her demeanour, today, her jet-black mane flowed down the sides of her face. Last week it took on a stark peroxide blonde, almost albino, and closer to her natural colour. It was hard to keep up with the fast changes, and I recall that it took on a much-preferred wavy, copper-coloured style a few weeks ago. If I didn't know better, I could have assumed she was styling herself each week on one of the three Witches of Eastwick – the latest film Jenny was super keen on seeing when it hit the screens next month. I'd turned my nose up at that suggestion, but like all films and TV shows due for release, Jenny was clear that I kept my opinions to myself and not spoil the surprise.

Colin caught up and joined the party as George placed the drinks on the table. Now, on the subject of the Witches of Eastwick, there was nothing Daryl Van Horne about Colin. Although, to be fair, he may have been *your average horny little devil*, but hey, that was for Jess to know. However, although he was a competent teacher, a great step-dad to Faith, and seriously made my daughter happy, he was more of a Forrest Gump type than an audacious eccentric trickster-cum-shape-shifting devil.

As Jess's latest style resembled the Cher look and presuming her panicked state directly linked to the news George had just relayed regarding Patrick, like Cher, I guess she wished she could turn back time, so she'd never got involved with the bearded grim reaper's twin brother.

"Hang on there, lass. Calm down. Come on, calm down." George gently folded his giant hand around Jess's elbow, acting as her comfort blanket, smothering the imaginary 6:22 train vibrations which visibly tramped through her body.

Whether in this life or my first, George always possessed the ability to bring situations off the boil. He was like the British Gas adverts that were about to flood the TV screens *'Don't you just love being in control'*, I half expected him to click his finger and a blue flame to appear at the end of his thumb.

At least the *'Tell Sid'* commercials had now finished following the privatisation of British Gas last year. George had taken some persuading to invest as he'd said share dealing wasn't for the likes of the working class. However, with my insider knowledge, so to speak, he accepted that my time-travel credentials would ensure he would net a tidy profit.

"Right, come on. All of you sit yourselves down. Colin, lad, get you and your lovely lass a drink and let's pull a rational plan together," calmly stated George, as he handed Colin three pound-coins he'd thumbed from the plastic pound coin holder he plucked from his wallet.

"Come on, Jess," whispered Jenny, as she reassuringly smiled and patted the seat beside her.

Jenny sat on one side, rubbing Jess's hand as if trying to warm her up following a bout of hyperthermia. George the other, his calming demeanour now reducing the heat levels in the atmosphere of the pub. They could do with a few George-type characters at the Paris Climate Change Conference in 2015; then, the one-point-five-degree target would be a piece of cake. Unfortunately for Jenny, she would definitely have to hang on to her winter sweaters.

"Jess, did you read it in the Chronicle about Patrick?" asked her comfort blanket who sat beside her.

"No!" blurted Jess, as she swung her head from side to side.

"Where's Faith?" calmly asked Jenny, still stroking Jess's hand. An action that Ernst Stavro Blofeld would have used to comfort his white, blue-eyed Persian cat.

"She's with Beth. Christopher said it was fine to leave her with him."

"Yes, Chris will be fine with the girls," I threw in.

"Who told you about Patrick then? Has it been on the wireless, lass?"

"No ... I saw him!"

"What?" all three of us questioned.

"What d'you mean you saw him? Where? When?" questioned my Blofeld impersonating wife.

"Today ... about an hour ago!"

"What the hell did you say to him? Oh, hell, tell me he doesn't want visiting rights to Faith!"

"No, I didn't speak to him. I'd just picked up Faith from a friend's house and was getting out of the car when we'd arrived home, and there he was. He just stood across the road gawping at us."

Colin placed a pint of snakebite and blackcurrant in front of Jess. My daughter was ahead of her time in enjoying cider and berry-mixed drinks. Drink deposited, Colin then squeezed in next to me. He seemed to be nursing an Appletiser with a cherry on a stick – see, as I said – more Forrest Gump than Daryl Van Horne.

After gulping down half her snakebite, Jess carried on with her news about the evil Shirley Colney, *other* Jason's half-sister, only-surviving-or-at-liberty son. Well, that's assuming the nut-job Paul had not been reincarnated like my loose cannonball mate, Martin.

"We just stared at each other for a couple of seconds. It was so weird! He looked like he hadn't aged, although … somehow different. Odd-looking. I know that sounds nutty."

"You sure it was him?"

"Well, yes. I didn't have my glasses on – as you know I hate wearing them – but it was him. I'm sure of it … I know … I know that doesn't make any sense. Neither of us said anything. Then he just walked off, whilst I stood there holding Faith … I was terrified! As soon as Colin came home, we dropped Faith off and nipped up here as we guessed this is where you'd both be."

You know you may have a drinking problem when people come to the pub looking for you as their second port of call. Note to self – reduce my frequenting of the Three Horseshoes to no more than five nights a week. Until I get a mobile phone, it would be good to keep a few people guessing regarding my whereabouts.

"Watcha. Where is he then? Fucked off and done a runner already 'as he? Should have guessed he was a shag-and-run type of bloke."

All five of us halted our conversation and peered up at Randy Mandy, who stood chewing gum, holding that hand-on-hip-pose she seemed to have perfected. She blew a sizeable pink bubble that ballooned until bursting on her lips before she seductively ran her tongue across them, sucking the pink blob back inside, thus allowing her mouth to continue its concrete-mixer impression. It's fair to say it wasn't a sophisticated look.

Apart from what I presume must have been an extensive session of back-combing to achieve the required lift to her hair, and her bright electric-blue eye-shadow framed with black eyeliner delivering that smokey-eye look, her appearance hadn't changed from the previous evening when she'd accosted Martin.

"Well, where is he? Harry Houdini done his disappearing act again ... gone up in a puff of smoke?" she asked, whilst we all presumably waited for her to perform her next rendition of the bubble gum balloon blowing. "I want what's owed. He can't shirk his responsibilities, you know. I knew he'd be a crap father, but he can damn well help out with a few quid."

Now to be fair to Randy Mandy, I agreed that I had rarely witnessed any behavioural traits in Martin that might suggest he could be a candidate for the Father of the Year award. Also, I certainly didn't see him challenging Mrs Doubtfire for that coveted trophy, which presumably he or she would have been a front runner to receive. However, Randy Mandy hadn't given him a chance, and I thought he would be better than the axe-wielding Jack Torrance – no, that was more akin to Patrick or Paul Colney – I shuddered at the thought.

"Darling, where is Martin?"

I glanced at my watch. "Jesus! I said to be here an hour ago."

"Jess, have you seen him?"

"Martin? He's dead! Don't you mean Leonardo, his brother?" Jess fired back, unable to take her eyes off Bubblegum woman.

"Oh, err ... yeah ... shit!"

"Who the fuck is this Leo bloke? Martin s'posed to be 'ere. So where is he?" stated a pissed-off looking Randy Mandy before blowing one of her signature bubbles – quite a large one this time – impressive.

"Err ... Mandy, he's running a bit late. He said he'd be up in about half an hour," I threw out, not knowing how to scramble out of this particular mess.

"Smells like bullshit in 'ere. Half hour ... he better be 'ere. Right, you can get me a drink. I'll 'ave a double Malibu and Coke while I wait."

I thumbed out a fiver, waving at her. "There you go; you can get it," I said, whilst desperately trying to get her to disappear.

"Dad, who the hell was that? And how does she know Leonardo?"

"Who's Leonardo," chirped up Jenny, George and Colin, as if they were performing the chorus in this hellish tune that was playing out.

"Oh, Christ!" I pronounced, before rubbing my hand over my face. Not only had I not prepped Jenny and George regarding the younger brother story from South Africa, I stupidly hadn't thought about the consequences when Jess met up with us. Also, Martin had plumped for Leonardo and not Keith as his new name.

"Yes! Woohoo! I've got a cheese," announced a young lady on the next table. She looked well chuffed as she was handed the brown wedge-shaped plastic triangle by one of the other players. To be fair, she was well within her rights to whoop, as I thought the brown cheese was always the most challenging cheese to secure – I'd always struggled with the Art and Literature questions. I'd lost interest in Trivial Pursuit years ago, but back in the '80s, the general knowledge board game phenomenon was sweeping the country – everyone was playing it.

The excited cheese-achieving lady's whoop momentarily afforded me a moment to try and conjure up some bollocks to get me out of this mess – unfortunately, nothing came to mind.

"Err ... Leonardo is Martin's brother. He's over here and staying in Don's house at the moment."

"What? Lad, where's Martin gone then?"

"George, are you alright? Martin is dead!" exclaimed Jess.

As luck would have it, Jenny cottoned on. "George, you're getting their names mixed up. You know how this Leroy looks just like his older brother, Martin." She bulged her eyes as they pleaded for George to make to connection.

"Oh, have you met him as well? I thought he said his name was Leonardo, not Leroy," said Jess, as she swung her head to look at Jenny, which afforded me the opportunity to draw my fingers across my lips, indicating to George to zip it.

"Yes, it's Leonardo," I corrected, praying this conversation was coming to an end. However, that would not resolve the issue of Bubble-gum girl who would be back at any moment with her double Malibu and Coke.

Although I could see George hadn't quite joined all the dots, at least he followed my non-verbal instruction to keep shtum. Colin continued nursing his fizzy apple juice, thankfully not complicating the conversation further.

As for my returned loose cannonball with the stupid Teenage Mutant Ninja Turtle name, a deep sense of foreboding settled on me. He was late; Martin was never late to the pub or anywhere that involved alcohol – where was he?

I heard the rest of the gang return to their conversation whilst I contemplated that something was afoot with my old employee.

My gaze caught sight of the two lads on the Pac-Man video game table, one leaning over the screen whilst the other's body jerked back and forth as he attempted to negotiate his yellow Pac-Man through the maze.

Even in this era, the video table could be classed as ancient. Christopher and my elder sixteen-year-old brother, Stephen, could be considered an authority on arcade games due to the unacceptable amount of time they spent in the arcade gaming hall in town. As we careered towards the '90s, Beat'um and Motion Simulator games were now in vogue – already, only a few years from inception, poor old Pac-Man was ancient history.

Whilst the two lads enjoyed the outdated technology, I imagined Martin as the Pac-Man whizzing along the maze with the four coloured ghosts in the shape of Paul, Patrick, Shirley and this person Frenchie had mentioned, Ralph, as they once again chased him down to eliminate his existence.

"Right lass, let's have a plan about Patrick," stated George, distracting Jess and Colin, which also hauled my mind from Pac-Man and allowed me an opportunity to whisper my concerns with Jenny.

"Something's not right ... I can just feel it! Where the hell is Martin?"

"Darling, d'you think something's happened to him?"

"Shirley Colney? Or worse, Paul?" I shuddered as I said it, instantly causing the colour to drain from Jenny as if a plug had been pulled.

Without answering, Jenny jumped up, making a beeline for the cigarette machine. I know this was stressful, but I considered this an odd moment to grab a packet of fags.

"Jen?"

"I need to phone home," she bellowed over her shoulder, alerting the whole pub of her intentions.

George, Jess, and Colin looked up. The Trivial Pursuit crowd momentarily stopped as one player asked another to name the capital of Yugoslavia, clearly a blue cheese question – my favourite category. However, a defunct question from my time.

The concentration camps of the Bosnian war had often featured on the agenda of the Time Travel Believers' Club meetings. However, like everything else, we had no idea how to avert the disaster that was now only a few years in the future. George found it head-spinning that parts of Europe seemed to be planning to repeat history within fewer than fifty years since the Nazi concentration camps of the Second World War.

Jenny grabbed the payphone mounted on the wall next to the cigarette machine, ferociously punching out the number, balancing the coin in the slot, whilst ramming her finger in her free ear and tightly squeezing her eyes shut.

"Oi! Is she warning the weasel not to turn up? Guess he's about to hop on his flying bike and piss off to some far-flung planet! Anything to escape sticking his hand in his pocket!" exclaimed Randy Mandy before delighting us all with a golf-ball sized bubble that appeared out of her mouth before once again splattering her lips.

"What?" I asked the bubble-gum woman who continued her relatively poor impression of the bohemian drifter character played by Madonna in *Desperately Seeking Susan*, now holding her drink, and I presume with no intention of offering me the change from the fiver.

Mandy pointed at Jenny. "E.T! Phone home!" she chuckled.

"Oh." I didn't get the film the first time around, and it didn't improve on the second attempt, although Beth had loved it in both lives.

We all held our breath as Jenny dialled home, praying Christopher would answer. The poor boy would presumably wonder why his mum was phoning and perhaps be somewhat concerned regarding her hysterical, panicked tone when asking if Cruella de Vil or a dead psychopath had come calling.

"Lad?"

"Hang on, George." I dismissed him with a wave of my hand as I intently watched Jenny whilst grabbing my car keys, ready to dash home.

"Lad. Lad!"

I afforded a cursory glance in his direction to appease his persistence. George held his arm aloft as if saluting Adolf Hitler, which I thought unlikely. Nevertheless, I followed his pointing finger that traced through to the public bar, widely considered the rough side of the pub.

Through the clouds of hazy blue smoke, I spotted Cruella de Vil, who stood chatting to a large man who could have been the Incredible Hulk, although he wasn't green in colour.

"Oh bollocks ... of all the backstreet boozers—"

21

Live And Let Die

"Hey, what's going on?" exclaimed a concerned Christopher, as the three founder members of the Time Travel Believers' Club, plus Jess and Colin, all barrelled through the back door.

Fortunately, Chris had answered the phone when Jenny had called from the pub. He'd stated all was well and apparently sounded more concerned about his mother's panicky tones than what Beth and Faith were up to in his sister's bedroom. His mother had demanded that he run upstairs and check that the girls were actually there, even though he could hear them giggling.

Regardless of Christopher's assurances that both girls were more than fine, Jenny's panic had now firmly set in, resulting in her insisting we decamp back home immediately. So, we'd shot out of the pub, disappointingly leaving half-consumed drinks. Although relieved to escape the company of Randy Mandy, who shouted that Martin wasn't going to duck out so easily, and the evil Shirley with her non-green-skinned Incredible Hulk holed up in the public bar.

"Nothing, Chris. It's fine. We're all fine," blurted Jenny, the first to barrel through the door, now tramping her way to the stairs to check for herself that the girls were okay. Then, as Chris turned around from following his mother's speedy flit through the kitchen, a second tornado knocked him clean out of the way as his half-sister, Jess, torpedoed herself through whilst hot-footing her way in Jenny's wake. Like any half-decent Formula One driver, Jess used the slipstream created by Jenny to gain on her as they both negotiated the chicane of the breakfast bar before breaking at the bend of the kitchen doorway, then disappearing from view into the hall.

∼

As Jenny burst into Beth's bedroom, both girls, positioned cross-legged on Beth's bed, hid their hands under the covers, appearing suitably caught out.

"Mum!" exclaimed Beth, protesting about her mother's intrusion into her private space.

"Mum?" questioned Faith, as Jess's head peered over Jenny's shoulder.

For a brief moment, the silence held. Then, Beth and Faith, fearful of being caught out, shot each other a look as they swivelled their eyes, then back at their mothers who still hadn't said anything, both catching their breath and appearing to be recovering from running the London Marathon.

Beth's bedroom could be described as being in the transitional stage. Perhaps that moment of lost identity as it morphed from a little girl's bedroom, with My Little Pony wallpaper and shelves lined with an extensive collection of Care Bears obediently sitting neatly in a row, through to a teenager's squat that now donned the poster of Bananarama promoting their recent album release, *WOW*, showing Sara, Siobhan and Keren hugging naked-chested men.

Jenny had refused to allow Beth to plaster the poster on the wall, stating that her ten-year-old daughter was being sexed-up by the debauchery of half-naked pop stars destroying young girls' moral standards.

Jason had stated in his previous life that Beth had very much been part of that half-naked trend. He'd suggested to Jenny that she would realise how innocent Bananarama were when Madonna released her Sex Book in the early '90s.

Jenny reluctantly relented on the erection of the Bananarama poster. She was also somewhat surprised her husband could describe all the pictures in the not-yet-published one-hundred-and-thirty-six-page book, which sounded like a debauched porn magazine that only dirty-old-men dressed in flasher macs would be interested in.

Certainly, times were changing fast. Beth was only ten but already had bare-chested men on her bedroom wall covering up My Little Pony, which, not so long ago, she'd seemed obsessed with.

When a young teenager in the early '60s, Jenny could recall being somewhat red-faced by the sight of those saucy postcards on the stands next to the bucket and spades and sticks of rock positioned outside the seaside shops where her parents took baby Alan and her on Sunday outings. Also, with their saucy innuendoes, the Carry-On films already seemed innocent and outdated compared to her ten-year-old daughter's choice of bedroom poster.

Her mother, Frances, hadn't helped. When visiting earlier in the week, she cooed over the tanned muscley men on the poster and stated that Beth was coming to that age, advising Jenny that she should go with the flow and not be such a prude.

Shockingly, her mother had asked what she thought she and her father got up to when they regularly had their close friends around, stating Jenny needed to loosen up a bit. Jenny had shuddered at the thought of her parents in some debauched '70s style porn-movie foursome.

At the time of the poster and Madonna's Sex Book discussion, Jenny had rummaged under their bed and at the back of the wardrobe, concerned to see what Jason might be hiding. However, her worst fears were not realised and was suitably relieved to only discover a tatty Haynes Car manual for a Triumph Stag and one, not so well-thumbed, Playboy magazine, which she suspected was significantly more innocent than how Jason had described Madonna's book. Or, for that matter, how she now imagined her parents entertained themselves on a Saturday night with their friends and neighbours – once again, Jenny had shuddered at the thought.

Judging by how well-thumbed both publications appeared, it seemed her husband was turned-on more by the drawings of engine parts and the big end of a 1976 sports car than the significantly less prominent end of a nude pose depicting the beautiful Jane Seymour.

However, Jenny was surprised that the stunning Bond girl had shed her clothes but did think the pictures were quite erotic. Subsequently, Jenny found herself sitting on the bed for some time as she, in some detail, read the publication. However, she didn't bother thumbing through the Haynes manual before placing both publications back in the nether regions of her husband's wardrobe.

Anyway, back to Bananarama and Madonna – Jenny had grave concerns for young girls' morality as they headed towards the millennium.

"Mum, what's up? What's all the fuss? First Chris, and now you?" asked Beth, concerned why her mother and Jess were gawping at them.

With the relief of seeing the girls happily chatting and not disappearing after being caught and whisked away by Cruella de Vil, Jenny turned her attention to what the girls were clearly trying to hide under the covers.

"What are you hiding?"

"Nothing!" both girls blurted, as they blushed.

Jenny stepped into the room and repeatedly clicked her fingers, demanding that whatever was hiding under the covers be handed over. Reluctantly Beth surrendered the magazine she and Faith had been poring over. Jenny snatched up the magazine, a publication aimed at teenagers, not ten-year-old impressionable schoolgirls. The headlines disturbed her—

How to be a model.

How to look great in a little black dress.

When is the right time to say yes to your boyfriend?

Less disturbingly, there were free posters of Michael J Fox and Five Star included, and Jenny was relieved to see they were fully clothed.

"Oh, Mum," whined Beth. "Dad doesn't mind," she added in a less whinging tone.

Jenny turned her nose up at the content of each page and loudly tutted as she read the agony aunt page regarding a girl's concern about her parents' reaction about her having a negro boyfriend.

Jenny knew her husband wouldn't be happy about the magazine printing the word negro. He often pulled George up when he referred to his 'darkie' workmates and had a right go at Brian, the landlord at the pub, who called Guinness, Nigerian Lager. Then, of course, there was the Robinson's Jam 'Golly' badges argument – Jason had flatly refused for Christopher and Beth to collect them. As for the Black and White Minstrel Show back in the late '70s, well, don't even go there.

At first, Jenny struggled to understand Jason's viewpoint. However, education prevailed, and now Jenny found these references just as abhorrent as her husband did. And, even more so, with the knowledge that in the time he left, thirty years in the future, Jason had stated that society still hadn't learnt its lessons.

"Mum?"

Jenny looked at Jess, who shrugged.

"Alright. However, young lady, if you want advice about boys, you talk to me," stated Jenny whilst handing back the magazine to her beaming daughter.

If the truth be known, she couldn't care less if Beth was thumbing through that Playboy magazine hidden at the back of Jason's wardrobe, because all that mattered was both girls were safe – for now.

"Mum?"

Jenny and Jess peered back into the bedroom, both raising their eyebrows, responding to what was clearly going to be a pleading request from the girls.

"Can you order the Freemans Clothes catalogue? Look, there's a cut-out coupon we can send off. You also get two pounds off your first order! See, there's a crop top in there just like Sara's," stated Beth, as she pointed to the blonde on the poster, dressed in a black and white crop top, half smothered by a naked man.

"We'll see," said Jenny, as she closed the door, hearing both girls exclaim "Yes!" knowing full well they'd succeeded.

~

"Dad, what the hell is going on?"

"Chris, I don't know," I lied.

Colin sat at the breakfast bar whilst George brought up the rear, closing the back door, then sliding across the top bolt.

"Lad. The boy's not a child anymore," stated my wise counsel, advising that I shouldn't be lying to my adopted son, even if I had good intentions.

"What?" asked Chris, as his eyes darted between us. "Mr Poole?" he questioned, probably hoping Colin would enlighten him as his father and Uncle George seemed to be holding out on replying.

"Chris, call me Colin. We're not at school now," answered Colin.

"Yeah, alright, Colin. But I tell you, it's confusing. I have to call my dad, sir, at school! Some of the guys take the piss out of me for calling my dad, sir!"

"Nothing wrong with that, lad. Respecting your elders is part of a proper upbringing."

If only Chris knew, I thought. He might find calling me, sir, a bit odd, well, that's not as bizarre as having your older brother in the fifth-form, and your ex-wife as a second-year student, with my best friend now my daughter, and my grandfather, my best friend. Now, that's what I call confusing!

"Are we having any tea tonight? I could eat a scabby horse," questioned Christopher, eager, I guess, to change the subject.

"Yeah, your mum will do it in a moment, but first, I need to talk to you."

Out of the corner of my eye, I spotted George give a slight nod of his head, indicating he approved I was about to be honest with Chris. Well, honest to a point, because I had no intention of ever issuing Time Travel Believers' Club membership forms to either of my adopted children.

Christopher grabbed a packet of crisps from the cupboard, and going by the spent packets on the kitchen worktop he'd already devoured quite a few. It appeared he was on a mission to burrow his way through the snack cupboard. As he pulled open the blue packet, I was struck by what flavour they were. Cheese and onion or salt and vinegar? Well, I knew that Walkers never changed the colour of their packets, which in my day had been a confabulation of psychiatry, or colloquially known as the *Mandela Effect*. But now, I really had no idea what colour went with which flavour.

"What flavour are those?"

"Cheese and onion. You want one?" offered Chris through a mouthful he'd just rammed in.

"Oh God, no!" I screwed up my face as if offered some hideous delicacy from a Bush Tucker trial. "I can't stand cheese and onion."

George coughed and started playing a tune with the loose change in his pocket. However, there was no particular melody, but rather like an orchestra tuning up, preparing to bash out some long symphony, which I was fully aware George was capable of playing with the coins when nervous. He coughed again, louder this time, indicating I was procrastinating.

I cleared my throat, preparing to make my speech.

"Oh, per-lease, not an attempt at an embarrassing Dad chat about girls and how to use my ding-a-ling!"

"Christopher! Some respect, lad!"

"Sorry, Uncle George," apologised Chris, waving a crisp in acknowledgement of his unwelcome smutty language.

"No, Chris. Far worse, I'm afraid."

"Oh!" exclaimed Chris, through a mouthful of crisps with a look on his face that suggested he was super surprised there could be anything worse than your father talking about sex.

"Chris …" I huffed. My train of thought now lost.

"Lad?"

I nodded to George, then back at Chris, who'd stopped mid-chew, probably now realising that hideously this conversation *was* going to be far worse than discussing sex with your parents.

"You remember when you lived with your mum?"

Chris nodded, and instantly his whole complexion changed. The movement of tiny muscles in his face transformed my confident, handsome son into a mere shadow. This rapid morphing would always happen when his real mother's name, Carol Hall, dropped into a conversation.

"Well, there was a woman who lived on that estate who you probably don't remember, but she believes that her son is Beth's father—"

"Shirley Colney!" he blurted, causing a spray of crisp mulch to fire out in all directions.

I nodded.

"She left the country years ago. I remember going to her flat with Carol when I was about four or five. I'll never forget it because she nearly threw Carol over the balcony … I remember crying as I watched her beat Carol and threaten to kill her!"

"Carol was your mum … it's okay to call her that, Chris."

Tears formed as his eyes watered.

We had adopted Chris from Lexton House Children's Home when he was just five years old. However, the terror that he'd often experienced from a long succession of Carol Hall's abusers had scarred him, and I feared it would live with him forever.

The Colneys and their associates had not only tormented many through extortion and intimidation, but they'd also left a long trail of destruction that many children would have to deal with throughout their adult lives – my adopted son, Christopher, would know that better than most.

He dropped the bag and rubbed his eye with his greasy fingers, I imagine, causing them to sting and water some more. Of course, this was a big deal for my sixteen-year-old son – adolescent men don't cry.

George, who finally reached the interval in playing the tune with his pocketed loose change, stepped towards Chris but halted as I held up my hand. I knew for Chris that tears which had involuntarily welled up were bad enough – George offering comfort would be too much. Chris was becoming a man, and he would want to cope as such. Well, that's how I knew Chris would see it.

"Jenny Apsley is my mum ... not Carol Hall," he stated with calm authority.

"She is. Never forget, though, Carol did her very best for you in her short life. Chris, she had a very tough life, and she would be proud of you."

Chris nodded.

"Anyway, Shirley Colney has returned to Fairfield."

"Why?"

"I don't know, but as you can imagine, your mum and I are a bit concerned. Now, not a word to your sister, mind." I pointed in his direction.

Chris nodded.

"You remember my friend Martin? He was around when me and your mum adopted you?"

"Err ... vaguely. Yeah, sort of."

"Well, his younger brother, Keith ... err ... Leonardo. Leonardo Keith ... he's over from South Africa." Christ, why had Martin decided on Leonardo! No one is called that! And where the hell is he? Although we'd left Randy Mandy supping her Malibu and Coke when we'd shot out of the pub, she wouldn't let this rest, that's for sure.

"Oh, okay, cool. Odd name, though!" chuckled Chris. "What's he got to do with Shirley Colney?"

"No idea. But he might be around for a bit over the next few weeks while we deal with this situation."

"Okay, will he be staying with us? Where is he?"

"Chris, good point ... where is he?" I muttered out loud. However, I was referring to Martin, not Leonardo Keith. A name I thought sounded more like a bad '70s folk singer that would fit nicely into George's hideous record collection.

"Where is who?" asked Jenny, as she walked back into the kitchen. "Oh, Chris, make yourself a sandwich, not systematically chomp your way through the snack cupboard like some gluttonous Augustus Gloop! Oh, and what's that all over the worktop? You've made a right mess! Come on, Chris, this isn't fair. I work all day, and I don't expect to come home to this bloody mess—"

"Jen," I called out to halt her rant.

With her hands still aloft at the carnage of spent crisp packets and spat crisp mulch, she turned to see her son's tears as they dribbled down his cheeks. Instantly she guessed the conversation I'd just had with him. Stepping forward, Jenny wrapped her arms around him, hugging him tightly.

Even though Christopher was already nearly a foot taller than his adopted mother, he held on to Jenny like a frightened child. At least a minute passed before they broke their embrace, tears in both their eyes.

Jess stood behind Colin, who'd remained seated at the breakfast bar, resting her head on his shoulder, whilst George and I watched Jenny and Chris comfort each other.

Jess broke the silence. "Colin, our nine-year-old daughter is now reading magazines about pop stars, boys, and she wants a crop top like Bananarama."

"What?" exclaimed Forrest Gump.

22

The Eagle Has Landed

After Colin had recovered from the shock that his innocent adopted daughter was growing up far too quickly and, now under my maturing daughter's influence, had acquired a thing about Bananarama, Bros, New Kids on the Block, and, God forbid the Beastie Boys, we settled down to prioritise our actions – that said, he was visibly disturbed by the crop-top idea Beth and Faith had floated as their choice of weekend attire.

Incidentally, I did warn my colleague, Jayne Stone, that she should protect the badge on her VW Golf as there soon would be a spate of badge thefts as the emblem was about to become an iconic rap symbol. Jayne laughed it off even though her husband Frank agreed with me, and God knows how he would have any idea of the future. Anyway, Jayne ignored our warning, and within a few weeks, sure enough, the badge was duly removed, and now I suspected it took pride of place around some teenager's neck – hopefully not my daughter's.

After Jess had spotted Patrick, and George had spied the evil Shirley Colney supping her drink only feet from where we were sitting, this left us with three urgent priorities. Firstly – check the girls were okay – tick! Secondly, feed the kids before Christopher gorged through a month's worth of snacks – Jenny was on the case. And lastly – find Martin, although we now called him Leonardo, and thankfully George had cottoned on.

Jess thought it odd that Randy Mandy knew Leonardo, a point I managed to gloss over. However, I did state that I wasn't too fond of the connection of him being AWOL along with Patrick and Shirley reappearing.

As the conversation flowed, of course, Jenny, George and I had the other dread festering in the pit of our stomachs that also Paul was back to muddy the waters, so to speak.

Like in any good Scooby-Doo cartoon, we split up to investigate. Jenny, AKA Daphne Blake and Colin, AKA Scooby (simply because all other characters were assigned, so I decided he had to be the dog ... unfair? Hmmm ... maybe) stayed back to organise tea and, with Christopher's support, protect the girls if Cruella de Vil and the Incredible Hulk came calling. George, AKA Fred Jones, Jess AKA Velma Dinkley, and me, AKA Shaggy Rogers, jumped in the Quattro, AKA the Mystery Machine, to search Don's house to look for clues about the strange disappearance of the time-traveller, Leonardo. That said, Velma had no idea about Martin's true origins.

"Dad? I know Colin will be a bit miffed, but I think I'd feel safer if we stay at yours tonight? I'm too spooked after seeing Patrick today," asked Jess pensively, as she leant through the gap between the front seats as I sped the Mystery Machine over to Don's house.

"You know you can. We'll give Jenny a call from Don's to get the spare bed sorted."

"Thanks. You sure Jenny won't mind?"

"No, course not."

"Okay, I'd better grab a bag of stuff for Colin and Faith."

"Lass, I'll come in with you," offered George, as I parked the Mystery Machine on the drive of Don's house, which appeared to be set in ghostly darkness.

"I'm not sure he's at home, lad. The curtains are all open, and I can't see any lights on."

Silence.

George turned in his seat to glance at me in the fading light of dusk. "Lad, you alright?"

I shook my head to release the trance I'd fallen into. "Yeah. It was only two days ago I was chatting with Don up there in his bedroom. Now he's gone," I whispered, as if not wanting my old dead friend to hear me as I leant forward, pointing out of the windscreen up to his bedroom.

Silence once more, as the three of us all had that private moment to remember our lost friend. Jess snivelled, digging out a scrunched tissue from her jumper sleeve, then repeatedly wiped the end of her nose.

Although George was AKA Fred, tonight he wasn't in charge of the gang on the mission to locate Martin. No, for one night only, Shaggy Rogers took the lead role. A storyline that the creators of the original series of animated shows for Hanna-Barbera could never have envisaged.

George and Jess patiently waited until I was ready to move. But, unbeknown to them, I was having a chat with Don in my head, asking for some advice.

He didn't answer.

"Right, come on then." I pinged off my seatbelt, ready for action. "We'll all search Don's and then go together to yours, Jess."

My team nodded.

There was no way we were splitting up, as I recall that Fred and Velma never seemed to get into the same scrapes as Shaggy, and I wasn't facing a cartoon monster prowling around Don's house on my own.

Reality is, the house was probably empty, and Martin had gone on a bender in town and was now doing what he did best – chatting up a group of young ladies, which he probably had eating out of the palm of his hand.

"Mar ... Leonardo?" I called out. I had that Déjà vu feeling of ten years ago when I'd entered the house next door and found Martin and Jenny in the garden – the day that Jenny started to believe I was a time-traveller. This time, as the three of us stood in the dim light of Don's old hallway, the house had a feeling of death. Perhaps it was the eerie feeling a home holds onto when the owner dies, or maybe we were about to find a gruesome discovery.

"Hello, anyone home?" I called again, whilst George quietly closed the front door, holding the Yale lock back and gently clicking it into the frame. We all stood in silence.

The hall light snapped on, causing Jess to squeal. My heart leapt as I peered up the stairs dreading who or what had flicked on the lights. I held my breath, suspecting any moment now some hideous monster would appear out of the gloom of the upstairs landing.

"The house is empty, lad," stated George from behind me, his finger on the light switch.

"Christ, George, you'll give me a bloody heart attack!" I hissed.

"Sorry!" chuckled George.

"Come on, let's have a quick spin around, then we'll nip next door. He must have gone out and forgotten to meet us at the pub. Now, switch the light off in case there's someone else in here," I whispered.

"Like who?" whispered Jess, whilst George again plunged us into darkness.

"No idea," I replied. I crouched and stepped forward, dreading the thought that Paul Colney was alive and well – and on the prowl.

With me at the front, Jess in the middle, and George bringing up the rear, we gingerly moved forward, commando-style towards the kitchen, tiptoeing our way along whilst hugging close to the wall. I abruptly halted at the lounge door to peek inside, causing Jess to bump into me, and in turn, George into her.

"Ouch! I banged my nose!" hissed Jess in protest, as she shot her hand up to her face causing her elbow to involuntarily collide with George's nose as he straightened up behind her.

"Oh, bloody hell!" exclaimed George. "Do you mind!"

"Sorry, George, but Dad just stopped!" Jess grabbed my arm. "You need to signal if you're slowing down ... like they do in the war films when the lead soldier holds up his hand!"

"Like Michael Caine did in *Where Eagles Dare,*" added George, still rubbing his nose, trying to recover from colliding with Jess's elbow.

"No, he was in *The Eagle has Landed*, not *Where Eagles Dare,*" I hissed back down the line.

"You sure, lad?"

"Yes! Anyway, I don't recall Michael Caine creeping forward and holding up his hand to halt his troops' advances."

"Yes, he did, Dad. It was the scene when they were attacking the church," whispered Jess from behind.

"No! He played a German Colonel. They were in the church, not attacking it!" I once again hissed back down the line.

"Michael Caine's a German! I don't think so, lad! What you talking about?" added George from the rear.

I halted once again, using my raised hand as instructed by Jess. I turned, needing to put an end to this bizarre conversation. I felt we were in danger of performing Chinese whispers, which reminded me of the First World War instruction to *send reinforcements we're going to advance* that purportedly ended up as *send three and fourpence we're going to a dance*. "Look, can we discuss Michael Caine's and Richard Burton's war film castings later?"

"Alright, lad. But what the hell Richard Burton's got to do with this, I have no idea! And I can inform you that Michael Caine is very British!" George somewhat belligerently whispered up the line.

"JR was in that film. You know, him out of Dallas," added Jess, seemingly wanting to get the last word in.

"Who?" George whispered back up the line.

"Alright. Alright," I hissed. "Just keep your bloody voices down!"

We returned to our formation and proceeded. After my hand signal coaching session from Jess, I waved my left arm, indicating my next move was to turn into the lounge. I signalled over my shoulder with my right arm for Jess to circle around me and take up a position at the other side of the door opening before we proceeded – it was a solid plan.

I guess we hadn't practised our movements. Hence, as George and Jess stepped forward, they collided mid-hallway, causing the telephone table to topple, resulting in the phone, a copy of the Yellow Pages, and a particular favourite photo frame of Don's wife, Peggy, to crash to the floor.

"Christ! We'd be shite burglars! We're making enough noise to wake the bloody dead! I reckon Don can hear this commotion!" I blurted, as I snapped on the lounge lights, no longer concerned that we were about to discover anything grisly, be jumped by some madman, or succumb to satanic forces like in the Amityville House of Horror.

"Oh, George, are you alright?" fretted Jess, as she bent down to help George up from the pile of debris where the contents of the telephone table had landed.

"Buggerations! I've cut my hand on some ruddy glass!" exclaimed George, as he knelt, then removed a sliver of glass from his palm.

"Oh, Christ. Hang on. I'll get the first aid kit. Don kept it in the sideboard."

"Come on, George, sit on the sofa and let me get the glass out with some tweezers. I've always got a pair in my bag."

"Jess, here you are. It'll have some plasters and whatnot in there." I waved the battered, dented Family Circle biscuit tin at her before placing it on the sofa's armrest. Don had glued a red cross to the tin lid, although the Woolworths price label was still visible at 2/6.

"Jesus, George, are you okay?"

"Yes, lad. Don't fret," he chuckled. "I don't know what we were thinking."

I started to laugh. "Ha, no. We were acting like a scene from a spoof spy movie! Christ, Jonny English and Austin Powers, eat your heart out!"

"Never heard of them, lad."

"Oh, that's no surprise. Dad makes these things up all the time! Hold still! I've got it," stated Jess, as she worked on George's hand extracting a sliver of glass with her tweezers.

George raised an eyebrow at me. I nodded, confirming I'd spouted off without thinking of my audience. Fortunately, Jess was well used to my occasional odd statement and thought nothing of my, not so rare, time-travel cock-ups.

"Look, this is a waste of time. Let's lock up, get your stuff from next door and head home. I'll pop around tomorrow and see what he's been up to … there'll be some logical explanation why he's disappeared."

"There, you're all done. It's not too deep."

"Thanks, lass."

"Right, come on then, let's go."

"Dad, I'll just pop this in the kitchen," called out Jess, as she waved the pre-decimal tin of biscuits in the air and headed off down the hallway.

"Christ, now I feel guilty. That was the frame I bought Don about ten years ago," I muttered to no one in particular as I knelt to retrieve the picture of Peggy that now sported a splash of George's blood across it.

"Dad …"

"Dad … Dad!"

"Uh-huh. Give me a second, and we can go," I replied, as I wiped the blood from Peggy's black and white smile.

"Lad."

"Dad!"

The tremor in her voice caused my head to shoot up where I spotted Jess backing out of the kitchen towards me. As she stepped back, I could see a man standing in the doorway covered in blood, dripping from his hands, with splatters across his face.

"Pa-Pat-rick?" stammered Jess.

As I glanced up, I suspected the man wasn't Patrick. The man I presumed to be Paul Colney sneered; the blood splattered across his face morphing the vision in front of me to that of The Joker.

23

The Italian Stallion

Jess screamed.

"Ye gods and little codfishes," uttered George before his mouth gaped open, impersonating Bananarama, Beth's new pet, not the pop group with semi-naked men as per her bedroom-wall poster.

Faced with what appeared to be a grinning, blooded mad axeman, Jack Nicholson style, I joined Jess, hearing an involuntary scream exit my mouth.

Then, so as not to be left out, Paul Colney joined in and screamed as a tartan-patterned flask appeared to have materialised out of the darkness, crushing down on top of his head. I'm no expert, but as the flask bore a pattern of a mixture of red and greens, I'd plump that the design was the classic MacGregor tartan popularly used to decorate the thermos flasks of choice from the '60s and '70s.

Without looking around to assess whose hand held the flask, Paul bolted past Jess, hopped over my crouched body, nipped past George, who I think was now screaming as the axeman advanced, then bolted into the night out of the now flung open front door.

For a brief moment, we all stopped screaming. However, that became short-lived when Jess restarted her damsel-in-distress shriek as Martin appeared at the kitchen doorway, replacing Paul and looking just as menacing as the man who he'd just smashed a picnic flask on his head.

Leaping up, I grabbed Jess's arm as she appeared stuck in a trance, her screams now repeating as if the needle had stuck on the scratched record, and it just required a nudge to move it on.

"Jess! Jess, it's alright. It's alright," I blurted, grabbing the sides of her face, trying to stop her shakes which now had complete control of every muscle – she was hyperventilating.

"Bloody hell, Martin, lad, are you alright?"

"I've had enough of that sick bastard. I reckon, as Jenny suggested, we're going to have to cut him up into small pieces. Clearly, sending his head through a car windscreen and burning the sicko in a cremation oven wasn't enough to kill him! Christ, I need a fag," babbled Martin, as he rubbed the back of his head. "Oh, great!" he exclaimed, pulling his hand from his hair that appeared smeared with blood. "Look, the bastard's split my skull!"

The frightened rabbit look, that Jess had displayed in the pub earlier, returned, now fully perfected. Wide-eyed, still shaking, she gawped at Martin as he belligerently moaned about what Paul Colney had done to the back of his head.

"Lad, sit down and let me take a look," instructed George, as he shimmied past me, flicked the kitchen light on, then guided Martin to the only chair that was upright and appeared to be in one piece. "Bloody hell, lad. It looks like you've been burgled! What a mess," tutted George.

Martin complied with his request, allowing George to take a look at the top of his head. Although we had all stopped screaming, Jess was in no fit state for me to let go of. If I did, I felt sure she'd crumple into a heap. So, leaving George to assess the damage to Martin's head, I held Jess tightly whilst I considered my next move.

Whether I liked it or not, clearly, I was about to issue Jess a Time Travel Believers' Club application form. Now, as for her wanting to complete the said application and pay the subs, well, that was a very different matter. However, she had just seen Paul Colney close up, and she would know the Joker lookalike wasn't Patrick. Also, it was clear that dead Martin was now sitting in Don's kitchen whilst George assessed the state of his head. By the looks of his prodding and poking, coupled with Martin's constant stream of profanities, George was poorly applying his extremely limited first-aid skills.

I eased her head up from where she'd buried it deep in my chest. "Jess. Jess, look at me." Still, with her rabbit eyes, she complied. "We're going to sit you down and put the kettle on, okay? Let's have a warm drink, see to Martin, and then we can have a chat, alright?" I suggested, as reassuringly as I could, whilst holding her head in my hands and flashing my best comforting smile – she wasn't convinced.

Jess discovered the ability to offer a slight nod. Although complying, she now glanced back and forth between the three of us; I presume contemplating the possibility she was experiencing a strange hallucinogenic experience after a heavy session on the magic mushrooms, which I am aware she used to partake.

The other option that may have started dancing around her head was perhaps she now considered some of us had started some weird shapeshifting routine with newly acquired abilities like the plasticine men, Morph and Chas, who regularly changed their appearance on *Take Hart*, a particular favourite children's TV show of mine and Beth's in more than one childhood.

After retrieving an upturned kitchen chair, checking the legs were still attached, I guided Jess down, offered my cigarettes, supplied an ashtray, shut the front door to stop the shapeshifting Colney from re-entering, and stuck the kettle on.

The unforgiving light from the double undiffused bare fluorescent tubes above, illuminated the carnage that was once Don's orderly kitchen. With their blue hydrangea floral pattern, Don's white enamelled saucepans lay strewn across the brown carpet tiles. To complement the saucepans' floral design, they now sported an added splash of rouge, donated by either Martin or Paul or perhaps both. I considered taking a whack from one of those would have more than hurt, as would the Pyrex baby-pink with white floral pattern dishes that now lay smashed across the worktops.

An upturned bowl of potpourri lay mingled with the smashed glass jar of tricolour pasta. Both of those kitchen additions, which now lay across the top of the smoked-glass lid of Don's relatively new cooker, were an inspired addition by Jenny some years ago. They were that old, I suspected the pasta, potpourri, and glass would probably now all taste similar. I don't think Don had been aware that the pasta was actually food and not a decoration like the potpourri.

"George, how's it looking?"

"There's a lot of blood, but head wounds bleed a lot," he replied, as he dabbed Martin's head with a tea cloth. "I don't think you'll need stitches, lad. It's stopped bleeding by the looks of it."

"Oh, bloody hell, George! That hurts! Not exactly Florence Nightingale, are you!" blurted Martin, as he ducked his head from another potential tea cloth attack from George. "I reckon that bastard Colney might need stitches! He might have had the upper hand the last time we fought ten years ago, but I'm confident I won the rematch on points!"

"What actually happened?" I asked, whilst placing four cups of hot sweet tea on the table.

"The bastard just burst into the kitchen. He came from nowhere!"

Grabbing George's elbow, I nodded in Jess's direction as he looked up. Then, I mouthed, "She's in shock."

George nodded.

"I was just having a cuppa before coming to meet you up at the pub, and there he was, diving through the doorway wielding a garden spade like the Tasmanian Devil!"

"It looks like it, lad," offered George, as he surveyed the carnage that was once Don's, the old soldier's, perfectly clean, perfectly orderly kitchen.

That did explain why Don's bloodied garden spade lay abandoned on top of the ripped under-sink gingham curtain which, like the nets at the window, had a splattering of blood arced across them – a forensics scene-of-crimes technicians' paradise.

"To be honest with you, after that, it was all a bit of a blur. He was intent on killing me, that much I do know. It was like the Rocky and Apollo Creed re-match. I think we ended up knocking each other out because we both must have come to when Jess came in the kitchen."

George guided a mug of tea to Jess's hand whilst she tentatively dragged on a cigarette.

"Come on, lass. I know this is all a bit of a shock, but have a sip of this tea. That always does the trick."

"It was Paul. It was Paul," a whispered chant started, as she held the mug handle in one hand and the cigarette in the other, now shooting looks at me, then at George. "It was Paul."

"Yes, Jess. It was Paul."

"Is she alright? I'm the one with bloody concussion! What's the matter with you, woman?"

"Martin! The matter with Jess here is you're supposed to be dead, remember! And the bloke who just ran out of the house with a tartan picnic flask embedded in his scalp is also supposed to be dead!"

"Oh, yeah. Shit, sorry," he cheekily grinned. "Hi, Jess." Martin offered an almost embarrassed wave across the table at her, whilst Jess repeated the mantra about the real identity of The Joker.

"You're dead too," she stated, pointing her cigarette causing ash to ping off into Martin's tea.

"Oh, cheers. Lovely!" Martin sarcastically pronounced, as he watched the ash sink.

"Lass, look, as I said, this is all a bit of a shock—"

"Shock! Shock? What's the matter with you two? That man is dead! Dead! Can't you see that he should be dead! And a few minutes ago, I was faced with Patrick's evil bastard brother who should also be bloody dead!" delivered with anger but concluded with tears.

"He should be dead. Dad ... why isn't he dead?" a tearful question that I was fully aware was going to be super tough to answer.

"George, this is your area of expertise."

"I don't know about that, lad. Last time I told this story, Jenny stormed off saying how disappointed she was with me."

"She did. But why don't you have another go ... practice makes perfect, as they say."

George huffed, glanced around the room, then back at me.

"I think as we've got dead Martin in the room and a dead psychopath in the shape of Paul Colney running around Fairfield, you've at least got a good starting point. Jess needs to know, now we've got this far."

"Okay, lad. You'd better pull out a bottle of Don's whisky. Also, the lass here is going to need a large brandy."

"What's going on? Tell me, Dad. What's going on?"

"Jess, listen to George. However, before he goes any further, I'm not your real father."

24

The Omen

The dented, faded, various shades of blue Venetian blind announced DS Farham's arrival into DI French's office as it completed its clanging routine.

Before the blind finished its jangling sequence, Danny hurriedly blurted whilst he hung onto the door handle. "Guv, the Divisional Super is on the blower. You want me to tell him you're out?"

"Ohhh … Christ," huffed the DI, as she peered up from a stack of reports. "No, put him through."

"Okay, Guv."

"Oh, Danny," called out the DI, as the blind started its out-of-tune clanging routine again.

DS Farham stuck his head back in. "Guv?"

"When you put him through, come in; I might need you."

"Guv," nodded Danny, leaving the door open as he nipped back to his phone, patched the call through and hopped back into the DI's office, holding the blind in an attempt to silence it as he closed the door.

"Good morning, sir," stated the DI in her formal voice, which she always saved for the Divisional Superintendent, also aware of the need to project it a few decibels above her normal tones due to the fact that the ancient crown-epauletted dinosaur who should have retired years ago was as deaf as a post.

DI French despised the man, who, in her opinion, and all of her team's for that matter, displayed the competence of Inspector Clouseau, possessed the arrogance of Shere Khan, the brains of Worzel Gummidge, and oozed a power-hungry megalomaniac trait that made George Orwell's Napoleon seem almost agreeable. Damien Thorn could be described as angelic when compared to the Divisional Superintendent. And to top it all off, his breath stunk like Pepé Le Pew, so contact via the phone was always preferable over face-to-face visits – thank God for small mercies thought the DI.

"No, sir. I understand it's not a good morning," stated DI French, which preceded a brief moment of silence.

"I said, I understand it's *not* a good morning—" she repeated at one or two decibels higher.

"Yes, sir. I did say, *sir*, the first time." The DI plucked up her pen, scoring a large exclamation mark on the well-worn leather-bound blotting paper desk pad, causing the paper to tear.

Danny feared that the Super had already wound the Guv up, which did not bode well as the call had only just started.

DI French listened to her boss as she watched Danny clinging to the Venetian blind. He'd now got himself tangled up, and the only way to extract himself would be to cause a tumultuous clanging that would put the cymbals in the percussion section of the Philharmonic Orchestra to shame.

Peering around at her, Danny nervously grinned, now thankful for his boss's nod, which indicated he could extract himself and allow the crash of Venetian cymbals to fill the quiet room.

"Yes, sir. I understand, sir, but—" DI French rolled her eyes.

Danny quietly sat in the chair opposite whilst watching her expressions morph, suggesting the Super was on one of his famous rants.

"No, sir. What I said in my report was—"

"Yes, I do agree that was unfortunate, and I—"

Danny raised his hands, non-verbally questioning what the now heated exchange was regarding. Heather French wasn't known for her humour, so DS Farham was somewhat surprised when the DI pulled a face as she motioned that she was hanging herself with her free hand. Although, that said, all her team were fully aware that DI French held an extremely diminutive opinion of the Super.

"As I said, sir, I don't believe DC Reeves or Taylor intended to cause offence to the Shah family—"

The DI slapped her hand on her forehead in frustration, as once again, the Super interrupted her.

"Oh ... Christ. They said what?"

Danny could detect the pain which now radiated from the DI's face. Whatever the Super was relaying, clearly, it wasn't good news. Danny feared a shit-storm of gale-force proportions had just nudged over the horizon.

"Yes, sir, I agree. That was unfortunate—"

The DI slowly closed her eyes whilst continually shaking her head as the Super presumably ramped up his verbal rant.

"Yes, as you say, forcing them to remove their turbans was totally unacceptable, and I *will* be dealing with Reeves and Taylor through the disciplinary procedures."

Danny's jaw dropped and performed a bug-eye expression in disbelief at what he was hearing from this one-sided conversation. The Guv had instructed Reeves and Taylor to 'shake down' Susan Kane's neighbours. But unfortunately, it was apparent from the snippets of the conversation that *Fonzie* and *Flintstone* had taken the Guv's instruction literally. Reeves, called *Fonzie* due to always having his jacket collar upturned, was anything but cool. As for Taylor, well, yes, he was as immature as the cartoon character, demonstrated by the fact that he and his wife had actually named their daughter Pebbles.

"Yes, sir, absolutely. Absolutely. I will arrange to visit the Shah family with DS Farham and try and make amends."

Danny groaned inwardly. Visiting the Broxworth Estate was painful at the best of times. However, when the purpose of the visit was to grovel and apologise for police officers' actions, well, that just hit the bottom of any to-do list.

Whilst Danny dreaded the impending visit the Guv had mentioned, the two senior officers' conversation seemed to move on to a different subject.

"No, sir. I was quite clear that although the car had the same index number, *obviously,*" stated in frustration and rolling her eyes, "It couldn't be the same vehicle as it was crushed ten years ago—"

"But—"

"Yes I—"

"No, sir. No, I wasn't suggesting for one moment that I thought you were stupid—" she calmly stated, probably realising she was heading for hot water. Whilst nodding and chucking in the odd "uh-huh" here and there, the DI scrawled out on her now shredded blotting-pad—

The man is an idiot!

Danny smirked. Although the DI was a straight as a bat, which sometimes he and the team found frustrating, Danny considered her the most competent officer he'd ever had the pleasure of working for throughout his years of service. However, Danny always enjoyed it when the Guv let her guard down in front of him. It gave Danny the feeling that she trusted him, and he treasured that trust.

"We're picking up with Patrick Colney today, sir. Yes, I know—"

"Sir … sir. Patrick is not a suspect. He was in Havervalley nick at the time of the murder, so—"

"No, sir, I'm not suggesting that. However—" DI French held the phone receiver away from her ear, allowing Danny to hear the Super rant down the phone although the actual words were not decipherable.

The DI just shook her head whilst Danny contemplated the fallout that was surely coming Reeves and Taylor's way.

A few seconds passed before the DI reapplied the handset to her ear. "Sir, that is not the case—" She clenched her fist. "My team have been on this since Monday morning. I have cancelled all leave, and most of my officers are pulling in eighteen-hour shifts!"

From DS Farham's side of the desk, it was clear from the constant tinny sound emanating from the handset thrust to a pissed-off looking DI's head that the news her team were pulling in long shifts was not cutting the mustard with the Super.

"Sir, my team are the best you can get. I can assure you we will get results!"

Danny thought of Reeves and Taylor; they could not be categorised as the best you can get. However, Danny was not surprised that the DI strongly defended her team in front of the Super – she demanded loyalty, which she received back by the bucket load.

"Well, yes, I accept Reeves and Taylor may not fit into that category based on their intimidation of the Shah family. However, the rest of my team—"

Interrupted again, Danny thought the blood vessels that now stood proud on her temples were about to burst, which would result in more blood splattered about the office than was up at the crime scene where Susan Kane had been discovered.

"No, I understand, sir. Yes, I agree your wife and the Fairfield branch of the Women's Institute could probably do a better job than Reeves and Taylor."

Danny looked away, fearful that he might burst out laughing at hearing the DI's sarcastic comment. Although, to be fair, the Super had a point.

"No, sir. Absolutely not. I wasn't being disingenuous. I certainly didn't intend to come across like that."

Danny raised his eyebrows.

"No, sir, I didn't go to university."

Danny held his hands aloft, wondering what tangent the Super had now sent the conversation off on.

"No, I don't think disingenuous is a posh word, and I would never intend to mock you, sir!"

Danny shook his head in disbelief. The Divisional Superintendent had always grabbed every opportunity to bore anyone, who was prepared to listen, regarding his working-class background and the underprivileged upbringing he'd endured in the East End, which, according to him, provided the life skills, as he put it, to be an effective senior officer. But clearly, disingenuous was a word outside of his vocabulary.

"Yes, sir, I guarantee—"

The DI picked up her pen and motioned to Danny for paper. He turned over a roughly torn manila envelope, placing it in front of the DI whilst firmly holding down the corner to the desk so she could write her message.

'Get Reeves and Taylor back here now ... I'm going to castrate them!'

DS Farham read the note upside down, looked up at the DI, nodded and swivelled around to hunt down the soon-to-be-eunuch detective constables.

As the Venetian blind precision set clanged in the wake of DS Farham's departure, and with one last "Yes, sir," boomed down the phone, DI French slammed the receiver down.

With her eyes closed, a deep-breathing DI Heather French calmed herself, ready to deal with the two idiots who held warrant cards but could not, in any shape or form, be described as detectives and fell well short of the capabilities of PC Plod. She very much doubted either would be capable of delivering effective police work in Toytown.

DI French knew her team weren't the greatest. However, Taylor and Reeves would have to be dealt with because they were dragging the whole department's reputation to the gutter.

"Guv."

"What?" barked the DI at DC Megson, who stood in the doorway.

"This morning, me and *Fawlty* plan to pick up Bowen, Susan Kane's boyfriend. Word on the street is he's laying low, but we turned over a few rocks and got a tip-off he's squatting in the derelict houses up at the back of MFI and Do-It-All."

"Good. Although, something tells me he's not our man. Susan Kane was murdered by a psychopath. Bowen's a low life, but he's not that sick. That said, he's a piece of crap, so give him a damn good shake because I'd bet my bottom dollar, he knows something."

"Will do, Guv. But that's why I'm here. We've got another body. Do you want me with you before we pick up Bowen?"

"Where?"

"It was discovered up on a derelict piece of waste ground at the back of some warehouse near Havervalley Prison."

"It?"

"Yes, Guv. Uniform are there, and they say the body is so severely beaten and burnt, it will take dental records to identify if the body is male or female."

"I want DS Farham and you with me. Tell Sergeant Farham to send Taylor and Reeves to pick up Bowen."

"Guv," nodded Megson, as she swivelled around and hot-footed across the office to radio the sergeant.

Grabbing her jacket and bolting out of her office, the DI had one of her hunches that the body discovered up near Havervalley Prison would have a connection to Susan Kane.

Of course, letting Taylor and Reeves loose before she had the opportunity to castrate them was risky. But hell, it was only the low life Bowen they were picking up, so surely, they couldn't cock that up – could they?

The DI answered her own question – yes, they probably could.

On a positive note, as far as the DI could remember, Bowen didn't wear a turban, plus, she really couldn't give a shit if he lodged a complaint about the way her two incompetent Toytown officers had handled him.

25

A Spoon Full Of Sugar

Raised in the old town of Fairfield in a two-up-two-down Victorian terraced house by parents who had little money left after paying the rent, food and his father's Woodbines, Ralph had learnt to take what he wanted from life. Nothing came to a man through wishing and hoping. You either worked hard like his father, or you just took what you wanted.

At an early age, Ralph realised that working for a living in a conventional way was not for him. The plumbing apprenticeship his father had secured him in Darwin had only served to confirm this. His only other experience of work was helping his father with his early morning bread deliveries before school that, at the time, Ralph believed was akin to slave labour.

The law had changed in the last century, prohibiting the use of children to clean chimneys. However, his father insisted that young Ralph help him put bread on the table – literally. So, every day he would be up and out of bed at four in the morning, resulting in the twelve-year-old Ralph falling asleep during afternoon lessons.

Both short-lived excursions into working for someone else had taught Ralph that work paid little, or nothing in his enforced slavery when delivering bread. Also, both employment opportunities offered little excitement.

His years in Australia had paid well. Ralph's intimidating size and height, which he'd inherited from his maternal grandfather, served as a critical advantage over most, resulting in the highest-paid work always being available. Moreover, those who operated outside of the law and required certain skills, which Ralph's stature offered, always appreciated his talents. Therefore, Ralph became well respected and highly sought after in his field of expertise – namely, protection and intimidation services.

Twenty-five years of plying his trade for the organised crime gangs of Northern Australia had set Ralph up comfortably and, not to push his luck too far, he'd got out while the going was good.

Ralph sipped his coffee in the Palace Bar of the Maid's Head Hotel whilst waiting for his Shirl. He pondered what his father would have thought to his son staying in a five-star hotel, drinking coffee from a dainty bone-china cup with an array of sweet pastries on offer. Not to mention the attentive service from a young lass dressed in a red waistcoat and a short black skirt, who Ralph enjoyed ogling at when she bent over to serve the guests in the opulent bar furnished with plush, red velvet, Queen Anne chairs.

After enjoying their full English breakfast, Shirley returned to their room to freshen up whilst Ralph waited in the Palace Bar and perused the daily papers.

This morning they were due to meet with one of Shirley's old acquaintances. Once this meeting was concluded and the proper legal support put in place for her son, Andrew, they would be jetting off home at the end of the week.

Shirley had intended to spend some time with her close friend Susan Kane. However, unfortunately, it appeared someone had decided to remove Susan from this world by obliterating her skull on the very day Shirley and Ralph had arrived. This news, which his Shirl had received from one of many in the town who regularly kept her up to date with events whilst she enjoyed the Spanish sun, had uncharacteristically upset his Shirl – an emotion Ralph rarely witnessed from his feisty British bird.

Although Shirley appeared bothered about her friend's death, Ralph knew his girl was holding back on something else, and he fully intended to find out what that was.

Ralph had planned to settle an old score whilst Shirley visited Susan. However, now Shirley's plans had changed, he considered he might have to come clean with her regarding the revenge dish he planned on serving.

Last night after taking in a few local pubs, they'd stayed up drinking in the Palace Bar with some of the other guests. Many had retreated from the couple, and Ralph was fully aware his appearance could be quite intimidating – that physical presence which had earned him a tidy sum over the years.

So, after Ralph had unwittingly terrified and scared away many of the guests, the evening continued into the early hours culminating in a heavy drinking session which involved slugging back copious amounts of brandy sours bought by an apparently famous comedian who was appearing in a week-long run of shows at the Theatre Royal in town.

Although Ralph found the man annoying, Shirley had appeared to enjoy the cockney comedian's company. She'd constantly laughed at the man's smutty jokes and lewd innuendoes, leaving Ralph half tempted to punch his lights out. However, the Palace Bar in the most prestigious hotel in Fairfield wasn't the place to start a brawl, and he could ill afford a night in the cells.

The comedian had his girl eating out of the palm of his hand, and a pissed Shirley had let slip the real reason for their trip which, prior to a drunken night in the posh hotel bar, Ralph had been blissfully unaware of.

When they'd concluded this morning's meeting with the slithery brief, he would be questioning his girl about what she really intended to do over the next few days. He now feared the reason he'd been invited for the trip was for his muscle and not to keep his Shirl warm at night.

Although Ralph had revenge planned, he certainly wasn't prepared to put himself in the spotlight of the British authorities just so that Shirley could address the issue of two long-lost granddaughters. The two granddaughters who last night Shirl had cooed over when she and the smutty comedian babbled on whilst proceeding to get pissed into the early hours – leaving the disgruntled barman of the residents' bar to longingly and silently implore them to bugger off so he could close up for the night.

"Right then, pour me a coffee. I've still got a head splitter!" growled a fully made-up Shirley as she sunk into the chair next to her man-mountain partner.

"What time is the brief due?" he asked, as he picked up the silver pot, pouring out the thick black coffee whilst Shirley threw in handfuls of sugar cubes that piled up and stood like brown icebergs in the black-sea coffee.

She pointed to the ornate grandfather clock that started its chiming routine as it struck ten o'clock. "Now," she bit back. Shirley could be super feisty at the best of times; add in a mother of all hangovers, and she became ferocious.

"Well, he's late, then."

"Ralph, do me a favour," asked Shirley, as she rubbed her temples. "The penguin playing the piano. Be a love and smash his fingers. That bloody tune is killing my head."

"I'll let him finish this tune. It's Eye Level ... you know, the music to that Dutch detective series I like on TV."

"Shoestring? Eddie Shoestring?"

"No, he's not Dutch! Van Der something."

"Whatever. I couldn't care less what his fucking name is, but if you don't shut the penguin up, I will!" growled Shirley, as she reclined in her chair and continued to rub her temples in a rhythmic circular motion.

"Alright," stated Ralph, as he headed for the poor unsuspecting pianist.

Shirley wasn't sure what Ralph did, but the piano music abruptly halted mid-tune. There were no screams or cracking-finger noises, so she assumed Ralph had just applied threats rather than snapping the pianist's digits. Unfortunately, before Ralph returned from re-educating the pianist, the now more relaxed atmosphere was duly destroyed by the introduction of piped music that Shirley considered just as hellish as the screeching piano. T'Pau banged on about *China In Your Hand,* which was kind of apt as Ralph once again tried to negotiate the silly coffee cup, which somewhat resembled a thimble in his gigantic fists.

"Can I get you a refill, madam?" The attentive waitress in the short skirt stood leaning forward with her hand hovering by the coffee pot whilst delivering her well-trained I'm-happy-to-help smile. Although in reality, she probably didn't give a shit if Shirley was dehydrated or ever took another breath.

Shirley nodded. "And another cup. I'm expecting another guest."

"Of course, madam."

"Girl. What's your name?"

"Sharon, madam," stated the young lass, as she pointed to her name badge pinned to her waistcoat above a plethora of smaller badges which Sharon knew, full-well, she wasn't allowed to pin to her uniform.

CND, Free Nelson Mandela, Nuke Thatcher, Anti Nazis league fight against fascism, and Solidarność badges all clustered around her gold name-badge. Shirley guessed Sharon was one of those university types who planned to save the world – well, good luck with that, she thought. She also suspected that when the girl married an investment banker and lived in a posh house full of Habitat furniture with two kids in tow, she wouldn't give two shits about an imprisoned anti-apartheid campaigner or the rights of the oppressed Polish shipyard workers.

"Well, Sharon, if you don't want me to wipe that smile off your face, you better stop calling me a madam!"

"Oh, no, no, sorry, ma—" the young lass blushed before swiping up the pot and scuttling away.

"For God sake. She's in her twenties! You might as well have been fondling her!" spat Shirley, as she watched Ralph letch at the young waitress who almost ran from their table.

"What?"

"You! Looking up her skirt. Christ, you men! All of you … dicks for brains!"

"I wasn't. I—" protested Ralph, but his girl's attention had moved on.

"Ah, the snivelling tosser has arrived," interrupted Shirley, as she spotted her man who strode across the plush, albeit somewhat dated, Axminster carpet, wearing a solicitor's regulation pinstriped suit, carrying his Samsonite briefcase.

"Mrs Colney," he nervously grinned but failed to offer his hand, presumably wishing to avoid physical contact.

Shirley nodded to the vacant chair as the young waitress returned, almost abandoning the coffee pot and cup as she sped out of sight behind the bar.

"Ralph Eastley," offered the man-mountain, as he stuck out his hand to the city-style-suited man with monk-ring styled thinning hair, who regarded Ralph with disdain as he peered down at him, turning up his nose. As did everyone who met Ralph for the first time, the suited city gent appeared fixated by Ralph's white, sightless shark-eye.

"I know who you are, Eastley."

"Then you'll know getting on the wrong side of me is a bit fucking stupid, won't you!" barked Ralph, who'd taken an instant dislike to the slippery git – lawyers were all the same.

The weasel, as Shirley had referred to him, pursed his lips, seeming unintimidated by the giant creature that now appeared ready to crack his spine in two. "As you are accompanying Mrs Colney, I assume you will be fully aware that her husband is Mr Colney. So … assuming you know who I work for, threatening me is a bit, as you say, fucking stupid, would you not say?" he mocked, grinning at the beast, presumably assuming that Ralph was as stupid as he was big.

Ralph decided to let this one slide. Years ago, he would have folded the man in half for such a comment. However, with the benefit of wisdom and no desire to spend time incarcerated at Her Majesty's pleasure, he bit his tongue. What the slithering little weasel wasn't aware of – Ralph never forgot and never forgave. Mr Colney's bent solicitor had just signed his own death warrant and, at some point in the future, Ralph would ensure that warrant was executed – after all, he had his reputation to consider.

After winning the staring game with the Incredible Hulk, Mark Hawkshaw, a well-known solicitor with dubious connections, turned his attention to Shirley.

"Your husband sends his regards," he pompously stated as he sat, undoing his jacket and crossing his legs. Mark Hawkshaw was cocksure.

"Say hello to him for me."

"No. No, I'm not doing that," stated the confident brief, grinning and pausing for effect. "You'll do it in person … tomorrow. Mr Colney will be expecting you during the weekly visiting session. Do you understand?"

A pregnant pause held whilst Mark grabbed the coffee pot and awaited a response from Shirley, but nothing came.

"Have I made myself clear?" calmly stated Mr Hawkshaw, as he poured his coffee without taking his eyes off Shirley, not spilling a drop and not overfilling the cup.

Shirley nodded.

Ralph shot her a surprised look. Never had he seen anyone talk to his girl in that way. Well, not without dire consequences, that is. And now she was going to visit her husband because he'd demanded it! Ralph now started to acquire a feeling of uneasiness about this trip. This wasn't panning out as he'd expected, and he began to wonder if he was some pawn in Mr and Mrs Colney's twisted game.

"Mark, let's get down to business. Where are we with Andrew?"

Mark shook his head, sipped his coffee and gently placed the cup back on its saucer before reclining into the winged-back Queen Anne chair. "Your boy is bang to rights. You've heard of DNA evidence?"

Shirley shrugged her shoulders before replying. "Sort of."

"Okay. There are a few cases where DNA is considered sufficient evidence to irrefutably prove guilt. I have it on good authority that your boy's case is one of them. The newly formed Crown Prosecution Service are keen to make Andrew Colney their first landmark case and secure a conviction with DNA evidence. There are a few other cases that could pip your boy's case to being the first but, as you see, they're going hell-for-leather on this one to get it to court."

"What does that mean for Andrew, then?"

"They've got his DNA, Shirley. Your boy raped those women. He's a nonce. And, I can assure you … your husband isn't going to protect him inside."

"Then he can rot in hell along with Paul. I didn't raise my boys that way, so I don't care."

"Shirl?" questioned Ralph, shocked that his girl didn't seem to care about her boy.

"What?" she aggressively spat back.

"What the hell have we come for, then? If you're happy to let Andrew rot in a cell, why have we made this trip? I thought the point of coming was to get him a solid brief?"

"Oi, Eastley, can I remind you I represent Mr and Mrs Colney. So why don't you piss off?" spat the weasel with the smug look.

"Ralph!" Shirley caught hold of Ralph's hand, held it and nodded, indicating that her big fella needed to stay calm.

Ralph turned and faced her.

"Let Mr Hawkshaw finish, and I will explain."

"So, Patrick. He's signed in at the probation hostel last night. I'll be visiting him later, and I suggest you come with me. Your husband has some jobs Patrick needs to attend to, and I believe it will be in your best interests to join me. Anyway, good for a mother to see her son."

Shirley nodded again, at the same time squeezing Ralph's hand, which didn't go unnoticed by her husband's weasel solicitor. Shirley didn't care what he thought because she knew she held all the aces.

"Okay, so as I instructed you last week, where have you got with the investigations which I asked you to carry out regarding the Apsleys?"

"The who?" barked Ralph, now confused where this conversation was spinning off to. More to the point, Shirl said the name Apsley – a name that one owner of that name had a cold dish of revenge coming their way – coincidence perhaps, thought Ralph.

"They're a rock band, you gorilla," chuckled the poncy solicitor as he revelled at his own quick wit.

"Who?" repeated Ralph.

"Exactly! The Who. You really are a lump of Neanderthal gristle!" chuckled Mark. "Shirley, I suggest you ditch the idiot." He thumbed in Ralph's direction. "We've got a whole army of loyal lads who can protect you. So, let's ditch the gorilla."

"You fucking piece of shit," growled Ralph, who shifted forward in his seat, causing Mr Hawkshaw to flinch.

Shirley knew this was a possible outcome of today's meeting. And any second now, if she didn't act fast, Ralph would be a wanted man after he'd killed slithery Hawkshaw.

"Ralph!" she barked.

"There's a good dog. Sit!" commanded a now more assured Mark Hawkshaw. "You've got your Aussie dingo well-trained. Does he go around sniffing for babies near Ayers Rock when you let him off the leash?" chuckled the solicitor as he lit his cigarette, once again reclining in his chair, now confident Shirley had control of the ape-like man with the milky shark-eye.

In one swift movement, Ralph's arm shot forward, grabbing Mark's collar, hauling him out of his chair, twisting as he pulled. Ralph's bicep pulsed as Mark's crimson face darkened, and his eyes slowly started to pop. Ralph held him, inspecting his face like an insect he held between his thumb and forefinger before crushing the life out of it.

"Ralph!" hissed Shirley.

He let go, allowing the slithery piece of shit to fall back into his chair. Mark Hawkshaw, for the first time, appeared concerned for his safety.

Ralph clicked his fingers, gaining the barman's attention, who appeared to be held in a trance as he grabbed the phone receiver whilst gawping at the incident. Ralph shook his head and pointed his finger downwards, indicating to the barman, who'd probably messed his trousers, to replace the phone in its cradle, and that attempting to use the phone to alert the hotel management of the incident would be an extremely unwise move.

With the young barman now fully compliant, Ralph assessed the insect, who attempted to straighten his tie and shirt collar following Ralph's wardrobe realignment.

Hawkshaw's earlier confidence appeared to have ebbed away. Now he just displayed pure fear, which was the look Ralph was more accustomed to seeing in his prey.

"When my Shirl has concluded her business with you, I'm going to cut your cock off, alright?"

The terrified solicitor once again flinched. Ralph wouldn't be surprised if the pompous git hadn't shit himself – for sure, he wouldn't be the first to self-defecate when at the receiving end of one of Ralph's threats.

"So, about that bloke Apsley. What have you got for me?" questioned Shirley, before lighting a cigarette and delivering her signature cold stare.

Mark Hawkshaw finished straightening his collar then took a sip of his coffee as he tried to compose himself.

"Mark, if you value your dick, I suggest you answer me. Ralph wasn't joking," calmly stated Shirley, as she dropped her cigarette in Mark's coffee cup, which he held to his lips. She'd made her point.

Hawkshaw shifted his chair a further inch from Ralph's. Not that this helped, but he felt the need to distance himself, and an inch was an inch – it was better than nothing. He peered at his cup, which now sported Shirley's drowning cigarette butt, then cleared his throat. "Your husband instructed me not to pursue that. He wants it left ... he ... he thinks it just complicates matters for no reason," he whispered, as if stating this surely unwelcome news in a hushed tone would soften the blow.

"*I* asked you to do the work ... this has nothing to do with my husband! I paid you, not my husband!" she bit back, shifting forwards and stabbing a slender finger in his direction.

"Yes, that may be so—"

"Ralph, his hand!" barked Shirley without taking her eyes off the weasel and shifting further forward in her seat, knowing what was coming.

Before Hawkshaw could blink, the man-mountain had his hand pinned, palm-up on top of the table, between the coffeepot, the plate of Danish pastries and the half-full glass ashtray. To any onlooker, it appeared two men were concluding a business deal, one hand in the other.

Shirley lit another cigarette, taking a long drag, whilst eyeing up her husband's solicitor, who'd stupidly chosen to disobey her. She blew a plume of smoke at his face before holding her cigarette at Mark's wrist, his hairs melting as she guided the lit end to his skin.

The barman could see there was no business deal conclusion but, before he could make a dash for it, Ralph beckoned him over with the nod of his head. The barman hesitated then tentatively stepped around the bar, hovered and glanced around at the other patrons who were oblivious to the somewhat irregular events that were transpiring in the lounge bar in a five-star hotel.

"Oliver. That's your name, son. Oliver?" questioned Ralph, as he smiled at the lad whilst keeping the pressure on the weasel's hand.

The barman shifted nervously after he lifted his name badge pinned to his chest as if checking that he was, in fact, called Oliver. His right leg twitched as he stared bug-eyed at the lit cigarette end, managing a slight nod confirming his name.

"Struth! You lost your tongue?"

Oliver shook his head but still chose to say nothing, completely mesmerised by the glowing cigarette end that nudged its way ever closer to the suited man's skin.

"Alright. I'll assume your ears work, even if you've lost that tongue. Now, listen up. This is how today is going to pan out. There are six other guests in the lounge. When I tell you to, you'll go over to each table and apologise, but state there is a flood behind the bar and instruct them to move out to the veranda. When you've done that, you'll close the door, with you still in here."

Oliver didn't move.

Hawkshaw stayed motionless as he implored with his eyes for Shirley not to burn him. Shirley had crossed a line, and there would be consequences for her when he relayed today's events to her husband. However, at this precise point, those thoughts had to sit on the back-burner because Mark feared Shirley had lost control, and there was a real danger that her and her pet gorilla could cause him some serious harm.

Although the pay was good, the holidays in the Caribbean were wonderful, and he especially liked the fast cars, which always gave him an erection, Mark Hawkshaw knew the risks.

Unfortunately, there was always the potential for days like today, because working for the local mafia had its downside.

"Look, mate. You hear me?" asked Ralph to the young barman, who by the state of him, Ralph considered might have gone into shock. "Oli, I hope you understand me. Otherwise, you could end up with the same fate."

Oliver nodded. Shooting his hand to his stomach, he breathed out, just avoiding pebble-dashing the three of them with his breakfast. He turned and complied with the order.

Fortunately, the six guests didn't seem to mind their enforced relocation. Oliver had performed well with his hospitality training coming to the fore. He suggested to the more befitting guests of a five-star hotel that the veranda now benefited from the morning sunshine which flooded it with warmth and light.

"You're crossing a line, Shirley," calmly stated Mark, as the heat started to melt his skin.

Shirley nodded to Ralph.

Ralph reached into his jacket pocket, produced his flick knife and pressed the blade release button. Then, in one swift movement, he arced the seven-inch blade through the air before plunging it through Mark's palm, a nanosecond after Ralph had skilfully removed his hand at the last possible moment, resulting in the weasel's hand lying skewered to the ornate marquetry tabletop – true Godfather style. Ralph had loved the two films, Brando being his idol.

Mark squealed like a strangled piglet.

Oliver lost his breakfast.

Shirley smirked and took another long drag on her cigarette.

Mark Hawkshaw stopped squealing only to involuntarily release his bladder, which was evident because the front of his sharp-creased suit trousers darkened. He opened his mouth to scream in agony as the pain had registered with the vision of his hand pinned to the table and the blood seeping out and soaking into the Maid's Head monogrammed linen napkins. Ralph clamped his hand over Mark's mouth to silence him.

Shirley leant forward and calmly refreshed her cup, slowly pouring the coffee from the silver pot, whilst her husband's brief's cries of pain stayed muffled by her lover's large hand. She took another long pull on her cigarette, allowing the smoke to drift from her mouth as she eyed up the tears that trickled down his cheeks.

A few feet to Shirley's left, Oliver continued to choke up bile as he knelt on the well-worn Axminster.

Shirley stubbed out her cigarette where the blade entered Mark's hand. He writhed in pain, his eyes bulging as Ralph held him tightly in position.

"Get this, you weasel. No one tells *me* what to do. You can inform that husband of mine that he and his perverted sons are dead to me. And if he thinks he can take me on, he might want to check out some of my connections. Many of my acquaintances will eat him alive, and their pets make Ralph here look like Mary Poppins. You get all that?"

In muffled tones, Mark nodded, as tears flowed and snot frothed in his nose as he desperately tried to breathe.

"I was quite clear that I wanted action taken against the two families who stole my granddaughters … you chose to ignore my request, so the consequences for your decision are going to be dire."

Mark's eyes widened further as he presumably contemplated what could be more dire than his current situation.

Shirley reclined in her chair, crossed her legs, and grabbed another cigarette. Before lighting, she surveyed young Oliver, who still knelt praying to his now regurgitated breakfast.

"Clean it up. It stinks."

Oliver didn't move, preferring, it appeared, to continue to stare at the carpet whilst gently rocking back and forth as if in some trance and about to chant his allegiance to the Hare Krishna movement.

"Clean it!" spat Shirley, jolting the barman back into the land of the living.

Shirley turned back to face the whimpering Mr Hawkshaw. She noticed a trickle of urine reach the end of his seat pad before dripping to the carpet below. "You know it's wankers like you that makes what's wrong with this country. Weak men who can't think for themselves. You're just like my husband – and yes, you can tell him that. I've spent my life getting that tosser out of scrapes, then standing by him while he's banged up. Well, no more."

Swiftly she yanked out the blade, then thrust it towards his soaked trouser fly. Shirley had witnessed terror in a man's face on many occasions. Often, she was the cause of their agitated state. However, the terror etched in the expression of Mark Hawkshaw was a level up, the penthouse suite of terror – what a great feeling.

"Now, I could cut your dick off, or Ralph could break your neck. The other option is you work for me for a few days, and I'll see if Ralph thinks you're worth keeping alive."

Mark Hawkshaw continued his whimpering like an abandoned puppy stuck at the bottom of a hundred-foot well.

"Did he nod, Ralph? Or was that just the trembling?" questioned Shirley, as she nudged the blooded blade a smidge harder into his soaked crotch whilst raising her finger to her lips, mockingly trying to answer her own question.

"He nodded," confirmed Ralph, whilst keeping his hand clamped over Mark's mouth. Ralph wanted answers. "Shirl?" he questioned.

"Uh-huh," she replied, as she held the blade to the terrified man's crown jewels.

"Apsley. How do you know a man called Apsley?"

Shirley raised her eyes from where she'd been enjoying bathing in the man's torment to lock eyes with Ralph.

"I just do … he owes me."

"Well, Shirl, if he's the same Apsley, that makes two of us."

Part 3

26

1954

The Artful Dodger

Other Jason

"Jason! Come on, Apsley, what you doing in there?" called out Roy, as he checked his hair in the mirror, then wiggled the knot of his tie, straightening what was already perfectly straight. Looks were important – girls would only dance with clean-cut looking chaps.

"Alright, Clarky, I'm having a crap! I'll see you back in there. Keep your hands off that lass, Ruth, though, I think I'm in there," replied Jason, as he pulled out a few sandpaper-textured sheets of Izal toilet paper while he perched inside the only working cubicle in the gent's toilets of the Festival House Dance Hall.

"Well, you better hurry, otherwise I might just steal her from under your feet," replied Roy, who yanked open the toilet door, allowing the sound of the band who were attempting a rendition of *The Crewcuts Sh-boom* to waft in from the dance floor.

Roy Clark knew that although he said he might steal the blonde from under Apsley's feet, there was no chance of that happening. Jason always pulled the hot chicks, where Roy was happy to grab pretty much any girl who would agree to step out with him.

Enjoying a week-long break from university and back in his old hometown of Fairfield, tonight was the climax of the week's partying for Jason and his old mates from Eaton Grammar School.

The group of university lads were determined to let their hair down and have some fun. Also, this was one of their last opportunities because, come the end of their next term, they would all have to start their National Service.

Jason and many of his university pals had delayed their service to complete their education. They had all dodged a bullet, so to speak, when at the end of last year National Service was once again reduced from two years to eighteen months after the end of the Korean War. Jason really wasn't looking forward to being drafted in, and the reduction of six months was extremely welcome.

Tonight, they started at the Festival House with the weekly Saturday night dance where he and a few mates were hoping to pick up some girls and then persuade them to go drinking with them.

If he was lucky, perhaps one of the girls might be what the lads called 'easy', and he could sow some wild oats. The young blonde girl, Ruth, was definitely making eyes at him and, before the evening was done, he thought she looked innocent enough to be wooed by his worldly charms.

~

"Come on, Freddie, he's not looking. We can sneak in," suggested Ralph, as they approached the dance hall.

The three lads proudly wearing their Teddy-Boy jackets, who'd been waiting for an opportunity to sneak into the dance hall, made a dash for it, hoping the distracted doorman would miss them as they crept along the sidewall. Of course, they were well aware even if they did sneak in, the posh older lads would soon throw them out. However, they thought it would be a hoot because the small Hertfordshire town of Fairfield offered very little in the way of laughs, so anything was game to relieve the boredom.

"Oi! Stop. Where d'you think you three louts are off to then?" called out the doorman, as he swivelled around pointing to the group of Teddy Boys who now hovered near the entrance.

"What me, sir?" asked Freddie, innocently pointing at his chest, mockingly appearing aghast that the doorman could describe him as a lout.

"Yes, You three! Be off with you!"

"Oh, no, sir. You've got us all wrong, sir. Not us, sir," mocked Freddie, who stood his ground, smirking at the now flustered doorman.

"Who'd you think you are? The Artful Dodger? Now, come on, be off with you. This ain't the place for the likes of you lot."

Freddie eyed up the now nervous-looking vertically challenged doorman wearing a brown uniform. "Shouldn't you be punching tickets up at the ABC, you old-duffer!" he mocked before leaning towards the doorman's face. "Boo!" he added, which caused his mates Ralph and Dick to immaturely fall about laughing, holding their stomachs.

Now sixteen, Freddie was the super-confident one of the three lads, modelling himself on the James Cagney character from the film *White Heat*.

"Right, you lads, off you go. This is a young adult dance, and not for the likes of you lot!" demanded the doorman, as he tentatively dragged his hand over his thinning hair whilst involuntarily stepping backwards. Although slightly concerned about the lad, who seemed far too confident and appeared intent on trying to intimidate him, he kept half an eye on the others. One of them clearly hadn't suffered slow growth during the rationing years – he was the size of a giant.

"Oh, yeah, grandad. Is that so? And who's stopping us, then?" confidently challenged Freddie, who glanced around to soak up the adoration which poured from his subservient mates, Dick and the giant Ralph.

Alf Hurst, the hapless doorman, stood his ground whilst the cheeky young lad tried his best to browbeat his way past. For Alf, depressingly, life had come to this, a Saturday evening job on the door at the Festival House Dance Hall.

Alf was one of the lucky chaps who returned home in October 1945 after recovering in a Burmese military hospital following on from life in a POW camp under the vicious rule of the Japanese. He'd suffered for three years at the hands of his captors after the horrific capitulation of the British forces in the battle of Singapore in 1942. After miraculously surviving the hellish journey on the prisoner transportation ships, Alf ended up in Burma, building the Burma-Siam railway along the Kwai river. Unfortunately, most of his comrades, friends and acquaintances had not returned in 1945 – Alf was the lucky one.

He was the lucky one ... well, that's what he kept telling himself. However, after being demobbed, he found life in civvy street difficult, discovering that adapting back into life in a near-normal Blighty was a continuation of the hell he'd left in Burma.

Those lads who defeated Hitler and his army returned to a tumultuous fanfare celebration of their heroic efforts in Europe. However, by the time Alf was well enough to travel and make the journey back to this green and pleasant land, there wasn't any fanfare, no girls rushing up to kiss him, or any celebrations to welcome back another war hero. There was, in fact, no one. The day he arrived home, he discovered he'd lost his wife and son earlier that year.

Alf's family weren't victims of the Luftwaffe bombs. However, they were in the way of a pissed army major who ploughed his six-cylinder Morgan through them, scattering them like skittles, when driving home from a VE party one morning. The major had led his depleted platoon over a heavily guarded bridge that crossed the Rhine, allowing the allied army to advance into Germany. To the cheering masses back home, the major was considered a war hero, resulting in no action being taken regarding the unfortunate deaths of the woman and little boy who stupidly ended up under the wheels of the decorated war hero's car.

The trauma, nightmares, and constant embedded terror in his mind of the ordeal he'd suffered in Burma, resulted in Alf struggling to complete a full day's work. Positioned outside the Festival House Dance Hall wearing a dowdy uniform, whilst being disrespected by cheeky teenagers who thought it fun and acceptable to mock a war hero, was all he felt capable of.

Alf had practically laid down his life for their freedom. Now in his mid-forties, with no job prospects, no wife and son, no young ladies interested in him, and fading health, Alf found it all rather depressing. The only thing he could look forward to was a game of dominoes and half a mild on a Saturday lunchtime up at the Three Feathers.

"Right, you ruffians, off with you. You know the dances are for lads and lasses over eighteen, so come on, be off with you," repeated Alf, as he ushered the three unruly lads back down the steps.

"Hey, easy, grandad. You don't want to get your nice suit all ruffled," mocked Freddie, as he ran his fingers down the faded gold braid on the lapels of Alf's doorman's jacket.

Alf swatted the lad's hand away. "Get off. Now look, you're not eighteen, and as you can see on the sign, you're not welcome. You're not appropriately dressed," asserted Alf, now frustrated as he backed the boys away whilst pointing to the dress code rules pinned on the entrance door.

<u>Festival House Dances</u>

Youths wearing

Edwardian dress

Will NOT

be admitted

To Saturday Night

Dances

"What? Ain't my suit good enough for your poncy dance then?" questioned Freddie with mock horror whilst holding the lapels of his Teddy Boy jacket, known by the establishment as Edwardian coats.

"Just be off with you. You lot ain't coming in." Alf's frustration bubbled up, causing him to shove Freddie. The latter stumbled backwards, ending up on his backside with his precious Teddy Boy jacket soaked from the puddle he'd unceremoniously landed in.

A somewhat stunned Freddie sat motionless, shocked that he was now on his arse on the street. Like all bullies, Freddie wasn't used to this situation. He shot a look to Dick and Ralph, who both stood gawping at the unusual sight of Freddie being dumped on his backside.

"Well?" bellowed Freddie.

Dick offered his hand and helped the surprised bully to his feet whilst Ralph stepped forward towards the doorman, who seemed unperturbed by the situation.

"You're dead! No one shoves me," spat Freddie, whilst scrambling to his feet then inspecting his soaked coat. "Ralph, hit him!" ordered Freddie, fully expecting his mate to land the doorman one.

Ralph, an obedient lieutenant to Freddie, pulled back his fist, ready to comply with the request.

~

"Where we off to then? Somewhere fancy?"

"Wait and see, ladies! Roy and I are going to give you a whale of a time!" Jason winked at Roy, conveying in that action to his mate that he thought they could perhaps have their wicked way with the girls tonight. Now they'd prised them out of the dance hall, Jason and Roy would take them drinking and then, hopefully, his luck might be in.

"Well, I hope so," giggled Ruth, as she nervously tucked her blonde hair behind her ear. "You know Mary and I can't be back later than eleven. Our landlady's a stickler for timekeeping!" she added, as she held onto her new man's arm.

Although she and Mary hadn't planned on leaving the dance this early, the two lads said they knew of a swanky new club they could go to, so the girls had agreed. Ruth thought Mary was a little unsure about Roy but agreed to step-out with him because she could see Ruth was smitten with Jason. So, the girls agreed, linked arms with their new fellas and headed out of the dance.

"You girls are in for a right treat, ain't that right, Roy?" announced Jason, as he stepped through the dance hall front doors with his new girl on his arm.

"Ooo, lovely," giggled Ruth.

"No funny business though, d'you hear," stated Mary, delivering her warning shot by poking Roy in the ribs, who now looked like the cat who'd got the cream with the vivacious Mary hanging on his arm.

The foursome stopped on the stone steps as the two lads lit a cigarette. Jason offered the girls one before relinking his arm with Ruth.

"Who'd you take us for?" questioned Ruth, declining the cigarette. "Respectable ladies don't walk along the street smoking!"

Jason popped his lit cigarette between his lip, then patted Ruth's hand before traversing down the steps. "Come on, let's go."

"Oh my!" exclaimed Mary, as she took in the scene in front of her.

The party of four halted their jaunt – Jason and Ruth on the lower step, Roy and Mary bringing up the rear. A perfect foursome pose, as if a photographer had been present to snap a picture of the happy couples. However, the scene in front of them was not a joyous affair.

"What's going on here, then?" Roy questioned three lads – Teddy Boys – which usually spelt trouble.

"Oi, naff off. This ain't your fight," bellowed one lad at the precise moment that another significantly larger youth, more the bulk of an outhouse brick-built privy, sent his fist into the face of the doorman, flattening the poor fellow.

Jason and Roy didn't hesitate. Both released their arms from the girls and barrelled down the steps, grabbing hold of the abnormal-sized hulk. The other two lads turned and scarpered, hot-footing their way down the road, leaving their mate to take the rap.

"Jason!" shrieked Ruth, before her hands shot to her mouth.

Mary, who demonstrated she was somewhat more practical than Ruth, pirouetted down the steps to attend to the poor chap who seemed to be out cold.

"Grab his arm, Apsley," screamed Roy, who'd managed to cling on to the youthful goliath's left arm, forcing it up his back.

Although he was only a teenager and, between them, Roy and himself should be able to restrain him before someone could call for a constable, Jason feared they wouldn't be able to control the giant.

Instinctively Jason sent his fist towards the lad's face, resulting in sparks flying as the cigarette in Jason's hand connected with Ralph's eye. Not so much through the force of the punch received, but the searing pain in Ralph's right eye sent the Jack-and-the-Beanstalk giant reeling and screaming. Ralph's right eye now sported a bright orange glow, caused by the lit cigarette end that stuck to his eyeball as it melted its way through like a hot knife in butter.

~

The police doctor attended to young Ralph while he languished in Fairfield station's cells. His concerned parents also attended and, while his mother fussed with her blinded son, Ralph's father negotiated with the desk sergeant. Mr Eastley, who delivered bread to the sergeant's wife every morning, suggested he would take the strap to his son if they could see their way clear to only issuing a police caution, rather than arresting their son for assaulting the doorman.

Whilst Ralph's father negotiated his son's terms of release, which included a discussion regarding the severity of the corporal punishment he planned to inflict, Ralph's mother continued to fret over her son's eye, as any mother would.

The police doctor's assessment suggested a trip to the hospital was required, as Ralph complained he had lost vision and was in some considerable pain.

The surgeon saved his eye, which soon morphed to a solid milky-white colour. This newly acquired unwanted facial feature came to define him. All who were unfortunate enough to face Ralph would be fixated by his eye just before Ralph dispatched them. The white-eyed man affectionately became known as Shark-Eye.

Ralph adapted to his one-eyed vision. Although sometimes blindsided when in a particular ruckus, this never proved to be a disadvantage. Often an assailant used Ralph's half-sight handicap to try and gain an advantage over him, although that was still a risky tactic as they would have to win with one strike – they never did. Shark-Eye was simply too large a tree to fell with one blow – all assailants suffered at the hands of the white-eyed monster.

Just like the heavyweight champion, Rocky Marciano, Ralph remained undefeated – well, discounting the altercation with Jason Apsley and a lit cigarette. The events of that evening back in 1954 always stayed fresh in Ralph's mind. Well, they would for anyone. Losing an eye at sixteen was life-changing.

That evening the blonde girl had called out 'Jason', and the guy who'd grabbed his arm had called out 'Apsley'– Ralph would kill the man who took his eye.

Of course, Ralph's thirst for immediate revenge ended up sitting on ice when forced to emigrate to Australia early the following year. The dance hall incident had been the final straw for his parents, who struggled to control their son despite his father's liberal use of corporal punishment. Determined to make a new life and extract their son from the gangs he'd managed to entwine himself with, Ralph's parents forced their wayward son to a life as far away from Fairfield that was physically possible.

However, Ralph never forgot that evening in 1954. They say revenge is a dish best served cold.

27

1987

Through The Looking-Glass

It's fair to say that George's recounting of mine and Martin's time-travelling adventures to Jess didn't go well. Even with Martin doing his tattoo reveal routine, Jess thought we had all lost it, storming off to the sanctity of her home next door.

I'd called to pre-warn Jenny of the situation whilst George tried to coax Jess from her house in a pleading tone through the letterbox. This act, in turn, unfortunately had attracted the attention of a couple of nosey neighbours from across the street. After they'd twitched their curtains a few times, we then had a few of them venture out to assess the commotion, which led to a small posse forming at the garden gates observing George, whilst I'd performed crowd control duties.

As it became clear from the lack of response from Jess that George had failed with his coaxing method, Martin had waded in with more threatening techniques. This second, slightly more aggressive, attempt to coax her out had still involved communicating through the letterbox but centred around Martin reminding Jess that Paul Colney was still on the prowl.

Whilst this charade took place, I'd had to continue to perform crowd control duties because the posse of neighbours had doubled in size, all of whom I'd had to reassure there was nothing to concern themselves about, and there was no need to call the police.

Martin's somewhat less than engaging attempts to persuade Jess to open the front door bore fruit. I guess however ridiculous George's recount of my time-travel adventures were, there was no denying Paul Colney had stood only a few feet from her earlier that evening.

After Martin had successfully coaxed Jess out of her house, I'd applied our non-existent crowd dispersing techniques which involved corralling the neighbours away from Jess and repeating the mantra that there was nothing to see here.

Martin didn't believe he needed any further medical treatment following George's expert tea cloth dabbing routine and stated he was okay with staying in Don's house. He would secure the place and, considering Paul was skulking about, he felt someone needed to keep an eye on the Poole's home.

We'd decamped back home, with Jess less than chatty as she sulked in the back seat on the way. However, I did achieve a concordat in the respect that Jess kept my time-travel tale from her husband for the time being, whilst I agreed to remain schtum about Paul or Patrick, or whoever he was, standing in the kitchen doorway earlier. Judging by Colin's reaction to me over breakfast the following day, it appeared Jess had honoured that agreement.

As Shirley Colney and, as far as Colin was concerned, Patrick were on the prowl, Jess and Colin agreed to stay through the weekend. I brought Jenny fully up to speed with events whilst we decided it was best for Jess to inform Colin that we'd located Leonardo and all was fine.

Jess was somewhat displeased to hear that DI French demanded our presence the next day for questioning regarding the reoccurring Cortina incident. However, Colin felt it was a perfect opportunity to raise our concerns that Patrick had violated his terms of release. If only he knew, I thought.

My time-travel friends were, at best, limited – Martin being the only one, and at times I struggled to refer to him as a friend. That said, I was sure if there were others like me, none could possibly have such a complicated life as mine.

My home now became separated into three factions. Firstly, there was the fully-fledged believers: Jenny and I. Secondly, we had the absolutely-no-idea-what-was-going-on team, which consisted of Colin, Beth, Faith and Christopher. And thirdly, there was poor Jess firmly stuck in no man's land, probably wondering why she'd become the central character at a tea party in a Lewis Carroll novel.

Beth and Faith, both suitably buzzed up about the continued sleepover arrangements, which had never previously been sanctioned by either set of parents on a school night, appeared to be the only inhabitants of the Apsley household who thought everything was just dandy. Their excitement presumably related to the fact they could continue to plan their early leaps into womanhood and how to quickly bypass their early teenage years – a frightening thought, I mused, based on how I remember Beth at that age the first time around.

Colin and I set off for work on Thursday morning, leaving Jenny and Jess to have a chat. The saying *I would like to be a fly on the wall* could have been invented for just this very moment.

I'd given George some investigative homework which I was hoping he could tap up his mate, Harold Bates, for some insider knowledge – newspapermen were always the nosiest of gits.

So, I was hoping Harold could do a little digging with those in the know. Perhaps, like Private Walker, he could offer up a few tins of black-market Spam, or a few pairs of nylons, in return for some information regarding the whereabouts of Patrick Colney since leaving prison. Although, I do accept that since the end of food rationing in the early '50s, Spam may well have lost its place as a valuable black-market commodity, now a ubiquitous product, just like the unsolicited junk email we would all face in the-not-too-distant future.

George had stated that the authorities, in their infinite wisdom, released Patrick on Wednesday, so where was he now? This was the burning question because we assumed the man Jess spotted across the road that evening wasn't Patrick, but rather his dead twin brother, Paul.

Along with Martin, it seemed Paul had rematerialised from the dead. Also, the delightful Shirley was back with what looked like, through the haze of cigarette smoke in the public bar, her pet Godzilla. Who this Godzilla bloke was would be a question for Frenchie later today. Although I had a sneaking suspicion, he may be called Ralph.

So, some nosey muckraking pressman had to have the inside track on what was happening in the Colney family world and the whereabouts of Patrick Colney. Whatever information could be purloined by some snivelling nosy reporter, that knowledge needed to be referred to George's spiv mate and on to me – the Apsley family needed the inside track to keep ahead of the game.

I'd had a wasted trip out during lunch to check on Martin. He was out somewhere, so I presumed he'd recovered from his injuries. However, I became concerned about what calamity he might be causing and where and with whom the nailed-on certainty of a disaster was happening.

Of course, I couldn't call him because we were still some years from mobile phones becoming an item no one could live without. So, I resigned myself to the fact that I would have to delay dealing with the latest Martin-induced disaster.

I returned to school to complete my next mission, namely, calling Jenny and seeing how her storytelling session with Jess had panned out. However, after parking up the Quattro in my usual spot, and not performing the handbrake-turn manoeuvre Martin favoured, the vision on the school steps suggested my day would perhaps spiral to new, never previously achieved, lower depths.

~

"Jess, I think we need to walk the girls to school this morning. I know they're not going to like it, but—"

"Agreed. But we need to talk when we get back!" demanded Jess, who hadn't cooled from last night.

"I know Jess, I know. But your father is who he says he is … I promise you."

"Well, last night, he said he's not my father! You two will make your mind up in a minute! Christ, I can't believe I'm actually going to say this, but I should have believed my mother when she said not to get involved with him because he's a waster!"

"Jess—"

"Oh, don't Jess me! I'm furious!"

"Jess, come on—"

"No, Jenny. If it wasn't for the fact that I came face to face with that monster last night, I would be going straight home!"

"But you did, didn't you? You stood and looked straight at a dead man. Jess, that can only happen if something unexplained is going on."

"Yes, but—"

"Mum?" called out Beth from the top of the stairs. Beth and Faith exchanged questioning glances, both disturbed by the scene at the bottom of the stairs. They'd never seen their mothers raise voices to each other, and both girls were worried.

"Girls, come on. We're walking you to school this morning."

"No way!" blurted Faith. The horror etched on her face.

"You're joking? Why? We'll be the laughing stock of the whole school! Mum, no one in the top year has their mums walk them to school!" announced Beth.

"I'm sorry, but that's what's going to happen. And listen, young lady, we will be at the school gates to collect you this afternoon … no arguments."

"Noooo! No, why?" pleaded Beth.

"Because we said so. No arguments. There's something going on and, for a few days, we need to make sure that we're all safe."

"What? From who, Aunty Jenny?" politely asked Faith. Although, in reality, she was in a strop, as was Beth. However, her mother had taught her manners when a guest in another's house.

"Never you mind, young lady. And mind your manners!" scolded Jess.

"It's my real dad, isn't it? He's out of prison ... does he want to take me away?" asked Faith, knowing full well that when her mother had scolded her, answering back was very stupid. Expecting her mother's wrath, Faith chewed her lip and could feel the tears welling up.

Beth grabbed her hand.

Jess opened her mouth to bellow at her daughter. However, when feeling Jenny's hand on her arm, she stopped herself.

"Faith, sweetheart. No one is ever going to take you away. Your mum and dad, your grandfather and I will never let that happen."

"Mum?"

"Yes, Beth."

"It's our real grandmother who wants to take us, isn't it? We heard you talking to Christopher last night."

Beth's question stumped Jenny, who glanced at Jess. Jenny would usually scold Beth for eavesdropping. However, the enormity of her statement was way bigger than her naughty ten-year-old daughter listening in on private conversations. Jenny glanced back up the stairs to where the two girls stood holding hands in their blue, primary-school uniforms. Beth had reached up to one of the metal wire pictures of sailboats that adorned the staircase wall, plucking at the wire.

Jenny had purchased those pictures when they moved into the house, at the same time buying the children a Spirograph set so they could copy the patterns. Jenny pondered how seemingly time had moved on so quickly from those days. Christopher was now nearly a man, and Beth was about to blossom into a vivacious young lady – an up-and-coming event that Jason was concerned about based on his recollections of how Beth conducted herself when they were friends in his previous life – a few years in the future in this world.

The thought of trying to convince Jess of this complicated world of time travel and dead men coming back to life, filled Jenny with dread.

Beth absentmindedly continued to pick at the wire picture as the silence hung in the air from her disturbingly true statement regarding Shirley Colney.

Jason loved those pictures, saying they were just like the ones his parents had when he was a little boy in the late '70s the first time around. Anything that reminded Jason of his parents he lost when he was so young was precious to him. So, when Beth picked at them, which she often did, that would generally result in a telling off. However, wire pictures that evoked warm memories for her time-travelling husband now paled into insignificance.

Jenny knew she couldn't walk Beth to school every day. She couldn't be by her side every minute, twenty-four hours a day. Somehow, Shirley, Patrick and Paul would have to be eliminated, wiped from the face of the earth – forever.

Last night, Jenny had suggested involving her father because his police connections could be helpful. Also, her brother, Alan, a serving traffic officer, could be enlisted to help them out of this predicament. However, taking that path was fraught with danger with its potential risks and pitfalls, which only a time-traveller could know. Therefore, Jenny and Jason decided many years ago never to dish out application forms for the Time Travel Believers' Club to any of her family.

Beth's statement regarding her true paternal grandmother had quashed the conversation. Nevertheless, Faith hadn't moved from her position on the top step, presumably contemplating what it meant to have her real father potentially back on the scene. Jess, now quiet, probably had the same thoughts as her daughter.

Jenny called up to her daughter, this time in a significantly softer tone than a few seconds ago. "We don't know, sweetheart. But your father and I will not let any harm come to either of you, we promise."

Notwithstanding her determination, Jenny had no idea how she would keep that promise.

28

Crocodile Dundee

After the knife incident, which resulted in an extremely pale-faced gentleman stumbling out of the bar holding a blooded Maid's Head monogrammed linen napkin around his hand, the one-eyed monster had wrapped his gigantic hand around Oliver's throat whilst stuffing a wad of folded notes in the young barman's waistcoat pocket.

Oliver could still feel those hands around his neck, even though the beast of a man, who surely had connections to the Corleone family, had now left the scene. The petite woman with the streaked black and white hair, who Oliver presumed was the giant's handler, had instructed him to clean up the mess where the skewered man's hand had bled across the art-deco-styled mahogany table causing blood to soak into a half-eaten Danish pastry.

Oliver knew the right course of action was to immediately hunt down Mr Lodge, the hotel manager, and inform him of the events in the bar that morning. Surely then, the ever-efficient hotel manager would call the police and the knife-wielding maniac and evil woman would be duly arrested.

However, the sicko nutter called Ralph had made it quite clear to Oliver, as he wedged the wad of fivers in his pocket and crushed his windpipe, that if he uttered a word to anyone, he would slice out his tongue, then fry it up with a touch of his favourite Australian BBQ seasoning before eating it. After witnessing the events this morning, Oliver was in no doubt that Ralph would carry out his threat.

The other consideration was the wad of fivers amounted to seventy-five quid, which would nicely top up his car fund. All his mates were getting *Hot Hatches,* and Oliver was close to amassing the cash needed to pick up a 1983 Ford Fiesta XR2, with a massive 1.6lr turbo engine, wheel arch extensions, rear spoiler, pepper-pot alloy wheels, and red seatbelts. Thinking about his desired new motor, Oliver daydreamed how cool he would look riding around town. He imagined the windows down and a quality Sharp radio system banging out The Communards, Pet Shop Boys, or even a bit of Cutting Crew through the parcel shelf mounted speakers.

Oliver saw himself as a bit of a Nick Van Eede and had acquired a pair of white boots in his attempt to look the part.

He set about preparing for the lunchtime trade whilst humming *Died In Your Arms,* thinking about his new car, and trying to put the horrific scenes from the morning out of his mind.

To stave off hunger pains, Oliver plucked up a couple of bags of pork scratchings from the back of the bar. He'd not usually help himself to stock, but whether as a result of losing his breakfast over the Palace Bar carpet, or the rush of adrenaline caused by this morning's events, Oliver was absolutely starving. To quote his grandfather, he could eat a scabby horse.

"Hope you're paying for those, sunshine?"

Oliver spun around, shocked that he'd been spotted stealing from the bar and dreading that Mr Lodge had sneaked in and caught him red-handed.

"DC Paddon, and this is DC Suggett," stated the younger of the two men who now leant on the bar whilst Oliver tried to hide the packet of post-puke much-needed stolen snacks.

Both officers held up their warrant cards. The one who'd spoken wore a light-brown, soft-leather jacket which Oliver thought was pretty cool. The other most certainly didn't, as he rammed his hands in the pockets of an old blue rain mac that didn't appear too dissimilar to the style-lacking crappy old thing his father wore to the office each day.

"I ... I can put them back," stammered Oliver, whilst still chomping through a mouthful of pork scratchings, with one hand in the bag delving for another handful. His attempt to conceal the evidence had been futile, so he'd quickly opted for the pleading option.

"Well, son, unless you're going to gob them back in the packet, that will be a bit difficult, don't you think?" questioned the officer in the old blue mac.

Oliver froze, his hand in the packet and, his mouth motionless now he'd stopped chomping. Only a few minutes ago, he'd considered this could be a lucky day when almost a week's wages had been thrust in his pocket by the one-eyed monster, presumably to buy his silence – now he was about to lose his job and get arrested for pork-scratching theft.

Oliver withdrew his hand from the half-eaten packet and approached the officers who still leant on the bar, hoping he could talk his way out of this one. As luck would have it, the bar was empty – that lull time between morning coffee and lunchtime aperitifs. Oliver prayed the two plainclothes detectives had more significant issues than two missing packets of pork scratchings.

"Son, don't panic. We're not here about your light fingers. Although if you're not overly cooperative, we might have a word with the manager."

"How can I help, officer?" beamed Oliver, now relieved there seemed to be a way out of this predicament.

"You know these two?" asked the younger officer in the cool brown-leather jacket, as the miserable mac-wearing officer laid out two grainy pictures on the bar. Oliver had met these people – the colossus ogre and the petite witch once more stared back at him.

"Err … um …" stammered Oliver, as he involuntarily tapped the seventy-five quid still burning a hole in his waistcoat pocket, also considering how attached he was to his tongue and would prefer it to stay that way.

DC Paddon filled the silence whilst Oliver weighed up his options. "Up until this morning, they were guests here. The manager says you've worked the bar today and last night. Now, these two will have been here at least one of those times. So, you remember them?"

Oliver swallowed hard whilst continuing to weigh up his choices. It wasn't easy. There was the threat of dismissal for the pork scratchings theft, set against the danger of having his tongue cut out by the Australian cyclops.

"Of course, son, we could talk to the manager about your fetish for pork scratching," stated the miserable officer, as he folded his arms across the front of his blue mac.

Now furnished with the information that Ralph, the knife-wielding nutter, and the tiny witch had left the hotel, Oliver decided he needed to keep his job. He glanced back down at the two pictures and then nodded. "Yes, they were drinking here late last night and then took coffee at that table this morning," he replied, whilst pointing to the table to his left, now sporting a split in the ornate top which Oliver had earlier covered with an ashtray.

Both officers didn't glance away from Oliver, seemingly disinterested in where they had taken coffee and pastries.

"Good. So, who did they meet here?" asked the detective constable with the leather jacket, whilst the blue-mac officer retrieved the photos, securing them in his inside pocket.

"What makes you think they met anyone? Anyway, I remember them, but to be honest, I can't really say I took much notice of them," stated Oliver, deciding that being economical with the truth might be a wise decision, now recalling the threat to his tongue.

"Oliver. It is Oliver, isn't it?" asked the younger officer, as he stabbed around with a cocktail stick in the bowl of stuffed olives.

"Ye-yes," he replied, annoyed that his stammer had returned. But that was the same line Ralph-the-knife had used earlier, and Oliver was slightly concerned about what would happen next.

"Well, you see, Oli. Those two aren't the sort to sit in a bar and enjoy coffee. Those two would be meeting associates, and I want to know who they were. Also, I think you told my colleague and me that you didn't take much notice of them," he paused, raising his eyebrows, non-verbally questioning Oliver's earlier statement, plus it afforded him the opportunity to pop the stuffed olive in his mouth that he had successfully skewered. "See, that's not very likely, is it?" he stated before wincing, presumably as the olive spilt its stuffed content of anchovies – DC Paddon detested anchovies.

"Err, sorry, what d'you mean?" asked a nervous Oliver, whilst the officer spat the errant olive out into his hand, then lobbed it to the carpet – well, the carpet had suffered worse today.

"My point, Oli, is that Ralph Eastley is the size of a brick shit house with a strong Northern Territory Australian accent … a kind of huge Crocodile Dundee type fella. He's got a milky-white eye and a fondness of knives."

Oliver had seen that movie last Christmas. Now he recalled the knife scene when Mick Dundee saw off some hoodlums with his big knife – Ralph Eastley's face seemed to replace Paul Hogan's in his recollection of the scene.

"Also, the woman he was with is only about five-foot-tall, with long dark hair and the tongue of a viper. Out of the two, she's far scarier than this giant Aussie bloke. Never be fooled, Oli. The female of the species is always deadlier than the male. We've both got wives, so we should know, son," stated DC Paddon, as he waved a cocktail stick between him and his partner.

The blue-mac officer nodded and cracked a smile, presumably agreeing that his wife was deadly.

Oliver remained silent, weighing up his options.

"So, son, don't get married. Just play the field. Mark my word, no bird is worth it. Anyway, based on that description, I think it's pretty unlikely you didn't take much notice of them, don't you?" accused DC Paddon, now waving the cocktail stick in Oliver's general direction.

Lowering the small wooden spike, he stabbed a cube of cheese, now avoiding the olives with their fishy filling. He turned to his partner, who still had his arms folded across his blue mac. "What d'you reckon? You think young Oli here is telling us the truth?"

Blue-mac man pulled a face as if he'd now eaten an anchovy-infused olive, then shook his head.

"Me neither. So, son, let's try again. Who were Crocodile Dundee and the Black Widow meeting?"

29

Crackerjack

"You two! Come on," bellowed Sergeant Farham down the corridor after sticking his head around the door when spotting the two missing DCs, Suggett and Paddon, as they fought with the coffee machine.

DC Suggett swivelled around, spilling his coffee which slopped from the white plastic cup across his hand. "Oh, bollocks!" he announced, shaking the brown sludge from his coat sleeve.

"Pissing machine!" muttered DC Paddon, as he stuck his boot into the bottom of the machine's already heavily dented faux wood-grained front panel, trying to coax the ageing contraption to deliver the coffee that so far had only dribbled out a thimble full of grey tar-looking sludge. "Coming," he called out as he prepared to launch his boot into the machine in one more attempt to encourage it to pour the required drink.

"Come on. Guv's been waiting for you two to return."

A cheer went up as Suggett and Paddon bounded into the CID office. Only Suggett carried a coffee because Paddon had given up after accepting his ten pence was lost to the machine, which was a lottery with woefully poor odds of receiving a drink. If you were lucky enough in the unlikely event of the machine dispensing some hot liquid, all selections from hot chocolate through to white-with-sugar tasted and looked the same – shite.

"Did you get lost, *Mudda*?" jibed DC Taylor.

Suggett ignored him, just nodding to the DI, who stood at the front with her folded arms resting on her tray-of-beer chest. Suggett considered that the DI didn't look too happy and prayed that someone else on the team had caused her apparent stern demeanour.

Suggett was commonly referred to as *Mudda,* due to his fading Glaswegian accent and how he pronounced 'murder', just as the actor, Mark MacManus, did in the Scottish detective TV show, *Taggart.* He placed his vending machine sludge on his desk then threw his blue mac over the typewriter after retrieving his pipe and pouch of St Bernard tobacco.

"Good of you two to join us!" boomed the DI, causing a few sniggers to rumble around the room. "This morning, I've endured a particularly hellish conversation with the Divisional Super. It would be putting it mildly to say that he's not happy! So, I'm praying you lot have got something tangible from your enquiries!" Then, starting at what she suspected would be the lowest point, and before she hacked off their testicles, DI French addressed her two Toytown cops. "Reeves and Taylor, update on Bowen, please."

"Guv," announced Reeves, as he stubbed out his cigarette before reaching for another from the packet of Gauloises on his desk. Reeves only smoked the pungent aroma cigarette in an attempt to impress a new girlfriend, feeling the need to project a more sophisticated look than he usually did. "We picked him up from a squat where *Gladys* said he'd be.

Although, the little scumbag doesn't know anything. He reckoned Susan Kane booted him out a couple of weeks ago and ain't seen hide nor hair of her since. *Flintstone* put the squeeze on him," Reeves held out his hand, cupping it and squeezing, mimicking the action DC Taylor performed on Bowen, which everyone knew referred to a constriction of the testicles – an information gathering procedure that didn't fit into any police handbook, but was super effective when persuading male suspects to talk. "Apart from whimpering, Bowen said nothing worth noting." Reeves waved his pocketbook, indicating he'd written nothing down.

The DI wasn't surprised to hear that her particularly useless DC hadn't used his pen. Even if Bowen had details of who leaked the confidential information on the Westland Helicopter Affair that nearly brought the government down last year, Reeves still wouldn't have noted that down – DC Reeves and his standard police-issue notebook were rarely acquainted.

"Guv, door-to-door didn't provide any information. No shock really, as we know none of the scum up on that estate talk to us," called out DC Taylor, taking up the story whilst Reeves took the opportunity to light his cigarette. "There's a turban lot living in the flat next to Susan Kane, which is where the Colneys used to be holed up back in the day. Anyway, couldn't understand the old girl who just babbled on a load of old gibberish. But one of the lads, who I think was the old girl's son, said they had to chase out some geezer who broke into the flat on Monday morning."

"When on Monday?" demanded DS Farham.

"Err ... hang on," replied DC Taylor, whilst he consulted his notebook.

Thank God for small mercies, thought the DI. Suitably amazed that one of these two idiots had written something down.

"So, it was about 7:30, the geezer reckoned, although he wasn't sure. He's one of those turban types," DC Taylor swished his hand around his head to demonstrate what a turban was, in case any of the team were as stupid and thick as he was. Apart from Reeves, they weren't. "Anyway, I reckon those towel things they wear on their heads must squash their brains because he couldn't remember the exact time of forced entry and also reckoned he couldn't describe the bloke apart from he was youngish with a beard."

"Christ, all-bloody-mighty!" exclaimed DC Brown. "Are you that much of a fascist Nazi wanker? I bet you'll be marching through town on Saturday with those skin-head dicks from the National Front! Zieg Heil!" he proclaimed whilst jumping up from his desk and proceeding to impersonate Basil Fawlty's goose-stepping routine across the office with his finger placed under his nose.

"Alright, *Paddington*, keep your fur on! I'm only joking!" called out Taylor.

"Well, you might be, *Flintstone*. But it's comments like that, which gives the National Front their credibility!"

"Oh, shut it! No one's got a sense of humour anymore!"

"That's because it ain't funny! They're Sikhs! And they don't wear towels on their heads, you prat!" threw in Megson in support of Brown, who'd now stopped goose-stepping.

This earnt Megson a collective "Oooo," from several officers.

"*Gladys* has got her knickers in a twist!" chuckled Reeves.

"Quiet!" boomed the DI. "And just so you're abundantly clear, any officer joining in on a National Front march will face disciplinary procedures!"

"Anything else sensible to add?" demanded DS Farham, as he addressed Taylor, who unfairly thought the Guv's bark was squarely aimed at him.

"Yeah, the turban boy ... err Sikh lad, reckoned after they chased the geezer off, he stepped into the flat next door ... Susan Kane's flat," added Reeves after blowing a plume of smoke in the air.

Megson dropped her head in her hands, knowing full well what was coming next. She really couldn't understand how *Flintstone* and *Fonzie* kept their jobs because both were the stupidest officers she'd ever encountered.

"Are you telling the Guv and me that you've both known since yesterday that you have a witness to someone entering Susan Kane's flat around the time of her death? And in your infinite wisdom, you both haven't mentioned it for a whole twenty-four hours?" boomed DS Farham.

The two DCs exchanged a glance but didn't respond.

DI French audibly exhaled, appearing ready to rip her two Toytown officers limb from limb, only holding off when noticing her dependable sergeant was moving in for the kill. However, this was good news because they now had a lead. With a bit more digging from a couple of capable officers, she might have enough information to keep the Super at bay.

"Christ, you two! This is key information!"

"Sorry, Sarge," offered the two officers. But, going by the DI's thunderous expression, both officers expected that another bollocking would be heading their way after the briefing.

Reeves mused about this latest fuck-up which disappointingly probably didn't help his bid for firearms training. Of course, neither Reeves nor Taylor knew that the DI already had plans to castrate them.

"Right, anyone else got any startling information that we should know about?" bellowed the sergeant.

Suggett waved his pipe in the air. Yes, *Paddy* and I just tracked down the last sighting of Shirley Colney."

"Good work," threw in the DI before Suggett could continue.

"Shirley and Ralph Eastley, the big Australian bloke, have been staying at the Maid's Head in town."

"Very swanky! She's gone up in the world," called out Dawson.

"Too right, *Fawlty*. That's a few rungs up the ladder than Fawlty Towers! She must have a bob or two to her name to stay in that place," called out Brown.

"Suggett, get on with it!" boomed the DI, shutting down the chatter and giving a clear path for Suggett to continue.

"So, here's the thing. We had a chat with a few of the staff, and a young barman was most helpful. It appears this morning Shirley and Eastley had a meeting with someone unknown. That meeting turned violent, and the barman witnessed all of it. From what the lad said, the conversation became heated. Then Eastley stabbed the unknown man's hand with a knife, pinning it to the table." Suggett pointed with his pipe across to Paddon. "*Paddy* closed the bar down, and we've requested a forensic team immediately to attend. Sorry Guv, I was going to run it by you for authorisation but couldn't get hold of you."

"Right decision. Well done. Do we have any idea who the victim was? Have you checked Fairfield General?" demanded the DI.

"Done it, Guv," stated Paddon, or *Paddy* as he was known to the team. Not that he originated from anywhere near the Emerald Isle, but just a shortening of his surname. "No one has attended hospital with that kind of injury. But listen, apparently, he was wearing a pinstriped suit, in his mid-forties with a monk-style hairdo."

"Shady Hawkshaw!" blurted the DS. "Old man Colney's brief and links with the Gowers."

"Precisely! Me and *Mudda* nipped around his office, but his secretary was a bit tight-lipped. That said, fair play to Hawkshaw, he can't 'alf pick 'em. She's a fit bird with a nice set. Anyway, she scarpered as soon as we left his office. I reckon Hawkshaw is holed up somewhere nursing that hole in his hand—"

The DI interrupted, ignoring Paddon's reference to Shady Hawkshaw's secretary's anatomy. "Right, this is escalating. We've got an eyewitness to a man with a beard entering Susan Kane's flat in or around the time of her murder. We've got Shirley Colney and the Australian dishing out GBH to the Gowers' highly paid brief in a five-star hotel. Now, that means Shirley no longer feels threatened by anyone over here and is prepared to take drastic action. I want to know why." Thrusting her hand on her hips, the DI continued. "What could Shirley possibly want that she's prepared to take this risky action? So, regardless of whether Edwina Currie thinks they're all infected with Salmonella, as sure as eggs are eggs, having

Mark Hawkshaw stabbed was one hell of a risk. The Gowers will now get involved and, if we're not careful, this will escalate as Hawkshaw is their man. Yes, Benson," she called out as DC Benson waved his hand from the back of the room.

"Guv, we visited the bail hostel Patrick Colney is assigned to. We've spoken to the hostel caretaker," he glanced at his notebook before continuing. "A geezer called Adam Henderson. He reckoned Patrick checked in yesterday, then went out about an hour later, only to return just before the curfew in what he described as one hell of a state. He only copped a quick glimpse but reckoned he had blood on his hands and neck. Patrick had gone out again this morning just after nine but hasn't returned as of yet. I made it clear to Henderson that he must call me as soon as he returns."

"Good work, you two. Haul Patrick Colney in as soon as he returns and get a call out to Uniform ... I want all units on the lookout for him. If he's involved, he's broken his terms of parole. If he had blood on him, something is up."

"Check for any reported assaults from yesterday. They might link to Patrick," ordered DS Farham.

Benson nodded, taking the instruction.

"Guv, didn't he have a girlfriend? He might have gone and seen her?" called out Brown.

"That was Jess Redmond. She's now married, but I'm led to believe she has a daughter with Patrick, who her husband has adopted. Now, you know I'm not too fond of coincidences, but Jess Poole, née Redmond, is due in with her father this afternoon. Her father, who Danny and I had a chat with yesterday, is Jason Apsley, who just happens to have received a police caution in 1954 along with a certain Ralph Eastley for a fight outside a dance hall. In that fight, it's reported that Ralph accidentally lost an eye."

"Guv, do we know why Apsley only received a caution? That surely has got to be ABH?" questioned Megson, as she tucked into a Crawford's 54321 chewy biscuit bar. She'd been saving the treat for later but now relented as she just couldn't resist because her lemon curd sandwiches really hadn't satisfied her stomach rumbles. Unfortunately, one of the uniformed officers at the scene by Havervalley Prison had lost the content of his stomach at the sight of the pulped body. However, Megson was made of sterner stuff and never suffered from a queasy disposition, which was a blessing due to her love of chocolate.

"No, we don't. The records are poor. However, it appears that Jason Apsley stepped in to protect the doorman when a fight broke out at the dance hall. Unfortunately for the young Ralph, he caught Apsley's cigarette in his eye."

DI French moved over to the pinboard where Danny had stuck up various case photos. She pondered on an image of Patrick Colney, then tapped his picture as she swivelled around to face her team.

"Right, listen up. We have further developments. This man's twin brother died in an identical Cortina with an identical index number to the one discovered abandoned on Coldhams Lane on Monday." DI French let that statement hang in the air for a moment. Of course, Reeves and Taylor would struggle to see the issue, but she knew the rest of her team would now have had their minds blown apart.

"Guv, how the hell—"

"Precisely!" replied the DI to Paddon's question, who'd been the first to realise the impossibility of the statement.

"Guv, someone must have slapped some false plates on it," called out Megson with a mouth full of chewy caramel fondant.

"What about the chassis number?" questioned Dawson.

"Exactly! The chassis number and index number of this car we found on Monday match up. We don't have the chassis number of the car that Paul Colney died in ten years ago. So, it would suggest that car, which Jason Apsley reckons was owned by the driver, Martin Bretton, although there is no record of that, must have had false plates – something I will be discussing with him this afternoon." The DI nodded to Danny to continue.

"Okay. So, this morning we have another body. This one was discovered next to a disused warehouse at the side of Havervalley Prison. The time of death is suggested to be sometime on Wednesday morning. We'll have a better idea when the PM is completed this afternoon."

"Sarge, that's miles away. What's that got to do with Susan Kane?"

"Everything. We can't identify the body due to the ferociousness of the attack. However, it's the same MO as the attack on Susan Kane. Although, would you believe, delivered with such tremendous force, we'll need dental records to identify the body … it was that bad. What we do know is the deceased was probably an IC1 male, approximately six feet tall, and aged somewhere between twenty and forty."

"What about clothes and any ID?" asked Suggett, pointing the end of his pipe in the sergeant's direction.

"Nothing, *Mudda,* the body was stripped naked, and set alight with, what we presume, was the contents of a large jerrycan full of your finest four-star."

The DI once again moved to the large pinboard, tapping the picture of Shirley Colney. "Okay, this woman has to be the centre of our investigation. We have a witness placing her as an accessory to grievous bodily harm on Mark Hawkshaw—"

"Couldn't have happened to a nicer bloke," called out Dawson.

"Agreed," nodded the DI. "Dawson and Megson, find Mark Hawkshaw."

"You got it, Guv," enthusiastically replied Dawson.

Megson nodded, unable to reply as she'd just taken a bite out of a toffee flavoured Trio bar, which she'd started on after devouring her 54321 biscuit.

"Paddon and Suggett. Follow up with forensics on the Maid's Head Hotel. Although we know who the three in that bar were, I want fingerprint evidence."

"Guv," replied both officers in unison.

"While you're on it, I want you to ensure that any snivelling members of the press keep their noses out of this. So, any reporters come sniffing, move them on. I'll have to update the Super this afternoon, and I don't need this morning's events splashed across the front of the local rag."

"Got it, Guv," replied Paddon.

"Benson and Machin. Find Patrick Colney. I don't care if you have to turn the whole town upside down. I want him in an interview room before Crackerjack starts."

"On it, Guv. You're showing your age a bit there; Crackerjack ended years ago!" chuckled Machin.

"That's as may be. But if anyone is in doubt what time that is ... it's five to five!"

"Bet you've got one of their pencils as well!" threw in Benson, as he nudged Machin, indicating it was time to go and hunt down a Colney.

"Two of them, I'll have you know! Right, Brown, pick up with Uniform. I want every pair of eyes in this station looking for Shirley Colney. I want Traffic pulled in from cruising up and down the M1. I want every beat officer turning over every rock and stone to find her."

"Got it, Guv," replied Brown.

"When you've done that, rake through every missing person report over the last two weeks, and get hold of the Met, see what they've got. We've got to identify that body ... I just know whoever they were, they must link back to Shirley Colney."

"Guv," nodded Brown, who was used to these sorts of assignments. With retirement looming, his days of apprehending armed blaggers and knife-wielding yobs were well gone, and he was thankful to the DI for her consideration when assigning tasks.

"Guv, where do you want us?" called out Reeves, as he pointed between Taylor and himself.

A brief moment of silence descended whilst the DI stared at him. "I want you two in my office."

Although the DI commanded respect, she did allow some banter to flow through the team. She knew how to get the balance of teamwork without allowing anarchy. Often the team were self-regulating, so she wasn't the constant one barking at them. For example, DC Brown had pulled up DC Taylor when he'd used derogatory terms regarding the Sikh family. Also, she could always rely on DC Megson to vocalise her objections where necessary.

However, occasionally when the DI made a statement, she announced it with such force and dictate that the team knew not to offer any comment. Stating, as she had, 'I want you two in my office,' was enough to cause the rest to jump into action and distance themselves from what was about to happen to *Flintstone* and *Fonzie*.

Megson clenched her fist, delighted the two tossers were about to be ripped apart. Then, grabbing the half-squashed chocolate marshmallow Tunnock's Teacake she'd spotted under a heap of files, she nodded to *Fawlty* as he one-handedly wrestled his jacket from the back of his chair whilst stubbing out his cigarette; preparing to join her on their quest to locate a dodgy solicitor with a hole in his hand.

DI French nodded to the two officers indicating they were to step into her office. Once she'd dealt with these idiots, she would have to update the Super on this morning's developments. Before she met with Jason Apsley and Jess Poole, she had a particularly difficult encounter with the Shah family, where she would need to apologise for her dippy officers' actions and hope they wouldn't be demanding compensation for police brutality.

She prayed that their actions up at the Broxworth Estate yesterday morning didn't escalate, as had the Broadwater Farm incident in Tottenham a couple of years back. That particular hellish incident was still very clear in all police forces' minds, demonstrating how one incident could lead to catastrophe.

As for police brutality – well, that was precisely what she was about to dish out to Reeves and Taylor.

Heather French stepped into her office, closing the door so calmly that the Venetian blind stayed quiet as if recognising the sombre mood of the impending meeting where the DI was about to castrate two useless detective constables. Both officers sat quietly whilst awaiting the DI. With their heads bowed, they presumably were attempting to guess the reason for the bollocking that was soon to be received. They stood as she walked around her desk.

"Ma'am," they stated in unison.

DI French didn't respond. Instead, she plucked up an envelope from her desk. The handwritten addressee stated—

<u>Detective Inspector French.</u>

<u>Private and Confidential</u>

<u>Open by addressee only.</u>

30

Who Wants To Live Forever?

"I don't see how this proves anything! It could just be Dad's rambling guesses. We know he's obsessed with motor racing, so he would have a good idea who will win the races," spat Jess, before pouting and lobbing Jason's motor racing predictions notebook across the kitchen breakfast bar towards where Jenny stood.

"Jess, your father has listed every race for nearly fifty years! So far, he's only got one wrong! He could only know this if those races have already happened!"

"Oh, Jenny, come on. This is so silly. And why on earth would Dad say he's not my father! He *is* my father! My mother knows he *is* my father! Why are you both doing this?" Jess turned her face away, now sensing tears were starting to form. Rummaging through her jeans pockets, she found her cigarettes, then opened the back door and lit up. Jess sucked hard, inhaling the smoke as she tried to calm her heart rate before blowing a plume of smoke out to the garden.

"Jess ... Jess, look—"

"No!" Jess interrupted. She didn't turn around but held her hand aloft, indicating she needed some space, stopping Jenny's advance.

"Okay, I'll be back in a moment."

When Jenny returned a few minutes later, Jess hadn't moved position and continued to aggressively puff on her cigarette.

"Jess, I want to go through these with you." Jenny had retrieved a stack of dogeared, yellow, school-exercise books, which they kept locked in a filing cabinet in the study. Jenny and Jason guarded the keys with their life, as the thought of the kids getting hold of these was too terrifying to consider. As far as Christopher and Beth were concerned, the locked cabinet contained confidential School and Council information relating to their parents' work. In truth, it contained twenty exercise books full of scribblings made by Jenny when she'd recorded events that Jason predicted to happen from 1977 through to 2019.

Regularly they would review the books and add any updates as world events started to unfold and Jason's memory could predict what happened next.

George was the only other human that had laid eyes on these books, and they formed part of the strategic planning at the Time Travel Believers' Club's regular meetings.

The Club, which now had passed its tenth year since formation, could describe its success rate of changing world events as hopeless. Jenny had commented their performance was akin to Neil Kinnock's Labour party, who miraculously lost the general election this year after enjoying massive leads in the opinion polls at Christmas. A perfect example of snatching defeat from the jaws of victory, she'd said.

At the back end of last year, during one of the Club's meetings, she'd said to Jason that he must have mis-predicted this one because there was no way the country would elect Mrs Thatcher for a third term. However, as nearly always, Jason's predictions were correct.

"Why doesn't Dad place massive bets on those races if he knows the future?" questioned Jess, as she flicked her ash outside the back door before turning to face Jenny. "You could be multi-millionaires!"

"He does from time to time. Although, saying that, he has to be careful because over the last ten years he's been banned from most of the betting shops in town! Now he gets George to place the bets, but even he's getting noticed, and questions are being asked. Anyway, your dad wants a normal life, not like that football pools winner who they made that film about."

"*Spend Spend Spend*! I remember that. It was that Viv Nicholson woman who won something like a hundred grand in the '60s."

"It was her husband who won the money. But yes, she did say that when they won. See Jess, that's Jason's point. He doesn't want untold riches ... it doesn't always bring happiness. Your dad reckons that we'll have a national lottery in a few years. Unbelievably, someone actually wins about twenty million quid in the first few weeks!"

"Twenty million!"

"Yes, and apparently, just like Viv Nicholson, that didn't end well either."

"Okay, so has Dad remembered the winning score draws so I can win the lottery? Because I wouldn't mind twenty million quid!"

"No, it's not a football thing. I think he said it's numbered balls like bingo."

"Blimey, bingo! That's changed a bit! I think the top prize up at Mecca Bingo Hall is usually two pounds of crappy prime steak and an Our Price Records voucher!"

"Jess, I don't know. But your father does strategically place bets around the country, mostly on motor racing. How the hell d'you think we can afford a house like this on a teacher's and council manager's part-time wage!"

Jess glanced around the kitchen. Not that she needed to because she knew the house layout well. However, with its centre island and marble worktops, it was all state-of-the-art stuff. They even had a glass-fronted wine fridge, which she remembered her father insisting on installing. It was the sort of thing you'd only see in a high-end restaurant. But, of course, Jess had never thought about where the money came from. Dad and Jenny had nice things, and they were always generous to her – far more than they could probably afford.

"The holiday money Dad gave us this year. He said it was an old endowment policy paying out."

"No, Jess, he placed a bet back in 1985 that Coventry City would win the FA Cup in 1987, beating Tottenham. As you can imagine, the odds were huge. No endowment policy, just a football bet."

Jenny plucked up one of the exercise books; the front cover stated 1986-1990. She opened the page at 1987, laying it on the worktop next to Jess, who still stood by the open back door despite that she'd already flicked the cigarette butt in the drain. Then, applying her glasses, Jenny started to read her own text written some years ago with the odd updates annotated in the margins.

"So, the next few months. The UK has a hurricane on the way. It will inflict huge damage and cause loss of life. Your dad's not certain of the exact date, but it will be in October and at the same time as the great stock market crash which he calls Black Monday." Jenny looked up to assess attentiveness, peering at Jess above her glasses. "You remember back in the summer Colin said he wanted to invest Faith's nest egg in some blue-chip companies and your dad urging him to hold off until next year?"

"Yeah, something like that. Colin said he didn't know how Dad suspected there'd be a bit of a financial crash at the end of the year."

"Well, that's Black Monday; it's coming in the next few weeks."

Jenny pulled out a letter from a buff-coloured file, handing it to Jess to read. "We've sent hundreds of letters like these over the years. Always anonymous, always typed on the same old typewriter that belonged to my mother, which we keep locked away for this very purpose." Jenny pointed to the letter, which Jess now held. "That letter we sent in January this year." Jenny shook her head dismissively, "It's always the same. None of them get taken seriously."

Jess glanced down and proceeded to read the letter addressed to the London Underground, The London Fire Brigade and the Manager of King's Cross Railway Station.

"Jason said a couple of weeks ago when he was down there that nothing had changed. The wooden escalators were still there, and so many commuters were smoking. We did send another letter in August, but we think it will be ignored. George suggested we do a hoax bomb call and clear the station, so no one dies, but your dad said that won't work."

"People die? What d'you mean," questioned Jess, looking up from where she was reading.

"You see, the fire started by a dropped match on the escalator. If we go with George's idea and do manage to clear the station, then no one will drop the match and there won't be a fire."

Jess scanned the letter to the end. "Well, if this is true, then George is right, isn't he? No one in the station, so no fire!"

"No, Jess. Your dad said after the fire there were wide-sweeping changes made. Smoking banned—"

"Smoking is already banned on the underground!" interrupted Jess, whilst waving the letter in Jenny's face.

"No, it's not. It is on the trains, but not on the platforms or escalators. Also, all fire training was changed and upgraded because of the fire, and all wooden escalators and panelling was removed." Jenny tapped the letter that Jess had glanced back at. "If this fire doesn't happen, potential worse fires will happen in the future. It's like everything else ... until there's a disaster, nothing changes!"

"Hang on, according to this letter you've written, in a couple of months there'll be this devastating fire at Kings Cross Station. What, so you're going to let people die!" exclaimed Jess, astonished Jenny and her father could stand back and allow these things to happen.

Jenny smiled, remembering her reaction when she stood in Jess's shoes. "That's how I reacted when I found out about your dad."

"Found out what? That you're both deluded, crazed nutters! Come on Jenny, really?" questioned Jess, as she lobbed the letter down and plucked up an exercise book that stated 1990-1992, flicking through the pages at random.

"Look, Jess—"

"Hang on. You've written Margaret Thatcher gets booted out by her own party in 1990! Unlikely, I think!"

"She must do. If you look in the margins, each entry has a star rating. Five stars denote a nailed-on certainty. One star is a rough guess, and two, three and fours, just grade up from there. I think you'll see that Mrs Thatcher being booted out has a five-star rating."

"Oh ... hang on, what's this about Beth and Jason finishing school in May 1992! Dad reckons he was at school with Beth!"

"Jess—"

"Oh, you're joking! Freddie Mercury dies? Colin will be devastated! He loves Queen," announced Jess, as she thumbed back a few pages to 1991. "And it's got a bloody five-star rating!"

"Jess—"

"How does he die? Can't that be stopped? Does he have some accident, or ... hang on, he's not murdered like John Lennon, is he?"

"Jess, please—"

"Have you warned him that he's going to die, written a letter or something?"

"Jess! He dies of pneumonia. It's a bit bloody difficult to warn him of that!"

"Oh, that's odd. I thought only the elderly died of that."

"It will be complications caused by HIV."

"What?"

"AIDS, Jess. Essentially Freddie will die of AIDS."

"Really? That disease ... that those men get?"

"Yes, Jess. And look, times change. When your father was your age ... there was no stigma attached to what you call *those men.* His best friend at Uni was gay. He can get quite touchy about the subject."

"Oh," Jess pulled a face, now stumped at what to say.

"Look, I don't think many people realise, but your dad said Freddie Mercury had been bisexual. Unfortunately for him, he lived in this era when contracting HIV kills."

"Did you see on the news a couple of weeks ago when Diana shook the hand of that bloke who's got AIDS?"

"Yes, your dad said she did that to prove to the world that you can't catch aids from touching people, which is what so many idiots still believe!"

"Dad's not bisexual, is he?"

"Good God, No! Look, Jess. It's really hard to understand the future when you come from the past. But there's stuff your dad has told me that seems so fantastic to believe. I really can't understand how the world can change that much in such a short space of time. But I trust what he's saying because pretty much everything he said would happen, has!"

Jess plucked up one of the exercise books labelled 1978-1980. She flicked through it like you would if watching a story unfold in kineograph. "Everything has come true?" she questioned.

"Yes, pretty much ... there were the odd few things that haven't happened as he expected, but on the whole, yes, everything. Although, he still can't get his head around England winning the football World Cup last year. He's adamant that West Germany beat Argentina in the final and England lost in the quarter-final. He's been bemused by that one, something about the hand-of-God incident that never took place. But, anyway, apart from that, yes, every prediction that has a four and five-star rating has been one hundred per cent correct."

"Well, all this aside," Jess waved her hands over the strewn exercise books. "I can't see how Dad is a time-traveller. I can't even believe I'm saying it!"

"Well, he is," announced Jenny whilst picking up Jason's motor-racing book and flicking through to the 1987 page. She slipped her glasses back on to read the entry regarding the next race. "So, when an Alain Prost, after taking the lead on the second to last lap, wins the Portuguese Grand Prix next Sunday, when apparently he beats Jackie Stewart's record of race wins, you will have your first proof he is who he says he is." Jenny looked up over her glasses to judge Jess's reaction.

Jess huffed, then fished around for her cigarettes. Plucking them from her pocket, she offered one to Jenny.

"I shouldn't, but go on then."

"What does Dad say about Diana as queen?"

Jenny lit her cigarette, then pursed her lips whilst she thought. "I think that's in the book 1996-1998," she said, pointing to the scattered heap of exercise books.

"Oh, is that when the Queen dies? She can't have been that old," Jess threw over her shoulder as she plucked up the relevant book. "What page am I looking for?"

"I think that entry is 1997. Try August of that year."

Jess returned to the back door, joining Jenny as they both huffed out their smoke, most of which just filtered its way back in.

"No! You're joking! These books are full about people dying!"

"I know. I thought that was a really sad one when he told me."

"Prince Charles wasn't in the car with her?"

"No, no. I think Jason said they will split in the early '90s."

"Oh, that's a shame. Although I'm not surprised. He's so much older than her. Shame about that wasted wedding dress, though. That was beautiful, wasn't it?"

"What d'you mean about their age difference? Your dad is twelve years older than me, and Colin is nine years older than you!"

"Ha, yeah, okay. But he's not my dad, according to him!"

Jenny rubbed Jess's arm as they stood on either side of the doorway. She knew first-hand how hard it was for Jess to believe what she was being told, and Jenny also knew the only real weapon they had to convince Jess was time itself. As it had been for her, the passing of time and events happening made believing Jason easier until it became a certainty that her husband was a time-traveller. However, with the Colneys at large, time was something they didn't have.

"Jess, honey. Jason was born in 1977. You were born in 1956. Who your father is, we don't know. However, he has the same name and we expect must look identical to your dad, but was born in 1934." Jenny held up her hand to stop Jess, who looked about to launch a verbal tirade at what she'd said. "And before you say it, I know that's nuts. However, your father, Jason, my husband, loves you as his own, as I do."

Jess nodded and took another long drag on her cigarette whilst fighting the tears that had again sneaked into her eyes in a surprise attack, completely catching her off guard.

Jenny reached out and wiped away a tear that dribbled down Jess's cheek – Jess didn't flinch. "Martin died that day in '77. The man you met yesterday is the same man, not his imaginary younger brother called Orinoco or whatever."

"Leonardo," chuckled Jess, "You're thinking of the Wombles!"

"Yes, well, whatever. But that man was, unfortunately, Martin, and my God, I wish he wasn't! The bigger issue is the man that stood in that kitchen doorway was Paul Colney, wasn't it?"

"Well, it can't have been, can it! I must have been hallucinating!"

"But you weren't, were you? Yesterday evening you stood next to a living and breathing, dead Paul Colney, didn't you?"

Jess nodded. "I did. And to copy Dad's rating system, that can have a triple five-star rating in the margin ... I'm certain beyond doubt."

For a moment, the ladies puffed away on their cigarettes, alternatively trying to blow the smoke out of the kitchen doorway. However, the late summer gentle breeze was winning this particular battle as the smoke continued to waft its way back in.

"Afternoon, thought I'd catch you both here."

"You!" blurted Jenny and Jess in unison.

31

The Ecstasy Of Gold

I killed the engine of the Quattro, never once taking my eyes off the stone steps which led up to the school entrance. Cruella de Vil and her Bruce Banner shape-shifting sidekick stood staring at me through the windscreen of my car. Although the woman was small in stature, she had an aura that towered above the colossus of a man who stood by her side.

I gawped back at them.

Apart from the brief glimpse last night, I hadn't seen Shirley for ten years. Not since the day she stood on my doorstep that Sunday evening when advising me that her granddaughter, David Colney's daughter, Beth, would be taken away from us.

The school courtyard stood empty now that all the students were back inside attending their afternoon lessons. I'd planned to call Jenny before completing some admin work during a lesson-free period. However, as I exited and stood by my car, I feared my next hour's planned activities might have altered. I considered my next move.

The three of us held our positions, approximately the length of a bowling alley between us, our eyes nervously flitting from one to another. There appeared to be something odd with one of the big fella's eyes that had a kind of death-shark milky-white appearance to it.

I lit a cigarette, never lowering my eyes from Shirley and Shark-Eye. Repositioning it with my teeth, I moved the cigarette to the corner of my mouth. Our eyes still locked, only allowing mine to flit alternately from one to the other. Shirley stepped sideways, then stopped. The three of us now in position as if preparing for a final shootout at high noon. Just like *The Good,* I confidently narrowed my eyes to study the *The Bad and The Ugly* – seriously ugly, and seriously bad.

With a minute passed in our static positions, the gentle breeze picked up, tantalisingly swirling particles of dust between us – our eyes flicked from one another – I nervously chewed the end of my cigarette. The breeze increased its tempo, now producing a haunting whistling tune through the leaves and branches of the two giant sycamores – it seemed to fit the scene.

My mind joined in as if producing the backing harmony vocals to Ennio Morricone's famous Spaghetti Western movie score. I now wondered what part of nature would join the whistling trees to provide the 'Ooo-Ha' sound and ultimately the 'Ahhh-ahhh-ahhh' accompaniment as we reached the point of drawing weapons and the tune came to a close when we would form our Mexican standoff positions. Would we all reach for our imaginary army-issue Colt revolvers – could I take out Lee Van Cleef, AKA Shirley, before Eli Wallach, AKA Shark-Eye, took me down?

The *Bad* drew first—

"So, we meet again, Mr Apsley," delivered like a proper Bond villain.

'Christ! What movie was I in?'

'One where the bad guy wins ... I think!'

'Oh, and while we're at it, as stated by a certain Chief of Police character, and assessing the large shark-eye creature to your left, I might suggest you are going to require a larger seafaring vessel!'

Whilst agreeing with my mind talk on the metaphorical size of boat required to avoid Shark-Eye, I removed my cigarette, which, whilst I impersonated Clint Eastwood, had caused smoke to drift into my eye, now causing it to water. Not a great look to be crying even before the Great White had sunk his teeth in. An event that surely was only a few seconds away from occurring.

"This is private property. You have no business here," I stabbed out.

'Sorry, old son, that's not going to cut it with these two. You sound like a right pompous git!'

Shark-Eye advanced, presumably moving in for the kill. Fortunately, Shirley held onto his arm, not that she had the physical force to stop him, but clearly, she held the reins.

"We need to talk. You and I have some unfinished business."

"No, we don't. We have nothing to discuss now and never will have. So, I suggest you leave."

'Better, more confident. Come on, Apsley, keep this up!'

"We've got plenty to talk about, Apsley. So, listen up, or Ralph 'ere is going to turn you upside down!" cackled Shirley, as she closed the gap between us whilst her pet shark followed her movements. Both halted their advance when within ten feet of me. Shirley folded her arms, so did the Great White.

Although ten years had passed since our last meeting, the hideous woman, who'd produced four of the town's evillest men, appeared not to have changed a great deal. Not in the time travel sense like Martin, but her twiggy-shape figure and trowelled-on make-up were how I recall her on that Sunday afternoon in '77. Glancing at the shark, I now had a close-up view of that hideous white eye which afforded a ghostly Jaws-like stare to it – with his greying teddy-boy quiff, richly tanned, lined skin, he owned a face which any casting director would have paid handsomely for when searching for the perfect Bond villain.

"What d'you want. I can't talk for long ... I have a class waiting," I lied.

"I couldn't give a fuck if you've got the Queen waiting. You've got big ears, so use 'em," she spat back, adding an aggressive chicken-style nod of her head as if attempting a head butt. Although, due to her low stature, she'd have hit my sternum. Rather pathetically I flinched.

"My solicitor is preparing some documents that will be served to you tomorrow morning. They'll be the start of the legal process so that my granddaughters live with me, their grandmother ... where they should be."

"Granddaughters?"

"Good, you're listening. Yeah, Beth and Faith."

"Ha, you've got no chance! Beth is my legally adopted daughter, and Faith is with her natural mother and adopted father. No court in the land will ever give you custody!" With that, I stepped between them, confident this charade was finished. Shirley Colney was utterly deluded into thinking she could take custody of the girls. A wave of relief flooded over me as I stepped past them, heading for the school entrance.

"You wanna risk it?" Shirley called out, stopping me in my tracks.

I spun around to find they'd stepped forward, closing the gap. Again, the Great White towered over me – his fisheye probing.

"What d'you mean?"

"Well, as I see it, a court would find against you for refusing access. I'm their grandmother, and I have rights you can't deny."

"You want access?" I asked, disappointingly detecting a tremor in my voice.

Shirley swished her head to move her long salt and pepper, Cruella de Vil styled, hair from her face. The action revealed her hidden ears … large sticky out ones, just like mine. A family trait, perhaps? Well, if I was somehow a clone of *other* Jason, and Shirley and *other* Jason were half-siblings, then maybe their natural mother, Mary Apsley, had also owned a set of dubiously large ears. But where did I come into this? But then, come to think of it, my parents had normal ears, so who the hell knows.

Shirley grinned. "I can see you're a schoolteacher. Cleva ain't he, Ralph?"

"Why would you want access?"

"Cos they're my flesh and blood! David was my flesh and blood … my beautiful boy! But we both know what happened to 'im, don't we?" she spat back, as she closed the gap to within a couple of feet. The shark closed in with her, circling his prey – his Brylcreemed grey quiff appearing like a large glistening dorsal fin.

"I don't know what you mean!" I blurted, taking an involuntary step back from the white-eyed predator that now loomed large on my right-hand side.

"See, this is how it's going to play out. I get access," she waved her hand in the air in a questioning manner. "We can work out the days how often at a later stage. You voluntarily agree, then my bid for custody goes away." Shirley grinned, as she pointed a bony finger at my chest before continuing. "And, big ears, you avoid going to prison for murdering my son."

"I didn't murder your son!"

"You did. You were on that roof the day David fell."

"You can't prove that."

"You wanna risk it?"

Shirley's statement hung in the air. Back in the late '70s, I knew Frenchie was damn close to proving I was on the roof the day David died. Now, I know Frenchie would like nothing better than to see the demise of Shirley. However, she would also put me away for killing David if Shirley could prove it. DI Heather French was as straight as a bat and wouldn't hesitate to arrest me. Could I call Shirley's bluff? Could I risk it?

I feared she had me hemmed in a corner, with my only option to agree to her demands and give in to awarding weekend visiting rights to these two monsters.

'Told you on many, many occasions, old boy ... you're fucked. However, on this particular occasion, you're super fucked!'

'Oh, and can you imagine what Jenny and Jess will say to that!'

I shuddered at my mind talk, which was disappointing because I could see Shirley enjoyed the tremor she'd witnessed as it traversed through my body.

"The girls won't want to see you. You can't force them, even if you did have some access rights."

"That's my problem, not yours. Now, unless you and that slag of a daughter of yours want legal papers served on you, I suggest you agree to my terms."

"What are they?"

"Good, we're getting somewhere."

"Just tell me what you want!"

"Every weekend."

"No way! Anyway, you don't live here. You live in Spain."

"No, I'm back. And now I have a right as their grandmother to have the girls at weekends."

Shark-Eye moved his head to allow his good eye to look at Shirley. A chink in their armour, perhaps. Shirley moving back from Spain was new news to him, or was it a lie?

"You can't do this ... I won't allow it."

"Apsley, I've got you cornered. You've got no choice. Now, I'll pick the girls up here tomorrow night at, let's say, half-four. Make sure you're here, and they're ready!" she aggressively spat, before stepping back.

"No! No fucking way!"

Ralph stepped forward, reaffirming his threatening size, not that I needed reminding – the man could eclipse the sun.

"Even if we had some agreement, you can't have them without it being drawn up legally ... all above board, as such."

"Ralph!" commanded his handler, clearly stated in a tone that the beast could understand.

In one swift movement, the Great White lifted me with one hand under my left armpit, effortlessly carting me across the stone steps and slamming me against one of the white stone pillars.

The Great White opened its mouth – not to gorge on me but to finally speak. "Remember me?"

I detected an accent. Rolf Harris, perhaps? He'd been a discussion at one of the Time Travel Believers' Club meetings. However, I was super shaky on the dates, and George and Jenny point blank refused to accept what I was saying. They'd said, it was bad enough what I'd said about Jimmy Savile considering all his good work for charity, and they just weren't buying it – anyway, Beth and Christopher loved the *Rolf Harris Cartoon Time* shows, and Jenny would hear nothing more of it. I accepted that I couldn't win all my battles.

Returning to the matter in hand as this Australian shark held me against the pillar with my legs dangling, I wondered how the hell he thought we were previously acquainted. However, Frenchie had alluded to this yesterday afternoon.

"Err ... no, mate."

"My eye!" he rather aggressively stated, whilst using his free hand to point to the milky cold-staring orb.

"Put Mr Apsley down! And I'll let you know the police are on their way!" stabbed out Mrs Trosh, who stood at the school entrance with Sarah peeking over her shoulder.

Ralph glanced at Shirley, who nodded. He complied, allowing me to slither down the pillar into a crumpled heap.

"1954. Festival House. You blinded me!" boomed Ralph, as he pointed at my crumpled form.

I shook my head dismissively, wondering what the hell he was on about. But of course, in 1954, I wasn't even a twinkle in my parents' eyes who hadn't met and were still at school. However, *other* Jason would have been twenty and clearly had some altercation that caused colossus to end up with that shark-eye.

"My Shirl gets the girls, or it's an eye-for-eye," announced the Great White, as he pointed to his dead orb and then at my eyes with a two-fingered, *I see you*, action.

"Friday, Apsley. Make sure they're ready," spat Shirley before beckoning with her head, indicating to her pet shark that it was time to leave.

Shirley and Ralph fled the scene by jumping in a diarrhoea-brown Austin Montego with shit-brown go-faster stripes down the side – the '80s car market was hideous.

From my slumped position, I watched as they sped out of the car park, whilst Mrs Trosh and Sarah bolted down the steps to my aid as I lay still folded in a crumpled heap contemplating that I now only had about thirty hours to crawl out of this mess.

As the two school secretaries fussed, I pondered my options.

In thirty hours I would have to hand over Beth and Faith or, if I chose not to, it appears the Great White would blind me. Meanwhile, my daughter, well, *other* Jason's daughter, was probably now calling the authorities to have Beth and Christopher removed after Jenny had most definitely failed to convince her that I was a time-traveller. I expect by now she would consider her father and Jenny to be unstable and clearly unsuitable to look after their adopted children. To add to this steaming pile of hideous mess, my loose cannonball was not in Don's house when I shot around earlier. So, he was out there somewhere, causing more havoc, which he seemed to have a natural ability to do. Also, the psycho-nutter, murdering bastard Paul Colney was on the prowl, who also wanted to kill me. Well, join the bloody queue, mate, because I think your mother and pet shark have just taken pole position for that particular desire!

Oh, yes, and how could I forget, the other half of the Chuckle Brothers must also be out there, current whereabouts unknown. And to finish it off, I had DI French probing around, trying to discover how that bloody yellow Cortina ended up rematerializing after ten bloody years!

I considered I was in the eye of a bit of a shit storm.

~

"Struth, Shirl! Shirl? What's that all about? So, you're not returning to Spain? Thought we were going back at the weekend?" questioned Ralph, his giant bulk filling the passenger seat of their hire car, whilst Shirley spun out of the school car park.

"Ralph, keep up! Why d'you think I ordered that weasel Hawkshaw to organise a boat from Brightlingsea? Before dawn on Saturday, we'll be heading home from Dunkirk with the girls."

"We're kidnapping them?" Ralph shifted in his seat to look at Shirley with his working eye.

"No! They're coming to live with their grandmother. I've got a hold over Apsley … it's a long stretch inside for him, or he just accepts the girls are gone!"

32

An Inconvenient Relationship

"Don't fuss!" I quite unreasonably bellowed whilst Mrs Trosh and Sarah helped me back into the school office, each hanging onto an arm as they guided me through to a chair as if assisting a frail old-age pensioner across a pelican crossing.

"Alright! But we're just trying to help!" stated a now stroppy Mrs Trosh.

"I'm sorry. But I'm alright, honestly."

"Who were they? That man was horrible!" shrieked Sarah, who seemed to be in a worst state than I was.

"It was that Colney woman! I'll never forget that woman! Her four dreadful sons attended this school. Poor Mr Clark had several run-ins with that dreadful creature."

"Colney!" stammered Sarah, as she slowly guided herself into the seat next to me, appearing to be stunned at hearing that name.

"Oh, my dear. I'm so sorry, I forgot. It was Patrick who hurt your father all those years ago, wasn't it? I didn't mean to upset you. That was very remiss of me, my dear. But the unvarnished truth is there to see, that woman is the devil itself!"

Sarah looked up at Mrs Trosh, who now attended to both Sarah and I like a fussing mother. "Yes ... and all because that pervert, David ..." her voice trailed off, as the memory resurfaced of the assault which David Colney had inflicted upon her when an innocent schoolgirl.

"Oh, Miss Moore, I'm so sorry to bring it up." Mrs Trosh took hold of Sarah's hand, giving it a gentle, comforting rub. "Try not to think about it. David has left this world, and Patrick is locked away in prison."

I slowly shook my head.

"What? What is it, Mr Aps ... Jason?" questioned Sarah, presumably noticing my odd look.

Clearly, she wasn't aware. And I was about to piss on her strawberries, so to speak.

"Sorry, but haven't you heard—"

Before I could continue to ruin Sarah's day, two police officers burst through the swing doors. The spotty male officer, bringing up the rear, failed to hide his obvious leching as he eyed Sarah up and down – he was very unsubtle.

I mused that, in my eyes, both officers appeared to be still crawling their way out of puberty – or was that how they all looked now that I'd passed my fiftieth birthday?

"We had a call about a disturbance," called out a breathless female officer, who slapped her hand on her police issue handbag that now swung wildly from her exertions.

It still bemused me that in this era female officers carried a handbag which, apart from being able to batter a few armed robbers with, I couldn't see as an asset to any officer whilst giving chase to Fairfield's low life scum that oozed out at regular intervals from the Broxworth Estate.

"Delta Oscar five-nine-five to Delta Oscar, are you receiving? Over," the male officer called into his radio whilst he allowed his eyes to slowly remove every item of clothing from Sarah's body.

"Delta Oscar, receiving. Go ahead. Over."

"We're at the school now. The incident is no longer in progress. No further assistance is required. Over."

"Received. Over."

"Can you tell us what's happened here, please?" asked the female officer to no one in particular whilst extracting a notebook from her handbag.

"I called the police," confidently stated Mrs Trosh, whilst straightening up, shoulders back, and clearly delighted she had performed an important act in conducting her civic duty in reporting a misdemeanour.

"And you are?"

"Mrs Patricia Trosh. I'm the secretary to the School's Headmaster."

"And you are?" questioned the officer looking up at Sarah and me.

I nodded to Sarah, indicating ladies first.

"Sarah Moore."

"And you work here, Mrs Moore?"

"Err … yes. It's Miss, by the way."

I noticed the male officer soak in the information that Sarah was a Miss and not Mrs.

"Sir?"

"Jason Apsley. Deputy Headmaster."

"O–kay," stated the young officer as she finished scribbling our names. The male officer had placed his hands on his hips whilst continuing to make a detailed study of the younger of the two school secretaries.

"Mrs Trosh, you made the call about an assault. Have you been assaulted?"

"No! Didn't they tell you? I was very specific with the operator when I called. It's our Mr Apsley who's been assaulted!"

"Sir?" questioned the officer, her pen poised to make further notes.

"It's nothing. Just a misunderstanding that's no longer an issue."

Mrs Trosh shot me a look, presumably aghast at my dismissive stance regarding the incident when pinned to one of the school's white stone pillars by an enormous one-eyed Australian.

"We'll be the judge of that, sir. Who assaulted you, and where are they now?"

"I think our Deputy Head may have a spot of concussion. I can tell you, officer, that he most certainly was assaulted. One of the assailants was—"

"We don't know who they were, officer. As I said, it was a misunderstanding," I quickly interrupted before Mrs Trosh blurted out Shirley's name.

I was already knee-deep in shite. So, I could ill afford to allow Shirley's name to be uttered because that would surely filter back to Frenchie – clearly a situation I needed to avoid.

I had delicate negotiations to conduct if I was to keep the girls safe, my sight intact, and protect my liberty. Frenchie and her truncheon-wielding team marauding in with their size nines really wouldn't help my situation at this point in time.

The female officer glanced up from her notepad, flicking her eyes back and forth from Mrs Trosh and me, I guess, clearly detecting a cover-up on my part.

As cover-ups go, it wasn't huge and certainly not on the scale of the attempted official censorship that followed the reporting of the Queen's apparent *Uncaring Thatcher* comment reported in The Times newspaper last year. Along with the ensuing scramble at both the Palace and Downing Street to smooth over what was an embarrassing situation for all sides, according to the newspaper reports. However, I was desperately trying to stonewall Shirley Colney's involvement in this particularly delicate domestic-related incident.

The Times had reported *The Inconvenient Relationship,* between the two ladies, Her Majesty The Queen and our Prime Minister, Margaret Thatcher – a description I thought had a certain resonance to Shirley and me.

"Well, which is it? Assault or no assault?" asked the officer, her pen poised to note down the correct answer.

"Definitely assault! Mr Apsley, let me do the talking whilst you rest. It's been quite a distressing situation, and you need to get your strength back."

"Sir? You seem a little reluctant to lodge this complaint?"

I stood and stepped towards the officer, desperately trying to take control of the situation. "No, Mrs Trosh is quite correct. There was an altercation. However, apart from my shirt being grabbed, it was nothing more. So, you see, not really an assault ... more of a private matter. Handbags at dawn!" I chuckled.

"A private matter?"

"Yes, that's right. I'm sorry if I've caused a bit of a flap. But, honestly, it's nothing."

"Not according to these two ladies who look to be catching flies!" called out the male officer, sporting a smirk across his face, who'd now parked his backside on Mrs Trosh's desk. "Alright, love," he added, addressing Sarah whilst continuing to lech at her.

Not the best chat-up line I've ever heard. Although I wasn't coming from a position of strength in that area, so who was I to judge.

"Sir, did this non-incident have anything to do with the driver of a fawn-coloured Montego we passed at the school entrance?" questioned the female officer.

Personally, I thought diarrhoea was a better description. However, I do accept that if British Leyland had used my description in their car brochure colour charts, it could have dampened sales of their already woefully totally shite car.

"Yes, that was them! That woman—"

"Yes!" I boomed, verbally bullying to stop Mrs Trosh from uttering Shirley's name.

"We're all okay, officer. Perhaps you could go and apprehend them?" added in Sarah, who glanced at me, realising for some reason that I was desperate to keep Shirley's name from entering this policewoman's notebook.

We exchanged glances, and I detected that Sarah was willing to help. However, I feared she would demand an explanation, which I considered could be somewhat tricky.

"Okay. We'll be back later for full statements. Jock, come on," she stated to the male officer, who afforded Sarah one more visual undress before lifting his backside, leaning his head down, and calling into the station on his radio.

"Delta Oscar five-nine-five to Delta Oscar, are you receiving? Over."

"Delta Oscar receiving. Go ahead. Over."

"Yeah, I need a vehicle check. Index number ..."

The swing door closed as both officers left. Going by the tail end of that radio conversation, it appeared the officer had noted down the licence plate of Shirley's getaway car. So, presumably, they'd be apprehended pretty quickly. Was that a good thing? I didn't know.

"Jason?" queried Sarah, now presumably looking for answers as payback for her assistance in that particularly tight spot.

"Do *not* use first names in school hours! Golden rule, number one! This place is going to go to pot when I leave!" announced a red-faced Mrs Trosh. She aggressively thrust her hands on her hips as two wisps of hair simultaneously uncoupled from their position in her tight bun hairdo. The errant wisps of hair that had escaped and cascaded down the side of her head now appeared to resemble straps that held on to her bun-styled hair.

"Where's PoD?" I questioned Sarah, ignoring Mrs Trosh's rant, due to being more concerned PoD would've overheard the commotions.

"He's out. Don't you remember he had that meeting at County Hall this afternoon?" stated Sarah, in a much calmer manner than Mrs Trosh's outburst. The latter appeared to be now frothing at the mouth like some demented infected soul from the film *Contagion*. I recall Lisa and I enjoyed that film at the cinema, back in the day when we still liked each other and before my loose cannonball ex-colleague and her took up extracurricular bedroom antics.

"And what do you mean by the word PoD? Is this some code name for Mr Elkinson that I'm unaware of? Hmmm, well?" questioned our foam-frothing secretary, whose flustered state suggested she might suffer a coronary. Either that or had contracted rabies, which was a genuine worry of many concerned citizens of Kent who were convinced the disease would come flooding through the recently commissioned project to build a tunnel under the English Channel.

"Mrs Trosh, you're quite right. Please accept my apology. Yes, it's a silly nickname that I shouldn't have repeated."

"I should think not!"

"Jas—" Sarah halted as she clocked another Paddington stare from Mrs Trosh. "Mr Apsley, why didn't you tell those officers about Mrs Colney?"

Bollocks.

'Get out of this one, sunshine. As I told you earlier – you're super fucked!'

"Look, it's a delicate situation to do with ... err ... err—"

"Well?" demanded the foaming rabid Mrs Trosh.

"Martin. To do with Martin," I lied, thinking on my feet, and coming up with more bollocks that would probably drag me into deeper shite – if that was possible. Christ, this week really was spiralling down to new lower depths of hell.

"I knew it! There was always something odd about that man!"

"Hang on! You've always liked him! You swooned over the man!"

"Mr Apsley! I'm a respectable married lady. I'll have none of that talk, thank you!"

"Oh, come on, Mrs T, you do like him."

"Well, yes, he's a nice young man, I suppose." She returned one of the escaped strands of hair into the bun. "Mrs T, I like that. Ha, that sounds all official, doesn't it?"

"Yes, it does," I chuckled. "I can think of another person with that name!"

"Oh, who,"

"Well, our Prime Minister, of course."

"Oh, I've never heard of that. She's more the Iron Lady. However, Mr Trosh and I disagree on this subject. He rather annoyingly refers to Mrs Thatcher as *that woman*. We both vote at every election, as everyone must do, but we sort of cancel each other out."

Silence fell as the three of us exchanged glances. Mrs Trosh had always had an amazing ability to drag a conversation off-piste, leaving us all lost in no man's land and allowing the thread of our discussion to wisp away.

"I said to Mr Trosh back in June that I really didn't understand how he could want to vote for that dreadful ginger Welsh man – shocking man, can't understand a word he says. That said, I don't like our current MP. That Miles Rusher is a right shifty character, I just don't like him!" she announced, appearing satisfied she'd aired her views regarding the national and local political situation of the day.

There was something I just couldn't remember about the current MP. I do recall he was still the local MP when I left to go to university, and I'm sure there was some scandal that befell the poor chap, but what it was, and when, I have no idea. I know Frank, Jayne's husband, had an impoverished view of the man, but why that was, I never knew. As I pondered this irrelevant thought, Mrs Trosh continued.

"Now, as for the last MP, Mrs Stone, well, she was a lovely lady, lovely lady," she announced. Then, in true Mrs Trosh style, she leant forward after completing her signature furtive glance left and right and continued. "You know, of course, our Miss Hart married the last MP's husband ... a right old shady and shocking affair, if you ask me!"

"Yes, we all know that! That's why Jayne is now Mrs Stone! Anyway, Mrs T, before you cast the first stone, no pun intended, I believe that it was the MP, The Right Honourable Mrs Stone, who ran off with another MP, so I don't think you should judge Jayne and her husband too harshly!"

"Well, that as may be. But I'll have you know; Jayne is still the scarlet woman in my book!"

"Sorry, but can we get back to Martin, and what has he got to do with that bloody Colney woman."

"Yes, good point, Miss Moore. I will say there was a slightly shady side to Martin, you know," piously stated Mrs Trosh, as she raised her eyebrow at me, seemingly now turning her machine-gun character assassination views on Martin now she'd peppered Jayne's character full of holes. "God knows what his mother taught him!"

I glanced at Sarah, thinking we could ask her as she stood here. Hmmm, maybe not, because this conversation was already shooting up the nutty-conversations charts and interrogating Sarah about her parenting skills and what-on-earth she taught her son, which caused him to become a shady loose cannon, ex-wife screwing, woman chasing, and general pain in the arse, would be super tricky based on the fact she hadn't given birth to him yet, or ever would for that matter.

"Oh, I don't think he's shady. To be honest with you, when I was at school here, I had a bit of a girly crush on him. In fact, he's a bit of a hunk!" announced Sarah, who immediately blushed.

"Oh, my God!"

"Mr Apsley?" questioned Mrs Trosh, presumably surprised by my outburst, whilst ignoring Sarah's declaration that her son was a veritable babe magnet.

"Can this week get any bloody worse!"

"What now, Mr Apsley? You know you have had a bit of a shock; I think you should sit yourself down. Perhaps we can get you a nice mug of sweet tea?" she suggested whilst rubbing my elbow. "What d'you think, Miss Moore?"

"Oh, yes, of course, I'll nip along to the staff room. Anyone else whilst I'm at it?" announced Sarah, picking up on the nonverbal instruction to act as the tea lady.

Although Mrs Trosh had only a few weeks left in the role as the school secretary to the headmaster of the most prestigious school in town, it was abundantly clear she would not let go of the reins until the last minute.

"Sweet teas, all-round, my dear. Now, off you go, there's a good girl."

Sarah took her instruction, skipping out of the office through the swing doors. I heard her call out, "Oh, sorry, excuse me," as the doors closed.

"Now, Mr Apsley. What on earth is going on? You know you can't keep anything from me," she stated, still rubbing my elbow.

I took a deep breath, desperately trying to conjure up some inspiration – nothing was coming. However, I knew the ever efficient, super nosey Mrs Trosh would keep probing.

"Come on, what's going on? I only have your best interests at heart."

"Ah, Jason, Thank God, I've found you!" blurted out Colin, as he stumbled in through the swing doors.

"Mr Poole! Address the Deputy Head correctly! What's the matter with everyone? It's far too familiar to use Christian names!"

I spun around to see Colin with the back of his hand placed against his forehead, his eyes closed, producing a heavy sigh. This was not good. Clearly Jess had got hold of him and presumably broken her vow of silence regarding my ridiculous claim about my time-travelling capabilities.

"Jason, we're going to have to do something about that new girl! This can't carry on!"

"New girl?"

"That Lisa Crowther!" exclaimed Colin, still with his hand on his brow as if imitating some innocent well-to-do Victorian heiress who'd just been exposed to the vision of a naked man and finding it all too much to cope with – now verging on fainting.

"Oh, Christ," I sighed. What had my twelve-year-old ex-wife done now?

33

He's From Barcelona

With the day's lessons all completed, Mrs Trosh's questioning put on ice, two cups of sweet tea gulped, and Lisa Crowther's misdemeanour on the metaphorical back burner, I arrived home with half an hour to spare before needing to whisk Jess up to town to keep our appointment with Frenchie.

As luck would have it, Jayne had roped Colin in to support with the school play's rehearsals, so he was nicely tucked out of the way, leaving an opportunity for an open conversation between Jess, Jenny and myself before facing the rotund detective inspector.

After the Great White had not so gently informed me about how he obtained his shark-eye, I assume that the altercation with *other* Jason and him featured somewhere in an old typed report buried within police records, thus explaining Frenchie's comment when leaving the school office on Wednesday. So, the question is, did *other* Jason have a criminal record? And if so, by association, I now owned. Thursday 10th September just kept giving.

Of course, to add to the pile of issues, Martin was missing – again. Paul Colney was still at large, and I had Shirley's ultimatum to deal with – the clock was ticking.

It sounded like Jenny was taking all the suitable precautions as I listened to the unbolting sequence of the front door, which she performed before allowing me into the unknown. With all the fun at school today, I hadn't had the chance to call her. Also, as I wasn't that fly on the wall listening in, I now wondered – no scrub that – now dreaded how Jenny's conversation had panned out when trying to convince Jess I was a time-traveller.

Jenny had always fared well at poker and didn't suffer regular thrashings when playing Snap with Beth. Therefore, as she opened our Fort Knox-like front door, her dead-pan face gave nothing away.

"Well?" I questioned as a greeting, now that the extensive unlocking sequence was complete, whilst Jenny stood holding the front door peering past me up and down the street.

Jenny took hold of my hand, tiptoed up and kissed me, placing her hand on my cheek. "I love you, Mr Apsley."

"I love you too. But Jen, you're worrying me!"

"Come on." Still holding my hand, she dragged me towards the living room.

With great trepidation, I held on tight, a mixture of dread and excitement on what lay the other side of the door.

The sight before me wasn't what I expected. Martin lay splayed out on the sofa, hands behind his head staring up at the ceiling, casually posed with his ankles crossed as they lay propped up on the sofa arms. Jess sat cross-legged on the hearthrug.

The rug was not my idea; however, Jenny said all fires have a semi-circle rug in front, so we should have one as well. To me, it was an outdated item of soft furnishing – but hey, until another thirty years past, everything was outdated as far as I was concerned, that included my pleat-fronted trousers and Jenny's shoulder-padded blouses.

"Right, 1999," stated Jess, as she thumbed through one of the yellow exercise books which lay liberally scattered around her. "You should get this one! What happened in May ... it's football related?" she questioned Martin, whilst holding the book aloft, peering over the top of the book, and twiddling a pencil in her other hand.

"Ha, an easy one!" exclaimed Martin, shooting his hands in the air.

"Oh, hi, Dad," offered Jess with a smile before turning back to Martin, awaiting his answer. "Come on then, if it's that easy!"

Jenny retook my hand in hers, giving it a reassuring, gentle squeeze. Jess and Martin seemed to be entertaining themselves whilst they played a game of general knowledge, like a futuristic game of Trivial Pursuit or the TV show Blockbusters. Jess-Bob Holness-Poole took the role of quiz master whilst Martin was in the hot-seat. I wondered if he would ask, *I'll have a P please Bob*, as he battled his way to a *Gold Run*. It was one of Christopher's favourite TV programmes and one I'd enjoyed the first time around, albeit in the early '90s.

"United won the Champions League, of course!" exclaimed Martin, delivering his answer with his hands aloft.

"United? Which United,"

"There's only one United!" exclaimed Martin, sounding hurt, as he yanked up his trouser leg to display the tattoo of the Manchester United badge.

"Sorry, but that means nothing to me."

"Manchester United!"

"Okay. Who did they beat?"

"Easy! Bayern Munich, in Barcelona."

"Err ... nope. You haven't quite got that right. Manchester United *did* beat Bayern Munich. However, they won the European Cup, not some Champion League thingy. *And* it was played in Istanbul, *not* Spain."

"Ha, no, I'm right! Big ears here, has got it wrong again!" belligerently stated Martin, whilst pointing in my direction. "They changed the name from the European Cup to The Champions League in the early '90s."

"You sure?"

"Yes!"

"Okay. Dad, you want to counter this?" asked Jess, turning to me, now with her pencil poised at the page, presumably to make corrections.

I shook my head, accepting Martin's knowledge of Manchester United football trivia would steal a march on mine. Nevertheless, this was a good sign. Jess seemed to be enjoying herself and, presumably, this meant that Jenny had been far more successful than I would have believed possible.

"O-kay! I'll add a note in the margin," stated Jess. "Barthelonna!" she announced in broken English, copying Andrews Sachs when playing the poor abused waiter, Manuel, in *Fawlty Towers*.

"So, next question. Same month, same year. Something happened in space."

"Oh, not space again. I'm not good with these questions. Is it another shuttle launch or something?"

"No, not man-made."

"Oh, yes! Yes, yes, yes. The solar eclipse. However, your dad's got this one wrong as well! It happened in August, not May!"

"Yes, you're right, a solar eclipse! Are you sure about the month?"

"Defo! It was the school holidays, and Mum helped me and my mate make a pin-hole projector so we could see it. They showed how to make one on Blue Peter the day before."

"Blue Peter! I take it John Noakes, Peter Purves, and Valerie Singleton weren't still presenting," laughed Jess.

"Oh, Jess, that was your time. It's Caron Keating and that Peter Duncan bloke now ... not that Beth watches it anymore now she's speeding her way to womanhood."

I shot Jenny a concerned look.

"Yes, I know. I just can't believe it's still on the air in ten years' time!" threw in Jess.

"I think it carried on for many years after. Sarah Green and Simon Groom for me," I added to this completely pointless conversation. However, stating who your Blue Peter presenters were was like naming who your James Bond was. Although I was the eldest in the room, due to the time-travel conundrum, Jenny was technically the only one of us who actually predated the children's TV programme.

"Katy Hills and Anthea Turner." They were my era," announced Martin, not wanting to be left out.

"Who?" questioned Jenny and Jess.

"Oh, well, you won't know because that's in the future! So come on, Jess, next question, I'm on a roll!"

"This is like DLT's *Give us a Break*, isn't it! Snooker on the radio," announced Jenny, as we both took in the scene of Jess posing questions and Martin firing off the answers.

"What? Never heard of that. What's DLT?" quizzed Martin, shifting his gaze from Jess to where Jenny and I stood by the door.

"Dave Lee Travis, you berk! You'd get a *Wank-wank-oops*, for that answer," laughed Jess. "You know, the Radio One DJ show on Saturday mornings!"

"No, never heard of it."

"Really?"

"Really!" he exclaimed, once again pointing his arms in the air. "And do they really say wank on the radio?"

"Yes, well, that's what it sounds like. If you get a question wrong, you get the *Wank-wank-oops* sound!"

"Oh, I'm surprised they get away with that! Oh, hang on, now I remember him! Didn't he resign live on air or something?"

"Yes, he did!" I exclaimed, now enjoying having a fellow time-traveller to bounce memories around with. "When was that?"

Martin swung his legs off the armrest, shifting his prone body to face me. "I reckon I was only a kid at the time, but I remember Mum said something about him."

"I was about fifteen or sixteen at the time, so early '90s maybe?"

"Yeah, probably."

"Oh, really, darling? I like DLT. That's a shame. What was that all about?"

"Oh, hell, I have no idea."

"Wasn't there something …" asked Martin, but his question trailed off.

"I know what you mean, but I really can't remember."

"What?" questioned Jess and Jenny in unison.

"Forget it. Look, I hope you weren't followed? You could have led that psycho Paul here?" I questioned Martin, pointing at him. "Jen, are the girls okay?"

"Yes, darling, they're fine," she rubbed my arm reassuringly. "They're upstairs plotting how to grow up faster."

I shot Jenny a look, who smirked back.

"I'm not a total tit! Of course, I wasn't followed," stated Martin.

"That's still up for debate! How d'you know you weren't?" I pointed again, increasing the aggression asserted with my middle finger as I stepped towards my loose cannon, whose face still appeared heavily battered and bruised from last night's shenanigans with Paul. *Ten rounds with Tyson* was the phrase. However, that hadn't become popular quite yet because Iron Mike, as the papers were calling him, had just rocketed to stardom, taking the heavy weight title at the end of last year.

"I took precautions!"

"Well, pity you didn't with Randy Mandy!"

"Oh, Christ. I'd forgotten about her!"

"Yes, well. One thing at a time."

"Darling, because we're ex-directory, he can't find out where we live, can he?"

"Anyway, big ears, how d'you know he didn't follow *you* from school?" Martin asked accusingly, pointing his finger back at me.

Bollocks!

We held our positions for a brief moment. Both with our arm outstretched, pointing a finger accusingly like two opposing politicians across the floor of the House of Commons.

Christ, I just hadn't thought about that. With the altercation with Shirley and Ralph and the impending doom of what was to happen in about twenty-four hours, it hadn't occurred to me that Paul could have trailed me home when I left school.

'Told you, my old mucker ... you're super-fucked!'

"Jason?" nervously asked Jenny.

"No. No one tailed me," I confidently replied. Although in reality, I feared I might have cocked up.

"Good, I can't face that bloody man again. But Dad, I am worried where Patrick might be."

"Jess, do you ... well, do you believe ... believe what I've told you?"

"Dad, I don't know. It's mad, isn't it! But I will say Martin seems to agree with so much that's written in these books," she gestured her hand across the fawn-coloured hearthrug or was it more of a diarrhoea colour? "Although, he has performed much better than you with the '90s," she waved the exercise book, "Well, assuming he's not made it all up, that is!"

"They've been at it for hours!" stated Jenny, once again retaking my hand and guiding us both to the pastel-green coloured Dralon sofa under the window, which matched the one Martin still lay sprawled across.

"So, you think you can believe it?"

"Dad, I said I don't know! Martin did agree with so much of what you have written ... George and Jenny are sensible ... but ..."

"But what?"

"Look. I have to admit something isn't right. I did see Paul Colney last night, and I will admit these books, and what you two say, does seem to suggest you've both come from the future."

A blanket of silence descended, almost smothering what was coming next. Jess was the third person to try and convince that I was a time-traveller and, believe you me, it's not a straightforward task.

Jess waved her pencil in Martin's direction. "He's definitely the bloke who drove that car that night. I will never forget it! And he can remember the events as if they were yesterday!"

"Err ... well, as far as I'm concerned, it was only a few days ago!"

"Alright," I checked my watch. "Jess, we've got to get going. You remember, DI French wants to interview us both about that very same car crash."

"Yeah, not forgotten,"

"Come on then. We'll pull a strategy together on the way."

"Darling, I'll get some supper ready for all of us. Jess, what time will Colin be back?"

"Oh, I think he said about six-ish."

Jenny pointed at Martin. "You'll have to be Leonardo from now on, for the girls' and Colin's sake."

"Christ, what have the girls said about him?" I questioned, forgetting they were upstairs.

"Oh, they're too busy. I don't think—"

As the chimes from the front doorbell pealed out, Jenny abruptly stopped in mid flow. We all glanced to the hallway and then at each other – I guess we all held the same unspoken question on our minds – Paul Colney.

"It's not him. It can't be," I answered their unspoken question.

"Darling, you sure he didn't follow you?"

"No," I replied, shaking my head. "Anyway, I don't think murdering psychopaths ring the doorbell."

34

Dirty Den

In the vast majority of Agatha Christie's Hercule Poirot murder mysteries, which I could recall watching many a TV adaptation in both my lives, the tale's finale would feature the brilliant detective summoning the characters to a suitable location – perhaps in the drawing-room, or the library of a stately home, or even the deck of an opulently decorated paddle steamer. Once assembled, the waxed-moustached Belgian would then ratchet up the tension as he relayed his outstandingly complex discoveries, culminating in a proclamation of the identity of the murderer.

Suppose Agatha Christie had wanted to create a brilliant and inquisitive Detective Inspector who had the ability to bore a piercing I-don't-believe-you stare into your eyes. In that case, she could have done a lot worse than modelling her character on Frenchie.

There was no stately home's drawing-room or paddle steamer in this version of the gathering; instead, just our front room. DI French took on the role of Poirot, with her sergeant slotting into the Captain Hastings character. Leonardo, AKA Martin, Jess, Jenny, and I made up the group of suspects, whilst the tension in the room ratcheted up a few notches now we enjoyed the pleasures that Frenchie's company provided.

The once again thirsty sergeant held his notebook and pen at the ready. Jenny had offered drinks to which the sergeant had gleefully requested a cup of tea with two sugars, only for his boss to advise Jenny that both she and Sergeant Farham didn't require any refreshments.

DI French positioned herself on the edge of the sofa which Jenny and I had vacated whilst Martin continued to lay splayed out on the opposite sofa. Jenny, me, and the thirsty sergeant all stood whilst Jess held her position on the hearthrug as she surreptitiously attempted to gather up the array of yellow exercise books – an action that now took centre stage as the room took on an eerie silence following the DI's drinks refusal.

Frenchie tipped forward on her seat, gathering up one of the exercise books, I guess to help Jess as she corralled them to a pile in front of her. However, rather than passing it to Jess, she held onto it. Neatly penned on the front cover, in Jenny's handwriting underscored with two thick lines, was written 1989-1990.

I shot Jenny a look, which the thirsty sergeant clocked as the DI held the book poised to flick through.

"As I said, my sergeant and I were just passing, so I thought we'd save you a trip into town," she stated, still peering at the cover of the exercise book.

I feared her thumb appeared to be a nanosecond from flicking through the pages, which would display an account of the events of the up-and-coming end of the decade. The sharp intake of breath became almost audible as the four of us sucked in air whilst watching Frenchie's thumb slowly move across the fore-edge of the thin book.

"I must say, Mrs Apsley, I am surprised you thought your husband and step-daughter had already left, considering they're both here and your red Audi is still sitting on the drive," she stated, removing her thumb from the closed pages of the book, allowing the four of us to exhale.

A few moments ago, when the doorbell had run through its chimed sequence and after we'd decided that psychopathic murderous nutters indeed don't ring doorbells, Jenny had peeked through the net curtains to spot the two detectives at the door. Relieved that the murdering bastard, Paul Colney, or any other member of that family weren't now alternately ringing the bell and hammering the door knocker, Jenny had raced to open the door. In her panic, she'd informed the two detectives that Jess and I had already left to meet with her at the station. A lie which soon unravelled as Frenchie pointed to my car on the drive and her sergeant nodded to where I conspicuously peered around the net curtains.

"Yes, I'm so sorry about that, Heather ... err Detective French. I meant to say they were just about to leave," stumbled Jenny in an attempt to recover the situation.

DI French nodded and returned a tight smile. She and Jenny had known each other for many years, and I guess they would have regularly used their first names in the early days.

The first time I met Jenny when answering the door in that God-awful flat up at the Broxworth, Frenchie had been with her as they tried to hunt down Carol Hall. Little did I know that day that Carol was Beth's mother and how life would pan out with both Christopher and Beth now my adopted children with Jenny as my wife. However, what I did know that day,

PC French was on her game. As the years rolled by, and as she'd risen up the ranks, Frenchie had continued to sharpen her inquisitive mind.

My old friend, Don, only three days ago, had urged me not to concern myself about David Colney's death. However, as DI French's thumb once again hovered over the edge of the exercise book, I feared she was closing in on the truth.

"Okay. So, you're Leonardo Bretton?" questioned the DI, nodding at Martin, who remained relaxed as he once again had splayed himself out on the sofa.

Frenchie had met Martin in 1977, the day we had that stand-off with Paul Colney outside the school, similar to today's event with his mother and the Great White. However, although Frenchie was super sharp, surely, she wouldn't remember Martin? No, I was confident she couldn't, as it had only been a fleeting glance. That brief encounter had taken place over ten years ago, so I felt sure even the sharp-minded Frenchie wouldn't recall that.

"You look rather familiar. Have we met before?" she questioned, whilst her thumb slipped back, ready to open the pages of the book.

I groaned.

Martin shook his head, bowing it slightly to lose eye contact. As far as he was concerned, he last saw Frenchie a few days ago in 1977.

"And you came in from South Africa this week, you say?"

"Yep, that's right," stated Martin, as he swung his legs off the sofa, shifting his bum to get comfortable. But, unfortunately, none of this repositioning had the required effect of causing his trouser leg to drop from where he'd yanked it up earlier to show Jess his tattoo of the Manchester United badge.

Jess shot me a look, indicating Martin's exposed calf.

"Err ... Martin," I whispered, trying to grab his attention.

"Martin?" quizzed Frenchie.

"Sorry. Ha! Leonardo ... your ..." I nodded, indicating his trouser leg.

Frenchie was way too sharp to miss this flash of body art, pointing at it with the exercise book still firmly in her grasp. "Interesting tattoo, Mr Bretton. I believe your late brother had an identical one?" she quizzed, still waving the yellow book, which I could see Jess appeared now half tempted to take a swipe at to remove it from her clutches.

"Err ... yeah. Yeah." Nodded Martin whilst pulling down the leg of his jeans.

"Do you have any other tattoos like your brother?"

"No! None ... not one," he blurted, as he firmly smoothed down the other leg of his jeans before tugging the cuffs of his shirt.

Thank God he wasn't wearing shorts and a t-shirt. I feared Martin would also be shite at poker as he now sat grinning like a demented pillock, his lie causing a neck flush as bright a shade of red which adorned his Manchester United tattoo.

"And which flight did you arrive on?"

"Flight?"

"Yes, flight. I'm assuming you flew from South Africa and didn't walk? I presume you landed at an airport?"

See what I mean? Frenchie was as sharp as a new pin.

"Oh, yes," chuckled Martin, who now seemed obsessed with tugging at his shirt cuffs.

"Well, Mr Bretton," questioned Frenchie whilst still waving my version of Nostradamus's publication – this one detailing the events of a two-year period in the near future.

"Stansted," he replied. However, Jess had blurted 'Heathrow' in unison with Martin, and Jenny stated 'Gatwick.'

"Oh, Christ!" I blurted in frustration at our collective stupidity.

Rather stunned at how idiotic we all appeared, the four of us turned to Frenchie awaiting her next move.

DI French's thumb stopped strumming the pages, allowing the book to fall open. I noticed the page stated a list of events that I thought would happen that year – a sort of initial head-dump list with star ratings, which preceded more detailed pages.

Without trying to draw attention to the book, I glanced at the open page, spotting where Jenny had previously penned Lockerbie Bombing with a few question marks around it. Just above the next entry stating Dirty Den gets killed in EastEnders, and below details of the Tiananmen Square protests. Circled in red pen I could see an entry about the release of the second *Back to the Future* movie. I accept that these four events don't carry the same gravitas – however, Jenny just noted them down as I recalled them.

Throughout the pages of all the yearbooks, there were a high percentage of entries with question marks, usually where I couldn't quite decide if I had the correct year. Not that I really gave two shits when Dirty Den got killed but, as I waited for the impending doom of this ill-fated conversation to continue,

I feared that I'd incorrectly noted down the year when the Pan Am flight exploded above Lockerbie.

After today's events, and if I wasn't arrested or carted off to a secure unit, somehow manage to protect Beth and Faith, dispose of Paul Colney, and avoid being blinded by the Great White, I felt sure the Lockerbie bombing had better slot back onto the agenda for the next meeting of the Time Travel Believers' Club.

I considered there were a lot of 'ifs' there, and perhaps the Lockerbie bombing may well never be a problem that I had to consider. The way today was panning out, I doubted I would enjoy much more of a future.

Rather than glance down at the open page that her thumb had landed upon, Frenchie shifted her gaze between the four of us. She pointed at Martin. "Never heard of Stansted." Then swivelling her podgy-pointing finger in my direction, she continued. "And for that matter, I've never heard of an airport called 'Oh Christ', either!" Then, like a well-drilled Gunner in a Panzer tank, she swivelled her finger back in Martin's direction. "I think all of us know full well that you didn't arrive from South Africa this week. I'm guessing if my sergeant here checked every flight manifest over the last two weeks, your name wouldn't appear. Am I right, or am I right?"

"DI French, Leonardo has actually been staying here for a while now. He's had a rather messy split from his girlfriend in South Africa, which has been somewhat complicated due to the involvement of a rather influential wealthy to-do landowner's wife with connections to the government. So, it's all a bit of a scandal," I chuckled.

Jenny shot me a look, probably concerned that I seemed quite proficient at trotting out any old bollocks at the drop of a hat.

I continued. "You see, we're trying to keep his whereabouts under wraps, so to speak. There's nothing criminal involved, just reputations at stake. But, with all the anti-apartheid uprisings over there at the moment, Mar … err … Leonardo thought it best to take refuge here. We offered to help, you know, as we knew his brother." I nodded in Martin's direction, then back at Frenchie, who glanced around at her sergeant raising her eyebrows.

Not for one moment did I consider she'd buy the lie. However, I needed to gently corral her forward and away from the subject of the former dead time-travelling loose cannonball who I was sure would cock up big-style at any moment.

"His brother, Martin, that is?" questioned Frenchie.

"Yes, that's him."

"The man you claim drove that Cortina the day Paul Colney died."

"Err, yes."

"Hmmm." Frenchie pointed the open exercise book in Martin's direction. "As they say in all the good westerns … don't leave town until I say you can. Understand?"

"You got it. I ain't going nowhere, sheriff," replied Martin using his best American southern-drawl accent. I half expected him to spit out some imaginary chewing tobacco to finish off with.

As Frenchie still held the book, pointing it at Martin, Jess seized the moment. Akin to the lightning speed of a lizard's tongue snatching a fly, her hand shot upwards and recovered the book from the clutches of the DI. "Thank you," she sang, before placing the book face down on top of the pile on the hearthrug.

The returning of the book lowered the tension in the room – similar to that feeling of relief Marty McFly had experienced when wrestling that sports almanac book from Biff – a film I could enjoy again when released in a couple of years if the entry in that exercise book was correct. I'd awarded that entry a five-star rating, so I was pretty confident I had the correct year.

"Now, you wanted to talk to Jess and myself. Shall we go into my study?"

"Yes, Mr Apsley. Wherever is comfortable for you both. However, there is another matter I need to discuss with you all."

"Oh?" I responded, dreading what was coming next. Christ, what was the matter with this week? Surely nothing could be worse than now only having about twenty-four hours to save Beth and Faith, avoid being blinded, stop Shirley from convincing the police I killed David, and all the time avoiding Paul Colney.

"Yes, it's regarding a written confession I've received about the murder of David Colney in 1976."

35

The Dam Busters

"Bloody hell, Jason! Why on earth didn't you bloody well tell her what that hideous woman threatened us with, for Christ sake?" fired out Jenny, as we all stood in the kitchen where I'd relayed the events about Shirley's visit this lunchtime.

"I couldn't! Could I? Shirley reckons she's got evidence that could put me away for murder! Christ, if I told Frenchie of the threat, I could end up going to prison!"

"She knows it was Dad on the roof that day," blurted Jess. "Paul Colney worked it out before Martin and him were killed." Jess thumbed in the direction of Martin, before turning to look at the twice-dead enigma. I guess she still struggled to understand how he'd somehow come back to life.

"But she's got a confession! That letter states you had nothing to do with it!" Jenny fired back whilst thumping her hands on her hips.

The invisible steam rising from Jenny's nostrils and the tossing of her head from side to side afforded my wife the look of a rather pissed-off bull about to charge. I half expected her to start to scrape her foot back and forth, pawing at the tiled kitchen floor in preparation for an attack.

"I don't think for one moment Frenchie believes that letter! Anyway, if I tell the police about Shirley's threat, I'll have that hideous one-eyed man gouging my eyes out. You should have seen him. He's a bloody big bloke!"

"Look, if you two have come from the future, then you know the future! So, surely between the two of you, you know what happens and can avoid Shirley?"

"Jess, it doesn't work like that. I was only ten the first time around, and Martin wasn't even born! So, knowing what happened on 11th September, for one, isn't possible, and secondly, can be of no help what … so …ever!"

"Nine-Eleven, and Mum's birthday," stated Martin, who, now positioned on the bar stool, vacantly gawped out of the kitchen window into the back garden.

"Nine, what?" questioned Jess.

"It's the date the twin towers in Manhattan were destroyed by terrorists when they slammed two planes into the World Trade Center in 2001. They call it Nine-Eleven, as that's the date of the attack. The Americans reverse the month and day, hence nine-eleven."

"Oh. Well, that doesn't help much," replied Jess, whilst waving her hand in front of Martin's eyes who seemed transfixed by something in the garden.

"Darling, we have to do something! We can't hand the girls over to Shirley. Christ, we'll have to go on the run! We need to go into hiding."

Grabbing Jenny's hand, I pulled her towards me, hugging her whilst she nestled her head on my chest. I'd run out of ideas, now feeling cornered with no escape route.

"Last time Shirley threatened us, we camped out at Don's. That's not going to work this time, is it?" asked Jenny without looking up.

"No. No, it's not," I replied, whilst gazing at the heap of letters that Jenny had laid out on the breakfast bar.

Martin seemed fixated by the view of our rather average suburban back garden, whilst Jess picked at her fingernails. For the umpteenth time, the sound of Bananarama banging out *'I Heard a Rumour'* drifted down the stairs from Beth's record player.

Earlier, when DI French and her sergeant departed, we were left in a state of confusion.

The interview with Jess had been relatively straightforward, with Jess confirming the exact details as I had yesterday about the crash in the Cortina ten years back. Frenchie was clear that both of us should have stayed at the scene of the accident but confirmed no further action would be taken against either of us. Sergeant Farham completed our statements, which we both duly signed, and the matter was closed – hopefully.

However, we knew that Paul Colney was back, and the car found on Monday morning was the same car – the time-travelling portal machine that my old Beemer back in 2019 seemed to share the same miraculous time-shifting properties.

What DI French thought about that car, I had no idea. However, she knew something was afoot. Let's face it, crushed vehicles don't just vanish and then reappear ten years later in almost mint condition – or do they?

Frenchie had excused Jess from my study, which became her satellite office, no longer my man-cave that acted as my sanctuary from life. With the three of us remaining, she'd probed further regarding Ralph Eastley and the incident from 1954. Unfortunately, I had no idea what she was on about apart from what the beast had said to me earlier about some incident at the Festival House Dance Hall when *other* Jason had blinded him. I claimed to be unable to remember the incident that well, which was true because I had no idea. I also lied when the sharp detective questioned if I'd had contact with him since his return.

Of course, if those two officers who'd shot out of the school office earlier had apprehended Shirley and Ralph in that diarrhoea-coloured car, my lie would unravel, as would my whole life.

Jess now informed us that she'd dropped a bundle of letters in the post box at the end of her road on Tuesday morning. She'd not taken much notice of the addressees, just popped them in the box as instructed by Don. Jess had said Don handed them over to her a few weeks ago, asking her to post them upon his death. She'd assumed they were letters regarding his estate and just complied with Don's instructions and thought nothing more of it, only remembering there were five envelopes secured with an elastic band with the top letter addressed to a firm of solicitors in Fairfield.

We knew the location of three of those letters. Presumably, one lay in the in-tray at Brockett and Sons solicitors in the High Street. One lay in possession of DI French, and one lay unopened on the breakfast bar, delivered earlier that day along with a heap of bills and circulars.

Jenny nudged my arm, jolting me from my trance. "Jason. Jason, are you going to open it?"

Bananarama had started singing again, the same song repeating as it had for at least half an hour as Beth presumably lifted the record needle back and forth every three and a half minutes – you couldn't ask your record player to repeat the last song, which I recall was something I often asked Alexa to do for me.

"Darling, I said, are you going to open it?"

"You don't think Frenchie believes what Don wrote?" questioned Jess, without shifting her focus from what appeared to be a particularly stubborn piece of pink nail varnish that refused to ping free.

No one answered the question which hung in the air. Don had confessed to pushing David Colney off the roof of the flats in 1976. He stated that I had arrived only minutes after he had returned to his flat, just as he'd completed painting over the daubed 'Dead Junkie Whore' graffiti that David had painted across Carol Hall's front door.

"Well?"

"No, Jess. I'm sure DI French thought it was very convenient that a dead man just happens to confess to killing David."

Jess nodded as she reaffirmed her efforts with the stubborn nail varnish. "Hmmm, I think you're right."

"Martin, you alright?" I questioned whilst plucking up Don's letter. I presumed the content would be as per the letter Frenchie had received advising me that he had intended to take the rap for David Colney's death. I thumbed open the envelope removing the two sheets of notepaper filled with Don's handwriting, shakily written with a fountain pen.

"Martin?" I questioned once more, concerned about his catatonic state and now wondering if he'd suffered a stroke because there was nothing that interesting in the garden where he continued to focus.

Martin failed to answer. So, leaving him to gaze at a redundant rusty garden swing and Swingball, I held the letter so Jenny and I could read through together.

Don's letter started with his thoughts about my true origin. Presumably penning this in case he didn't get the opportunity to have the conversation we shared on Monday evening. This section of the letter didn't suggest I was a time-traveller but did raise questions and affirm that I had a step-sister in the guise of Shirley Colney. Well, *other* Jason did, but when Don wrote the letter, he wasn't to know that. Don went on to state that he had written to DI French confessing to David's murder, and now I must stop worrying because that case would now close forever.

Don had been filled with good intention when confessing, but perhaps his senior years had clouded his judgment. I knew, as Frenchie knew, she was way too sharp to fall for that.

However, I did believe DI French was focused on solving the murder earlier this week of that Susan Kane woman up at the Broxworth Estate and probably regarded David's death as a failed investigation consigned to history. So, if I found a way to shut Shirley up, I hoped that's how it would stay.

Paul Colney's history of violence strongly suggested he could be responsible for Susan's murder. However, I think implying to the rotund DI that a ghost was responsible was somewhat stretching the bounds of possibilities, albeit the probable truth.

As I was fully aware, Don went on to write about the fact I was the executor of his final will and testament, with a few details around his wishes regarding the division of his extremely modest estate.

I'd often wondered why he had lost touch with his two daughters and thus had nothing to do with their lives and family. All became clear in the final five paragraphs.

"Listen to this," I announced, breaking the silence and grabbing the attention of both Jess and Martin. "This is why his daughters never had anything to do with Don."

I read aloud for the benefit of Jess and Martin.

"I'm not proud of this, and knowing you as I do, I'm sure you won't judge me too harshly as my girls have. In the mid-1930s, I strayed from my beloved Peggy, something she wasn't aware of, and I'm thankful for this because she didn't deserve my betrayal. After Peggy left this world, I confided with the girls about my past. A decision I now regret, but I hoped at the time they may help and perhaps forgive.

A product of that betrayal was another daughter. She never knew me to be her father because her mother, Laura, and I kept that a secret from her. Another decision I regret. My relationship, or affair for want of a better word, spanned six years, only ending in 1940 due to the onset of war. Peggy and I took the girls away from London, and I never laid eyes on Laura or my daughter again.

As part of my investigations each week up at the library, I dug around to see what had happened to them both. Sadly, I discovered Laura died of tuberculosis in 1948, leaving my thirteen-year-old daughter languishing in St. Peter's Orphanage – the very same place as your newly acquired half-sister – Janet Shirley Curtis.

So, my boy, I ask one last favour of you. Although it's not much, I have left my entire estate to the daughter who never had the chance to get to know me. I failed to find out what happened to her after she left the orphanage. So, as my trusted friend, I implore you to find her and perhaps paint a picture of her father that I know you will.

I don't have much information to work with, hence probably why I failed to locate her. She was born on 12th July 1935, and her name is Beryl Backman, although I assume she will be married now. I implore you to find her and apologise for my absence in her life – perhaps she can forgive me.

Take care of yourself.

Your honorary father

Don.

"Poor Peggy," muttered Jenny.

I looked up, but no one else said anything. Don was quite correct. I wouldn't judge him – we all had our skeletons, and no one was perfect. However, I'm sure Jenny and Jess would be a wee bit disappointed in him. I would, of course, do as Don requested and try and find this lady. I knew in my heart, although disappointed with him, Jenny would help with that search. However, we had some rather more urgent pressing matters to deal with.

"You remember when they replaced the Carrow Road Bridge?" stated Martin, who appeared to be continuing his study of the Swingball in the garden.

"Hmmm, no, not really. Not sure what that's got to do with Don's dallying or what the hell we do about Shirley!"

"What d'you mean, replaced the bridge? That bridge is about a hundred years old. I don't think it lifts up anymore as the river is only used by small boats these days," questioned Jenny, as she plucked the letter from my hand whilst perching on a bar stool.

Martin turned his attentions towards me. "The old bridge collapsed on my mum's birthday."

"Okay, if you say so. But so what?"

Jess shot Martin a look. "Hang on. A moment ago, didn't you say your Mum's birthday is tomorrow ... 11th September, same day as that terrorist attack in the future."

"Yup," he nodded whilst pursing his lips, still deep in thought. Although presumably no longer contemplating a game of swing tennis.

"I'm so disappointed with Don," muttered Jenny, with her head down, rereading his confessional letter.

"Martin, get to the point," I announced, frustrated with Jenny's comment, although not surprised – Don *had* badly let his beloved Peggy down.

"My point is that after it collapsed, the Council or Highways Agency pissed about for weeks deciding what to do regarding demolishing the rest of the structure and plans to replace it. It was heralded as a miracle no one was killed when it collapsed as it happened during rush hour."

"So!"

"Jason. Listen. The reason I know about this is because it happened on Mum's birthday. The story goes, she was driving home from work the day it fell. Mum worked at the Council and crossed that bridge every day. That particular day, she was stuck at the traffic lights and just before they changed to green, the left-hand side of the bridge collapsed ... she saw it happen!"

"Martin?" questioned Jenny, who glanced up from reading.

"What's the punchline, mate?"

"The punchline is due to the Council's procrastination, two people were killed a few months later when the remaining part of the bridge structure collapsed." Martin shifted forward on his barstool, clearly excited as he recounted his tale. He pointed his finger at me and continued. "After the bridge fell, they obviously closed the road but left the rest of the structure in place as it was deemed structurally sound. However, what they didn't know was a few weeks or months later, strong winds would blow the rest of it down."

"And as I said, what has this got to do with us," I questioned, raising my palms, becoming slightly exasperated.

"Look, listen. There was a massive storm that caused two iron girders and stone slabs to fall and crush a young couple when walking home after leaving the Woolpack Pub—"

"Oh, not that awful place; it should be closed down. It's just a den of underage drinking," threw in Jenny, as she continued to reread Don's confession.

Martin ignored the interruption and continued. "Mum relayed the story many times, probably because the initial collapse happened on her birthday. Apparently, the excrement seriously hit the air-conditioning, and one of the structural engineers that had assessed the collapsed structure in September of that year was later convicted of manslaughter."

"So, the bridge collapsed during rush hour on your mum's birthday, which is tomorrow. The same year that there was a great storm a month or so later?" I asked, already knowing where this was leading.

"1987!" blurted Jess. "It's in your books. Dad, you've written it down! The great storm of October 1987."

"Err ... why is everyone excited?" questioned Jenny. "No one was killed initially, so what has this got to do with us?"

"Jenny! Don't you see?" exclaimed Jess, as she swivelled around, no longer concerned that the errant piece of pink nail varnish refused to budge. "I said that they knew the future, so use it to stop Shirley!"

"Oh ... we get Shirley on that bridge?"

"Precisely! We get her on that bridge tomorrow evening. Hopefully, this time two people will be killed the day it collapses," exclaimed Martin.

George barrelled through the back door, looking somewhat ready to burst and rather flushed. Either he had some significant developments to convey from his investigation errand or had simply just got hammered whilst up at the Three Feathers enjoying an afternoon of drinking and playing shove-ha'penny.

"George, you alright?" I questioned, whilst also concerned that Jenny had secured the front door like the gates of Troy, only leaving the back door unlocked and as vulnerable as the Möhne and Edersee dams. Fortunately, only George had barrelled through, not Paul Colney disguised as a bouncing bomb.

"Yes, lad. I met up with Harold Bates at lunchtime and had an interesting chat!"

"Oh, pray tell," I asked, pleased that it appeared George had cracked on with his homework assignment I'd given him.

"Well, I think I may have located a Colney!"

36

Up Pompeii!

"Go on, what's happened?" I questioned George, as I sprung across the kitchen to barricade the back door whilst Jenny filled the kettle – George drank more tea than the vicar – not that I knew the vicar, but they all drink tea, don't they?

"Well, lad. So, as it happens, Harold has a few contacts up at Fairfield Police Station who regularly feed him tit-bits of information. It just so happened his contact nipped in the pub for a swift half this lunchtime and brought him up to speed with the latest developments."

"Christ, George, get on with it!" spat Jenny. Clearly, after the stress of the last few hours she was now running out of patience, causing her worry to spill over and morph into aggression.

"Alright, Jenny, lass, I'm getting to it," stated a somewhat hurt-looking George. However, he didn't know the events of today.

"Sorry, George. But we have a few shocks to tell you about as well."

"Oh?"

"George, we'll bring you up to speed in a minute. I'm calling an impromptu urgent meeting of the Time Travel Believers' Club."

"Oh, err ... what about the lass here," questioned George, raising his heavy eyebrows and placing his hands on the small of his back, performing a pretty good impression of Frankie Howerd as he nodded in Jess's direction.

Hopefully, he wouldn't add an *'Oooh Noo'* when I brought him up to speed with events. That said, I didn't see George as the Lurcio type in the slightly risqué comedy riddled with double entendres. Ha, but then I wondered what George would have made of the erotic uncut Spartacus Saga series, which I seemed to recall Lisa enjoying, and I reaping the benefits afterwards – if you get my drift.

"I think Jess has joined the club ... fully paid-up member?" I suggested, glancing at Jess for confirmation that her quiz-filled afternoon had been enough for her to believe the unbelievable.

Silence – Jenny held the kettle mid-air, ready to pour – if it had been tipped at this point, I was sure the boiling water would freeze in time as we all held our breath in anticipation of Jess's response. I glanced at George, who continued to hold his Frankie Howerd pose, whilst Martin looked at Jess as we all awaited her response to my suggestion.

"Jess?"

She chewed her lip whilst glancing around the group, then nodded.

"Good."

"Bloody hell! If you'll excuse my French," exclaimed George, as Jenny poured the water now time had restarted. I chuckled at his choice of words.

I recalled one lunchtime in the school staff room when Jayne relayed a particular story regarding a class she'd taken earlier that day. It was fairly typical for Jayne to entertain the rest of the teaching staff with her humorous tales. In this particular class she'd stood in for Miss Clayhorn, one of our language teachers. Jayne didn't usually conduct language lessons, but needs must for that particular day. At the start of this French lesson for a group of first-year students, she'd asked the class who knew of any French words. A young, innocent lad, who'd excitedly thrust his hand aloft, confidently stated '*Bollocks*' – apparently, a word his father often used and apologised for using French.

"George, here's your tea."

"Thanks, lass," replied George, pleased that Jenny seemed to have lost that bullish aggression. "Now look, Jess, my lass, this might be true, and then again, it might not." George waited for a reaction, which thankfully none of us complied to this rather bizarre statement, probably fearing George could drag this out to become one of his long shaggy-dog stories, which he was prone to doing. "Well, Harold reckons that the police discovered another body this morning with a similar MO as that poor woman up on the Broxworth. Battered to a pulp before being set alight."

"Oh, grim!" announced Jenny, as she retook her seat.

"Yes, grim indeed. They discovered the body next to the Havervalley Prison, and their initial investigations were centred around that area and released prisoners. But apparently, they've moved on from that line of enquiry because only three prisoners were released this week, and all three can be accounted for."

"Sorry, George ... but what's that got to do with me?" questioned Jess.

"Patrick?" I threw into the conversation.

"Lass, your father's got it," replied George, pointing his full mug of tea in my direction.

"What about Patrick? You think he murdered this person they've found? He wouldn't have murdered Susan. Patrick is a lot of things but, there's no way he would've killed Susan Kane, no way—"

"Jess, honey," interrupted Jenny, as she placed her hand over Jess's on the breakfast bar. "George and your father aren't suggesting that Patrick has murdered anyone."

"But—"

"Now, lass, don't get upset, because as I say, I could be wrong."

"George, I won't be upset ... Patrick is all in the past. But I take it you're suggesting Paul murdered his brother to steal his identity?"

"They're identical twins. But to someone who knew them well, could they tell them apart?" I questioned, whilst trying to fathom whether this could actually have happened.

"Oh, loads of people got them mixed up. But they weren't totally identical. I could tell the difference," Jess replied.

"Who else could?" I fired back. "I mean, who would easily know which was which?"

"Well, actually not that many. Most people knew Paul because of that horrible black biker-jacket he always wore. Of course, dressed in the same clothes, they did look identical. I reckon only his family, me, and ... well probably, Susan Kane could spot the difference."

I glanced up at George, then Martin. All three of us now understood why Paul Colney had been prowling around trying to find Jess. He'd bludgeoned Patrick to death and set him on fire to destroy his identity. If he was to continue life ten years after dying in that Cortina, he had to be safe in the knowledge no one could prove who he really was. If Paul thought his mother still resided in sunny Spain, and his father and brother languished in prison, that only left two people who could spoil the party, so to speak. Susan Kane and Jess Poole would have to be eliminated – he'd already ticked off one of those tasks.

"Jason, how do we protect her? We have to go to the police!" blurted Jenny, as she scooted around behind Jess, hugging her tightly like a protective mother.

"Wha-what do you mean, protect me?"

"Lass, if we're right, Paul is killing off those who could identify him as Paul and not Patrick. If you reckon that only a select few could be certain, he only has you left to deal with because he thinks the rest are either in prison or in Spain."

"Oh my God!"

"Right, listen up. This is officially a TTBC meeting, okay," I announced, then glanced around the room, gathering affirmative nods.

"TTBC?" vacantly questioned Jess, who appeared to be digesting the news that once again Paul Colney was probably trying to kill her.

"Time Travel Believers' Club ... of which you are now a fully paid-up member."

I brought George up to speed with the afternoon's events. He threw in a few more 'bloody hells' followed by requests to excuse his French but, other than that, he soaked up the story. Beth and Faith seemed to be content and continued to amuse themselves in Beth's bedroom. Although, at last, they'd given Bananarama a rest, and I think I could hear Samantha Fox banging out, *I Surrender*, an apt song title for our current dilemma, I mused.

I did consider that Martin would be super disappointed not to have had the opportunity to follow Miss Fox's page three career, which she'd recently abandoned to focus on destroying teenagers' eardrums. Although Martin, over the few weeks he'd spent back in time, was super into that particular page of the daily newspaper, I thought he'd have to wait for the busty glamour model to appear in Playboy in the next decade – that's assuming any of us made it that far because today's events had seriously shortened the odds of that happening.

"Right. So, as I see it, we have to get Shirley and her big fella on that bridge at rush hour tomorrow."

"Darling, how the hell do we do that?"

"Martin, you said your mother was driving home at rush hour. Do you know the exact time?"

"Err ... well, no, not really. She worked at the council offices. So presumably, it was a nine-to-five type job, I guess. I dunno," he shrugged.

"Dolly Parton. I love that film," added Jenny.

"Dolly who? Dolly the sheep?" quizzed Martin.

"Dolly the sheep! Who's that? No, Dolly Parton, and that Nine to Five film. It's so funny."

"Oh, think I've heard of her. Sorry, I thought you were talking about the sheep."

"What's a sheep got to do with all this?" asked Jess, now joining in on this pointless conversation.

"Christ! Come on. We need to focus, not be comparing a blonde bombshell Country and Western singer to a cloned sheep!" I stabbed out, concerned the TTBC members weren't as focused as they should be. "This is a crisis situation!"

"Blimey, lad. Do they clone animals in the future? It's all a bit Frankenstein, isn't it?"

"George!"

"Sorry lad," offered George before slugging the last of his tea.

"Another, George? Anyone else?" asked Jenny, taking George's mug out of his hand, knowing that he would require an instant refill.

"Lad, does it change things that this time around Sarah Moore doesn't work at the Council anymore?"

"I don't know. I think it will just mean she's not sitting at those traffic lights. Apart from that, everything should just be the same, shouldn't it?" I questioned the group, now concerned the act of Sarah changing jobs may have altered the timeline.

"Jen, sweetheart, do you know what hours Sarah worked?"

"Oh, darling, I have no idea. She was in a different department. That said, everyone pretty much does nine to five."

"Dad, everything you've written in your books has come true, yes?"

"Yes, pretty much."

"Have you got everything right … you know, events, dates, bets you've made?"

I thought for a moment. "Yeah."

"What about the World Cup, darling? You got that wrong."

"Oh, yeah. But that's the only one I can think of."

"What was that about the World Cup?" questioned Martin, now perked up as the discussion seemed to be heading in a football direction.

"Well, you won't believe this, but last year England won the World Cup!"

"No way! What about Maradona and the hand of God?"

"Didn't happen!"

"Bloody hell! What about the *Football's Coming Home* song and all that stuff about thirty years of hurt?"

"Dunno. But we did win the World Cup! I placed a bet on the quarterfinal that Maradona would score two goals. I bloody well lost fifty quid on that one. I can tell you; I was stunned!"

"Christ! Get in! Come on, England," chanted Martin as if standing on the terraces at Wembley, which we still could for a few more years until the Hillsborough disaster due at the end of the decade – an event planned for discussion at the November TTBC meeting.

"Lad, you never lost another bet, though, have you?"

I shook my head dismissively, still bemused how it could have happened. Jenny placed mugs of tea down for all of us even though none of us had answered her question regarding who wanted one.

"What d'you think caused that change? Y'know, something must have happened to cause that game to change its result?"

"Martin, I don't know. But look, I think Jess's point is what we know will happen in the future is more than likely to repeat itself, yes?"

Jess nodded before taking a slurp of tea.

"So, even though Sarah has switched jobs, in this timeline, the Carrow Road Bridge will still collapse tomorrow afternoon. We just have to work out what time. I'll meet Shirley as planned and tell her to meet you and the kids on the bridge," I stated, as I pointed at Jenny, who nodded. "Of course, you won't be there. However, hopefully, Shirley will wait on the bridge. If we get the timing right, and with a bit of luck, she and that monster will end up in the river along with a mass of concrete and iron … and hopefully that will be the end of her!"

"What about Paul Colney?"

Martin's question hung in the air, dampening the mood. None of us had any idea what to do about him. Samantha Fox now rested whilst Billy Ocean had taken up centre stage. *'When The Going Gets Tough, The Tough Get Going'* permeated down from the first floor.

37

Bunny Boiler

The impromptu meeting of the Time Travel Believers' Club, with its newest member Jess, concluded with a somewhat loose plan to hopefully deal with Shirley and her big one-eyed fella. Fortunately, Colin arrived home from assisting Jayne with this year's school play rehearsals just after we'd wrapped up proceedings.

Colin was obviously concerned regarding Patrick's whereabouts following the incident where he believed Jess had spotted him outside their home on Wednesday evening. He suggested rather than camping out at our house, we should be calling the police to ensure Patrick was not allowed to approach them. Clearly, for two reasons, that wasn't going to happen. Firstly, we believed that man was Paul and not Patrick, and secondly, if it had been Patrick, he technically hadn't broken any laws by turning up at their house.

Fortunately, we were able to persuade Colin regarding point two, and suggested we wait until George had managed to glean some information from his contacts regarding Patrick before they made any rash decisions. We all thought a little white lie to keep Colin in the dark and not pestering Jess to shoot back home was a small price to pay – also, it bought us some time.

Of course, we couldn't let Jess out of our sight now we firmly believed Paul had her in his cross-hairs. Also, taking Colin through the initiation process to join our group was fraught with problems. Frankly, at this stage, and after initiating Jess, none of us possessed the energy to try.

Martin, AKA Leonardo, stayed for supper and fortunately managed to eat his meal without causing any calamities, which was a relief and somewhat surprising given his tendency to cause havoc with his well-tuned loose cannon skills. Martin then decamped back to Don's old home with a plan to return tomorrow after Colin and I had left for work.

More than any of us, Martin was capable of squaring up to Paul. So, we felt our safest option was to have him act as a bodyguard for Jess in case the deranged nutter came calling. Unfortunately, at this point, we had no concrete plans of how to deal with Paul because eliminating time-travelling murdering psychopaths wasn't an issue the club members had previously had to contend with – we'd entered new territory.

I'd suggested that Jenny took a duvet-day on Friday, also proposing we kept the girls off school with a faked stomach bug excuse – for sure, Beth and Faith could easily entertain themselves in Beth's bedroom. Jenny questioned the term duvet-day, which I explained was throwing a sicky. Even after living ten years in the past, from time to time, I was still prone to using language from the 21st Century, leaving many wondering what the hell I was talking about.

On Friday, just before the allotted time stipulated by Shirley, I hunkered down in the Quattro and waited for her and the big fella to show. We'd calculated the first time around that

Sarah Moore had reached the traffic lights at approximately 5:15 p.m., assuming she would leave work at 5:00 p.m. on the dot. She'd confirmed that her job at the Council had been a nine to five job when I casually questioned her earlier in the day – so we were set.

The plan was to tell Shirley that Jenny would meet her on the bridge just after 5:00 p.m., and as long as the evil woman and her side-kick stayed on that bridge waiting, they would end up in the river under a mass of twisted iron and concrete.

The plan did have some issues and certainly wasn't bulletproof. Shirley could be late, or not wait, or even refuse to go there. Also, the two officers that attended school yesterday may have apprehended them last evening, which may mean Shirley doesn't turn up at all. However, it was our best shot, and we had to take it.

Shirley and her pet shark were seven minutes fashionably late – seven minutes in which I'd checked and rechecked my watch every few seconds, concerned the plan would fall at the first hurdle. They'd ditched the diarrhoea-brown Austin Montego with shit-brown go-faster stripes in favour of a new Ford Sierra RS500 Cosworth in a rather fetching moonstone-blue, sporting a whale-tail spoiler. Clearly, an upgrade from yesterday's mode of transport, also suggesting this wasn't your average hire car. Presumably, Shirley had tapped into her extensive dodgy connections to supply what seemed the perfect getaway car – I doubted the police had anything in their fleet that could catch that beast. Not that she was ever going to have Beth and Faith in the back seats of the high-performance car, but it made me wonder where she had planned to speed off to with a thumping two-hundred-plus brake horsepower under the hood.

I stepped out of my car as Shirley and Ralph exited theirs. Here we were again, the good, the bad, and the ugly. However, I think we'd moved on from our spaghetti western scene. Frenchie had stated that my family and the Colneys seemed dangerously intertwined. She was right. Shirley Colney and I seemed to have some kind of fatal attraction. Not in a romantic sense, but our lives had an intense draw hauling our fates together. However, I felt sure she and her partner were somewhat more dangerous than a bunny boiler.

"Where are they then? You mess me about, Apsley, you know what'll happen!"

Her pet shark didn't wait for instructions, instead making his move whilst flexing his fingers, presumably preparing to perform his Kill Bill styled eyeball snatching move. I wondered if he'd been trained in the art by Pai Mei, or would he just thrust his hand towards my head and rip it off.

∼

After ventilating the centre of the snivelling weasel Mark Hawkshaw's right palm, Shirley knew they would have to maintain a low profile until they had secured the girls and were away on that boat across the North Sea.

Knowing the place would be crawling with filth, they'd checked out of the Maid's Head Hotel. Also, after delivering her ultimatum to Jason Apsley, they'd ditched the hire car and camped out at the dodgy solicitor's posh home on the New Dunstable Road – probably considered the most salubrious part of town. Not that Mark Hawkshaw had invited them to stay because that was unlikely after Ralph had skewered his hand to an antique mahogany table, but because they afforded him no choice. Apart from being able to hide out there, she could also ensure the shady solicitor complied with her demands.

The last ten years, most of which she enjoyed all the luxuries and trappings that ill-gotten gains can provide, Shirley had learnt that life in Fairfield, running small-time protection rackets and low-level drug distribution, hadn't paid well. Her time living in that shit-hole of a flat on that estate had delivered slim pickings, along with suffering the relentless aggro from having to constantly bow to the Gowers. And all that time, Mark Hawkshaw was living it up in a swanky part of town with his dollybirds, plush house, outside pool and endless parties. It had taken Shirley far too long to wake up and smell the coffee, so to speak.

Well, not any longer. Hawkshaw had confirmed their boat ride was secured and ready for them, after which Ralph had re-encouraged him to remember where his new loyalties lie with the snapping of a couple of digits and removal of his little finger.

However, Shirley knew once they were away and across the sea, there was the potential for Hawkshaw to become a turncoat. So, to make extra sure he didn't perhaps consider doing something stupid, Ralph had taken him for an early morning dip in the opulent kidney-shaped pool. Ralph had said it was a little chilly, although Mark didn't comment, probably because he lay floating face down after their little swim.

The police had drifted by, probably following up on the back of the hotel incident. Ralph and Shirley hadn't answered the door and, although Mark now lay bobbing about in the pool, Shirley was confident they would be long gone before any of the filth would return to discover his bloated body.

She hadn't quite got the measure of this meddling schoolteacher. He'd been a thorn in her side and, over the years, he and his ginger bitch of a wife had caused Shirley far too much heartache. Also, the few encounters they'd enjoyed hadn't suggested he was capable of blinding Ralph – he seemed too wimpy. However, that incident had taken place over thirty years ago, and she suspected the older Jason Apsley had mellowed over time.

Really, she should let Ralph snap him in two and be done with it. Notwithstanding her desire to inflict violence on the man, securing her granddaughters had to be the priority. She would consider her next move when she had the girls safely out of the Apsley's and the British authorities' reach. Perhaps she could send her colossus Elvis look-alike back on a clear-up mission. If he got caught in the act, well, so be it, no skin off her nose – there were plenty more *Ralphs* back in Spain.

Now, as they all stood facing each other once again, it was clear the girls weren't with him, causing Shirley to become concerned about what game this Apsley bloke was playing. However, she couldn't afford Ralph to bend the man in half before she had her granddaughters. So, disappointingly, she'd have to stick a leash on her man for the moment.

"Ralph! Hang on."

38

Mack The Knife

"Megson, Dawson, update please," boomed the DI through her open door as the two officers trudged into the CID office. They'd spent most of the day interviewing witnesses to the fire which took hold in the earlier hours and destroyed a row of dilapidated buildings in a less desirable area of the town, which included the Black Boys Public House and a coin-operated launderette, both of which DC Adele Megson thought no one would miss.

The initial assessment from the Fire Service Investigators suggested a significant amount of accelerant must have been liberally splashed about to start the fire in the bail hostel positioned at the rear of the now blackened fire-damaged pub.

Adele Megson hadn't stepped foot in the Black Boys Pub for years, probably because it wasn't a destination of choice unless you held a criminal record in one hand and a weapon in the other. Earlier, when assessing the damage, she considered the décor hadn't deteriorated much from the last time she entered the hellish establishment. The purpose of that previous visit, when in uniform, was with five other officers to take down a violent thug after they'd received a tip-off that the said reprobate had surfaced there despite having an arrest warrant pending.

"Guv," replied both officers as they stepped into the DI's office. The fact her door was ajar indicated the DI was happy for interruptions and wouldn't demand certain formalities to be followed.

"It's not good, Guv. The place is a mess! The fire brigade boys hauled out three bodies from the flat above the Black Boys Pub. We think it's the landlord, Mack the Knife, and his wife and one other female," stated Megson, as she sunk into one of the chairs in front of the DI's desk whilst rummaging around in her jacket pockets.

The landlord, Michael Greene, who was known to those who operated in certain circles as Mack the Knife, was an intimidating low life who kept a machete behind the bar to deal with pub brawls. He certainly wasn't known for his dulcet tones, and Megson suspected that he would probably struggle to match up to Bobby Darin or Frank Sinatra. However, the man could wield a knife. And although the large knife was classed as an offensive weapon, thus making it illegal, Mack the Knife would usually sort out his own issues. The arrangement suited Uniform because it was one less bar brawl they'd have to attend to. The fact that two female bodies were discovered along with his wasn't a total surprise because Mack the Knife was well known for the various ménage à trois type relationships he enjoyed.

"What about the hostel?" questioned the DI.

"Two bodies, Guv. Both are badly burnt, and one of them looks to have been bludgeoned to death."

"Identity?"

Dawson stepped back to the door to light up a cigarette as Megson grabbed a Yorkie bar from her jacket pocket, taking a trucker's sized bite. Dawson really couldn't understand how *Gladys* could consume such vast quantities of chocolate and still stay as skinny as a rake. His overbearing wife, Sybil, only had to glance at the pick and mix fixture in Woolworths to add three inches to her already sizeable childbearing hips. Whilst allowing his partner to munch her way through her fifth chocolate bar of the afternoon, he picked up the story after blowing the smoke away from the office door.

"Guv, the body was in a similar state to the Havervalley incident ... burnt to a crisp. Reckon they couldn't have done a better job over at the crematorium. Anyway, although the skull had been pulverised, it's pretty clear it was a he, and huge. So, it suggests it was Adam Henderson, the caretaker geezer."

"Christ! What about the other one?"

"Same, Guv. Although, unlike a nice fish supper, that one was just fried, not battered. No ID at the moment, but the forensic boys are on it."

The DI thumped her hands on the armrest whilst pushing back in her swivel chair. "Could it be Colney?"

"Ooo owes," stated Megson with a mouth full of chocolate rolling around.

However, as she'd raised her palms, the DI could decipher that her protégé was attempting to say 'Who knows' whilst trying to avoid pebble dashing her desk with a mixture of chocolate and saliva. DI French thought she might have to work on Megson's etiquette before pushing the highly capable DC through her sergeant exams.

DS Danny Farham poked his head around the door, appearing slightly out of breath. "You two," he panted, addressing the two detective constables. "You went to Mark Hawkshaw's house yesterday when you tried to locate him?"

Megson's hand hovered in front of her mouth, holding the last two chunks of her Yorkie bar. "Yes, of course we did, but no one was there. We swung by this morning as well." She slotted in the two hefty blocks of chocolate and continued, although slightly less coherently. "The house seemed to be all closed up as if he's gone away somewhere."

"We tried all the usual haunts, and he's not showed up at any of them. I've got a couple of snouts putting some feelers out, but I reckon after yesterday's incident he's gone to ground," added Dawson, before stubbing out his cigarette in the floor standing spinning ashtray which guarded the entrance to the DI's office like a Sphinx that prevented any evil cigarettes entering her office.

"Well, you can stand your snouts down because we found the bent bastard."

"Good! Is he here now? I fancy a crack at him myself," stated the DI, now feeling relieved that after a fruitless day, they perhaps had the break they needed.

DS Farham shook his head. "Sorry, Guv. One of Hawkshaw's birds found him an hour ago floating face down in his pool. He's been dead for some hours, I'm afraid."

"Oh, Christ!" growled the DI before she shot Megson a look, "Didn't you check the rear of the property when you swung by this morning?"

Megson shook her head, due to once again having a mouth full of chocolate, before shooting a frustrated glance at *Fawlty*.

"No, sorry, Guv. The side gate was locked," replied Dawson, wishing he'd now climbed over the gate as *Gladys* had suggested.

"Bloody hell—"

"My fault, Guv. *Gladys* suggested I scale the gate. But I didn't fancy ripping my trousers because Sybil would give me what for, and I'd never hear the last of it."

"Who's there at the moment?"

"*Mudda and Paddy*. I just spoke to *Paddy,* and he said Hawkshaw appears to have lost his little finger. That said, the cause of death is likely to be drowning," stated DS Farham, after shooting a disappointed glance in Dawson's direction.

"Little finger?"

"Yep, *Paddy* said it appears to have been cleanly cut off within the last twenty-four hours. My guess, Guv, it's by the same person who shoved a knife through the palm of his hand."

"Ralph Eastley?"

Danny nodded.

"So, twenty-four hours have passed since we issued warrants for Shirley, Patrick and Ralph, and we still don't know where any of them are. We have Susan Kane, Adam Henderson and A N Other all bludgeoned to death in the space of four days plus a probable arson attack causing four more deaths, one of whom could be Patrick Colney. Plus, we have another murder, in the shape of Shady Hawkshaw, but with a completely different modus operandi."

"Yes, Guv. That's about the size of it."

Megson swallowed the last of her Yorkie bar whilst raising her finger, indicating she was about to speak. "Guv, I think we can assume Ralph Eastley murdered Hawkshaw."

"Agreed."

"However, he didn't kill Susan Kane as he wasn't in the country at the time. So, that would suggest he didn't kill Adam Henderson or the A N Other up at Havervalley Prison because they have the same M.O. Also, he didn't start that fire."

"Yes, your point is?"

"So, we have another killer on the loose who is probably responsible for all these deaths, which means Patrick Colney can't be our man as he couldn't have killed Susan Kane as he was still inside. Guv, we have an unknown killer on the loose who is probably already responsible for seven deaths, including Susan Kane, Adam Henderson, the unidentified burnt bodies at the hostel and the prison – oh, yeah, not forgetting Mack the Knife and his two women. So, my point is, Guv, we need to get Eastley for Hawkshaw's murder, but none of the other three individuals we have warrants for are responsible for those seven other deaths."

DI French stopped rocking back on her swivel chair, shifting her weight forward and thumping her elbows on her desk. "All of you. Mark my words … Shirley Colney is involved. I don't know how, but she is."

DC Brown joined the sombre party now taking place in the DI's office, entering just as DI French delivered her statement regarding one of Fairfield's most infamous matriarchs of post-war history.

"*Paddington*, what's up," questioned DS Farham, noticing Brown sported a pallid complexion.

"Guv, sorry."

The DI raised her eyebrows whilst the others all held their breath and fully anticipated that Brown wasn't about to spread good news.

"Well, Guv, it's like this. Couple of Uniforms responded to a suspected assault yesterday afternoon, where a witness provided them with a car description and Index number—"

"I'm not going to like this, am I?"

Brown shook his head. "Not a lot, Guv."

"Christ. Go on."

"Well, they didn't track down the car until this morning up at Jenson's Car Hire at Luton airport."

"Bloody hell," muttered DS Farham, realising as everyone else did that this linked to Shirley and Ralph.

"Turns out the car was hired on Monday morning by one Ralph Eastley. An Australian national, with a home address somewhere in Costa Del Crime."

"Don't tell me the car place doesn't have an address for them here?"

"Correct, Guv. Also, Ralph Eastley returned the car yesterday afternoon."

"Returned it! Did he take another one?"

"No, Guv. Also, I've checked all the other hire companies. He didn't hire another car from the airport. And before you ask, neither he nor Shirley have left the country because I've checked."

"So, why if we have the whole Force looking for them, am I only hearing about it now?" boomed the DI, throwing the question to the whole room.

The four officers hung their heads.

"Guv."

"What, Dawson?" fired back the rather red-faced DI.

"Guv, they've got to have wheels to get about. I wouldn't mind betting they've taken one of Hawkshaw's cars. On his drive, I clocked a rather snazzy brand-spanking-new moonstone-blue RS500 Sierra Cosworth and an older British racing-green convertible XJS, although still a nice motor. I reckon it might be worth checking if they're still there."

"You got the index numbers?" questioned DS Farham.

Dawson shook his head.

"I did," stated Megson, pulling out her notebook.

The DI gave a wry smile. Megson once again showed why she was sergeant material and a cut above the rest of the DCs, even if her confectionery piranha-style consuming skills could quickly empty Wonka's factory.

"I'll check with *Paddy* and *Mudda* if those motors are still there. But my guess is that one of them is missing. *Paddington*, get the index numbers out there. We need everyone searching for those cars as a top priority."

"Will do, Sarge," stated Brown, as he grabbed the notebook Megson held out.

"Well done, both of you. Now let's see if Uniform can pick them up without cocking up!"

Brown noted down the Index number and spun around, ready to zip off.

"Oh, hang on, Brown. You said there was an alleged assault reported. What was that about?" shouted the DI, stopping Brown before he had a chance to scuttle away.

"Err ... it was reported by someone up at the Eaton City of Fairfield School. Apparently, one of the teachers was assaulted by some large bloke with one eye."

"Apsley!" exclaimed the DI, as she thumped her hands on her chair's armrests.

"Guv, he never said anything yesterday about that," stated DS Farham.

"No, he didn't, did he! Right, you two, get back out there and pick him up. I want Jason Apsley back in an interview room within the hour!"

"Guv," affirmed both DCs in unison.

"Oh, and while you're at it, haul in their new lodger. Some weird bloke called Leonardo Bretton. There's something not right about him. And if I didn't know any better, I'd say he's related to the Colneys ... he looks just like them."

"Are we arresting them or asking for help with our inquiries?"

"Arrest them! I've had enough of Jason Apsley. Arrest him!"

"What for, Guv?" questioned Dawson, as Megson shot past him, making a beeline for her desk.

"Perverting the course of justice."

"Got it. And the other bloke ... Leo, whatever?"

DI French pondered this thought, but her mind was clouded by her frustrations with Jason Apsley. "I don't know. Just think of something!"

"Will do," grinned Dawson. Loving it when the DI gave them free rein to act.

"Arrest him for possessing a stupid name!" called out DS Farham before muttering, "Christ, his parents must be some weirdo Renaissance Art fans."

"What?" questioned Megson, who hovered at her desk for a quick rummage to locate a Mint Club Biscuit she thought she'd earlier stashed under a pile of paperwork.

"Leonardo Da Vinci!"

"Oh, okay. Whatever," she threw back over her shoulder, clutching the chocolate biscuit and following Dawson out of the office.

DC Brown, the only one in the team with any credible knowledge of the arts, turned to the sergeant, quite impressed *Bergerac* knew Da Vinci could be used in the same sentence as renaissance art. "The Vitruvian Man, I might suggest."

"What?" quizzed the DS. Although instantly regretting asking, knowing there was a real chance *Paddington* could bore the pants off him with his public-school knowledge.

"Brown! You still here?"

"No, Guv," replied Brown, as he shot off to find the location of both cars belonging to the now-dead dodgy solicitor whilst leaving DS Farham bemused.

"*Paddington* needs the love of a good woman. His head constantly stuck in books and listening to classical music ain't healthy."

DI French didn't answer. Instead, her brain whirred, trying to fathom the connection to these events and a schoolteacher.

39

Hinge and Bracket

Ralph immediately came to a halt at the command of Shirley, looking somewhat disappointed he wasn't about to rip my eye from its socket.

"Where are they, Apsley? We had a deal. I get the girls for the weekend, or Ralph here has his fun."

I involuntarily held up my hands and backed away. Not that this action would stop the giant colossus, but I just needed to be out of his reach.

"Look, you can have the girls for the weekend, but we need to know where you're taking them." Not that this really mattered, but I had to coerce Shirley into believing she held all the aces and thus go along with the plan.

"Never you mind. You know what Ralph will do to you. Remember, any police involvement will get you arrested for David's murder. Stop pissing about. Where are they?"

I glanced at my watch. I needed Shirley on that bridge in seventeen minutes, which was a ten-minute drive away. "The girls are with my wife. They'll be on the Carrow Road Bridge at five."

Shirley stepped forward, passing her man, and stopping only a few inches from me, invading my personal space. I backed up to the door of my car; I had nowhere else to go. I was now pinned in by the evil woman, with Ralph the colossus blocking any escape route.

"What game you playing, Apsley?"

Peering down at her, then back to her frozen-in-time pet shark, I feared our plan was going to collapse at the first hurdle. Shirley wasn't going to buy this.

'Jesus, boy. Now you're fucked!'

"You there! You!" came a shout from the school steps.

All three of us spun around, spotting a woman barrelling out of the school entrance whilst aggressively wagging her finger in my direction. For a brief moment, I had no idea of the identity of this pugnacious intruder. However, as she marched towards me, followed by a student, I recognised my ex-mother-in-law with my twelve-year-old ex-wife trotting behind.

"Jesus," I muttered.

Yesterday, after my last encounter with Shirley, poor Colin had relayed the particularly difficult lesson that afternoon where Lisa had splattered the classroom walls with pictures taken from a men's top-shelf type publication. This resulted in Colin spending some time removing them, much to the immature students' amusement.

Within her first few days, Lisa had already reached cult status with a loyal following of male and female students. Needless to say, PoD had requested Lisa's mother attend the school to discuss my ex-wife's behaviour. Clearly, that meeting had just concluded, and it appeared Mrs Crowther wasn't best pleased with the outcome.

"You were supposed to be supervising my daughter!" she aggressively spat, whilst muscling her way into my personal space and rather stupidly shoving Shirley out of the way.

"Oi, bitch. Fuck off!"

It was perhaps a predictable reaction from Shirley. I fully expected, any second now, for her to give my ex-mother-in-law a slap. Lisa's mother's mouth dropped in horror. Again, a reaction I fully expected. Lisa smirked whilst she took in the scene in front of her.

In my two lives, I had met two wholly repugnant females, who both now appeared to be squaring up to each other like some comic scene with Hinge and Bracket, who were still all the rage on prime-time TV. However, there was nothing humorous about this situation. Mrs Crowther, who possessed the most vicious tongue of any woman in history, didn't know what the petite, viperous, salt-and-pepper-haired monster was capable of – or her pet shark, for that matter.

"You might want to have a word with your husband. I'm guessing the salacious pictures that your daughter plastered all over the classroom came from some mucky-mags that your husband stores in a briefcase which he hides in the garage behind the chest freezer," I suggested to the mouth-gaping woman.

Back in my old life, Lisa had stumbled across the briefcase stashed in her parents' garage when searching for a suitcase her parents had said we could borrow when preparing for our honeymoon. Lisa, at the time, had been shocked by the extensive stash of porn but never mentioned it to her father. I guess in this life, Lisa had discovered the briefcase a good fifteen years early. By the look on Mrs Crowther's face, she was also fully aware of her upstanding pious Masonic-leader husband's mucky stash. So, presumably embarrassed and wondering how the hell I knew about the briefcase, she quickly scuttled away, roughly manhandling her daughter in the process.

"Yeah, go on. Fuck off!" shouted Shirley before returning her attention towards me. "Right, you get in the motor. You're coming with us," she spat, whilst pointing up at me. "Fuck me about … you're done for."

40

Quantum Of Solace

"Thank you, Mrs Hall. I'll see you next week," stated the butcher, dressed in his bloodstained blue and white striped apron, after he'd handed over the bag he'd just spun and tied containing two lamb chops and a pound of stewing steak.

Before serving the next customer, he removed the 'Lamb Chop' sock puppet from his hand that he always donned when selling lamb. He would put on a silly voice and attempt the Shari Lewis ventriloquist act, which all the regulars would laugh at even though his act was poor and rather old-hat.

Mrs Hall placed the meat in her shopping bag, whispering a thank you as she exited the butchers and stepped into the High Street. She checked her watch, concerned about the time and knew she'd now have to hurry.

Earlier, when taking her usual Friday afternoon shopping trip into town, she hadn't been able to grab a parking space in the High Street, thus having to park in the multistorey car park next to Carrow Road Bridge. Beryl Hall had never been a confident driver, and the impossibly tight corners and the frighteningly small parking bays in the multistorey car park terrified her.

Last Christmas, in that very same car park, she'd scraped the bumper on a concrete bollard. The resulting wrath from her husband now caused Beryl to shake as she recalled the violent beating she'd received.

Unfortunately, it didn't take much for her husband, Graham, to lose control, something that she'd learnt to live with. Beryl hurried along with the heavy bag of groceries, praying she'd make it home unscathed and in time to have Graham's tea on the table before he arrived home from the office. Not having his tea ready was unthinkable.

She knew he'd be furious tonight because Graham demanded that Friday's evening meal consist of a large pork chop, new potatoes and carrots. However, unfortunately, the butchers had sold out of pork chops, leaving her in a state of panic about what to purchase. Only because of the long queue behind her, who belligerently moaned about her dithering, had she eventually asked for lamb chops – Beryl knew it would be a painful mistake.

For the last twenty years, she'd followed the same routine. Monday was washing day. Tuesday, she hoovered and polished. On Wednesdays, she collected her husband's shirts from the dry cleaners, where he insisted his shirts were taken because she wasn't competent with the iron to ensure the collars and cuffs were adequately pressed. Thursday was ironing day for the rest of the laundry, an odious task because she knew Graham would inspect his socks and underwear, checking for unwanted ironed-in folds. On the odd occasion she had incorrectly ironed his Y-fronts, it had taken extensive make-up application to her cheek to hide the bruising.

This left Fridays, which was her grocery shopping day. Fridays petrified her for two reasons. Firstly, she had to drive into town in her husband's Talbot Alpine. And secondly, she had to mix with other people. Beryl had always found socialising quite taxing. Just the thought of conversing with strangers could bring her out in hives. Graham repeatedly stated that she was a stupid woman and, to save embarrassment, he'd suggested she kept her mouth shut.

Every evening followed the same routine. After preparing and serving his evening meal, she would clear the table and perform the washing-up duties before asking her husband to inspect the kitchen to ensure it was to his satisfaction. Then she would polish his shoes to a parade-ground shine, ready for the next day. Finally, after he was satisfied his shoes had acquired the required gleam, they watched television together – as that required a prolonged period of time in her husband's company, it was the time of the day that Beryl dreaded the most.

Her only quantum of solace was the weekends, a time when Beryl had no stipulated chores, so she could visit the library and read her books. Although she loved the arts, especially classical music, she knew a visit to the opera would be a treat she would never experience. Graham, who spent the weekends on the golf course, wouldn't know the difference between a sing-along to *The Good Old Days* and Puccini's Madame Butterfly.

Graham had stipulated when they married that they wouldn't be having children because he expected his wife to look after him and not be distracted by messy, boisterous, and unwanted offspring. She suspected that Graham had chosen her as his wife to replace his mother, who'd died when he'd still lived at home when in his late twenties.

Of course, when their daughter was born, life for Beryl and the child deteriorated. Graham had no paternal desires and therefore no interest in the child. Although Beryl tried her best, their daughter, Carol, rebelled. By the time she had turned eighteen, Carol resided in a squalid flat on the Broxworth Estate, had a young son, and a drug addiction.

Graham had firmly stipulated that Beryl could have no contact with their daughter or grandson. The one time she had disobeyed her husband and visited Carol, she'd then spent two days in hospital nursing a broken jaw.

Tragically, when Carol was only twenty, and a few weeks after giving birth to a daughter, she'd taken her life via a heroin overdose. Beryl lost her daughter and her grandchildren, who were taken into care. She'd bravely left her husband that year, only to be dragged back and repeatedly beaten. As long as Beryl complied with her husband's demands, the regularity of the beatings subsided. Her daughter was dead, and she was forbidden to enquire about her grandchildren – Graham had broken her.

Beryl had no other family as her father was unknown, and her mother died when she was a child. The years had rolled on by, and Beryl had come to realise she was perfect for the role of subservient wife that Graham required. Not unattractive, although certainly not a looker, but totally controllable.

Her upbringing in a girl's orphanage had sucked out any remaining confidence she had as a child. So, by the time she'd reached courting age, Beryl was perfect for any man looking for an acquiescent wife to pander after him.

Beryl often reflected on her time at St. Peter's Orphanage and how those few years had defined her life. The torment she'd suffered at the hands of the 'head girl', Janet Curtis, had ultimately led to marrying a controlling bully who made her life a living hell.

Beryl had lost count of how many times, with trembling hands, she'd buttered his morning toast. Her body would ache and be covered in bruises caused by the previous evening's thrashing. Holding that butter knife, she'd imagine sticking it in her husband's throat – just as she wished she had Janet's, all those years ago.

After depositing her bags of groceries on the passenger seat, Beryl prepared to negotiate the tight turns of the multistorey car park. Terrified she might be late she prayed the traffic lights before the bridge would be on green. Arriving home late and not having her husband's evening meal prepared really didn't bear thinking about.

Trying to hurry, Beryl swung the car around the last turn before the exit barrier, only to hear the sound of concrete on metal. In her attempt to race home, she'd stupidly caught the rear wing on one of the concrete stanchions. Braking hard, then releasing her hands from the steering wheel, she covered her mouth and howled in fear of what her husband would do to her.

41

You've Been Tangoed

Being a self-confessed petrol-head, having an opportunity to drive the Cosworth would usually tick all my boxes. However, this wasn't the right set of circumstances to enjoy driving an iconic '80s rally car. You might say it had kind of lost its appeal because I had the evil Shirley on the back seat and the cyclops man-mountain riding shotgun.

I swung the Cosworth into the multistorey car park, a brutal grey monolithic concrete disaster, which Jayne boasted her husband, Frank, had designed. Personally, if I'd have created the piss-ridden, drug-den shit-hole, I'd have kept that particular fact well hidden.

So far, the plan was on track. I'd fully expected Shirley to demand I join them on this fool's errand, also hoping they would insist I drive so they had control of the situation. This afforded me the opportunity to park in the multistorey and walk to the bridge. Once there and in position, I would nip to the phone box less than fifty yards away with a ruse to ring home and check Jenny had left. At which point, we hoped time would repeat and send the bridge, along with Shirley and Ralph, into the river below.

What could go wrong?

At three minutes to five, and now worried the altercation with Lisa's mother concerning the early discovery of her husband's stash of porn had put us behind schedule, we hot-footed our way through the concrete layers and out of the multistorey towards the bridge.

I had a momentary pang of guilt as we passed a brown Talbot Alpine and the distressed female driver who clearly needed assistance. After colliding with a concrete post, she'd brought her car to a halt, causing a tailback of horn-thumping frustrated drivers producing a cacophony of blasts that I suspected wasn't helping the driver compose herself. In any other situation, I'd have stepped in and offered assistance. But guiltily, I glanced at her tear-streaked face as she stared back at the three of us whilst we trotted past.

"Silly cow," muttered Shirley, almost laughing at the poor woman, whose distress appeared far more than a scraped wheel arch should cause.

"Come on," I urged, not wishing them to be late for their deaths.

"What's the hurry, Apsley?"

"Err ... nothing, nothing," I offered over my shoulder, praying I hadn't made it too obvious I wanted to get her on that bridge. "Cool it, cool it," I muttered to myself, relieved Shirley didn't have a follow-up question.

Just fifty yards away from Frank Stone's architectural disaster, which doubled up as a car park and rough-sleepers' hotel, stood the Carrow Road Bridge, which I expected had entered its last few minutes of existence in its long life serving the town as a reliable river crossing.

"Ralph!"

The statement was a familiar command that I heard Shirley use before, knowing it was her instruction for her pet shark to strike.

Fortunately, we were in the centre of town and during rush hour. So, there were plenty of witnesses about, resulting in the Great White only hauling me back with his colossus hand and not gouging out large chunks of flesh from me.

"What's your game? You pissing me about, Apsley," spat Shirley, any pleasantries that may have been lurking underneath that concrete make-up persona had now fully evaporated. She could see the girls weren't on the bridge. I guess she'd smelt a rat, so to speak.

"No, look, I promise you. I promise you they'll be here any minute," I blurted, a little too desperately, whilst glancing at their feet and almost wishing them to move forward to the bridge.

"By God, Apsley. You play any games here, and I'll let Ralph off his leash," she warned, then nodded to her pet shark to let go.

I detected a hint of disappointment radiating from Ralph and perhaps a dislike of the control she clearly exercised over him.

We stepped onto the bridge as the traffic lights turned to red, halting the long line of commuter traffic. As we stopped in the centre of the bridge, I noticed the first car in line waiting at the lights was the Talbot Alpine, now feeling less guilty that the upset lady had composed herself and driven out of the car park. I hoped she'd recovered and wondered if it was going to be this sequence of light changes when the bridge would fall.

Clearly, I had to move fast. Otherwise, I would join Shirley and Ralph for a dip in the river seventy feet below.

"Well, where the fuck are they?"

Before suggesting to Shirley that I nip to the phone box and call Jenny, I glanced around at the early evening scene in front of me.

Something was amiss – this wasn't right.

Criss-crossing their way over the bridge must have been at least thirty people: a woman with a pushchair, a road sweeper and his barrow, a group of yuppies who appeared to have spent too long enjoying the new-world wines on offer in the wine bar on Elm Hill. I spotted two blokes carrying squash rackets who looked like they could audition for the future 118 adverts. Walking straight at me were two young lads drinking Tango whilst playfully pushing and shoving each other, perhaps pioneers for the *'You've been Tangoed'* adverts soon to hit the TV screens. In their droves, similarly dressed office workers also barrelled their way across the bridge, blissfully unaware of what was about to transpire.

The bridge was teeming with people crossing both ways, presumably on their way home. Martin had said no one was killed, and it was deemed a miracle at the time that the bridge had been empty. At this point, or very soon, the bridge pavements should be clear. However, as I glanced in both directions, assessing the swathes of commuters, I considered the chances of a lull at the point of collapse to be below zero.

I knew I had to escape from the bridge and leave Shirley and Ralph to fall to their deaths. However, the sight of potentially fifty people on or heading for the bridge dragged me into a state of panic. How could I just walk away and watch this disaster unfold?

I became mesmerised by the amazing shiny-black shoes of a middle-aged gent who strode towards me, just another innocent man who was about to die along with everyone else on this bridge. The plan had failed. I couldn't let this happen, even though that meant Shirley and Ralph would live and Beth and Faith would still be in danger.

"Get off the bridge," I shouted. "Get off the bridge!" Then, waving my hands in the air, I jumped up and down, performing weird star-type jumps, as I once again shouted, "Get off the bridge. Get off the bridge! Your life depends on it! Get off the bridge."

"Struth Shirl, he's lost it! What's the matter with the bloody Poms these days?" I heard Ralph shout over my repeated mantra, which had now attracted a small crowd of intrigued onlookers.

"The end is nigh," called out a man who joined me, performing similar star jumps. I presumed he held the view that the world was nearing its apocalyptical and eschatological end. So, I guessed he'd grabbed the opportunity to join what he thought was a like-minded individual in an attempt to convince the world of its impending doom.

Although my shouts and general wailing around had the opposite effect of clearing the bridge, now causing many to stop and watch, I continued in the vain pathetic hope that they would listen to my prophecy of doom.

The two Tango-swilling lads stopped and assessed the show. "What a twat!" chuckled one of them, indicating I was the person to whom he directed his vulgar derisory comment by pointing his can of fizzy orangeade in my direction.

As I stopped jumping, at last realising my attempts to clear the bridge had failed, I spotted Ralph move towards me –

Shirley had unleashed him. Stumbling backwards, I bumped into the shiny-shoes gent who I'd noticed a few moments ago. Before stepping by, he threw me an odd look, probably concerned about my previously performed weird gymnastic performance.

Ralph continued his advance. However, before I could turn and make a dash for it, I heard a deafening crack, followed by screams, and the panicked scattering of commuters – this was it – the bridge was going.

42

One Man Band

"Oh, *Gladys,* come on!" exclaimed DC Dawson, as he flung his hands in the air, frustrated at her for shoving her chocolate wrapper down the side of her seat.

DC Megson shrugged, looking away out of the side window, whilst savouring the chocolate, although disappointed she didn't have any more in her jacket pockets.

Rush hour in Fairfield, as usual, was a bloody nightmare. It could take another half an hour to get to the school to arrest Jason Apsley.

"Christ, come on, what's the matter with these bloody lights?" he muttered, frustrated by the logjam of traffic as they waited in their unmarked Ford Escort near the Carrow Road Bridge.

"Stick your light on," she suggested.

"No point. I can't get around that crap heap in front." He gestured to the brown Talbot Alpine, which sat patiently at the front of the queue waiting for the lights to change.

"You got this Apsley bloke's address?"

"Yeah, what you thinking? Nip up there first and nab Leo Sayer, or whatever his stupid name is."

"Well, it could save a bit of time. By the time we've got there, Apsley might arrive home and save us a trip up to the school."

"Jesus, *Gladys*! What's that bloody idiot doing on the bridge?"

Megson shifted her gaze from the side window through the windscreen and across the bridge where, as *Fawlty* had stated, some nutter was performing star-jumps and appeared to be shouting at the top of his voice.

"Jesus Christ! This town is full of them. D'you reckon it's something in the water?"

"Christ knows. But we ain't got time for this. Right, let's turn around and head up to Apsley's place as you suggested," stated Dawson, whilst he swung his arm over the back of her seat and peered out the back window, preparing to reverse a few feet to enable him to pull out.

"Oh, shit. Shit!" exclaimed Megson.

Dawson twisted his head around just in time to spot the Talbot Alpine accelerate through the red light heading for the melee on the bridge, who'd now gathered to watch, not one, but two nutters performing star-jumps. "What the—"

"Oh, shit. Noooo!"

~

Thirty-seven years. All that time had passed, but Beryl had never seen her even though she apparently still lived in Fairfield. Yes, she'd aged, but she'd never forgotten the face of that petite monster who'd terrorised her back at the children's home in the late '40s.

As she'd tried to compose herself with the queue of cars behind her all bibbing their horns, Janet Curtis had walked past her car, briefly locking eyes. Beryl didn't believe Janet recognised her. However, she definitely recognised the tormentor of St. Peter's Orphanage – a face she'd never forget.

Ignoring the damaged rear wing and the inevitable ferocious attack she would suffer at the hands of her husband, Beryl felt compelled to follow her. After taking a few deep breaths and wiping her eyes with the back of her hand, she shot out of the car park to the traffic lights, relieved to see that Janet, for some reason, had stopped on the bridge.

Beryl waited, all the time keeping her eyes on Janet, wondering why the bloody woman had stopped on the bridge and where she was going. Then, for some bizarre reason, one of the blokes who appeared to be with Janet walked onto the road in the middle of the bridge and appeared to be performing star-jumps.

That's when it happened. As if the planets aligned at the precise moment, almost presenting the opportunity to Beryl which she felt compelled to take. The idiot performing his gymnastics stopped jumping, then bumped into a middle-aged man who made his way across the bridge, briefcase in hand, heading home to beat his wife.

Within the same three-square yards stood Janet Curtis and Graham Hall. Although not holding a butter knife, she had the power and force of a 1.6-litre engine and a car bonnet at her disposal. After revving the engine, Beryl slammed her foot on the accelerator, aiming the car for those three-square yards in front of her.

The sense of euphoria and release engulfed her as the Talbot Alpine shot across the bridge with her two tormentors nicely positioned in the most beautiful three-square yards Beryl had ever seen.

43

Grand Theft Auto

As I spun around, I fully expected to see the left-hand side of the bridge slide towards the river, taking Shirley, Ralph, plus thirty others and myself down seventy feet to the dark waters below. However, although there seemed to be people running in all directions and general panic had ensued, the bridge stayed firm, upright and exactly where it had been a few seconds ago.

The loud cracking sound wasn't the road surface breaking, but the noise of Ralph and the bonnet of a car colliding. The brown Talbot Alpine with the distressed driver had jumped the lights and driven at some considerable speed onto the pavement where Shirley and Ralph stood. By some miracle, the driver managed to miss the lady with the pushchair and the two lads drinking Tango, only taking out Ralph, then Shirley, and unfortunately the gent with the shiny shoes.

My initial thought was the distressed driver had accidentally slammed her foot on the accelerator instead of the brake, causing her to shoot forward across the bridge. Ralph had now disappeared from view as he sailed over the bridge's ornate iron railings, presumably heading for the river below, and I guess joined by the shiny-shoes gent.

The car came to an abrupt halt as it collided with one of the three large iron Victorian lamps that decorated the bridge at regular intervals along the railings. Embedded between the crumpled bonnet and wrought-iron feature light was the small frame of Shirley Colney, appearing to be almost cut in half.

I gawped at her as she stared back at me. All around us, people dashed in every direction, still panicked and screaming. I presumed their chaotic running was an attempt to escape the scene and avoid the path of the mad driver who'd appeared intent on a killing spree. Shirley blinked before her head tipped forward, her body folding at right angles, causing her head to thump down onto the mashed-up bonnet. By some quirk of fate, a weird traffic incident had taken Shirley and Ralph – not the bridge and its imminent collapse.

"The bridge," I muttered. "Shit, shit. Shit. The bridge is going to go!"

I resumed my star-jumping routine whilst screaming out to anyone who would listen. "Get off the bridge. Get off the bridge. It's going to collapse. Get off the bridge!"

No one listened. Yes, many ran off the bridge in fear of the car, which had appeared to be playing some game of pinball as it bounced off the railing and rested up, pinning Shirley to a lamppost, but not because of my warning. As I continued to bellow my prophecy of doom, many ran back onto the bridge to inspect the scene, presumably to satisfy their predilection to morbid fascination. I noticed one woman try to help Shirley.

'Don't try too hard. She needs to be dead!' my mind bellowed to the woman who now gently lifted Shirley's head.

A white Ford Escort shot forward from the traffic lights, accelerating hard. I feared this was the second driver now racing across, intent to kill. Had the town gone mad? Was this a sick game of take your turn to kill as many as you can – each driver gets one go, and the one with the most kills score the most points? Was this some sick, real-life version of Grand Theft Auto? I will admit, a game I used to play on my Xbox when at Uni. Would the Ford Granada, now in pole position at the lights, be the third car to shoot forward and kill a few innocent people?

"Get off the bridge," I screamed again.

The Escort screeched to a halt. The driver hadn't followed the example set by the Talbot Alpine. Instead, it was now positioned in the middle of the bridge with its blue lights blazing.

I ran towards the woman who jumped out of the passenger seat, presumably a plain-clothed police officer. "The bridge is going to collapse! We have to get everyone off the bloody bridge!"

"Woah, woah, woah, calm down. Hang on, sir. Now, I need you to calm yourself," stated the officer, who held her hands defensively as she gingerly approached. I guess this was part of her training when dealing with nutters who seemed out of control, which I guessed is what I appeared to be.

"Noooo, no! It's going to collapse! We have to—"

"Sir! Calm down."

I noticed the other officer waving people away, getting them off the bridge. At last, someone was listening to me. However, I also needed to get the officers and myself off. Otherwise, we would be joining Ralph and shiny-shoes man down below.

"Sir. Listen. I need you to calm yourself and step back, please," stated the officer as she corralled me away from the scene.

Exasperated, I stepped back, thinking at least if I moved away and she followed, I would save one officer from falling to her death. However, I could do nothing about the other who now attended to the driver of the Talbot Alpine after a quick assessment confirming Shirley had left this world. Any minute now, the male officer and that poor driver were going to fall to their deaths and, because I was being corralled away, there was nothing but to stand and watch as the force of time took control, allowing history to repeat itself.

"Please, please, get that other officer off the bridge," I pleaded, as I backed away, frustrated and becoming angry at her stupidity. However, she didn't know what I knew.

Time travel comes with great responsibility along with unparalleled opportunity. However, I always struggled to cope with the great sadness of repeated events that caused needless misery and suffering. I had the knowledge of so many upsetting future events, which so often I witnessed from the sidelines as they repeated. Ten years on from my time leap, I knew time would not bend that easily. Once again, here I was, this time witnessing an awful repeat, but not on TV, or in the news bulletin, but live, and right in front of my eyes.

"Come on, sir. You seem a little emotional. We'll get you checked out when we've assessed the driver," stated the officer in her sing-song Welsh accent. She continued to back me off the bridge, holding her arms out wide and sporting a kind smile.

Two ambulances, followed by another police car, swung onto the bridge, their sirens and lights parting the crowds near the traffic lights like the command from Moses. Any second now, all of them would fall to their deaths.

∼

After witnessing the scene on the bridge, the driver of a British racing-green Jaguar XJS convertible slowly exited the multistorey car park. He glanced at the scene on the bridge and smirked at the sight of the crushed woman before speeding off up Carrow Road and away from the melee in his rear-view mirror. He had a clear plan – it was time to execute it.

44

First Blood

Two uniform officers assisted with crowd control, one on the far side near the entrance to the multistorey car park and one heading to my side of the bridge where I now stood with a modest crowd of onlookers. I checked the time – 5:25 p.m.

Martin had said his mum, Sarah, queued at the traffic lights when the bridge fell. If she'd left work on time, she would have been here about ten minutes ago. However, since the drama had unfolded, the lights had changed twice. So, if history was repeating itself, which it always did, why was the bridge still standing?

"*Rambo*, tape off that side of the bridge," called out the Welsh plain-clothed officer to the traffic officer walking towards me.

"Oh, shit. Alan!" I muttered. Jenny's brother was a traffic officer, and I knew his nickname to be Rambo based on the Sylvester Stallone character from the *First Blood* film. Christ! Now he was standing on the ruddy bridge that surely must now collapse.

"Alan! Alan," I bellowed to grab his attention.

Alan raised his hand and trotted the last few feet towards me. "Hi, Jason, what are you doing here? Is Jenny with you?"

"No. no, she's not."

"Did you see it happen? Looks a right mess!" The glint in his eye confirmed that nothing he liked better than the scene of a gory road accident.

"Alan, the bridge ... the bridge is going to collapse!"

"What?"

"The bloody bridge, it's going to collapse. You have to get off it!"

"Christ, you alright? You been on the sauce all afternoon?" he chuckled.

"No! But ... but, the bridge might collapse," my voice trailing off to almost a whisper, as I realised what I was saying must sound quite stupid.

The Carrow Road Bridge had spanned the river for over a hundred years. Built by the Victorians, made of offensively thick, heavy iron and supported by gigantic stone pillars – the bridge looked as if it could weather another hundred years, and one crumpled Talbot Alpine was a mere tickle to its robust structure. Notwithstanding my assessment of late Victorian civil engineering, Martin was correct. This bridge collapsed. However, it now appeared that today was not the day it was going to join Ralph and that poor shiny-shoes gent in the river below. I checked my watch – 5:32 p.m.

"Sorry, Jason. I need to cordon off this area. Tell Jenny I'll pop round at the weekend. I could take Chris out for a spin in the Rover. I reckon he'd like that!" he winked, then stepped away and continued to marshal the onlookers away from the scene.

The ambulance crew focused on the driver of the Talbot Alpine, who appeared to have miraculously survived the event, now walking unaided from the car to the back of the ambulance.

No one attended to Shirley, who now lay on the car bonnet covered with a blanket. We hadn't reached the days of camera phones. So, the only concerns the police had regarding unwanted sightseers were newspaper reporters and freelance cameramen. I suspected it would be a few more minutes before they arrived.

The bridge remained solid.

The driver sat in the back of the ambulance talking to the Welsh officer, who repeatedly nodded whilst making notes in her notebook.

Knowing Jenny would be climbing the walls with worry, I nipped over to the phone box, the one that I was going to pretend to use to call Jenny when I'd arrived at the bridge with Shirley and Ralph.

I patiently waited for a bloke, who sported a mullet haircut dressed in a grubby flasher-style mac, to finish his call. I groaned as he slotted in another coin to extend his conversation. Now living in yesteryear, I'd learnt that patiently waiting in line to use a phone box could be a fruitless task. There was the very real possibility of growing a beard or dying of boredom before the box became free.

With no other phone box in close proximity, I applied the tried and tested technique that had a proven success rate of persuading the caller to end their call early. Stepping up to the glass and eyeballing the mullet-man, I waved a ten pence piece, indicating that I urgently needed to use the phone. He shook his head, about-turned and faced the other way.

Unperturbed, I scooted around to the other side of the box and repeated the routine. We repeated this dance for another five full about-turns until I'd achieved success.

"Darling, I'm going to have to go. My money is running out, and this *wanker* is still trying to get the phone," stated the mullet-head, before replacing the receiver, exiting the box and reaffirming that I must masturbate a lot as he muttered obscenities before he trudged off towards the bridge, which incidentally, was still standing.

"Oh, Jason. What's happened?" screeched Jenny, who'd snatched up the receiver on the first ring.

"Are the girls alright? And you and Jess? Has anything happened? Have you seen that Colney bloke?" I machine-gunned out, now terrified that my luck was surely running out and convinced that Paul Colney would have murdered all my family while I'd witnessed his mother being squashed.

"No, we're all fine. What's happened?"

"They're dead. She's dead."

"The bridge collapsed then, as Martin said it would?"

I heard Jess and Martin cheer in the background as Jenny asked that question.

I explained the events, giving cause for Jenny to mutter a few 'Ohs', which ultimately led to breaks in the conversation as Jenny repeated what I'd said to Jess and Martin.

With a perpetual flow of questions coming back my way whilst my stash of ten-pence pieces quickly dwindled, an elderly lady with an umbrella used the other tried and tested tactic to free the phone box as she tapped away at the glass, informing me it was her turn. I ended the call, exited the box and refrained from accusing the senior citizen of performing obscene acts as the mullet-head had of me, leaving her grumbling, *'I should bloody well think so!'*

Jenny would now call George to collect me, so I strolled back to the bridge to wait. On both sides of the bridge, police directed the now backed-up traffic. The ambulance had disappeared along with most of the rubberneckers.

The bridge remained solid.

45

Ziggy Stardust

Colin had heard the news on the radio regarding the warrant for Patrick Colney's arrest. He'd suggested, that as every police officer in the land were hunting his tail, it was surely now safe to go home. As he said, Patrick wouldn't risk being anywhere near Fairfield. Jess agreed, knowing Beth and Faith were safe now that Shirley was dead. But, of course, this didn't negate the issue of Paul Colney, who was out there somewhere. However, Jenny and I reluctantly accepted that if Paul had killed Patrick, he would now be on the run for fear of being picked up by the law because his twin's mugshot was presumably imprinted in every police officer's mind after the report about the fire on Timber Hill.

George, Jenny, Martin and I mused over why the bridge had stayed intact. All of us struggled to believe our luck that the woman in the Talbot Alpine had driven headlong onto the bridge, fortunately killing those two people – an outcome which we'd hoped the supposedly collapsing bridge would provide.

"Lad, do you think you just got the wrong year?"

"No. Well, I don't think so. It definitely happens on 11th September, and the year of the storm," replied Martin.

"Darling?" questioned Jenny looking at me.

"I don't know." I dismissively shook my head. "I mean, Martin is right. The bridge does collapse, something I'd just forgotten about. I do remember it was when I was at school, but I really have no idea of the year."

"What about the storm, you predicted? Could that be a different year?"

"No. That was 1987, for certain."

"Martin?" questioned Jenny.

"Look, I wasn't born, but Jason is right on this one. Everyone I knew would say the storm was 1987."

George had started his loose change symphony as he jingled the coins in his pocket, the sound accompanying a mix of music floating down the stairs from Beth and Christopher's bedrooms. I couldn't be certain, but I'd guess it sounded like Bananarama were performing a duet with U2; an interesting combination, I mused.

"Well, look, before you lot lead me a merry dance, I need to get going. Ivy will have my guts for garters. But something in your predictions has gone awry."

"I don't know. But whatever that woman was up to, she sure has saved us a lot of heartache. I do hope she's okay. And then there's that poor innocent bloke who ended up in the river with Ralph."

"Yes, that's dreadful. I know we shouldn't revel in Shirley and Ralph's deaths, but they were evil. But that poor man, and what about his wife and family?"

The three men nodded in agreement to Jenny's statement.

"Christ, talk about merry dance. You should have seen me on that bridge screaming to warn everyone about the impending doom! Would you believe, but I actually had some nutter join in and shout the end is nigh!" I chuckled, lightening the melancholy mood as we pondered the shiny-shoes man and his family.

"Oh, look, it's on TV," exclaimed Martin, pointing to the portable TV, which Jenny had earlier muted but would always have on as she liked to watch *Wogan* when preparing a late supper.

"Turn it up, lass."

As Martin had pointed out, the early evening local news featured the events on the bridge. The newscaster reported three deaths, two of which had warrants for their arrests issued earlier in the week. Janet Shirley Colney and Ralph Eastley, who had both entered the country on Monday, were named. A third victim's body, believed to have no connection, was recovered from the river at the scene. A fifty-two-year-old local woman was assisting police with their enquiries. The presenter then cut to the reporter at the scene.

The TV crew positioned on the multistorey side of the bridge panned around the scene where the Talbot Alpine car remained embedded into the lamp post. However, Shirley's body had now been removed.

The camera panned around to a reporter, who stood with the bridge in the background.

"This is the scene from today's events, which the police are suggesting is not just a road traffic accident. Detective

Inspector French, can you indicate if you are looking for anyone else to help with your inquiries?"

The camera panned on to Frenchie, who I thought looked a little more rotund on TV than in the flesh – although that may have been a little unfair.

"We urgently need to speak with Patrick Leonard Colney in connection with the fire which destroyed several buildings on Timber Hill in the early hours of this morning, where tragically, five members of the public lost their life."

A mugshot of Patrick appeared on the screen as Frenchie continued.

"I'm appealing to the public to be vigilant and dial 999 immediately if you see or know where ... his whereabouts ... where this man is. He is extremely dangerous, and I urge no one to approach him. We're also urgently looking for the driver of a green convertible Jaguar XJS, registration number A763 YHF."

"Christ, Heather made a bit of a pig's ear of that!" stated Jenny, as she critiqued Frenchie's TV debut.

The screen cut away from Patrick's not so flattering mugshot and returned to Frenchie, who appeared highly uncomfortable with the camera pointing at her. Two lads about twenty feet behind her started to pump their hand back and forth from their waist, indicating they were performing an act that the mullet-head bloke had accused me of being earlier. The camera's positioning causing the lads to appear as animated wanking earrings hanging from Frenchie's ears.

"Inspector, can you tell us how this incident here relates to the fire last night on Timber Hill?"

"At this stage, I'm not at liberty to say. Although we have several inquiries that link this incident to the fire on Timber Hill and the murder of Mark Hawkshaw, a local solicitor whose body we discovered earlier today."

"Are you looking for anyone else in connection to these incidences?"

"Yes. We are making a number of arrests as we speak."

As if on cue, the doorbell chimed and was quickly followed up with a rapping of the door knocker. After checking psycho Colney hadn't popped around for supper and a bit of murder for afters, I took the front door through the Fort Knox opening procedure to be faced with the Welsh plain-clothed officer and her sidekick. I could only assume that Alan had said who I was, and they'd nipped around to gather a witness statement regarding today's events.

I was wrong.

"Good evening—"

"Hello," I stated, interrupting the officer, who looked a little surprised to see me.

"Oh, *Fawlty*, it's him. Starman!"

"Who, David Bowie?" replied the other officer, who'd stepped back from the doorstep and appeared to be assessing the windows and side gate.

"No, that bloke jumping on the bridge!"

The male officer turned his attention from the side passage to where I was standing. "Oh yeah, how weird. Come on, *Gladys*, get on with it."

"Jason Apsley?" the Welsh officer asked in her sing-song accent.

"Yes."

"Jason Apsley, I'm arresting you on suspicion of perverting the course of justice. You do not have to say anything if you do not wish to do so, but anything you do say may be used in a court of law. Do you understand?"

"What? Sorry, what!"

"You're nicked!"

46

Two weeks later

Don't Have Nightmares

"Well, what d'you think? D'you reckon you're down there?"

"I don't know ... it's weird, isn't it? I mean, I can't be because I'm standing here. So, how the hell can I be down there?"

"I have no idea, but it gives me the creeps thinking about it."

"Gives *you* the bloody creeps! What about me? I'm standing here, looking at my own grave wondering if I'm down there in a box!"

We stood in silence at the foot of his unmarked grave, where ten years earlier Martin had been laid to rest. Frenchie had drilled me regarding his grave and the fact that I never came forward to identify Martin after his death in '77. However, I'd stuck to my story about not wanting to be associated with the Colneys, and she left it at that.

That Friday evening when Martin and I were arrested, both for perverting the course of justice, we'd enjoyed a night in the cells along with a third prisoner, Beryl Hall, who I learnt was the driver who killed Shirley.

I might be naive, but I'm certain Frenchie bought my story about not informing the police regarding my altercation with Shirley at the school for fear of reprisals from Ralph. For obvious reasons, I never mentioned the evil woman's threat to fit me up for the murder of her son, David. From what Ralph had said about his eye, I was able to state that I did now recall the incident in '54, although I remained vague and feigned memory lapse where I was unable to remember the details of the assault.

As for the bridge incident, well, explaining Shirley's threats covered that, and I lied to say we were handing the girls over, complying with her demands for weekend access to her granddaughters. However, I was wholly incapable of explaining my star-jumping routine and the constant mantra that the bridge was about to collapse, which, incidentally, still stands.

Martin AKA Leonardo had once again suffered a grilling from Frenchie and her crew about his dead brother, Martin, and his time in South Africa. Of course, I had no idea what happened in his interviews, but the newly formed CPS must have suggested that Frenchie didn't have enough evidence, resulting in dropped charges and a swift release from custody.

The manhunt for Patrick Colney reached a conclusion the following week. The news reports stated a man's body found near Havervalley Prison, ten days prior, had been identified as Patrick. The police once again appealed for witnesses to the fire on Timber Hill, the murder of Patrick Colney and Susan Kane.

Harold Bates, George's contact, had heard that the shit had hit the air conditioning up at Fairfield CID. They had eleven murders to investigate, three of which were obviously attributed to Beryl Hall, and one had been pinned on Ralph Eastley. However, the other seven were unsolved with no leads. Apparently, the main line of their enquiries was centred around the bail hostel where Patrick had reportedly attended after he'd been bludgeoned to death a few hours earlier. This, I suspected, had Frenchie and her team spinning around trying to work out the conundrum of a dead-man-walking. To add to the CID's woes, the fire had destroyed any evidence along with the hostel caretaker.

All the reports in the newspapers and on TV indicated they were looking for one man – of course, the five members of the Time Travel Believers' Club all knew the identity of that man. But, unfortunately, and rather concerningly, like the police, we had no idea of his whereabouts.

The Crime Watch TV show's main feature on Thursday evening was about the events in Fairfield: the fire and the deaths of Susan Kane and Patrick Colney. A young Sue Cook, the presenter, interviewed Frenchie, who'd significantly polished up her performance from her TV debut two weeks earlier.

"Come on. Let's go and join the others." I nudged Martin, jolting him from his trance, as he stared at his own grave. He'd brought a bunch of flowers to lay at his own gravestone, which I thought was an odd act.

"Reckon the church will be packed today, don't you?"

"Yep. Don has left a big hole in many peoples' lives. They're all going to want to say their goodbyes."

"You said his daughters and their families are coming as well?"

"Yeah, both of them with their husbands. Jenny and I met up with them last night at the Maid's Head where they're staying."

"What about Beryl?"

"Yes, she'll be here. Handcuffed to a police officer, of course."

"Poor woman. She deserves a bloody medal, not standing trial for murder,"

"Agreed. We owe her so much."

I'd been busy after my arrest. Firstly, as requested by Don, I'd investigated what happened to his illegitimate daughter. George and his friend, Harold, had assisted, and we discovered Beryl Backman became Beryl Hall.

Discovering that Beryl Hall, Don's illegitimate daughter, was, in fact, Beth's and Christopher's maternal grandmother came somewhat as a shock. Although Don hadn't known Beryl in later life, he had, unbeknown to him, helped and often cared for his very own granddaughter and ex-neighbour, Carol Hall. My honorary father, Donald Nears, was my adopted children's great-grandfather. This was wonderful news, although, of course, saddened by the fact that he would never know.

Beryl had murdered Shirley as retribution for the torment that the evil woman had inflicted upon her at that children's home. In some strange quirk of fate, Beryl had also rid the world of the mother of the evil bastard who'd murdered her daughter. Paul Colney, although not proven, murdered Carol when he injected a lethal dose of heroin into her arm back in '76. I felt I would have to pick my moment to share that news with her. Beryl thought her daughter committed suicide, as that had been the official line – however, I suspected differently.

The truly great news was that although Beryl had lost her daughter, she had now gained two grandchildren. So, Christopher and Beth would be part of her life, even if that was only on visiting days in Holloway Prison, which is where Beryl and I fully expected she would spend the next twenty years.

Unfortunately, Beryl and I had only been able to meet once. However, I was able to relay the good news about her new family. Discovering that shiny-shoes man hadn't been an innocent bystander closed down the questions about why Beryl hadn't been part of Carol's life. Beryl had rid the world of an evil sadistic tormentor who thoroughly deserved the same fate as Shirley and Ralph.

Beryl was sad that she had never had the opportunity to know her father, Don, but was grateful that Don's two other daughters and I were here to support her through the trial and whatever that led to afterwards.

Martin and I joined the rest of the Time Travel Believers' Club outside the church, milling about as we waited for all the attendees and, of course, Don.

I spotted Beryl handcuffed to the Welsh detective, and waved at Don's daughters, before noticing DI French approach.

"Good morning, Mr Apsley," she nodded to the rest of the gang.

"Oh, God. Why are you here?"

"Jason!" exclaimed Jenny, presumably chiding my rudeness.

"No, that's okay, Mrs Apsley. I understand. We agreed to allow Beryl Hall to attend, so I'm here with a few of my officers." She nodded in Beryl's direction.

DC Brown, who'd been one of the officers who'd interviewed me when arrested, stood chatting to Beryl. I noticed him affectionately rubbing her arm, and Beryl returning a shy but warm smile. The Welsh officer rolled her eyes at the two of them. It appeared an interesting chemistry had developed between the middle-aged officer and Beryl.

"We watched you on Crime Watch, Heather. You were brilliant!"

"Thank you. We've already had a terrific response."

"Oh, that's good," I politely replied, not wishing for Jenny to berate me for my lack of manners.

"Yes, interestingly, about that car we've been trying to find, the Jaguar XJS. We've recovered the vehicle burnt out on a piece of waste ground at the coast in Brightlingsea, of all places."

"Oh," I responded, shooting a look at the others.

"We've also discovered a boat owner in Brightlingsea who had an illegal trip planned across to Dunkirk on Friday 11th September, taking two adults and two young girls."

Jenny grabbed my arm. "You don't think Shirley was—"

"I'm certain of it, Mrs Apsley. Shirley Colney planned to kidnap your daughter and granddaughter."

"Christ!"

"Excuse me," George interjected. "But what does that have to do with that burnt-out car?"

"Good question, Mr Sutton. The boat owner obviously didn't take the four across the water because they didn't turn up. However, he did make the trip with one passenger who apparently just happened to be the spitting image of your dead ex-boyfriend and his brother," she stated, pointing at Jess. "I seem to be chasing ghosts!"

The members of the club shot each other a look.

"So, Mr Apsley, Mr Bretton, who am I and half of Interpol chasing across mainland Europe?"

"No idea," came the chorus from the club members.

DI French raised her eyebrows at me before giving the same expression to each member in turn as she rotated her gaze around the group. "I give up," she muttered before stepping away to join her officers.

47

January 1990

Force of Time

"Jason, it's nearly half ten. I think we need to get going if we are going to be on time."

"What? I can't hear you." I shouted in her ear, unable to decipher anything over the din of the disco, which was now in full swing, with the dance floor full of pissed-up revellers all enjoying the party after seeing the bride and groom off just half an hour ago.

"I said it's gone half ten. We need ten minutes to get there, so I think we'd better go," screamed Jenny, cupping her hands around my ear.

I checked my watch, then nodded.

Saying our goodbyes to Don's daughters and their families, we exited the main ballroom of the Maid's Head Hotel to head off to complete our mission which we'd planned to military precision at the December meeting of the Time Travel Believers' Club. Earlier that evening, Jess and Colin had taken Beth and Faith back to their house. Christopher had lessons at college the next day, so he'd left before the disco started, saying he didn't want to cramp his style and needed to complete an assignment before the morning.

This particular mission had initially hit the agenda of the November meeting, where we had planned the same operation but hadn't expected to be attending a wedding on the same evening. That said, it had been a wonderful day, which I know Don would have enjoyed if still with us – certainly, he would have been proud.

In December the previous year, after campaigning by many groups, including an organisation that fights for changes in the law regarding domestic violence, Beryl's appeal to commute her sentence from murder to manslaughter was successful. Because she had served two years in prison, the trial judges released her immediately. It was headline news and considered a landmark case in the fight against injustice where women were tried and convicted for defending themselves against violent husbands. The evidence of her torment received at the hands of Shirley Colney was compelling and helped her case.

The newly promoted DCI French had also waded in to support Beryl. So, having an influential Detective Chief Inspector in your camp certainly helped.

Today, four weeks after release, Beryl Hall became Beryl Brown, marrying the now-retired detective constable, Steven *Paddington* Brown.

Scooting up to the multistorey car park, that monolithic brutal grey hell-hole, which looked far worse at night than during the daylight hours, we donned our overcoats and headed towards the bridge.

"Jesus, it's still really windy!" whinged Jenny, whilst stamping her feet to keep warm. A feat I suspected can't have been easy in four-inch heels.

"Well, it's supposed to be! I think we've got it right this time."

"The pub closes at eleven, so they should be coming out any minute now," she announced whilst shivering.

I pulled Jenny close into a tight hug as we waited for the pub to empty. The Woolpack Pub was a haunt for young drinkers. It was well known that, at any one time, half the people in there were still of school age, but it never got raided. Of course, underage drinking was illegal, but I guess the police had many more things to worry about, like finding their mystery man who fled from Brightlingsea two and half years ago.

At 5:22 p.m. on September 11th 1989, precisely two years after Beryl had played skittles with Shirley, Ralph and Graham, the lights at the Carrow Road Bridge turned red, stopping the traffic. For some bizarre reason, at that precise point, no one was walking across the bridge, just at the moment when three of the four primary wrought-iron supports shattered, taking the left-hand side of the ornate Victorian bridge seventy feet down to the river below. It was deemed a miracle that no one was killed.

There were grand plans for a new bridge, and although the main stone supports still stood on either side, they had been deemed safe until demolition and rebuilding work was planned for the spring of 1990. However, the Time Travel Believers' Club members suspected otherwise.

Before Martin, now known as Leonardo – a stupid name, which I told him was his own fault and should have called himself Keith – left this unremarkable Hertfordshire town to tour the world in '88, he and I regularly updated those yearbooks. Last September, during one of our regular catch-up calls, we'd discussed how we had mis-predicted the year that the bridge collapsed. However, we both remembered the Burns' Day storm of 1990. Now realising that history would, as it always did, repeat. The collapse of the bridge's stone supports, which would kill two youngsters, would happen on the evening of 25th January the following year.

So here we were, standing near the collapsed bridge, waiting for the pub to empty, so we could warn away a young couple who weren't aware they were about to die. The TTB Club achieved few successes. However, when we did alter time and save lives, it made up for all the failures.

Of course, saving the young couple who should be crushed to death would change history. They may go on to have children who could pioneer some great discovery or become serial killers – we didn't know. However, if we knew the precise moment when someone would die, as we thought we did in this instance, we felt compelled to act.

The pub light flicked off with the punters pouring out, making their way home in the opposite direction away from the collapsed bridge. We suspected very few would turn towards the bridge because now that afforded no access across the river, which is probably why the soon to be collapsing stone support had previously only killed two.

"I'll tell you … if it was our kids drinking whilst underage in that pub, I'd have their guts for garters," muttered Jenny.

"I'm pretty sure Christopher and Stephen used to go in there before they were eighteen."

"What? And you knew about that?" she exclaimed, pulling back from our cuddle.

"Oh, come on, Jen. Kids drink before they're eighteen all the time. I'm sure you did as well."

"No, I did not! My father would never have allowed that!"

"Ha, maybe. But I know your brother Alan did!"

"Hmmm, maybe. Did you?"

"Well, not for want of trying. But in the early nineties, it wasn't so easy. Depressingly, pubs had started to ask for ID. Your generation had it much easier."

"That still doesn't make it right. If Martin is right, and the two who we're about to save are school-age, we should be taking them home and having a strong word with their parents!"

"Well, oddly, I don't think we'll have that problem. Looks like the doors are locked, and no one else is coming out."

"Oh, well, that's it then. Martin must have got it wrong again! And here we are freezing to death after another fool's errand," belligerently moaned Jenny through chattering teeth.

"Sorry, sweetheart."

Jenny cuddled in close once again. "No, darling. It's not your fault. We had to check."

I turned and glanced back towards the towering stone support, which seemed unperturbed by the battering it had received from the wind over several hours. Due to our predilection to cocking-up our predictions, I wondered if Martin or I had once again misremembered.

"Okay. Shall we hang on and wait for that stone support to collapse?"

"Well, it's freezing, but we might as well now we're here."

We huddled together, staring up at the stone support in a deserted windy street in January. No cars passed us because of the storm, and no other idiots were predisposed to stand outside in a hurricane watching to see if a structure might or might not collapse.

"Excuse me, please," called out a male voice from behind us.

We both spun around to see a young couple with their heads down, presumably attempting to shield themselves from the wind and gesturing to pass us on the pavement. The young couple who appeared unequivocally unsuitably dressed for the weather hovered, waiting for Jenny and me to step aside. The young man held the hand of whom was probably his girlfriend. They indeed appeared far too young to be out at this time of night, or to be drinking in a pub, or be wearing a dangerously short sparkly miniskirt – the young lady that is, not the young man, just for clarity.

"Christopher!" exclaimed Jenny.

"Mum! Dad! Wha-what are you doing here?" my eighteen-year-old son stammered, sporting that *'oh no, this can't be happening'* look.

"It's not what are *we* doing here! It's what are *you* doing here?" bellowed my wife taking a step forward, presumably preparing to wring our son's neck.

"Err... err—"

"Don't you err me, young man! You've got college in the morning. And earlier you said you had to go home to finish your assignment!"

"Sorry," winced Christopher, now clearly embarrassed in front of his young girlfriend, who'd bowed her head.

The wind had now crept up a few knots and added a swirling rain to dampen the evening. Rather than tear a strip off our son whilst standing in the middle of an impending hurricane, I thought we could save his bollocking for when we arrived home.

"Jen. Jen," I bellowed above the noise of the wind. "Let's get home. We can straighten this out then. We're going to get soaked through in a minute."

Jenny nodded her agreement to my suggestion now the rain had set in. She roughly grabbed Christopher's arm, preparing to drag him and presumably his shy girlfriend back to the car.

"And how old are you?" asked Jenny, addressing the young girl who still did her best to avoid eye contact.

"Fifteen," she whispered.

"Sorry, I can't hear you," shouted Jenny, as we all made our way back to the multistorey car park.

Whilst Jenny still tugged at Christopher's jacket, his girlfriend clung to him, as the young and in love do. With her hand firmly clasped in his, Christopher's girlfriend jogged forward a couple of paces so Jenny could hear her reply. Now she'd drawn level with me, the wind lifted her hair, and I caught sight of her face.

"I'm fifteen," she stated, now almost in a light jog as we stomped along.

However, I'd stopped, now gawping at the young lass.

Her declaration of age halted Jenny in her tracks. "Fifteen! You're fifteen?"

"Yes, Mrs Apsley," she replied before turning to me. "Hello, sir."

"Do your parents know you're out at this time of night?" demanded Jenny, who'd let go of Christopher's jacket sleeve in favour of aggressively thumping her hands on her hips – Jenny's trademark stance indicating that all was not well. "Jason! Did you hear? Fifteen! The girl's only fifteen!"

The rain did its best to encourage us to get to shelter. However, all four of us had now halted our route march as we stood in a circle.

"Mum, Dad. We love each other," announced Christopher.

"Oh, God. You're both too young to start announcing declarations of love!"

"But Mum, we do. We do love each other." The young lass clasped both hands around Christopher's as if to reaffirm his declaration.

Jenny shot me a look, presumably wondering why I held a muted state whilst impersonating the now dead, toilet-flushed, Bananarama. "Jason, have you got anything to say? Or are you just going to stand there with your mouth open?"

"Oh, bollocks."

"What? Is that all you have to say? Your son just announced he and a girl of fifteen, yes fifteen, are in love, and all you can come up with is, oh bollocks!"

The conversation came to an abrupt halt as an almighty thud boomed down the road behind us. Swivelling around, I witnessed the remaining stone blocks collapse to the ground, following the first one that caused the initial thump. We all gawped at the dust cloud that had emanated from the collapsed bridge support, which now barrelled its way towards us.

"Fricken hell!" exclaimed Christopher.

Jenny grabbed my arm. I pulled her tightly to me, our mini argument now long forgotten.

"Jason!"

I nodded, realising the enormity of the situation. We'd saved the young couple from death, one of which was our son.

Jenny's anger at Christopher now evaporated as quickly as the high winds dispersed the dust cloud, relieved, I guess, that we had been here to stop our son from ending up under a pile of stone. In my mind, I thanked my loose cannonball nightmare time-travelling companion. If it hadn't been for Martin, we would have lost Christopher.

Jenny took Christopher's free arm. "Come on, let's get you two home."

"Hang on, didn't you see what just happened!" exclaimed Christopher, presumably shocked that Jenny and I seemed reasonably unsurprised about the bridge support collapsing.

Jenny shot me a look, I guess silently appealing for suggestions on how to respond. But, of course, it was no shock to us, as we'd been expecting this for years. Although we didn't know it would be our son who we saved.

"Chris, let's just get home. It's pissing down with rain, and I suspect your girlfriend will need to call her, oh-so-lovely, parents."

"Yes, come on, let's get going," agreed Jenny, as she grabbed my hand. "I'm sure your parents will be worried sick and will want to know you're safe. What did you say your name is?" she asked the young girl wearing the soaked-through sparkly mini-skirt, who now seemed fixated by the collapsed bridge support.

"Lisa. Lisa Crowther."

In my first life, fate had drawn Lisa and me together. Perhaps the force of time was pushing back as it fought to restore history. Lisa and I could no longer be a couple in this life, but maybe *time* had decided to force the next best option to fix time-lines by pairing my cheating ex-wife with my adopted son.

As we once again strode back to the car, I pondered what other effects Martin and I would have upon *time* and would it fight back to stop the changes we made. However, I feared we weren't the only time-travellers. My concern switched to consider what the third time-traveller might do.

What had *time* in store for my nemesis, Paul Colney, and would our paths cross once more?

I shuddered at the thought.

∼

What next?

It's Payback Time, the first book in a new time-leap trilogy, set in the unremarkable Hertfordshire town of Fairfield, will be published in the autumn of 2022. I hope you get the chance to catch that book as well.

Thank you for reading this book and my other books in the series. As an independent author, I don't benefit from the support of a large publishing house to promote my work. So, may I ask a small favour to help push me along? If you enjoyed this book, could I invite you to leave a review on Amazon? Just a few lines will help other readers discover my books — I'll hugely appreciate it.

For more information, and to sign-up for updates on new releases, please drop onto my website. You can also find my page on Facebook.

www.adriancousins.co.uk

Facebook.com/adriancousinsauthor

∼

I wanted to mention …

Regarding the comments and behaviours of DC Reeves and DC Taylor – I do hope you were not offended by these references, as that was not my intention. However, I used them to highlight the outdated attitudes that unfortunately still existed in pockets of our society at that time. Thankfully education has prevailed, and will continue to do so in eradicating sexist and racist attitudes. I'm quite certain the brilliant DI French dealt with both officers professionally, which didn't involve the use of a Kenwood.

∼

Other titles by Adrian Cousins: -

The Jason Apsley Series

Jason Apsley's Second Chance

Ahead of his Time

Force of Time

Standalone Novels

Eye of Time

<u>Deana – Demon or Diva series</u>

It's Payback Time

Death Becomes Them

Dead Goode

Acknowledgements …

Thank you to the following, your feedback and support has been invaluable.

Adele Walpole

Brenda Bennett

Tracy Fisher

Lisa Osborne

Patrick Walpole

Andy Wise

And, of course, Sian Phillips, who makes everything come together, I'm so grateful.

Finally – thank you for reading.

Printed in Great Britain
by Amazon